FORGET ME NOT

Marliss Melton

FOREVER

NEW YORK   BOSTON

Copyright © 2004 by Marliss Arruda
Excerpt from *In the Dark* copyright © 2004 by Marliss Arruda
All rights reserved. Except as permitted under the U.S. Copyright Act of 1976, no part of this publication may be reproduced, distributed, or transmitted in any form or by any means, or stored in a database or retrieval system, without the prior written permission of the publisher.

Cover design and art by Dale Fiorello
Book design by Giorgetta Bell McRee

Forever
Hachette Book Group USA
237 Park Avenue
New York, NY 10017
Visit our Web site at www.HachetteBookGroupUSA.com

Forever is an imprint of Grand Central Publishing. The Forever name and logo is a trademark of Hachette Book Group USA, Inc.

Printed in the United States of America

First Printing: December 2004

14 13 12 11 10 9 8 7 6 5

GABE FOUGHT
TO REMAIN CONSCIOUS . . .

He lay with his left cheek in a puddle of oil. His arms and legs were bound. His mouth continued to bleed. He would never have the chance to tell the world who was stealing weapons.

Gabe heard a noise that made every hair on his head stand on end. Someone somewhere struck a match. If he couldn't find a way to get out of there, he was going to burn like coal doused in lighter fluid.

He didn't know what was worse—burning alive or realizing he'd never have the chance to tell Helen he loved her.

Please turn to the back of this book for a preview of Marliss Melton's new novel, *In the Dark*.

Books by Marliss Melton

Forget Me Not

In the Dark

Time to Run

Next to Die

Don't Let Go

Too Far Gone

Acknowledgments

Special thanks to the following Navy SEALs for your professional input and encouragement:

Greg
Jeff Stratton and his wife, Paula Stratton
and Stephen White

My hero was inspired by Major Dave Reynolds, USMC. For a man with no gray crayon in his coloring box, you sure colored my imagination!

Heartfelt thanks to my fabulous agent, Pamela Ahearn.

And lastly, thank you to my editor, Devi Pillai, for remarking on the potential in this story and knowing how to summon it. You have a gift that will serve you well!

FORGET
ME NOT

Prologue

Gunfire rained down on the four-man SEAL squad, ricocheting off the concrete floor and metal walls of the warehouse in Pyongyang Harbor, North Korea. Bullets punctured holes in the barrels of crude oil stacked between massive metal containers, spewing slick liquid all over the floor.

Lieutenant Gabriel Renault, code name Jaguar, ducked behind a barrel as a bullet chipped the wooden pallet beside him. *Who the hell?* he wondered, his heart beating fast beneath his wet suit. Local tangos—terrorists—weren't likely to shoot up their own warehouse just to ward off intruders. Nor could they have seen the SEALs in the dark, camouflaged as they were to blend into the shadows.

Yet there were at least four shooters, positioned at opposite ends of the warehouse on catwalks that crisscrossed overhead. To have spied the four-man SEAL squad, they would have had to have night-vision goggles similar to Gabe's. And if that was the case, they were either lousy shooters or they had no intention of killing the SEALs, only scaring them, which didn't make sense if they were terrorists.

The executive officer's anxious whisper floated through Gabe's earpiece, sounding as uncertain as it did on the other scant missions he took part in. "Fall back," he told them.

Gabe grimaced in disgust. "We need to secure the rest of the cargo, sir," he reminded his senior officer. Christ, there were only four shooters; it wasn't like they were outnumbered. They'd faced more serious odds in the past and still fulfilled their objective.

"Negative. We'll be good with what we have. Repeat. Fall back to the SDV. Westy and Bear, do you copy?"

"Copy, sir." It was Chief Westy McCaffrey, who sounded as pissed off as Gabe was feeling.

"Roger, X-ray Oscar," Bear confirmed on a growl, using the XO's call sign.

"You two take the south exit," Miller instructed them. "Jaguar and I will take the west."

The message ended with a hiss of static that made Gabe flinch. Not again! He tapped his earpiece, concerned that his communication system, faltering for the last twenty minutes, had finally crapped out on him. "X-ray Oscar, do you copy?" he inquired, hearing nothing but static. "Shit!" He tapped the microphone three times, but no response.

At least his NVGs were working. He scanned the catwalks with the thermal sensitive goggles, spying an arm as it emerged from behind a steel girder and fired rounds in a random pattern, wreaking havoc on the barrels of oil, which emptied their contents in sluggish streams. Cautioning himself not to slip, Gabe backed out of his hiding place.

Leaving behind the fourth surface-to-air missile left a bad taste in his mouth. He finished a job, no matter what obstacles impeded the mission—and there was always something.

Quitting now was an act of cowardice. Westy was a good enough sniper to take the tangos out, one by one. They hadn't even tried a distraction, for God's sake! Why carry smoke grenades if they weren't going to put them to use?

He snaked out of his cover, flattening himself against the crate that housed the fourth missile. The fact that this surface-to-air missile, or SAM, was bound for the Middle East tomorrow meant that it might ultimately be used against the United States. Leaving it in this North Korean warehouse was not an option, in his mind.

With great reluctance, he slid his hand along the crate, feeling the rough splinters prick his palm. He rounded the corner and came face-to-face with his XO, and drew back in surprise. Miller was supposed to meet him by the out point.

Even with grease paint on his face, Miller looked nervous. The whites of his eyes shone in the darkness. "Let's go," he muttered, jerking his head toward the exit.

Gabe tried to tell him that his headset wasn't working, but Miller had already turned away. Gritting his teeth, Gabe followed. Every muscle in his body quivered in frustration.

Suddenly Miller pivoted. The butt of his Heckler and Koch flashed before Gabe's eyes and made stunning impact with Gabe's right cheek. Pain lanced through him. He staggered back, losing his footing on the oil-slick floor, and went down hard, the air knocked out of him. He tasted blood in his mouth.

What the fuck?

Miller bent over him, grabbed him by the belt, and turned him forcibly onto his stomach. Gabe struggled to inflate his lungs. He struck out a foot, landing a blow to the XO's knee. The man cursed and grabbed him harder.

The pain in Gabe's head seemed to swell, making thought impossible. *What the hell is happening?* He couldn't get beyond the question. Why was Miller turning on him? A tie-tie, a plastic cuff, snared his left wrist, then his right. Blood filled his mouth. He spat out a tooth and sucked a painful breath into his lungs. "What the hell are you doing, Miller?" he growled, thrashing as the man groped in the dark to latch his ankles together.

Miller didn't answer him. Through the waves of pain beating at his skull, Gabe was aware that Miller had immobilized him. The gunfire that had compelled their retreat had ceased. That held some significance, but in his pain-filled haze, Gabe couldn't fathom what it was.

Miller yanked his head back. Gabe could feel a tremor in the man's hands as he fumbled with duct tape. A sticky strip imprisoned his mouth, making speech impossible. He gagged on the blood that had nowhere to go but down his throat.

Miller released him and turned away. Gabe watched with dawning horror as the man stepped into the open and gave an all-clear gesture to the men on the crosswalks. Over the pounding in his head, Gabe heard their approach.

But his eyes were glued to Miller's back as he grappled with the realization that his own XO was the one stealing weapons worldwide. For months now, SEALs had gone to interdicts various armaments, only to find them missing. And it was Miller who was stealing them. Weak-willed, sallow-faced Miller!

He could hardly believe it. But there he was, telling the shadowy figures around him to take the SAM in its packaging out the side exit and be quick about it.

Gabe fought to remain conscious, to identify the other looters. But the darkness hovering at the corners of his eyes warned him that he was about to pass out. Miller turned, looking at him one more time before he, too, drifted away, presumably to rendezvous with Gabe's unwitting teammates.

Gabe lay with his left cheek in a puddle of oil. The NVGs had been knocked askew and were lying across his right ear. His arms and legs were bound. His mouth continued to bleed. He would never have the chance to tell the world who was stealing weapons.

For whatever reason, Miller had left him here to die. Why? It took a moment for his battered brain to supply an answer. It had to be the memo he'd found on Miller's desk pertaining to the requisition of an additional sub. He'd queried Miller about it, thinking the man was too inept to know that one sub provided sufficient cargo space for four missiles. He'd never suspected his XO was plotting to take a missile for himself.

With oil oozing between his eyelids and into his Kevlar diving suit, Gabe heard a noise that made every hair on his head stand on end. Someone somewhere struck a match. If he couldn't find a way to get out of there, he was going to burn like coal doused in lighter fluid.

He didn't know what was worse—burning alive or realizing he'd never have the chance to tell Helen he loved her.

Chapter One

Helen immersed herself in the bath so that only her eyes and nose cleared the layer of bubbles. Gazing down the length of the tub, she studied Gabe's picture, standing amid a ring of dancing candles. Mixed emotions stormed her heart as she stared into his eyes.

Even from a distance of a few feet, the eyes in the eight-by-ten portrait mesmerized her, just as they had when she and Gabe first met. Light green with a gold starburst at the center, Gabe's eyes had given him his code name, Jaguar. They were uncannily direct, making her blush whenever he'd stared at her, which had been quite often in the beginning. But by the time he'd disappeared last year, only two years into their marriage, he'd scarcely given her the time of day. He was too wrapped up in being a SEAL platoon leader and in saving the world.

Helen blew the encroaching suds away from her mouth, sending a bubble into the air. It drifted a moment and then disintegrated. *Like my love for you,* she thought, addressing the man in the picture.

He'd disappeared a year ago. The Navy wouldn't reveal where he'd been or the circumstances surrounding his disappearance. For twelve long months, they'd referred to him as MIA, missing-in-action, never as deceased. But all that changed last week when a young officer appeared on her doorstep bearing a flag.

With twelve full months gone by, the Navy was ready to declare Gabe dead. The flag made it official. Strange that a brand-new banner with crisp red stripes and bold stars would send Helen into shock. Not that she'd expected Gabe ever to return, but the way the flag had been folded in military fashion drove home the reality of his death like nothing else. Seeing the flag so tightly bound made it possible to imagine that Gabe's vitality had also been subdued.

Yet, on the heels of her shock came an inordinate sense of relief. She wouldn't have to surrender the newfound independence she'd discovered in recent months. She wouldn't have to give up the job that gave her so much satisfaction. She would raise her thirteen-year-old daughter alone, as she should have done in the first place.

It wasn't easy to admit, but her marriage to Gabe had been a mistake, an unnecessary detour. She'd thought she needed him to redeem herself in her parents' eyes. She'd wanted Mallory to have a father. But Gabe, with his drive to save the world, hadn't had time for a wife, let alone a stepdaughter.

Within a year of their marriage, the man who should have been her knight in shining armor had practically forgotten her. Three years in, he was dead.

So now it was over.

The mighty, indomitable Jaguar was gone, taken out by some faceless enemy. The flag made it evident. It was time to put the past behind her and to let it go. She didn't need

Gabe Renault to make her whole. She'd done just fine this past year on her own. Better than fine. And yet . . .

Even with her ears underwater, the words of the Natalie Cole CD playing in her bedroom reached her clearly. *"Unforgettable, that's what you are . . ."* A pang of regret pierced Helen's heart.

She missed him from time to time. Closing her eyes, she could still feel his hands on her, his hot, scandalous tongue. He'd known every pleasure point on her body and used his knowledge to his advantage, calling her back to him whenever her heart began to drift away.

"Unforgettable, in every way . . ."

He wasn't here to call her back now. She was free to go, to live her own life. With a deep sigh, she released her regret and sank into the water. Emerging moments later, she reached for the shampoo.

The telephone rang in another part of the house. Helen waited for Mallory to pick it up. She'd taught a step class in the morning and body sculpting in the afternoon. Arriving home this evening, she'd desperately craved a long, hot soak in the tub.

"Mom, it's for you." The bathroom door slammed open as Mallory marched in without knocking. In the light of the candles, her face looked waxen. Maybe it was just her complexion against the dye job she'd just given herself.

Black? "Oh, Mal," Helen cried, "what have you—"

"It's urgent," Mallory said, holding the phone out.

The size of Mallory's green eyes made Helen hesitate. She took the phone and leaned out over the edge of the tub. "This is Helen," she said quickly.

"Mrs. Renault, this is Commander Shafer over at Portsmouth Naval Medical Center, Traumatology."

Helen lifted her gaze to her daughter's shocked face. This had to be about Mallory. She'd acted out again, had to be.

"Ma'am, I'm calling to let you know that we've got your husband here. It's a remarkable story, actually. He washed ashore in South Korea, just below the DMZ. He was in pretty bad shape considering . . ."

The commander kept talking, but Helen couldn't hear him over the ringing in her ears. "I'm sorry, I think you've made a mistake," she said, cutting him off. "My husband's dead. He's been missing for a year."

"He's not dead, ma'am. The man we have is Lieutenant Gabriel Renault. He's been in North Korea all this time."

It couldn't be Gabe. Her mind flashed to the officer giving her the flag. It had been folded so tightly, so permanently. "Have you positively identified him? How can you be sure?"

"I understand that this is coming as a shock," the commander soothed. "But you can rest assured we IDed him thoroughly before making this call. His commander has been in to see him. All that's left is for a family member to do the same. He is alive, ma'am, and in pretty good condition, considering what he's been through."

Helen swallowed convulsively. Shock and amazement competed with powerful denial. The freedom she'd relished this last week was an illusion. Gabe was back. He'd been alive all this time!

"I'm sure you'll want to get down here right away," the commander prompted.

"Of course," she said, though she wasn't nearly as sure as he was.

Maybe they'd made a mistake. How could Gabe have survived a year in North Korea, of all places?

"There's something you should know, ma'am, before you see him."

She braced herself for awful news. He'd tell her now that Gabe had been tortured or mutilated.

"He's lost a portion of his memory, apparently. He doesn't have any recollection of a family of any kind. This sort of thing is normal, I want you to understand. It's an indication of post-traumatic stress disorder, nothing that can't be dealt with. We've got him on meds that keep him calm. Why don't you come down to the hospital tonight, and I'll go into more detail with you?"

Shocked into silence, Helen stared up at her pale-faced daughter. *He doesn't remember them?*

"Ma'am?"

"Yes." She forced herself to say. "I'll be there in about an hour."

"Great. We're on the third floor. Just ask for Commander Shafer, and I'll escort you in to see your husband. Maybe someone should come with you?" he suggested.

"I'll bring my daughter."

The commander hesitated, no doubt picturing a young child. "Okay, we'll see you soon."

The phone clicked in Helen's ear. It fell out of her numb fingers and hit the bath mat with a thud. The flames of the candles seemed to bleed together. Maybe she'd drowned in the tub and was experiencing some kind of hallucination.

"Mom!" It was Mallory, bending over her with midnight hair instead of chestnut. "It's Dad, isn't it?" she demanded. Her pasty complexion wasn't solely a result of the dye job. "He's back, isn't he?" Mal asked in a tight voice. Helen couldn't tell if she was overjoyed or upset. It probably wasn't that simple.

Poor Mallory. When Helen and Gabe were married, she'd been euphoric with the expectation of finally having a father. It had been a painful disillusion to discover that her new father had no time for an adolescent daughter.

"He doesn't remember us." Helen related what the doctor had just told her. "He's suffering some kind of amnesia from being . . . um . . ." She couldn't bring herself to say it.

"Tortured?" Mallory supplied.

"I think so. We need to get to the hospital." Helen levered herself upward.

"Mom, your hair's full of soap."

Helen cranked on the faucet and stuck her head under cold water. She dressed in record time, brushed the tangles out of her hair, and jammed her feet into her tennis shoes while Mallory waited on her bed.

"You want me to drive?" Mal asked, looking suspiciously composed.

"Yeah, right." Helen forced a laugh. For someone who wasn't even related to Gabe, Mallory was a lot like him. She took blows without a blink, seemingly unaffected by the harsh realities of life. But then the stress manifested itself in some self-destructive behavior that sent Helen scrambling for a counselor.

"It's not that hard to drive," Mallory insisted, following her down the hall and out the front door.

Helen drove the silver Jaguar that had been Gabe's exclusive property. It was nearly nine o'clock on a gorgeous August night. They chased the sun that was sinking fast behind the trees. Helen took Route 264 at eighty miles an hour, her fingers so tight on the steering wheel she had to pry them loose to turn up the radio.

Just pretend everything is normal, she told herself. She was aware of the fact that she wasn't feeling grateful. It wasn't every day that a missing serviceman reappeared. What kind of wife was she not to be thrilled?

She was wary, that was all. She didn't know what to expect. Gabe had been held captive for a year, caught by the enemy in what must have been a weapons seizure gone bad. North Koreans were notoriously unfriendly to outsiders. No doubt they'd worked him over good for information that could be used against the U.S.A. God knew what kind of effect that would have on his personality.

She glanced at Mallory and wondered if her daughter felt as tumultuous as she. Mallory looked composed, staring out the window at the Norfolk and Portsmouth skylines. It was impossible to tell what she was thinking.

"It's going to be all right, Mal," she said, if only to keep them on line and communicating. The counselors had all stressed the importance of communication.

Mallory said nothing. Glancing down at her lap, Helen saw that Mallory's fingers on both hands were crossed for luck. She tore her gaze away, wondering what Mallory was wishing for—that Gabe would be okay? That he'd remember them? Surely she wasn't naive enough to wish for more than that.

How awfully he must have suffered, so badly that he'd repressed his memories! She quailed to think of his agony. More than that, she shuddered to think how he must be now, a terrorized, mental wreck.

She could see her newfound freedom flying out the window. Just an hour ago, she'd admitted to herself that her marriage to Gabe had died of neglect. How ironic that the moment she'd put his memory to rest, he returned to her, perhaps to wring that last drop of commitment out of her before he shook her off again.

She wouldn't turn her back on him, not in his time of need. She'd do everything in her power to see Gabe healthy again. And when he was finally whole, she'd give him back to Uncle Sam, who owned him anyway. She'd tell him then that their marriage was over.

It wasn't like the news was going to destroy him. Gabe

didn't need her any more than she now needed him. It'd hurt his pride more than it would his feelings.

Blowing out a long, steadying breath, Helen felt better for having made a decision. This reunion was just temporary.

The knock on the door startled Gabe out of a drug-induced lethargy. He'd been staring at the empty TV screen envisioning a baseball game he remembered watching four years ago, wondering how he could remember that and not remember the three years in between. "Yeah," he called, pushing himself into a sitting position.

The knock had been charged with purpose. Gabe held his breath, thinking it just might be his wife and kid—the ones he couldn't remember. Dr. Shafer had warned him they were on their way. He'd bathed and shaved for the occasion, but he still didn't feel ready. How did a guy prepare for that kind of thing anyway?

A bouquet of flowers preceded his visitor through the door. Over a bright orange spray of lilies, he recognized the leader of SEAL Team Twelve, Commander Lovitt, and he started struggling out of bed to salute him.

"At ease, Lieutenant," Lovitt called, making formality unnecessary. Marching in, he deposited the flowers on Gabe's bedside bureau. "From the office," he explained, dusting a few fallen petals off his dress whites, as meticulous as ever. Obviously, Lovitt was on his way to some function. "How's the patient today?"

Lovitt had asked the same question yesterday, only Gabe had been too tranquilized to answer. "Better, sir," he said. "I apologize for not responding yesterday . . . "

Lovitt waved away his apology. "There's no need to explain, Lieutenant. You'll have bad days and good days. At least you remembered me." Lovitt's gray eyes sharpened, an implied question in his statement.

"Yes, sir. I remember being stationed here, working primarily with Echo Platoon, but that was three years ago."

Lovitt's long stare struck Gabe as grave. "Mind if I draw up a chair?" he asked.

Gabe's heart sank. "No, sir. Please do." Lovitt's somber expression made him nervous. It made him think his commanding officer was going to cut him from the team without giving him a chance to get his memory back.

Lovitt hitched up his perfectly creased trouser legs and sat, military straight, in the visitor's chair. "Tell me what you remember, son," he exhorted.

Gabe swallowed hard. "Of the mission, sir?" He'd been through this just yesterday, with an analyst from the Defense Intelligence Agency, a man whose questions had worked him into such a state of anxiety he'd had to be tranquilized. Gabe didn't want to be put through that particular wringer again.

"No, no," Lovitt corrected. "I mean everything. Start with the beginning. Where were you born?"

The tension in Gabe's shoulders eased. He had no problems with his long-term memories. His childhood—as much as he'd like to forget it—seemed like only yesterday. "I was born in New Bedford, Massachusetts, 1968."

"Go on," Lovitt prompted, giving him a patient nod.

"My grandmother raised me," Gabe continued, wondering just how much detail the CO wanted. Did he need to know that his young mother had died in a car accident when he was just six, that he'd never known his dad?

"We, ah, we lived in a tenement house on Acushnet Street." His grandmother had been an alcoholic who lived off her dead husband's pension. As far as parenting was concerned, she was about as influential in Gabe's life as Santa

Claus. Gabe had bluffed his way through school and was heavily into street crime when his first real father-figure interceded—Sergeant O'Mally of the New Bedford Police.

Gabe was certain Commander Lovitt didn't need to hear about Sergeant O'Mally, but it was chiefly due to him that Gabe had joined the Navy in the first place. If O'Mally hadn't talked the judge into dropping car theft charges, Gabe would just be getting out of jail. Instead he'd been given an opportunity to redeem his sorry life by joining the U.S. Navy.

"I enlisted when I was eighteen." Gabe decided to spare his CO the details. "I was an EW for about eight years," he added, referring to his grade as an Electronics Warfare Specialist.

Lovitt nodded, his short, silver hair reflecting the halogen light overhead. Gabe guessed the man already knew his background—he was just testing the patient's memory, the same thing everyone else had been doing since his medevac from the Korean Peninsula three days ago.

With a burst of impatience, Gabe summed up the rest of his life quickly. "I was recommended for BOOST," he added, referring to the Broadened Opportunity for Officer Selection and Training, a way for enlisted men to become officers. "And after four years at the Naval Academy, I went straight to BUD/S training." The Basic Underwater Demolition training in Coronado was etched so deeply in Gabe's memory, no amount of post-traumatic stress could erase that. "I remember all my training, sir," he felt compelled to add. "I can still serve my country with integrity."

Lovitt gave him a grim, pitying look. "Three years is a long time to forget," he commented solemnly.

It was, in fact, the longest span of time any man had forgotten due to PTSD, according to Gabe's doctor.

Gabe's blood pressure rose. He sat taller in his bed, hoping to look less like a starved skeleton and more like his former self. "It'll come back to me, sir," he swore.

"I'm not here to relieve you of your job, Renault," the commander soothed. "You're one of my men, and I'm concerned about you. According to Commander Shafer, there was damage to the frontal lobe that might also play a part in your amnesia. Now, I choose to believe that your memory loss is temporary. But you've got to keep in mind the possibility that it could also be permanent."

Gabe stared at Lovitt's stoic features and wondered what the man was really thinking. Lovitt was a good CO—capable and dedicated, but impossible to read. At least he didn't seem to be implying what the DIA analyst had hinted at yesterday: that Gabe had buckled under his captive's persuasions and blurted government secrets; that the amnesia was a convenient way to forget his disgrace.

Then again, did the CO have any idea what kind of scars were on Gabe's torso? He curled the fingers of his left hand toward his palm, hiding the fingernails that were just growing back.

"Do you remember anything about the night you disappeared, Lieutenant?"

Gabe had known the question was coming. Of all the puzzles he presented, this one troubled his interrogators the most. Where the hell had he been for the past year? The Navy had just declared him dead.

Gabe let out a breath and cleared his mind, desperate for even a glimmer of that mission, something to restore his commander's faith in him. For a second, an image formed— light blazing in the darkness—but then it receded, lost in the gaping hole of the past three years. He shook his head, ashamed to meet his commander's eyes.

Lovitt leaned forward and squeezed his wrist. "I don't

want you worrying about your career, Lieutenant. I want you to concentrate on getting healthy, getting back on your feet. It's a goddamn miracle you're here with us today."

"Thank you, sir," Gabe muttered. He appreciated Lovitt's show of support, but he heard plainly the underlying message: Lovitt didn't expect Gabe to recover. He didn't think Gabe would ever be a SEAL again. The realization made Gabe's stomach hurt.

"I hear they're releasing you tomorrow," the CO said, standing up.

"Yes, sir." His innards cramped at the reminder. He was going home, even though he didn't know where home was. He last remembered living in the BOQ—Bachelor Officers Quarters. Now he had a wife and kid. No doubt he lived with them, though he had no idea where.

The only family he remembered were his brothers in Echo Platoon. "Are the guys around, sir? Westy, Bear, and . . . the new guy, Luther?"

Lovitt gave him a wry smile. "Luther's now a lieutenant, junior grade," he said patiently. "The men are working coastal patrol. I've radioed in the news of your reappearance, and Master Chief León is flying in as we speak. I imagine he'll be by to see you before you're released."

Gabe nodded, relief flooding through him. "Thank you, sir." Master Chief was exactly the man to have around at a time like this. Unlike the CO, he wouldn't undermine Gabe's confidence. He'd bully Gabe into remembering the past three years, suggest he get his ass back on the job, double time. Gabe looked desperately forward to his visit.

"Well." Lovitt clicked the heels of his spotless white shoes together. "Take it easy, Renault. Your wife'll take good care of you. She's a lucky woman to have you back."

Gabe couldn't bring himself to answer to that one. He'd

seen what his captors had done to him. He couldn't imagine any woman wanting him, period.

"I'll leave you to rest." Lovitt turned toward the door.

"Good night, sir. Thank you for the flowers," he called, though he couldn't bring himself to even glance at them. Lilies. Christ, weren't those for funerals?

As the door thudded shut, Gabe collapsed against the pillow and cursed at length. His commander had pretty much eliminated him already. If he didn't recover his memory, and fast, he'd lose his job. He'd lose his identity. And then what?

With insidious depression, Gabe considered what he'd been before he'd been a SEAL—little more than a hoodlum, really. Becoming a SEAL had taught him self-respect, self-control. It had given him purpose and direction. It had given him the best years of his life. Before the SEALs, he was just a kid prowling around looking for trouble and picking fights to relieve the deep-down anger inside of him.

If he wasn't a SEAL, then what was he, a husband and a father? How had that happened?

He was the last man in the world any woman should marry. Not that he didn't like women. Hell no, he loved their bodies, loved the powerful way they made him feel. But he didn't know the first thing about intimacy. He didn't like it when soft, tender feelings stole over him. Feelings like that had a way of turning on a man, twisting his guts inside out, and he couldn't afford that. It'd taken him ten years of his adult life just to get his head on straight. He couldn't afford to let a woman mess him up again. So what was he doing married, with a kid already?

A knock sounded at the door.

Jesus, God. He was about to find out.

Chapter Two

C ome in." Gabe sat up, his heart beating erratically.

The door swung inward. Gabe saw the khaki sleeve of the doctor's arm as he held it ajar. Hospital sounds rushed in—the beeping of monitors, a doctor being paged, elevator doors opening. But several seconds elapsed before anyone entered.

Then a woman stepped inside. The adrenaline that jolted Gabe's system made him clutch the rails on the side of his bed. His gaze locked with hers across the room. God in heaven, no wonder he was married. One look at her and he never wanted it to end.

Honey-colored eyes regarded him from a heart-shaped face. Her lashes and eyebrows were subtly darker than the gold hair tumbling down her back. Her chin had a tiny cleft in the center. She wore a stretchy white top that clung to her neat breasts and shorts that accentuated slim, muscular thighs.

"Gabe?" she whispered, as if she didn't recognize him either.

He nodded his head, about to say the name they'd given

him—*Helen*. Helen was the perfect name for her. But then another woman stepped into the room, and he thought—wait, maybe this is Helen.

Only she was just a girl, taller and stockier than the woman. Her hair was dyed black. Her eyes, which were a dark green version of the first woman's, betrayed their relationship.

Hold up. The kid was in her early teens. If she was his, he'd remember her. He'd never been more confused in his life.

Jerking his gaze back to the first woman, he felt his panic subside. She was unquestionably the most beautiful woman he'd ever seen. The trials he'd suffered this past week paled in the face of this unexpected reward. Maybe he was up to being a husband, after all.

Helen suffered the urge to turn tail and flee. Thankfully, Mallory was right behind her, blocking the only exit.

Gabe dominated the room. After any extended absence it took days to get used to him again. Not that he was a giant at six feet one inch, but his magnetism filled the room. His vitality took up an enormous amount of space, making the hospital bed look like a baby carriage.

She inched toward him. Gabe was staring at her as if he'd been hit by a stun gun. His expression was so open, so unguarded, that she hesitated. Was it even him, or was this some kind of mix-up?

She inspected him carefully. Wearing a hospital gown, he looked different anyway, but the breadth of his shoulders was familiar, as were the arms sticking out of the arm holes. Despite the lean muscle on him, he looked thinner than she'd ever seen him. The hollows under his cheekbones sharpened his already precise features.

It was definitely Gabe. The angles and planes of his face were the same, but the eyes cinched it. A peculiar shade of yellow-green, they gleamed with the same intelligence and intensity that had drawn her to him, three years ago. She steeled herself to resist him now.

"Hey," she said, her voice strangely husky. "How are you?"

He gave her a familiar, crooked smile. "I've been told I should be dead, so I guess this is better."

Yep, same quirky sense of humor. It was definitely Gabe. His rough-edged baritone made the hairs on her nape prickle.

He was staring at her with such open fascination that she felt a blush coming. At the same time her scalp tightened, for she realized the doctor hadn't been exaggerating. "You really don't remember me, do you?"

"No." He stared and shook his head. Not remembering didn't seem to bother him too much.

With that elevator-dropping feeling in her stomach, Helen reached for Mallory and dragged her closer. "This is Mallory," she said. "You've been her dad since she was ten."

His focus shifted from her to her daughter and uncertainty usurped his amazement. Helen had never seen uncertainty on his face before. "Hi," he said, sticking out an awkward hand.

Mallory ignored the hand, leaned over the bed rail, and threw her arms around him. "Hi, Dad," she choked.

Clearly nonplussed, Gabe looked to Helen for help, but she was too surprised herself to save him. Mallory had given up a long time ago on being affectionate with Gabe. Why bother? It had gotten her nowhere. But this burst of emotion seemed genuine. She was hugging her dad for all she was worth and she wasn't in any hurry to let go, either. As much as he'd ignored her, she was thrilled to have him back.

Her daughter straightened, dashing a tear from her cheek.

To Helen's distress, Gabe's look of panic had turned to one of expectation.

He wanted a hug from her, too. She braced herself, knowing her body would betray her. The attraction was still there. Perhaps it would always be there.

She stepped forward, looping her arms around him lightly. Gabe, on the other hand, pulled her close, his arms like giant manacles. Burying his nose in her damp hair, he breathed her scent—she heard his indrawn breath in her ear. His body blazed with heat as it always had. He smelled like Ivory soap, rubbing alcohol, and a clean, familiar scent that made her head spin.

Dismayed by how good it felt to be held again, Helen struggled free. "Welcome home," she said, disentangling herself.

Comprehension flared in his eyes. All at once, he looked more like the old Gabe, cautious and secretive. "Yeah, well." He ran his fingers through his nutmeg-colored hair—it was longer than he usually wore it. "It'd be a lot nicer if I could remember."

"The doctor says it's temporary." Helen turned to the door, grateful that Commander Shafer was still there, eyeing the threesome with speculative, blue eyes. "How long before he gets his memory back?" she asked, inviting him to join them.

The commander strode to the foot of Gabe's bed. "That's not something I can say for certain," he replied, frustrating her further. "There's no set time, really. If it's just PTSD he's suffering from, his amnesia set in recently, most likely as soon as the danger was over. Why he's forgotten up to two years prior to his captivity remains a puzzle. It may indicate some kind of permanent memory loss due to a blow he took to the side of his face. There is trace evidence of damage to the frontal lobe. But the sooner he returns to a normal environment, the more likely something will jog his memories. Once that happens, we'll go from there. We'd like to release him tomorrow."

"Tomorrow?" she repeated. No, no, she needed more time to plot her future, to determine the best time for extraction.

"There'll be intensive therapy, of course," Commander Shafer added. "Dr. Terrien in Psychology will take your husband's treatment from here. He's already consulted him once," he added, nodding at Gabe. "Your husband will see him at his Oceana Clinic, which I understand is closer to your home. His first appointment is"—he glanced at the chart on the foot of Gabe's bed—"Wednesday at fourteen hundred."

Helen swung a look at Gabe, certain he would protest the need for therapy. In the past, he'd avoided psych evals like the plague.

Gabe regarded her earnestly. "Is that okay with you?" he asked.

She didn't see what she had to do with it. "Sure," she said, shrugging.

"You'll have to drive him to Oceana," Dr. Shafer explained. "In addition to the PTSD, he suffers from chronic fatigue syndrome—a result of sleep deprivation. Even with the meds he'll take to stay awake during the day, he really shouldn't drive. As for the memories, they're likely to return in bits and pieces called flashbacks. These can be prompted by a trigger or return to him in his dreams. He'll probably have trouble sleeping at night, so I've prescribed some sleeping pills, as well."

Helen pictured Gabe prowling through the house at night and shivered.

"Dr. Terrien will have more advice to give you the day after tomorrow," the doctor added.

She took a deep breath. "Okay," she said, rubbing her forehead. "I'm sorry. What time is that appointment?"

"Fourteen hundred."

Two o'clock. She'd have to leave work early to take Gabe to his appointment Wednesday.

Commander Shafer prepared to withdraw. "It was nice meeting you, Mrs. Renault, Mallory." He shook hands with both of them. "I'll leave you three to visit, and I'll see you tomorrow when you come—say, oh nine hundred? We'll need you to sign some papers then."

"Okay," she said again, though it was achingly apparent that her own life was definitely over, just as she'd known it would be.

The door snicked shut behind the doctor, and the three of them were left alone.

Gabe gave her a searching look.

Helen avoided it and looked around the room instead.

"Someone brought you flowers?" she asked, seeing a big bouquet of lilies on the bureau.

"Commander Lovitt," Gabe said with a faint twist of his lips. "He was just here to see me."

"That was nice of him."

"Master Chief's flying in tonight. I should see him soon."

Good, Helen thought. The more support from his team the better. It took some of the weight off her. "They had you on IV," she noted, seeing the empty sack beside his bed.

"Yeah, I've been on sugar water and antibiotics for a week. Today I graduated to toast." He gave her his crooked smile again and looked down at his feet almost shyly.

Helen noticed with a start that one of his teeth was missing. It ruined the perfect symmetry of his smile and gave him a roguish look instead. "You've been in the hospital for a week?" she asked, just processing the information he'd given her. "How come no one called me till tonight?"

"I was overseas. I had a fever and I slept for days. They had to match me to my dental records, which were apparently misfiled or something. No one believed me when I told them who I was."

"We thought you were dead," she blurted. The words slipped out of her before she could stop them.

He gave her a wounded look—another expression she'd never seen on him before. Studying him more closely, she saw other changes, too. There were several fine scars around his mouth and on his brow ridge that hadn't been there before. He'd been punched in the face, numerous times.

Dear Lord. "Is there . . . " She swallowed hard. "Is anything wrong with you besides your memory?" she dared to ask.

He shrugged, looking suddenly uncomfortable. "I'm thinner than I've ever been. I've got a few scars." He curled his left hand into a fist, hiding the stunted fingernails she'd already glimpsed.

Thinking of what he'd been through made her stomach queasy. But he prided himself on his independence, so she held her words of consolation in check.

Leaving them with nothing to talk about.

They both looked at Mallory, who was staring at Gabe with her heart in her eyes. Mallory who'd hugged her dad for the first time in years.

"So what grade are you in?" Gabe asked, surprising Helen with his interest.

"It's summer vacation," Mallory explained. "I'm going to go to high school in a month." This was said in a very adult manner.

"Wow," said Gabe. He looked at her intently. "So you're what, fourteen?"

"Almost. I have a late birthday, September second."

"Mine's in July. I remember turning thirty-three but not thirty-six. Pretty weird, huh?"

Helen couldn't remember the last time Gabe and Mallory had chatted so casually. A lump of regret clogged her throat.

"That's exactly how long we've known you," Mallory added. "Three years."

Gabe glanced at Helen. "I figured that," he said.

Helen experienced an undertow of attraction. If she had to do it all over again, she'd still have trouble resisting him. He was a modern-day Pied Piper. Even now, sitting there half-starved and stripped of his memory, he commanded their full attention.

"Listen," she interrupted, "I have to go and make some phone calls. I need to arrange to take the day off tomorrow so I can pick you up in the morning."

Gabe nodded, looking away. "Sure," he said. "Sorry about the hassle."

"No, it's all right." She felt a blush creep up her neck. "We'll see you in the morning, then," she added. "And . . . uh . . . try not to worry. You'll get your memory back." She hiked her purse strap higher onto her shoulder.

What now? Should she kiss him, embrace him, or just walk out?

She settled for a quick smile and a wave. "See you in the morning. C'mon, Mal." She practically ran for the door.

Mallory followed with obvious reluctance. "It'll be all right," Helen heard her say.

Oh, no, it wouldn't, Helen realized. There were way too many variables in this equation for things to turn out right.

Chapter Three

Gabe's eyes sprang open. Save for a soft line of light under the door, he was surrounded by darkness. *Where am I?* His sluggish brain would not supply an answer. He knew only that he'd heard something. Danger was coming, as it always did in the darkest part of night.

There it was again: the sound that had wakened him. A faint creak, like the sound of leather being stretched.

God, no. Not another flaying. Not an endless round of searing strips laid across his back. He couldn't go through that torture again, nor the hours following as he rode on waves of feverish agony.

Gabe grappled for a weapon, anything to fend off his captors, to dissuade them from taking him.

The creaking came again, louder this time. Gabe's fingers closed over the handle of an object. It felt like a pitcher, a pitcher full of liquid. He had no idea where it came from, but as it was the only object within reach he hefted it.

As a dark shadow loomed over his prone body, Gabe tossed the contents of the pitcher directly at the enemy. With

a startled exclamation, the shadow jumped back. Gabe
hurled the empty pitcher for good measure and scrambled
out of the strange contraption he was in, putting distance between him and his muttering attacker.

"*Madre de Dios!*" the man exclaimed, snapping on the
bedside lamp. "Jaguar, it's me," he added. "What the hell are
you trying to do? Drown me?"

At the sight of his master chief, Gabe sucked in a breath
of disbelief. He reached for the wall for something solid to
hold on to. A few darting glances corroborated where he was:
not in some dark cell with faceless captors, but in the
Portsmouth Naval Medical Center facing his beloved master
chief, who'd apparently just risen from the leather armchair
by Gabe's bed. "Sebastian," he whispered in dismay.

Sebastian León looked exactly the same. Tall and slim, he
regarded Gabe through eyes slightly lighter than his coal-
black hair. "You're okay," Sebastian said, falling back upon
his usual imperturbability. He rounded the bed slowly, coming to stand within a foot of his lieutenant. "I didn't mean to
startle you," he apologized, giving him a searching look.

Gabe took note of Sebastian's rough appearance. In complete contrast to Lovitt, he looked like he'd spent the last six
weeks aboard the coastal patrol craft. His hair was overlong
and curly, his chin in need of shaving. He wore an odiferous
battle-dress uniform, with the jacket cast aside. The green T-
shirt, drenched from the water Gabe had just thrown at him,
looked stretched and stained with sweat.

Gabe had never seen a more familiar sight in his life. He
knew a startling urge to throw himself into Sebastian's arms.
He also wanted to die with shame for having demonstrated
the pitiful state of his jittery nerves.

"You're still half-asleep," Sebastian said, offering an excuse. "Go in the bathroom and splash water on your face."

As an officer, Gabe outranked his master chief, but he obeyed all the same, thankful for a moment to pull himself together.

Dousing his whole head in cold water, Gabe sought to shake off the dulling effects of his sleeping pills. He rubbed his face briskly with a towel, and with his composure tacked back into place, he carried the towel out to his master chief.

Sebastian dabbed his chest with it. Draping the towel over his neck, he put a hand on Gabe's shoulders and turned him toward the bathroom light. His expression of tenderness put an immediate lump in Gabe's throat.

"Am I looking at a ghost?" Sebastian asked him.

Gabe laughed. "Yeah, maybe. I feel like I've been resurrected."

To his astonishment, Sebastian pulled him into a wet embrace. The tremor in his arms, the firmness in his grasp, made his heart swell. Sebastian's eyes glittered with tears as he put him at arm's length again. "I thought I would never see your ugly face again," the man admitted. "How can you be alive? The warehouse exploded with you in it."

Gabe tried to remember. He shook his head. "I don't know. I can't remember the mission at all. I don't even know my wife," he added, not bothering to conceal his dismay.

Sebastian tugged the towel loose and rubbed his shirt again. "It'll come back to you," he reassured him.

"Maybe." Gabe stepped away, assailed by uncertainty. "There was some damage to the front of my brain," he added, grappling with the frightful possibility. "I may never get my memory back."

"Never?" Sebastian scoffed, tossing down the towel. "I didn't think you knew that word, sir," he challenged. "Remember Kirkuk, when I was held by the Iraqis for two weeks before you liberated me?"

Gabe searched his memory, pleased when a crisp memory of that mission returned to him. He savored it, right down to the feel of sand between his teeth. "Yeah," he said. "I remember."

"It took me a year to recall those two weeks."

"You're shitting me."

"No." Sebastian shook his head in that very Latin manner of his.

"But you were debriefed and put right back on active duty."

"I lied," the master chief admitted. "I remembered small pieces at a time, mostly in my dreams. One day I woke up and it was all there. The same thing will happen to you."

"I can't lie about three years," Gabe said, dragging his hands through his hair. "Lovitt has all but dropped me from the team."

"Wrong," Sebastian retorted. "The CO wants you back as much as I do. He knows you, that's all. He knows you respond best to a challenge."

"I have to be a SEAL, Sebastian," Gabe grated as a shudder shook his body. "I have to get my memories back." He gripped the cold metal bar on his bed with the urge to shake it.

Master Chief nodded solemnly. "It'll happen, Jaguar. Just give it time. You need your rest," he added. "Get back to bed. I might as well use your shower," he added, turning toward the bathroom.

"Why aren't you at home?" Gabe asked him, tossing aside a wet pillow.

The master chief threw him an enigmatic look. "I have to sign papers before they release you," he explained.

"Disability papers," Gabe guessed.

"Permission for medical leave," the man clarified. He went into the bathroom and shut the door.

Clambering back into his bed, Gabe muttered self-directed curses.

Alone in the adjoining room, Sebastian let the shock of Gabe's appearance overtake him. Leaning heavily on the sink, he stared into the mirror, recalling the slight disfigurations on Jaguar's face, lingering traces of his torture. But the most telling of all was his startled reaction to an unknown presence.

Gabe had been severely traumatized.

Peeling off his sodden T-shirt, Sebastian remembered the last time he'd seen the lieutenant alive. Standing on a launch pad, he'd been watching men from Echo Platoon board a UH-60 Black Hawk, en route to the carrier in the Pacific. As Jaguar ducked into the chopper, followed by Miller, the executive officer, Sebastian had suffered a strange foreboding. When word came that the lieutenant had perished on the mission, his premonition had seemed a psychic revelation.

But Jaguar was alive. Never in his wildest dreams had Sebastian considered he might have escaped what the men had described as an inferno. He'd mourned the lieutenant for months. Hell, he was still mourning him, only Jaguar had returned from the darkness—crippled but still kicking.

Strangely, the uneasy feeling Sebastian had experienced a year ago was back, stirring the hairs at the base of his neck. His friend's reappearance was a miracle, *gracias a Dios*. But it was also a puzzle, a puzzle that raised some troublesome questions.

If Jaguar had survived the explosion, then what about the missile they had failed to interdict?

And there were other questions that demanded answers: like why Jaguar had stayed behind when the other SEALs left the building; who were the mysterious shooters who had driven the SEALs back? The only man who'd yet to testify was Jaguar himself, a man whose memory had retracted into darkness, driven there by unrelenting horror.

A surge of protectiveness shuddered through him. Sebastian twisted the knob on the shower to hot. If he'd listened to his premonitions a year ago, Jaguar might have been spared the nightmare of his captivity. His instincts warned him now to remain vigilant. The loose ends in this case left him more than a little perturbed.

"See if you can guess which house is ours," Mallory challenged from the backseat of the Jaguar—the car Helen wasn't supposed to drive. Gabe had paused with satisfaction to see his automobile again, which he clearly recognized, having purchased it five years ago in California. He didn't act the least bit upset that Helen had made it hers.

It was nearly noon. It had taken two hours to sign the release papers at the hospital. It might have taken longer if Master Chief hadn't been there to expedite matters, bullying and cajoling the hospital staff without once raising his voice. Helen had always liked Sebastian. His even temper complemented Gabe's more mercurial temperament. They had always paired up well together.

This morning, though, Gabe had been surprisingly patient, considering they'd waited more than an hour for his prescriptions to be filled. Maybe he was too depressed or too high on drugs to care. The Navy had relegated him to disabled status, meaning he was completely at loose ends until his memory came back. That could take anywhere from a day to a year, according to Commander Shafer. He hadn't wanted to give her such disheartening news yesterday.

Her freedom would have to wait, it seemed. And if it

wasn't enough to have Gabe around for God-knew-how-long, Helen had also agreed to escort him to and from his clinic appointments, as he was not allowed to drive.

By the time she'd signed her life away, filled Gabe's prescriptions, and stuffed him into the passenger seat, her goodwill was running dry. They'd still had a half hour's drive to get home, and with three years of Gabe's memory missing, she didn't know what to say to him. Mallory did most of the talking while Gabe looked out the window.

They were nearly home now, having turned onto Sandfiddler Drive, where the Atlantic Ocean rushed onto the nearby shore. It was a weekday, but the beach crawled with summer tourists who'd rented out the wooden castles at the edge of the sea for their week of freedom.

Their own home was in less peril of being swept away by hurricanes, positioned as it was, a hundred yards from shore where the road curved inland, nudging the back gate of Dam Neck Naval Base.

"This one?" Gabe asked, picking up Mallory's game. He gestured at the fairy-tale structure, complete with turrets and towers.

Mallory laughed. "No, not that one."

Helen tried not to look at him. Was he playing this game with Mallory because he had nothing better to do? He used to be preoccupied all the time, his thoughts a thousand miles away.

"Oh, I know," he said, sounding confident this time. "It's coming up now. It's this one on the left." He pointed out a high-tech structure that might have been a museum for modern art.

"No-ho," Mallory hooted, enjoying herself.

Helen flicked a look in the mirror. She'd thought her daughter had been happier without Gabe around. Apparently she wasn't. Her green eyes were dancing in a way they hadn't danced for months.

With too much to think about, Helen guided the Jaguar around the bend and pulled into their driveway, beside the Jeep that didn't run.

Theirs was a modest, wooden contemporary perched atop a dozen fat pilings. It was two stories high, with the laundry room, shower, and workshop on the ground level. Steps zig-zagged up to the front door. A balcony hugged the entire right side, overlooking a yard in the front and the Atlantic Ocean at the rear. Wildflowers splashed color onto the beige sand, creating an effect like a Monet painting. Helen had invested a lot of energy into getting the valerian, chicory, and black-eyed Susans to grow. She glanced at Gabe to gauge his response.

He was staring at the house like he'd never seen it before. How strange not to recognize his home, she thought.

Mallory leaned over the seat and peered at his profile. "You don't remember," she guessed.

"No," he admitted. "But I like it. Especially the flowers."

Helen blinked. She wouldn't have guessed Gabe would say something like that. He'd never slowed down long enough to notice things like flowers. She pushed open her door and jumped out.

Today she'd dressed in a denim skirt and a peach top. Warm sand crept into her sandals as she rounded the back of the car to fetch Gabe's stuff from the trunk.

The hospital had sent him off with a bag of souvenirs, including a business card from someone at the Defense Intelligence Agency. She'd dropped his prescriptions into the bag, and he'd left the hospital with just a few meager possessions.

Closing the trunk, she hurried to help Gabe to his feet, but Mallory was already putting her shoulder under his arm.

Helen paused at the picture they presented. She'd never seen Gabe lean on anyone, let alone a teenager.

Gabe could hear a dog barking frantically inside. It was a welcoming sound, almost as welcoming as the flowers waving in the wind. Helen hurried up the steps ahead of them, her sandals slapping against the soles of her feet. He found himself admiring her shapely legs and marveling that he was married.

"You got us a puppy before you left," Mallory explained. "You were going to train her to behave, but you never had time, so she's still a little wild."

Helen cracked open the door and a nose appeared. The dog pushed its way forcibly through the aperture and broke free. Gabe saw it was a yellow Lab as it scrabbled down the stairs and launched itself at him.

"Whoa!" he cried, catching himself from tumbling down the steps. "Hello there."

"Pris, down!" Helen scolded.

Mallory tried to pry the dog off. Gabe laughed under the onslaught of the dog's wet tongue. He'd never experienced a more joyous reunion in his life. He loved it.

"Pris!" Helen called again, her tone worried.

Mallory caught hold of the dog's collar and hauled it off. "Sorry," she said, looking contrite.

"That's okay." Gabe patted the dog, who now sat on its haunches grinning at him. "Good boy."

"It's a girl," Mallory said. "Her name's Priscilla. We call her Prissy for short, but you never liked that."

"Maybe I thought the dog would get a complex," Gabe explained.

"Yeah," said Mallory with an airy laugh.

He looked up at the front door of his house, just a few

steps away. Nothing about it looked familiar to him. But there was Helen, standing in the doorway, clutching his bag. Looking into her gold-brown eyes made his pulse accelerate. He found her riveting, right down to the way she breathed. He might not be a SEAL ever again, but his wife was a hell of a catch. Because of her, he could still keep his head up.

She shepherded the dog inside, and Gabe continued his climb. He was shaking with fatigue by the time he stepped through the door. As he paused to catch his breath, something familiar assailed him, easing his sense of disorientation.

It wasn't the appearance of the place; it was the way it smelled. He took a deep breath, scenting wooden beams and sea salt and Helen's disturbingly familiar fragrance. She was moving around in the kitchen, casting him quick little glances, but giving him time to get his bearings.

Mallory squeezed around him and shut the door. "Anything?" she asked, peering up at him.

He met her gaze and smiled. The spray of freckles across her nose made her look like a pixie—or maybe it was the short haircut, curving to fit the shape of her head. "It smells good," he told her, glancing around.

The dog raced deeper into the house and came back, barking.

The foyer was lined with marble tiles. A tall plant stood on his right, taking in sunlight from the window by the door. He moved left, into the great room.

The ceiling soared upward to a point, supported by wooden beams. Two lazy fans whirled over a combination living room–dining room. The furniture was white pine, with floral cushions in blue, yellow, and pink. Windows dominated the rear and side walls, offering a stunning view of sand and sea grass and a denim-colored ocean tumbling onto shore a hundred yards away.

The view uplifted him. He'd always thought of the Special Operations Building as his home, but this was definitely nicer, making it a pleasure to move in. In this peaceful place he would find the missing pieces of his memories, just as Sebastian had predicted. His family would help him.

His gaze drifted toward the kitchen, only to be arrested by Helen's gaze as she regarded him over the rim of her glass.

Or would they?

Her gaze was decidedly watchful and not as warm as he would have liked. "Are you thirsty?" she asked, moving over to the counter to pour him some lemonade.

He couldn't fault her on her hospitality. She'd been patient and concerned, but he sensed an invisible barrier that was meant to keep him at a distance. The barrier worried him. He would need her support if he was going to make it through this.

"Please," he said, moving toward her. She had left his hospital bag on the breakfast bar. He slid onto one of the tall stools and rummaged through his stuff, pulling out the baby cactus in a plastic cup, a gift from the hospital staff.

Mallory tossed a toy to the dog, who ran back and forth in a frenzy of joy.

Gabe put the cactus down and examined the kitchen. The cabinets were a light pine with Formica countertops in soft gray. A window over the sink gave a view of the wildflowers in the front yard. A door by the refrigerator gave access to the balcony.

"This place is really nice," he said, amazed that he could have forgotten it. Knowing how dedicated to the team he'd been, he must have worked too much. Mallory had already blamed the dog's exuberance on the fact that he hadn't made time to train her.

Helen placed his lemonade on the breakfast bar within his

reach. He took note of the fact that she hadn't handed it to him. Helen didn't want to touch him. He heaved an inward sigh. So, it was like that then, was it? He knew his life couldn't be as good as it looked.

"You don't want me here, do you?" he challenged.

Her eyes flared with surprise, and she took a quick step backward.

He studied her, wishing he could read her mind, but the fact that she held her tongue was confirmation enough. Suddenly he felt weary and defeated all over again. He didn't have the patience to play games, either. "Look," he said, rubbing his forehead as he propped an elbow on the counter, "why don't you tell me a little about our situation? You seem kind of . . . reserved."

Helen's amber-brown gaze shifted to Mallory, who'd flopped down on the couch and was watching them. "Mal, take Priscilla for a walk, will you?" she suggested. The Lab was still running amok, giving off intermittent barks.

Mallory rolled her eyes. "Fine," she groused, coming to her feet. "C'mon, Prissy," she called. "Let's go for a walk."

The Lab bounded after her. Seconds later the door thudded shut, and they were left alone.

Helen's heart pounded. This was it. She was going to tell Gabe what she'd decided. Apparently, he could sense something in the air; he'd always been terribly astute. She kept the breakfast bar between them, not trusting herself to see it all the way through. Just sitting there, he appealed to her—something about that wounded-hero look did it to her. She didn't know about the timing of this, but he'd probably realize something was up when she told him he was sleeping in the study.

"Okay," she said, letting out a shaky breath. "You've been

gone a long time," she said. "A whole year. We were led to believe you were dead."

She looked for a reaction from him. Nothing. He held still as if he were part of the chair, his yellow-green eyes watchful.

She twisted her hands together. "It wasn't like we were happy before you left, Gabe. We never did anything together. It was all about work for you. Mal and I, we just tiptoed around you, trying not to get in the way." She paused, waiting for something from him.

Still nothing.

She pushed ahead. "Things changed while you were gone. I got a new job, and I like what I do. I didn't realize before that I could do it on my own. But now I know, and . . . and I think our marriage was a mistake."

He blinked at the word "mistake," and she had to wonder if he felt some kind of response to it, because it was impossible to tell from his expression. "You've found someone else?" he inquired softly.

Was that disappointment she heard in his voice or jealousy?

"No," she said definitively. As if another man could take Gabe's place. "God, no." She was off men for a long time to come.

A thick silence settled between them. Helen swallowed hard. Gabe was staring at her in that same way that used to make her weak in the knees and hot in the face. It was having a similar effect now. She wished he would say something to break the tension.

"So, what, you want me to walk out right now?" he asked. This time there was an edge to his tone that betrayed some irritation.

"Of course not," she reassured him, wiping the sweat surreptitiously off her palms. "You're more than welcome to stay here until your memory comes back. I just—you know—thought I should explain why you're sleeping in the study and not . . . " *in my bed*. She couldn't seem to spit the words out.

His gaze slid down the length of her body. She experienced a pinpricking sensation clear down to her toes. It was obvious he was mentally undressing her. When he raised his eyes to hers, there was no mistaking the regret in them. "I see," he said. "So, you're saying you want to separate just as soon as I'm well enough to take care of myself." He said this with self-directed mockery.

Helen wet her dry lips. When he put it like that, it made her seem so coldhearted. "There's no hurry," she insisted. "It's important to me that you recover fully. I mean, being a SEAL is your life, and I want you to have your life back."

Resentment flickered in his gold-green eyes. She knew the signs of his volatile temper, and she barely caught herself from rushing in to beat down the flames. His temper was his own problem. She didn't need to wrestle with it anymore. "I'm sorry," she added, forcing her chin up. "I didn't mean for things to end up this way."

And before her courage could fail her, she quietly excused herself, making a dignified retreat to her bedroom, where she leaned against the door and stood there, quaking. She waited for the relief to wash over her. She'd done it: she'd given Gabe the ultimatum. Her best friend Leila would be proud of her.

Why, she wondered, wasn't she glad that part was over?

With the feeling that he'd taken a bullet in the gut, Gabe sat stunned on the kitchen stool. Bit by bit, his surprise shattered, sending shards of hurt under his skin and straight into his heart. This was why he'd never gotten close to anyone. Helen wielded a terrible power over him. He could barely breathe, his chest ached so much.

He tried to distance himself from the emotion. Why should he care what she thought? He'd just met the woman, as far as he remembered. He didn't know the first thing about her—what her favorite food was, what kind of music she listened to, hobbies, nothing. So what difference did it make that she considered their relationship over?

At the same time, he knew the answer: without her, he was even less than a former SEAL. He was a washed-up warrior, too beaten up to be recycled.

He gazed into his lemonade with the feeling that he was drowning. Then irritation kicked in and he wrenched his gaze upward. God damn it, he knew he wasn't lucky enough to have a wife like her just waiting for him to come home.

He couldn't blame her for not wanting him. He'd seen himself in the mirror; he knew what he looked like. Only that wasn't the reason she was calling it quits. She'd accused him of living his life for his team, of not making time for his family. Supposedly it had nothing to do with his state of mind now, or his disfigured body. Yeah, right.

He should never have married in the first place. He knew the kind of man he was; the kind of ruthless drive he had to excel. He even knew why he worked so hard—to make up for all those years he'd been a drain on the taxpayer's money. Given his family history, he knew he'd make a lousy husband and an even lousier father.

But then he'd met Helen, and apparently she was too much woman to let go of. So he'd compromised his private oath and married her. He could have written the end of the story himself.

And now who was sorrier for his neglect? He was. She'd

discovered that her life was better without him. And he needed her like a ship needed an anchor.

Anger flared in him, a welcome emotion compared to the pain that came before. Gabe rose on shaky knees to prowl around the kitchen. A sense of suffocation had him heading for the door. He needed fresh air to clear his head so he could think of a strategy.

He let himself out, squinting as sunlight bounced into his eyes. A balmy breeze ruffled his overlong hair as he moved down the steps. At the same time, he was struck by a sudden sense of vulnerability that had him scanning the quiet street for hidden dangers. But soon the mere act of walking upright took his mind off his uneasiness. He wasn't used to freedom—that was all.

Spying Mallory and the dog down at the beach, he moved painstakingly in their direction. As his tennis shoes filled with sand, he kicked them off and plodded on, barefoot.

Moving along the chain-linked fence, he noted the signs posted at intervals. WARNING: PROPERTY OF THE U.S. NAVY. ALL UNAUTHORIZED PERSONNEL KEEP OUT.

He suffered the same sense of inadequacy he'd lived with as a child. Being disabled, he could still get on base, but he wasn't authorized to set foot in Special Ops now, not without an invitation. He was an outsider, burdened with the dreadful possibility that he'd betrayed his country. As the DIA agent had implied the other day, why else would a SEAL lose his memory, except to forget the ignominious moment he'd disgraced himself?

Fuck, no. He shook his head in powerful denial. No matter what, he wouldn't have shared government secrets. He'd been trained to withstand torture, to keep silent.

He glanced at the two fingers where his nails were growing in. So pins had been jammed under his fingernails or maybe a hammer had smashed them till they bled. Big deal. He wouldn't have spilled his guts over that.

What if they'd pulled his tooth, though? He slid his tongue into the groove where his eyetooth had been. He'd had a bad experience as a kid, when the Novocain had failed to take. He didn't like people messing with his mouth.

By the time he reached the water, Gabe was quaking with fatigue. Mallory and the dog had headed down the beach to his right, too far ahead for him to catch up. They hadn't even seen him.

Dam Neck Naval Base stood on his left. Gabe studied the sweeping shoreline, relieved to recognize the missile detection drones rising from the dunes a short distance away. Farther down the beach stood the Shifting Sands, club and restaurant combined. Beyond that, the city of Virginia Beach.

Hallelujah! He knew this place. There wasn't any question he belonged here. This was his life. He planned to settle in and find himself. And then his wife could kick him out.

The strength leaked out of his legs, and he sat abruptly in the sand, brooding.

Not only was his career in jeopardy but his marriage was falling apart.

Unless he could fix it. She hadn't kicked him out yet.

As stubborn as he was, he didn't intend to bow out without putting up a fight. He shoved his feet into the sand and earned a nasty pinch on his pinky toe.

A crab scuttled back into his burrow. Gabe regarded the hole where the crab hunkered out of sight, kind of like his memories.

With a perverse need to expose the crab, he grasped a reed that had washed ashore, inserted it into the burrow, and teased the creature into grabbing on. Gabe tugged, but the sucker had a solid toehold. He tugged harder, and the crab let go.

Well, there you have it. He tossed aside the stick with disgust. Sebastian was right. His memories would have to come on their own.

But was he ready for them? The thought of remembering everything filled him with sudden dread. Was it just that he didn't want to relive the torture he'd endured? Or had he done something awful that he didn't want to face?

Aware that his jeans were growing damp, Gabe turned his head to eye his house, his cozy little cottage by the sea. He thought of the woman inside—gorgeous, strong in a way that both pleased and worried him.

Determination made him sit straighter. He didn't want to move out, not even when his memories returned. He liked what he'd done with his life, couldn't understand why he'd taken it for granted. He liked his house, his dog, his step-daughter. His wife was incredible, taking the time to care for him, even when it was obvious she had better things to do. Not only that, but she smelled good.

He wanted to keep her. Whatever it took, even if it meant sacrificing his commitment to the SEALs, he was determined to make her change her mind. He rose to his feet and beat the sand off his jeans.

Mallory had caught sight of him and was running toward him, dog straining at the leash. "What'd Mom say?" she asked, out of breath, as she drew up alongside him.

He was struck by the vulnerability in her eyes. "It was nothing," he said, forcing a smile. He could sense that Mallory needed careful handling.

"She's letting you stay, isn't she?" she asked, bending to pet the dog.

"Yeah, sure."

"Come on then." She gestured toward the house. "Let's go have lunch."

Grateful that at least the kid wanted him, Gabe fell into step beside her as Priscilla pulled her sled-dog style toward the house.

"You want some advice?" Mallory asked as they moved along the fence.

He glanced at her, intrigued. "Okay."

"If I were you, I'd take it slow. Mom still has feelings for you, you know. They just need to grow back." She gave him a sidelong look full of teenage wisdom.

Gabe's heart beat faster. Was Mallory right? Did Helen still have feelings for him? God, he hoped so. If she did, he would nurture those feelings the way Helen nurtured her wildflowers. But did he even know how? He'd married her, thinking he could make her happy and look what had happened. She'd stated herself that it wasn't his absence that had driven her love to extinction. It was the sad fact that he'd ignored his family, that he didn't know how to love.

Was he any different now than he'd been before? Yes . . . maybe. His imprisonment, though he couldn't remember it, had changed something inside him, something he couldn't put a name to. It was a feeling, really, just a quiet, patient *something* inside him.

He wanted to be a SEAL again, the best that he could be. But more than that, he wanted to be a husband to Helen and a father to Mallory. That would be his strategy, he decided, to nurture them both and prove he was someone in their lives worth keeping.

Chapter Four

He slept until late in the afternoon. Gold filaments of sunlight shot through the back windows of the house as Gabe ventured from the study, rubbing the sleep out of his eyes. "Hello?" His voice bounced off the high ceiling as he called for his family.

No one was home. Not even the dog came running.

He shivered, chilled by the unexpected isolation. Pausing in the kitchen, he poured himself a drink. Silence wrapped itself around him, giving him an eerie sense of déjà vu. He gazed out at the ocean, seeking comfort, but even the deep sapphire waves seemed far away.

Yet he belonged here, he assured himself. Other than Helen's ultimatum ringing in his ears, there wasn't any need to feel so adrift, so apart. *So vulnerable.*

He let his gaze wander, touching on the built-in bookshelves and furniture, seeking some hint of himself in this place. There were lots of books and school pictures of Mallory, but no pictures of himself.

He emptied his glass and wiped his mouth with the back

of his hand. He wanted to find proof that this was home, evidence that Helen once loved him, that a future for them wasn't impossible.

He'd found nothing in the study where he'd slept, save his college diploma hanging on the wall next to Helen's. The place to look, he decided, was the master bedroom.

He moved purposefully past the study and Mallory's room. The door to Helen's bedroom was partially ajar. He pushed it open wider, wondering if he'd recognize it. Her flowery fragrance floated out to greet him. It was the only thing familiar.

The room was practical, which pleased him. A king-sized bed dominated the right wall. The quilt and curtains were a collage of earth tones and canyon colors, and the four walls had been painted a dusky peach. There were more books here—romance novels—stuffed into oak bookcases, left on the bedside table. But most of them were old and worn, covered with a light film of dust. She hadn't read any lately.

He eyed the bed, his chest growing tight as he pictured Helen sprawled across it. The oak headboard, with its knotted rope design, matched the bureau and mirror. He realized his dresser, which was now in the study, completed the suite. It had gone in the empty space against the wall, here.

Surely there were traces of him in this room. But as he scanned the bookshelves and tabletops, he realized that other than a collection of Tom Clancy novels, there was no evidence that a male had ever lived here. There was nothing that he could claim as his own.

He probed deeper, desperate now. Surely Helen hadn't obliterated all of him—because if she had, then she'd already expunged him from her life; there was no way to win her back, despite what Mallory said.

He wandered into the walk-in closet and found some

clothing—a couple of dress shirts and slacks painstakingly wrapped in plastic, with matching shoes lined up beneath.

Was this him? The clothing struck him as vaguely familiar. Yes, now he remembered. He'd had himself fitted by the most expensive men's clothier in Coronado. He'd liked dressing up on his off hours. It had made him feel important.

Reaching under the plastic, Gabe rubbed a suit sleeve between his thumb and finger. The quality in the fabric did nothing for him. He doubted he'd wear it again, except maybe to a wedding or a funeral.

He turned away, dismayed to find so little of himself. He must have spent as much time away as Helen and Mallory had suggested. While he understood his drive for excellence, he couldn't understand why he'd have preferred the office to Helen's company.

Unless he'd been afraid of her and the power she wielded.

A familiar feeling coursed through him, as if he'd come to that same conclusion over and over again in the recent past.

He stepped from the closet and spied a bathtub through the open door across the room. It was a nice tub, big enough for two and fitted with jets. But what caught his attention was the standing picture frame, surrounded by half-melted candles.

There, among the candles, was a picture of himself. He approached the tub and studied the scene. The candles were melted to mere nubs. He doubted Helen had been praying for him, not when severing ties was at the top of her agenda. So what was this about?

He picked up the photo and regarded it. He felt as if he were looking at a stranger.

The warrior in the picture was someone to be reckoned with. He wore desert camouflage, his hair neatly shorn, and a confident smile on his too handsome face. He also looked like a man too revved up to slow down, eyes blazing with ambition.

Gabe's gaze slid to his reflection in the mirror. He hardly looked like the same man. Leaning toward the mirror, he compared differences.

There were new marks on his face: several white lines around his mouth from getting his lip split open; a scar just below his left eyebrow. He had dark circles under his eyes now, too. His cheeks were hollowed out. He pulled his lips back in a grimace. The missing eyetooth gave him a piratical look.

But the eyes were the same.

He stared at his reflection and those gold-green eyes stared back at him. *Jaguar.* The code name sounded in his head with the clarity of someone talking in his ear. He'd gotten the name before his memory failed him, five years ago when he'd joined SEAL Team Twelve.

For someone with such good vision, you can't even see what's right in front of you.

This time Helen's voice was unmistakable, coming out of the past. Gabe drew back, startled by the clarity of the memory and the aching accusation in her tone. They'd been arguing over Mallory, who'd done something wrong, something for attention.

"Gabe?"

Helen's voice had him turning in confusion. Was she really calling him or was he still remembering?

The sound of running feet was his only other warning. With a bark, Priscilla located his whereabouts, blocking his hasty retreat from the bathroom. Gabe cursed his sluggish reactions. He'd been caught, first by the dog who cornered him and then by Helen, who drew up short at her door, amazed to find him in her bathroom, clutching his picture.

At the sight of her, all thoughts fled his mind. Her skin was flushed from a recent run. Her long hair was in a ponytail. The spandex top she wore left her midriff bare and her nipples clearly delineated. "Were you looking for something?" she asked, still breathing hard.

Her frosty tone accused him of invading her space. He felt it important to explain his actions, but the sight of her nipples had narrowed his focus considerably and he had to struggle to think. "I was, uh, looking for a picture of me." He held up the frame to show her that he'd found it.

She glanced at it, myriad emotions in her eyes.

Gabe looked at the candles in the bathroom, then back at her, conjecturing, but unwilling to press her.

"I, um . . . " She licked a droplet of sweat off her upper lip, while coloring fiercely.

"You don't have to explain," he said quickly. He didn't want to hear what kind of ritual she'd enacted in order to forget about him.

"Is there anything else you need?" she asked, looking relieved.

He let his gaze drift deliberately down her scantily clad frame. "Not that you'd want to give me," he said, unable to check his self-pitying smile.

A haunted look crossed her face.

"Guess you want to take a shower," he said, having mercy on her. He headed out of the room, edging by her in the process.

In the same time, the dog bolted past him, knocking him into Helen, who hit the door. She sucked in a breath at the full-body contact and tried to melt into the wood. Only the tips of her breasts touched his chest.

"Sorry," he muttered, electrified by the feel of her pebble-hard nipples against his chest. Hot and sweaty as she was, she smelled delicious.

He was a lot sorrier to have to step away from her. "I'll be in the family room," he added, hoping against all odds that she'd call him back and indulge his fantasy of seeing her strip that top off. But as he drifted down the hallway, the only sound that followed him was the firm shutting of her door followed by the click of the lock.

The encounter left him weary. He paused by the study to stick the picture into his dresser, where he buried the handsome stranger under a pile of socks. He was no longer the confident warrior who'd taken his good fortune for granted. He was scarred and he was scared. He may even have betrayed his country—the ultimate traitor.

Helen struggled to focus on her cooking. She'd never felt at ease in the kitchen in the first place, but Gabe's presence in the living room made her feel twice as inept. She hadn't gotten used to his presence yet. Dishing the pork chops into the hot pan, she found herself regarding him from the corner of her eye.

She'd always been weak where Gabe was concerned. The breadth of his shoulders never failed to rouse her awareness of him. His virility charged the room with a sexual undercurrent that had been absent in her life for over a year. His presence caused an abrupt awakening of her libido that made it difficult to marshal her thoughts, made her feel awkward and unfocused.

She thoroughly resented his effect on her. She'd been perfectly happy to live a nunlike existence. It jarred her peaceful self-occupation to have him in her life again.

If Mallory wasn't sitting close to Gabe, looking happy as a clam watching a game show for kids, Helen would be tempted to order Gabe out of the house, right now, so she could at least draw a full breath.

"What is the name of the mythological bird that rises from its ashes into new life?" asked the host of Mallory's show.

"The phoenix," said Mallory and Gabe at the same time. They shared a quick smile.

"An illness which, in Latin, means 'inflammation of the lungs.'"

"Pneumonia," Mallory piped up, but the boy on the red team got the answer wrong. "Oh, my God. How dumb is he?"

Helen couldn't stand it any longer, watching Gabe and Mallory all cozied up before the TV. *It's not going to stay like that,* she wanted to warn her daughter. *Don't get your hopes up that he's going to be a father to you.* "Mallory, would you set the table for me?" she asked, hearing tension in her own voice.

To her surprise, both Gabe and Mallory popped up from their seats.

"I've got it," Mallory said to him.

Gabe wandered into the kitchen, causing Helen's blood pressure to soar. She already felt like a hormonal wreck. The last thing she needed was him hovering over her. "Is there anything I can do?" he asked, glancing with concern at the sizzling pork chops.

They were burning, Helen realized. "No, thanks," she said, hurrying to the stove to flip them over. As she lifted the lid off the pan, a fleck of grease flew out, catching the underside of her arm. Helen nearly dropped the glass lid. It clattered into place as she hurried to the sink to run her arm under cold water.

She found Gabe right next to her. "You okay?" he asked with evident concern.

Had he always been this tall, this attentive? She stepped quickly away, snatching up a paper towel. "I'm fine," she said, pressing the cool towel to the burn.

He trailed her over to the stove. "You might want to turn down the heat," he offered, doing it himself.

She whirled on him. "Don't tell me how to cook," she warned him, crushing the paper towel into a ball.

He stood there, clearly taken aback by her vehemence. "I'm not telling you how to cook," he said. "I just don't want you to burn yourself again."

"I know what I'm doing," she insisted. "I don't need you to micromanage me."

With a nonplussed look, Gabe glanced at Mallory who had frozen by the buffet, looking pained.

"I thought I ignored you," Gabe said quietly.

He had. He'd spent hours and weeks and months away from her, giving everything to his team. Self-pity strangled Helen abruptly. She turned around so he wouldn't see her stricken expression and stirred the rice without purpose.

The silence in the kitchen was suddenly bottomless, as was the despair in Helen's heart. Why did they have to go through this? she wondered. Gabe's presence only confused her senses and caused her daughter to wish for things that would never happen. Having Gabe home was pointless. He'd proven in the past that he wasn't meant to be a husband or a father. It was just a matter of time before he proved it again. It wasn't fair to either of them that they should have to relive their heartbreak.

Sensitive to Helen's upset and realizing that he was the cause for it, Gabe turned toward the living room and thumped into an armchair. It'd be easier on Helen if he just stayed out of the way. Clearly having him around was as unsettling to her as not having his memories was to him.

Mallory's show had gone to commercial. Gabe reached for the remote and flipped idly through the channels, pausing when he came to CNN. It disturbed him to think of how much he'd missed this last year—Jesus, the last three years!

"Relations with North Korea continue to deteriorate," relayed the newscaster. "South Korea's president continues endeavors to keep the peace between the two countries, but North Korean leader, Kim Chong-il, has yet to cut back the nuclear program. President Towers has stated that in order for the United States to give financial aid, North Korea must respond to the U.N.'s demands. At the present time, it is estimated that one in three North Koreans will starve this year if humanitarian aid is not resumed."

Gabe was aware that the news had moved on to other hot spots, yet he sat unmoving on the couch as a vision of Kim Chong-il, North Korea's leader, burned the back of his eyes. He'd stared at a picture of that face so frequently that he knew every line and wrinkle on it. Goose bumps ridged Gabe's forearms and spread. *One in three North Koreans will starve this year.* The words of the newscaster replayed in his head. A chill moved up Gabe's spine and gripped his scalp.

There was something significant about the hunger raging in North Korea. Something he knew. Something he had to remember.

He felt the tension gather in his muscles, making him rigid. He heard himself breathing hard, felt his hands curl into fists. He searched his empty mind and found nothing but vague shapes shrouded in gray; illusory images that flashed so briefly he couldn't recollect what they were. It was important. Christ, he had to remember!

"Dad!" Mallory's voice penetrated the fog in which he was trapped. "Are you okay?"

He felt her hand on his shoulder and he shook himself free, rousing to the present.

Helen rushed over and stood behind her daughter.

Gabe dragged in a steadying breath. His skin felt clammy. "Yeah, I'm okay." He came shakily to his feet. For a second he thought he was going to puke. He held perfectly still. The scent of burnt pork chops assailed his nostrils.

Helen's face swam before his eyes. "I'm calling the doctor," she informed him, heading for the phone.

"No," he said, waving her back. "It was a flashback. They said it would happen. I'm fine."

She searched his face. "Did you remember something?"

He found her concern encouraging. Or did she merely want this transitory stage over with, so she could move on with her life? "Not really." His thoughts went back to what he'd heard on the news, and he rubbed his forehead with exasperation. "But there's something I have to remember."

"You will," she assured him, touching him briefly. "Don't try so hard. It'll come in its own time."

He thought about the crab he'd tried to drag from its burrow that afternoon. He wasn't sure he had time to coax his memories to the surface.

But her palm felt warm and soft against his arm. "Dinner smells good," he lied. "Let's eat."

Her look of startled pleasure stayed with him for the remainder of the night.

"Mrs. Renault, would you join us?"

Helen frowned over the article she was reading on how to make a rock garden. Dr. Noel Terrien was standing at his door, a door that had been closed for some time now. Helen had been prepared to wait the full hour. She was completely caught off guard by the invitation to join in Gabe's therapy.

"It would be helpful to your husband if you would sit with us from time to time," added the doctor encouragingly.

Oh, bother. She was still distressed that she'd had to leave work early. The paperwork had piled up from her day off, and she hadn't even put a dent in it. The routine that she'd enjoyed when Gabe was gone was shattered. Once more, the world revolved around him.

She immediately chided herself for being so insensitive. Gabe was dealing with far more serious issues than inconvenience. She ought to be more supportive. The sooner he recovered, the sooner she could move on with her life.

On the other hand, she wasn't that eager to bring back the old Gabe. The man she'd brought home from the hospital might look like him, but he hadn't acted anything like him. He'd been patient, thoughtful, and attentive—attributes he hadn't exhibited in years.

The old Gabe had also refused to take part in Mallory's counseling. She didn't want to be guilty of the same crime, so she dropped the magazine on the chair and snatched up her purse.

Gabe was waiting in the doctor's office. He'd chosen the least comfortable chair and was sitting ramrod-straight in it with his arms crossed.

No wonder Dr. Terrien had asked for her help.

At her entrance, Gabe sent her an imploring gaze. He looked so utterly miserable that compassion welled up in her. She surprised herself by taking the chair nearest his and giving him an encouraging smile.

Dr. Terrien sat in a wingback chair opposite them. Leaning forward, he propped his elbows on his knees. He was a big-boned man with a head of salt and pepper curls, thick eyebrows, and eyes the color of the ocean on overcast days.

"Mrs. Renault," he said, "your husband has just been relating to me what it is he can remember, and his memory apparently stops about the time he met you. I'm hoping you can fill in the gaps. Whether or not he remembers is not as important right now as giving him a sense of continuity. He was just telling me of his years at Annapolis."

Helen took a cleansing breath. Okay, she thought, simple enough. She could color in Gabe's past without revealing her own naive belief that he would be her prince and make her life a fairy tale.

"Annapolis," she repeated, picking up the doctor's cue. "So, you remember your classes?" She addressed this question to Gabe, who nodded grimly. "One of your instructors' names was Commander Troy," she continued. "Do you remember him?"

He nodded slowly, his brow clearing. "Sure," he said. "Naval history. He was the one who encouraged me to be a SEAL."

"You were his favorite student," Helen explained, trying to keep the mockery out of her tone, "older and more experienced than the others. He obviously convinced you, so you went to Coronado for BUD/S training class 223 and you were one of the sixteen who actually graduated. You remember all that?"

"Yes," he said succinctly.

"Then you remember being assigned back on the East Coast," she added.

"I remember," he said, looking glum. "But I lived in the bachelor quarters."

"You did then," she agreed. "But the next summer you went back to Annapolis to visit Commander Troy."

Gabe's eyes roved her face like searchlights. It was clear he'd forgotten that part.

Helen plunged ahead, keeping her story as factual as possible. "And when you did, he introduced you to his younger daughter, and that was when we met."

She knew the second Gabe put her first and last name together, because the corners of his eyes crinkled with appreciation. *Helen Troy.* Yes, her father loved the classics—though she hardly lived up to her name, unless you considered the number of ships that had sailed *away* from her.

"Anyway," she pressed on, determined to put this chore behind her, "within a couple of months, we got married. We bought the house in Sandbridge. The first two years you were home maybe . . . six or eight months total? Then this last year . . . " She shrugged, hoping to give the impression that their marriage had been so brief, so uneventful, that it wasn't any wonder he'd forgotten.

But Dr. Terrien's steady gaze assured her that he was on to her. "Mrs. Renault," he said, "what was your impression of Gabriel the first time you met him?"

Drat. She forced her fingers to uncurl and placed them casually in her lap. A snapshot image of the other Gabe flashed across her mind. "He was . . . godlike," she admitted, smoothing the mockery from her tone. "He was handsome and smart and carried himself with so much . . . confidence." She'd toyed with substituting the word "arrogance," but then she'd chickened out. "I was drawn to him," she added, downplaying her infatuation. Gabe had dazzled her with his charisma and his knee-weakening good looks. His ambition to be the best SEAL ever had met with her approval, back then. He was so different from Zachary, Mallory's father.

"Did you know he would be gone so much?" Dr. Terrien asked. "How did you deal with that?"

Helen considered the question with private recrimination. "I guess I figured that a part-time father for my daughter was better than none at all," she said, misleading them both into thinking that was her main motive for marrying. She didn't want to reveal the truth: that she'd thought herself desperately in love. She could see Gabe out the corner of her eye, regarding her with unmasked astonishment.

"What happened to Mallory's real father?" the doctor wanted to know.

Helen sighed. "Nothing. He's out there somewhere. He's just never been there for her."

The doctor steepled his hands and rubbed his chin along his fingertips. "This case is extremely unusual," he admitted, taking a different tack. "In many cases of trauma, the victim will forget the violence he endured. That's perfectly normal, perhaps even desirable. But Gabriel has also forgotten the two years preceding his disappearance. X rays reveal that he took a blow to his right cheek. Trauma to the frontal lobe may have added to his memory loss. We really don't know.

"But here's what we're going to do," he continued, leaning toward them. "It's my recommendation that we leave Gabriel's memories of captivity dormant for the time being. It's entirely possible to lead a normal life and never remember them. However, you *must* remember the two years prior to that, or both your career and marriage are bound to suffer. Do I have your agreement on that?"

Gabe offered a nod, but he'd averted his gaze, clearly troubled by the doctor's words.

"Helen?"

"Yes, of course," she said quickly. The doctor had picked up pretty quickly that their marriage was on the rocks.

"Good," he said. "I have an assignment for you both."

Uh-oh. Mutual assignments required a degree of intimacy, and Helen wanted no part of that.

"This evening," he instructed, "I want you to pull out all your photo albums and go through them. If you don't remember anything in the pictures, Gabriel, that's okay. Your wife will interpret them as she remembers them. Let's see if the photos don't stir some memories or prompt some flashbacks. We'll discuss them tomorrow when we meet again."

Helen put a hand up. "Just one thing," she said. "I can't bring him here every day at two o'clock. I have to work." She tried not to sound too stressed.

"How about four o'clock?"

Reconciled to her duties, she gave an inner sigh. She could cancel the afternoon body sculpting and make it by four without too much trouble. "Fine," she agreed. "Four o'clock will work."

The doctor nodded and looked at Gabe. "Do you have anything to add, Gabriel? Any questions for me?"

Helen looked at Gabe to gauge his reaction. He hadn't said much at all since her entrance. His mouth looked grim. He'd tucked his hands under his armpits. "What's your prognosis?" he asked point-blank.

Dr. Terrien's shaggy eyebrows rose. "It's a little early for me to say," he answered honestly.

"Give a stab at it," Gabe quietly exhorted.

Helen's gaze slid back to the doctor. When Gabe demanded answers, people did back flips to ensure that he got them.

Dr. Terrien shook his head. "It's really too soon," he insisted. "You could get your memory back tomorrow. Or, it could take years. As I've said, we have no way to predict whether your amnesia is a result of brain damage or emotional distress or both. But with your wife's help"—his mysterious gaze slid over Helen—"we'll do our best to recover the earlier memories."

Helen's gut clenched. What was this, marriage counseling? She didn't want to rehash those earlier days. She wanted to move on with her life.

With sudden rebellion, she surged to her feet. But obedience had been drilled into her since childhood, and it kept her rooted to the carpet.

"Did you fill your prescriptions?" the doctor asked Gabe.

"Yes," he said, and he stood up slowly, as if the session had exhausted him.

"Dexamphetamine during the day," the doctor said, coming to his feet. "It'll keep you alert and focused."

"Already took it," Gabe said, thrusting a hand at the doctor.

Helen shook the doctor's hand as well and exited quickly. She stopped in the waiting room, long enough to tear the article about rock gardens out of the magazine and stuff it into her purse. One day, when she had time to herself again, she'd work on it.

She realized Gabe was holding the door for her and she hurried through it, thanking him, though she'd learned long ago that such formalities were taught in the military. He wasn't simply being thoughtful.

The sunlight was blinding. Helen shoved her sunglasses on. Gabe squinted. Once inside the Jaguar, she cranked on the air conditioner and turned up the radio, making conversation unnecessary. They drove back to Sandbridge in silence.

Helen spent the time reviewing what the doctor had told them. The longer she thought about it, the more worried she got. Dr. Terrien seemed determined to review the two years of their married life together. She wanted nothing more than to forget those hurtful years. She decided then and there that Mallory was going to walk Gabe through the photo albums.

They were just approaching the beachfront when Gabe shifted in his seat and faced her.

Helen's heartbeat accelerated. The directness of his gaze made her skin feel tight.

"Who was Mallory's father?" he asked, surprising her with his continued interest.

"His name was Zach Taylor. I dated him in college."

"And?" he prompted.

"And nothing. He dropped me like a hot potato when he found out I was pregnant. My parents were horrified and insisted that I deny Zach all legal rights as a father. He was more than willing to sign the documents."

"Why would your parents do that?" Gabe asked.

Helen gave a humorless laugh. "Zach was going nowhere with his life. Even though he was brilliant, he dropped out of college because he thought his professors were ignorant. He couldn't hold a steady job because he thought his manager was ignorant. He was the dead last person my parents wanted in my life or in Mallory's."

They drove awhile longer in silence. "That must have sucked," Gabe said with sympathy.

She shot him a startled glance. It wasn't often that Gabe considered other people's feelings. She shrugged. "I got through it," she retorted. True, but not without making one more mistake and giving her heart to a man who'd refused to give his in return.

"So they introduced me to you, thinking I'd make a better father?" he marveled.

Helen frowned. The old Gabe had always touted himself as the better choice. "At least you didn't run the other way," she pointed out, defending him. He'd been startled upon meeting Mallory, there was no denying that. But he'd recovered quickly, determined, it seemed, to claim Helen for his bride, regardless of the luggage she carried with her.

"Has he ever asked about her? Ever wanted to see her?"

"Zach? No, never."

Gabe shook his head, muttering something deprecatory under his breath.

"What's gotten into you?" Helen demanded.

"I can't understand a man running from his mistakes—not when there's a child involved."

His words struck a funny chord in her. "Why not?" she countered. "That's exactly what you did. You hid at the office so that you wouldn't have to face the fact that you were married." She couldn't believe she had the gall to toss that out, especially when Gabe was being so considerate.

His yellow-green eyes flashed in her direction. "Pull the car over," he said with resolve.

"What?" There were mounds of sand on either side of the road. She was not going to pull over and get them stuck.

"Pull over. Now." To her astonishment, he reached over and grabbed the steering wheel, driving two tires up the sandy embankment. Helen slammed on the brakes, and they came to a swerving stop.

"What are you doing!" she yelled, turning toward him and whipping off her sunglasses.

"Shhh," he said, catching her face with his hand.

Helen froze. What in God's name was he doing? He wasn't going ballistic on her, was he? Just what kind of effect had his captivity had on him?

His grip was gentle, thank God. His fingers strayed, caressing her cheekbone, the line of her jaw, her chin. Dazed, she stared into his eyes, snared by the web of sensual pleasure he was spinning on her face.

"I want you to know something," he said, very intently, his eyes burning into hers. "Whatever happens to you and me, if it doesn't work out between us, I'll still take care of Mallory. I'll never do what Zach did and turn my back on her."

Helen swallowed convulsively. Several times now in the short while that they'd been back together, he'd surprised her by saying the unexpected. Did he mean it? Why would he suddenly care about Mallory when he hadn't even given her the time of day before? There was only one reason she could think of. He was scared of losing his family; scared of being all alone with no career to occupy him.

"I know what you're doing," she said quietly.

He shook his head. "What?"

"It won't work, you know. Paying attention to us now won't change the past."

He released her abruptly and sat back.

She felt like she'd just slapped him. Doubt tugged at her anew. Maybe she'd read him wrong.

He looked out the window, averting his face.

Helen struggled with herself. Part of her longed to take those words back, but it was better to be forthright, to make it absolutely clear that she didn't want to backtrack.

Swallowing an apology, she fumbled to replace her sunglasses. She put the car into gear and drove them out of the sand, headed for home.

They completed the trip in silence. Silence so thick it would take a jackhammer to break through it.

She suspected she had actually hurt Gabe's feelings. That in itself was a novelty. For once, she was the one ignoring him and he was the one feeling rejected.

She frowned at the realization. Had they switched roles since his return? Was she doing to him what he had done to her in some kind of subconscious reprisal?

Darting him a glance, she caught a glimpse of his hopeless expression. Guilt pricked her anew. To think what the man had suffered this past year! Just because their marriage had been a disappointment, that didn't give her the right to be mean to him now.

She nosed the car into their driveway and killed the engine. Just as Gabe started to push his door open, she reached for him, putting a light hand on his forearm. "I'm sorry," she said quickly, meaning it.

He looked from her hand to her face. For several seconds, he said nothing at all, though his eyes were full of silent messages. "Me too," he said finally.

With that, he withdrew from the vehicle, leaving her strangely more regretful.

Chapter Five

She'd talked Mallory into taking her place.

Disappointment dragged Gabe's spirits down to an all-time low as he watched his stepdaughter pull a photo album from a shelf on the bookcase. "This is your wedding album," she said, flopping down on the study couch next to him.

Gabe looked down at the white cover with its gold trim, conscious of a great reluctance to participate in this activity, especially if Helen wasn't going to do it with him. "You know, I'm feeling kind of tired," he balked. "Let's look at pictures in the morning." He wasn't lying, either. Despite the medicine he'd taken every four hours, he felt weary down deep in his bones.

What he felt was defeat. The two things he wanted most right now seemed completely out of reach: returning to the SEALs and Helen's warmth.

Since her apology that afternoon, she'd been especially kind to him, but in a cool way that left distance between them. He'd forked down as much of her watery casserole as he could, his appetite having fled along with his energy. He wanted nothing more than to take his sleeping pills and seek oblivion on this lumpy couch.

"Just one album?" Mallory pleaded. She turned her big green eyes on him, and he knew he was a goner.

"All right. Just one."

She rewarded him with a smile, a dimple appearing on her left cheek. He found himself thinking she was going to break a few hearts one day. God protect the male race.

"Okay," Mallory said, cracking the cover, "here's Mom getting dressed for the wedding."

Gabe took a deep breath and plunged in. He was treated to a vision of Helen in a lace corset, complete with garters and sexy white stockings, standing beside her wedding dress. Her thighs were even more gorgeous than he'd imagined. His mouth went dry.

"And here she is putting on makeup."

Gabe lost himself in the close-up shots of Helen's face. She was younger, fresher, curvier than now. The pictures of her peering into the mirror, applying blush and eyeliner were subtly intimate. They caught a young woman performing that once-in-a-lifetime ritual of preparing for her groom. Helen glowed with expectation. Her honey-colored eyes were bright with excitement. No wonder he'd been unable to resist her.

Mallory turned the page.

"Here you are at the church. You're waiting for Mom to come in."

The picture was just like the one he'd taken from her bathroom, only this time he was a sharp-looking sailor in his dress-whites. The expression on his face was supremely confident. No last-minute sweats for this guy. The focus in his gaze was daunting.

Gabe felt as if the walls were closing in. He sat back on

the couch and steadied his breathing. Perspiration dotted his forehead and made his shirt stick to his back. He didn't want to see any more pictures.

Mallory turned her head and looked at him. She scooted farther back, so she was sitting snugly beside him. "You want to see what I looked like at ten?" she asked.

The kid was good. Gabe gave her profile a wry grimace and let his gaze be drawn to the album again. She was pointing to a girl in a garnet-colored gown, her chestnut hair shot with baby's breath, green eyes wide and sparkling.

Gabe felt the breath rush out of his lungs. "Pretty," he said. "I like the color of your hair."

She grimaced. "Yeah, well, this'll wash out." As she tucked a strand of dyed hair behind her ear, Gabe realized she'd punched holes all the way up the delicate shell.

"Does Mom know you pierced your ear like that?" he asked. He gave himself a start by calling Helen *Mom*.

Mallory covered the evidence with a toss of her head. "Yeah," she said warily. "It's just my left ear. I did it a month ago," she added defensively.

"Why'd you do it?" he asked, not seeing the point, especially when she kept them empty.

A sulky expression slipped over her face. "I don't know. My friends dared me to, I guess."

"What did Mom say?" He liked calling Helen *Mom*. It made their arrangement sound permanent, irrevocable.

Her look of disgust was almost comical. "She wigged out on me completely. That's why I don't wear any studs. I have to close the holes up."

He wanted to shake Helen's hand for holding her ground. "So you put yourself through all that for nothing," he pointed out.

She shrugged, a quick rise and fall of her shoulders.

Her silence nagged at him. "Do you always do what your friends say?" he added, goading something out of her.

"No."

He waited, sensing more.

"That's not really why I did it," she admitted quietly.

"No?"

Seconds stretched by as Mallory stared sightlessly at the photos. Suddenly she pushed the album off her lap and bolted, leaving Gabe sitting there by himself with more to think about than ever.

He wasn't an expert in child psychology by any means, but half a dozen holes in one ear was surely a cry for attention. Given Helen's accusations that he'd ignored his stepdaughter, he had to assume that he was, in some way, responsible for Mallory's actions, even though she'd thought him dead when she did it. If he'd been more of a father before he'd left on his last assignment, would she have pierced her ear then?

With a whispered curse he rubbed his gritty eyes. God, he was tired! The roadblocks in his future seemed higher and wider than anything he'd ever faced in his past—and that was saying a lot for a man who'd lived through Hell Week. Back in his days of training he'd had the energy to endure whatever was demanded of him. He was younger then. Right now, he felt about a million years old.

Through half-closed eyes, he studied his surroundings. The office had been converted out of the smallest of the three bedrooms. His bed was a burgundy and green sofa, lumpy but soft. The bookcases and computer desk were matching mahogany. An elegant valance framed the single window. It was paradise compared to what he'd likely endured. He really couldn't complain.

His gaze slid to the space beside him where the album

teetered on the edge of the cushion, still opened to where Mal had left it. He studied the pictures from a distance, keeping himself aloof.

There he was, a head above the rest of the men, posing for the camera with a possessive hand about Helen's shoulders. Curiosity prompted him to turn the page, and there they were, kissing.

Gabe's breath caught. He leaned toward the close-up shot, lured by the thought of kissing his wife. The expression on her face ignited a fierce heat in him. Her lashes were weighted with desire, her eyes glazed, lips softly parted. Jesus, she was beautiful like that!

Staring at her picture, he realized she'd tried purposefully to mislead him today. She'd told the doctor that she had married Gabe to give Mallory a father. But that wasn't the whole story, was it? These pictures made it obvious that she'd fallen head-over-heels in love with him. For a second, he reveled in the realization. But then he recalled his current physical condition, and his spirits sank. He wasn't the man he used to be; he was literally hatched with scars. No wonder she wanted nothing to do with him now.

Pushing to his feet, Gabe crossed to his chest of drawers and fished out fresh clothing. Resigned to a "cold" shower, he crossed the hall to Mallory's bathroom, more than ready to put this trying day behind him.

As it had last night, the sun and moon motif cheered him. He tossed his dirty clothes into the laundry basket, wondering when Helen had the time to do laundry. Maybe he'd help out while she was at work tomorrow. He'd also fix the brass hook that was coming off the wall.

Having assigned himself those tasks, he felt moderately better. If he made himself useful, Helen would be less eager to pawn him off. And if he played his cards right, he might even get to sleep with her one day. Not that he trusted himself to actually spend the night in her bed. He'd mistaken Master Chief for one of his captors. God knew what he might do to his unwitting wife.

But he was putting the cart before the horse. Step number one was to get Helen to appreciate him. To do that, he'd have to make himself indispensable. He'd take care of all the little odd jobs that needed doing. He'd be the perfect father to Mallory, who'd punched half a dozen holes in her ear for no apparent reason.

Refreshed from his shower and feeling better for his plan, Gabe donned his clothes. He was heading for the study when he noticed Helen at Mallory's door. He offered her a smile, which made her frown at him suspiciously.

She twisted Mallory's doorknob. "Honey, what are you doing?" She peeked inside.

"Reading." Mal's voice sounded like it came from the ceiling. She was up on her bunk bed.

"Really." On that skeptical note, Helen disappeared inside.

Gabe had peered in Mallory's room earlier. He pictured it in his mind's eye now: a sturdy white bunk bed drowning in stuffed animals, pink walls, white furniture. The innocent-little-girl setup was ruined by posters of pop stars, rap musicians, and bumper stickers with slogans like ALL STRESSED OUT AND NO ONE TO CHOKE plastered at intervals along the wall.

He pictured Helen approaching the bed. "*That* is not a book," she said. There came the sound of magazine crinkling.

"Hey, you lost my page!" Mallory protested.

"You want to read, get started on your summer reading list," her mother retorted.

"I hate those books!"

Seeing an opportunity to invoke his new plan, Gabe cruised down the hall and poked his head through the door.

"You haven't even tried them. How can you say you hate them?" Helen reasoned. She was bending over, searching through the bookcase, oblivious to Gabe's presence.

He sure as hell noticed her. Forgetting all about Mallory, Gabe ogled Helen's perfect—er, perfect assets. She was wearing a pair of jean shorts—so short, in fact, that when she leaned over to scan the bookcase, he was treated to two inches of sculpted buttocks—no panties in sight, unless she wore a thong. The possibility electrified him.

Mallory gave a snicker, and he ripped his gaze away. Helen looked around sharply. She straightened, clutching a book to her chest. "Don't sneak up on me," she scolded.

Gabe raised his hands in the air. "I thought I could help," he offered, his face hot.

"I've got it covered." Helen turned toward her daughter and thrust a book up at her.

"Not the biggest one!" Mallory wailed.

"What is it?" Gabe inquired.

"*Les Miserables.*" Helen held it insistently up to her daughter. "She should start on it now so she finishes it by the beginning of school."

"I agree," he said, looking pointedly at Mallory.

Mallory gaped at them. "Well, I don't," she said, "and I'm the one who has to read it!"

"You'll read it," said Helen firmly, "or you won't leave the house this week."

Gabe stepped forward. "I'll handle this."

"Excuse me?" She turned disbelieving eyes at him.

"I will," he said. "I'll get her to read the book."

"How?"

"I'll read it with her. It's a great book."

Mother and daughter stared at him as if he'd suddenly grown horns on his head. "Okaaay," Helen said faintly. "I'm going to take a shower." Then she sailed by him, handing off the book. Seconds later, her bedroom door clicked shut.

Was that a victory? he wondered.

Mallory propped her chin on her hand and smirked at him. "You were checking Mom out," she accused, her smile like a Cheshire cat's.

Gabe didn't bother to deny it. He shrugged instead, making light of his one-sided attraction. "You come down here"—he pointed to the bottom bunk—" 'cause there's no way I'm going up there."

She made a sound of complaint but started toward the ladder.

Gabe ducked into the dark space and switched on the reading light. "You're going to like this book," he said, putting his back to the wall. "I read it in high school and college." Déjà vu sacked him again, and he held still a minute, unable to escape the feeling that he'd sat like this, with his back to the wall, for many, many hours.

A now-familiar urgency niggled at him anew. He *knew* something. Something he had to tell the others. Something fraught with danger, that made him suddenly light-headed and damp with sweat.

Mallory leapt to the floor, and the feeling evaporated. She grabbed a pillow off her bed and settled in next to him. "It's more than three hundred pages," she complained.

With a shudder, Gabe focused on the present. "Take your shoes off," he said, seeing her sneakers. "You wore your shoes in your bed? That's gross."

Her shoes thumped to the floor. "You smell like strawberries," she answered, shifting the focus deftly from herself.

He'd helped himself to her Berry Bouquet body wash. "Wear your shoes in your bed again and they'll disappear," he warned, not falling for her ploy.

"Okay," she said lightly, straightening away from him.

He opened the book. "You want to read first, or do you want me to read."

"You." Her decision was immediate.

Clearing his voice, Gabe launched them into the novel. Soon they were both absorbed in the story.

As interesting as Victor Hugo's narrative was, Gabe didn't fail to notice when Mallory rested her cheek against his shoulder. A soft warmth stole through him, filling him—not with terror as he might have guessed it would—but with contentment. The feeling made him think that his prickle of danger earlier was just in his head. Being the world's most indispensable dad had its subtle rewards.

"Can I read to the end of the chapter?" she asked, reaching for the book.

"Yeah, sure." She'd taken the bait.

He knew a moment's regret when she shifted away from him. But her quick words and lilting voice reminded him again of just how clever she really was. He was taken aback by his sense of pride. She wasn't even his kid—not biologically, barely through marriage—but, damn, she was bright.

At some point, he was aware that Helen was listening to them out in the hallway. Only a faint shadow and the scent of flowers alerted him to the fact that she was there. Suddenly Gabe wasn't listening to the story so much as he was wondering why she was hiding in the hallway.

Mallory's voice died on the chapter's final word. "Cool," she pronounced. "Let's read some more tomorrow."

Helen chose that moment to sweep into the room.

She wore silky white boxer shorts with a matching pajama

top. Her hair was hidden by a towel twisted into a turban. Her neck looked incredibly slim and vulnerable. He knew a desperate urge to put his mouth on it.

"I'm going to bed," she announced with forced brightness. "Mal, you need to take a shower." She ducked her head under the bunk bed to kiss her daughter. Because of the turban, she had to bend low enough to clear the top bunk. Her pajama top gaped, and Gabe got a glimpse of her perfect breasts, dangling like ripe fruit.

Sweet Jesus. It was all he could do not to grab her and drag her to him.

She kissed her daughter on the cheek, then turned her head his way—probably by force of habit—and froze.

He didn't give her the chance to change her mind. On impulse, he planted his mouth squarely on her lips. Her eyes flared with surprise, and for a split second, they stared at each other.

A memory crystallized. He recalled, with the same shuddering pleasure of the moment, pushing himself inside her, only he'd made the mistake of looking into her eyes. Panic came out of nowhere, drowning him, pulling him down into a place where emotion ruled him. He remembered squeezing his eyes shut, willing the feeling away. Love was dangerous. It could make him hesitate before pulling the trigger; make him balk before jumping from a plane. He couldn't be a SEAL and feel this way.

Gabe drew back with a start. Helen stared at him, looking nonplussed.

Shaken by his memory, Gabe lurched out of the small space and left the room. He found himself heading for the front door, needing to clear his head.

He paced the length of the deck, sucking in deep breaths of salty air. Trailing the balcony around the side of the house, he saw that the crescent moon had cast a silvery blanket on the sea. He gripped the deck rail, finding it rough, in need of sanding.

Once his heart beat steady again, he allowed himself to relive the memory a second time. He was grateful for it, despite the disturbing emotions that accompanied it. The memory proved what he sensed already, that he belonged with Helen—that their lovemaking had been as incredible as he'd imagined it would be. So incredible that it had scared him to death.

He closed his eyes and relived the pleasure of loving her body, devouring every inch of sweetness, savoring every one of her responses. *For a while, she struggled to remain aloof, resisting his call to abandonment, but he wasn't satisfied unless she yielded herself completely. He sabotaged her self-control, licking, stroking, and probing her, until she thrashed in his arms and cried out her surrender.*

He was surprised to feel moisture on her face. He paused, gazing into her eyes to see why she was crying.

Her eyes were pools of amber. He made a point never to look in them when they made love. This night, he forgot. Instantly emotion clutched his heart. He couldn't look into her eyes and not feel her pain, not feel his overwhelming need for her.

Frightened by the power she wielded, he rolled abruptly away and stared at the ceiling, denying himself fulfillment, running from the fragments of love floating in her eyes.

The ocean wind blew across Gabe's bare arms and legs, rousing him to the present. Now he understood Helen's reluctance to have him back. He'd refused to give her the love he demanded in return. He'd feared his feelings would make him less of a warrior. And when he sensed her love fracturing, he panicked and ran, not wanting to see what his coldness was costing them.

With a groan for his own stupidity, Gabe put his face into his hands. What an idiot he'd been! Was he different now? He couldn't say. Possibly. He only knew that he would die of bliss if Helen welcomed him into her arms again. And then he'd take great pains to ensure that she kept him there!

But would she ever want him, scarred as he was, a man on disability?

Feeling defeated, Gabe moved to a lounge chair and collapsed upon it, like a patient in a hypnotist's lounge. The doctor had advised against hypnosis. In some patients it evoked memories so real it was like enduring the trauma all over again.

Minutes elapsed, but nothing happened. Only the one memory remained, torturing him with its sensuality, twisting his gut with the unavoidable truth that he'd disappointed her.

He threw an arm over his eyes, exhausted, but also achingly aroused. He thought of going back into the house, admitting to the memory and asking for another chance. But what would that accomplish? As she'd said this afternoon, *Paying attention to us now won't change the past.* She didn't want to relive her disappointment. She couldn't wait to be alone without him.

On top of that, she was getting up early tomorrow to go to work. He owed it to her to get a good night's rest.

While the wooden lounge wasn't exactly comfortable, Gabe's body didn't seem to mind. The air was tangy-sweet, as the perfume of wildflowers mixed with ocean brine. The warm wind ruffled his hair like a mother putting her son to sleep.

He drifted toward unconsciousness, vaguely aware that he hadn't taken his sleeping pill.

The first half hour's sleep was restful. But then images began to flicker through his brain like a terrifying slide show.

Shadows descending on him. A cold barrel pressed against his temple. He was yanked to his feet.

Dragged down a long hall. Blinded by halogen lights.

Shoved through a door into a dimly lit chamber.

Pushed into a chairlike contraption.

Strapped into place.

All the while, the awful recurring terror that this time, *this time* they might get something out of him.

A hand on his shoulder. *Not my mouth,* he silently beseeched as sweat poured off him in rivers.

The whispery footfalls of his chief tormenter.

His face gliding through shadows.

The man never spoke above a whisper. The others, those who manhandled him, never spoke below a shout. Gabe dreaded the whispered commands that floated from Seung-Ki's lips. He dropped his carrying case on a table and opened it lovingly. Metal scraped over metal. These were Seung-Ki's instruments of torture—like he needed them. The man's fists and feet had come close to killing Gabe already.

One of the tools looked like a scraper for probing teeth.

Oh, fuck, no! Gabe had figured it would happen eventually. He closed his eyes and scurried toward the corner of his mind where nothing could touch him—except possibly through a root canal. He owed that safe place to Chief Jeffries, the hard-ass who'd done his best to ensure the failure of every trainee at BUD/S.

Hold his mouth open.

The dreaded command reached Gabe's ears, and his entire body coiled like a spring, but it would do no good to fight the restraints. It would only sap his strength, and he would need his strength to recover.

Relax, he told himself in the voice of Chief Jeffries.

Suddenly he realized they'd forgotten to strap his left arm in place. *A miracle!* He held still, calculating the odds that he could free his right arm while disarming the two men who flanked him. Not likely. He was better off seizing a hostage first, then using the man to obtain his freedom.

Cool fingers settled against his jaw. Seung-Ki took a step closer. The instrument of torture glittered sharply while his face remained in shadow.

Gabe reacted. Moving his left arm in a lightning-quick arc, he grabbed the one who'd touched him, curved his fingers around the man's windpipe, and hauled him across his chest, so that he was held in front, like a shield.

But something didn't seem right. The Koreans were certainly smaller than he, but this man's strength was so puny that he felt like a child or a woman struggling in his arms. He'd fallen across Gabe's legs, and when he kicked and clawed, Gabe could tell, number one, that the man wore no shoes and, number two, that his nails were extremely long and sharp. His long hair spilled across Gabe's chest in fragrant waves.

Some deep-seated instinct caused Gabe to loosen his hold. He questioned the reality of what was happening and realized, with horror, that he wasn't where he thought he was.

He was lying on a deck chair on his own deck, and he'd been acting out this violence against a perfectly innocent human being.

His fingers sprang open, and his imaginary attacker slid off him. She collapsed onto the deck with a thud, clutching her neck and fighting for breath. Gabe stared down at her, not wanting to believe what he'd done.

Good Lord, he'd been strangling his wife.

Chapter Six

He dropped to his knees and reached for her. "Helen! Jesus, are you all right?" He held her by her shoulders, staring at the whites of her eyes shining in the darkness. No answer. His muscles flexed as he prepared to leap up and dial 911. But then he heard a wheezing intake of air, and he went weak with relief.

"Keep breathing," he urged. "Just . . . breathe, slow and easy. Christ, I'm so sorry. I was dreaming. I mistook you for someone else. I'm sorry."

Sorry didn't seem to cut it. Not when Helen couldn't even speak. With his gut twisting into knots, Gabe realized he would have to call 911, after all. He couldn't tell if she was getting enough air. If she couldn't even talk . . .

"I'm calling for help," he said, coming to his feet.

She reached for him and managed to grab the edge of his shorts. She shook her head, no. She didn't want help.

"C'mon, Helen, you can't even breathe," he argued, bending down.

She tilted her head up to implore him, and he watched

helplessly as she swallowed several times. "I'm all right," she managed to whisper.

It was the most horrible whisper he'd ever heard.

"Like hell you are," he snarled. "I crushed your goddamn windpipe!"

Again she shook her head. "I'll be fine." She started coming to her feet.

Gabe lost patience with her stoicism. Bending low, he scooped her into his arms, eliciting a hiss of indignation. He carried her into the kitchen, not caring when the screen door slammed behind him. Marching to the great room, he laid her gently on the couch, then reached for the lamp beside it, snapping it on.

Helen flinched at the sudden brightness. Her throat ached so badly, it felt like she'd contracted a severe case of strep. But at least she could inhale now. She didn't think he'd crushed her windpipe, only bruised it. At the same time, she couldn't help but cringe from him when he settled on the side of the couch and lightly put his fingers to her throat.

"I'm not going to hurt you," he said, seeing her reaction. *"Shit!"* He shot to his feet and paced the length of the room.

Helen willed the ache to go away. She knew she'd be fine in a day or so. It wasn't the specific injury that had shaken her. It was the shock of being attacked by her husband. Despite his deadly training, Gabe had never even hinted at physical aggression around her. Being on the receiving end of his fighting expertise had been a real eye-opener. He could kill her in a matter of seconds.

Again she wondered if his year in captivity had made him dangerous.

He appeared at the side of the couch again, his face unnaturally pale, his fingers curled into fists. "I'm taking you to the hospital," he said in *the voice of authority* that no one dared question.

"No, you're not," Helen whispered. God, it hurt to talk! "Think about it, Gabe." She swallowed against the unbearable ache. "What will the doctors suppose happened?"

She saw him absorb the meaning into himself. He put his hands to his face and rubbed his eyes as if they stung him.

He must be exhausted, she thought, feeling a twinge of compassion for him.

He sank down on the edge of the couch again, corroborating her guess. His normally erect posture was nowhere in evidence. He didn't touch her this time, just sat there with his hands over his eyes.

Helen hardened herself. She couldn't afford to feel sorry for him now. Not when she'd made up her mind about divorcing him, something she had more reason than ever to do.

"Ice," he said, shooting to his feet a second time.

She listened for him in the kitchen. His footsteps were still the same—utterly silent. If he weren't pressing the ice dispenser, she'd never know he was in there. She shivered at the potential threat.

He returned with ice in a bag and a drying towel.

"I'll do it," she whispered, trying to take the items from him.

He ignored her, folding the towel over the bag and laying it tenderly against her throat.

The cold was soothing at first. She lay perfectly still, letting him have his way. For now. Eventually he'd be out of her life for good . . . and then she could put ice on her own injuries. Boy, that was a cheering thought.

"It's too cold," she said after a while.

"Just a little longer," he coaxed, his gaze shadowed with worry as he hovered over her, his concern obvious.

She gave up trying to view him as dangerous. He'd mistaken her for someone else, just as he'd said. Everyone was entitled to a mistake now and then. Besides, it was a comfort to be coddled this way—a unique experience, actually. Gabe had never coddled her before.

But he was good at coaxing, always had been. That's what made him such a great leader. It was that same quality that had made her think he'd be an excellent father. That was before he'd transferred his attention to the team, of course. Before her feelings had cracked apart, like mud left too long in the sun.

"Talk to me now," he said, removing the ice at last. "Can you speak?"

He looked at her so tenderly that she struggled to maintain the last image. Her heart was hardened, wasn't it?

He'd just mauled her, for God's sake. He'd nearly killed her. She wasn't supposed to go soft at the sound of his concern. She cleared her throat. "I'm fine," she croaked.

He gave her a worried look. "You really should go to the hospital."

"No," she insisted. "I'm not going anywhere but to bed. I have to get up early tomorrow." She scooted to the end of the couch so she could swing her feet around him. But before they'd even touched the floor, he blocked her escape by putting an arm out.

"Helen," he said urgently.

His tone demanded that she look him in the eye. She did so cautiously, afraid of her weakness for him. "Please forgive me," he begged in a low voice.

His conviction tugged at her. She wanted to, but she couldn't. If she forgave him now, for even one of his transgressions, then she'd crumble like an avalanche, and she'd have to forgive him everything. She'd gone through too much heartache to risk doing it again.

She gave him a minuscule nod, but it didn't mean anything.

He knew it didn't. His lashes concealed his disappointment. Fixing his gaze off to one side, he said, "Don't come near me when I'm sleeping. I don't want to hurt you again."

"I heard you leave the house," she explained. She'd wanted to make sure he was all right. "Did you remember something in your dream?"

"Yes," he said after a second's hesitation.

She dreaded knowing what it was, but she knew she should ask, figuring he should talk about it. "Can you tell me?"

He looked her in the eye then away. "Seung-Ki," he said, on a note that sent a chill up her spine. "He's the one who tortured me."

Visions, sharp and horrific, flashed through her mind. She watched the muscles leap in his jaw, unsure of what to say. Again, she wanted to comfort him, but Gabe had always shrugged off sympathy.

He stood up suddenly, reaching out a hand to help her to her feet. She glanced at the unexpected hand, tempted to take it, to call a truce. Only, she couldn't trust herself not to go too far, not to capitulate to his demands as she'd always done. Besides, this new Gabe was too honest, too appealing. He was a threat to the independence she'd worked so hard to attain.

Ignoring it, she stood under her own power. "Good night," she said, moving past him en route to her room. She felt his gaze on her until she turned down the hall.

Helen locked her bedroom door, throat still throbbing from the episode on the deck. Strangely, her chest seemed to ache more—not for herself, but for the violence Gabe had endured this past year. For the first time, he'd given her a glimpse into that terrorizing world, and she felt guilty, terrible for not considering that he was still alive and enduring the worst physical pains, the worst kind of fear imaginable.

Gabe sat slowly on the couch that Helen had just vacated. Her warmth had already dissipated. He shivered, goose bumps racing over his skin, despite his T-shirt. His North Korean cell must have been hot in the summer and cold in the winter. He couldn't remember, but he hadn't yet gotten used to central cooling.

Furthermore, the memory of Seung-Ki's glistening tools was now fresh in his mind, chilling him from the inside out. He could still feel the wicked edges of those tools threatening his earlobes, the tip of his nose. He gasped at the recollection of a pointed hook piercing his right nipple, raking through skin and muscle as it scored his chest.

He slipped a hand under his T-shirt, feeling the raised scar where his nipple used to be. He followed it with the tip of his finger, shuddering as the memory replayed itself.

I didn't say anything, he comforted himself. They'd wanted to know more about the U.S. Navy's nuclear submarines. Gabe had known far more than he wished, but he'd refused to talk. They'd gotten nothing for their efforts.

And what did he get, besides a disfigured torso? The satisfaction of saving American lives, one day. Was that enough? It would have to be.

His fingers strayed to another scar, a deep indentation underneath his arm where a hunk of flesh had been torn from him. He shuddered, quelling his nausea as another memory began to surface. He quickly repressed it. He wasn't ready for more. He had enough to think about.

Standing abruptly, he hastened to the bathroom to find his sleeping pills. He shook an extra pill into his palm and regarded it with bitterness. *Look what I'm reduced to,* he thought. Helen wouldn't want him back, regardless of his apologies; regardless of how sincerely he apologized.

He tossed back the pills and washed them down with water. Averting his gaze from his reflection, he retreated to the study and extinguished the lights. Fear washed over him, leaving him covered in sweat. He reached out and snapped on the lamp by his head.

It's over, he reassured himself. *I'm safe now.*

Or was he? His heart feared otherwise.

His misadventure in North Korea wasn't over yet. He suffered the haunting certainty that a threat still lingered, and he would face death this time if he failed to remember what it was.

Just as terrifying was the realization that if he couldn't convince Helen to risk her heart to him a second time, his yearlong struggle to survive would have been for naught.

"We go left up here," Mallory panted as she jogged on the exercise path beside him.

"That's where the gym is," Gabe confirmed, remembering the way perfectly. He was discovering that he knew Dam Neck Naval Base like the back of his hand. His office had been straight down Regulus Avenue, past the Shifting Sands Club and the officers' housing. Soon he would work up the courage to pop in and say hello. He wondered at the welcome he would get, and uncertainty tugged at him anew, threatening to pull him back into the depression he'd wallowed in all morning.

Commander Lovitt hadn't called since his homecoming.

Despite Sebastian's conviction to the contrary, it seemed the CO had washed his hands of Gabe.

Surprisingly, he *had* received a call from the team's executive officer, earlier that morning. It had been a long distance call from their patrol coastal craft, the USS *Nor'easter*. In a voice devoid of any real warmth, Miller had welcomed Gabe home on behalf of the team. Gabe and the XO had never been tight, their relationship based on protocol rather than mutual respect. This morning's call was no exception. But Miller had sounded worried more than apathetic, as if Gabe were a threat to his leadership. Or worse, maybe Miller thought Gabe had betrayed secrets to the other side.

What if his platoon members thought the same? That stubborn question remained: why else would a SEAL lose his memory but to forget the ignominious moment he'd been broken by his captors?

The call had plunged Gabe into such a bleak mood that Mallory had steered clear of him all morning.

Finally she sought him out with the offer to show him where Helen worked. Remembering what he'd done to his wife the night before, Gabe recognized that he owed her an apology. He didn't want Mallory thinking he was a coward, so here they were.

"Wanna do this one?" she asked him as they ran, huffing, up to the next exercise station.

They'd tackled all the others. This station consisted of two wooden platforms, one flat and one inclined, for stretches and curl-ups respectively. "No way," he said. "The bench is warped on this side. It kills your spine to do sit-ups. Unless they fixed it." He jogged closer to get a look. "No, see, it's still warped."

"You remember that?" Mallory marveled.

"Guess so." He fell back into step beside her, lungs burning from the last mile or more that they'd already covered. His lack of endurance dismayed him. He'd obviously kept up calisthenics during confinement, but there were very few substitutes for a good hard run. "You tired yet?" he asked Mallory.

"No."

He glanced at her sidelong. Her cheeks were flushed. Sweat stained her T-shirt, and her fists were clenched. She was tired. But she was too competitive to admit it.

Damn, she reminded him of himself. "Well, I am," he admitted. "You want to walk for a while?"

She reined herself in at once and reached for him to slow him down. "You should've said so earlier!" She pushed a wedge of black hair out of her eyes and scowled at him. "Are you sure you're supposed to exercise?" she demanded.

"Absolutely. Exercise is the—"

"—key to longevity," she finished for him.

They smiled at each other, and a funny feeling washed through Gabe. He'd been a part of Mallory's life, and he couldn't remember it. According to Helen, he'd ignored his stepdaughter.

Recalling his fanatic drive to succeed, he believed it. But it wasn't just his quest for excellence that had kept him from cozying up to Mallory. It was his fear of failure. What did he know about parenting a daughter? His only father figure had been Sergeant O'Mally, a cop.

But some time between last year and now, Gabe must have understood what it meant to be Mal's father. He couldn't remember when the insight had come, or how; he only knew he wasn't afraid to parent her now. He could be there for her in a way that was meaningful and lasting. He probably wouldn't be a perfect dad, but he'd be good enough.

To his great fortune, Mal was willing to give him a second chance. He enjoyed her spunk, her sense of humor. He'd be happy to hang out with her all day.

"So, Mal," he began as the path took a turn around the corner. He was about to ask what things had been like between them.

She looked at him quizzically.

The words stuck in his throat. He didn't want to jeopardize the present by bringing up the past. "Er—" He thought of something else to ask her. "What's Mom's job, exactly?"

"She's the Fitness Coordinator," Mallory said, with obvious pride.

"Okay, so what's that mean?"

"She has her own office, and she doesn't just sweat."

Mal's response confused him further. "What do you mean, 'just sweat'?" he asked for clarification.

She gave him a quick little frown. "An officer's wife shouldn't have to sweat for a living," Mallory added, repeating something she'd obviously overheard. "But she doesn't just sweat. She organizes the marathons and the basketball tournaments—everything. She orders equipment and trains new people. She's the boss."

The boss, Gabe thought with no small amount of respect. "That's awesome," he said, meaning it.

Mallory gave him an approving smile. "I think so," she agreed.

He wanted to hug her so bad it scared him. He settled for a hand on her shoulder, relieved when she didn't shrug it off. They continued their walk in silence, the warm sun in their eyes and the murmur of the ocean behind them.

Dam Neck was a beautiful base. The usual nondescript, brick buildings were well spaced, separated by groves of bayberry bushes, walkways, little footbridges. It was also a wildlife refuge for white-tailed deer, gray foxes, rabbits, and assorted seabirds. Gabe wasn't in any hurry to be reassigned. He had a home on the ocean and worked on a fabulous base. What more could a warrior want?

Besides his job back?

And a wife who loved him?

Despair tugged at him anew. If he could just remember the last three years, then he'd be stricken from disability and given his job back. On the other hand, given the horror of last night's memories, he wasn't sure he could handle any more just yet. The niggling fear that the past would come back to bite him was still with him today. He could feel it lurking like the mother of all crabs.

Or was he paranoid now, like those Vietnam vets who suffered imaginary fears?

He hoped not. As long as he could help it, PTSD wouldn't drag him down any farther than it already had.

They approached the gym by cutting through a minimall of shops: barbershop, flower shop, bank, and food court. The recreation area was new. Gabe peered curiously inside.

"They've got Ping-Pong tables, foosball, and video games, now," Mallory pointed out. "It's all new."

"Cool," said Gabe. "Let's come here one night with Mom."

Mallory's face lit up, and he knew he'd said the right thing. Being a father wasn't all that hard.

"This way." She led him out the back door, through a courtyard and up the steps to the gym.

Gabe realized his palms were sweating and not from his run, either. He hoped Helen had forgiven him. The second they entered the two sets of doors, he could hear her voice. Even using a sound system, she sounded as though she were recovering from a weeklong flu.

"Flexibility," she was saying, "is the most important component of physical fitness."

"What's wrong with Mom's voice?" Mallory asked.

"IDs, please." Gabe was saved from answering as a female petty officer asked for their cards.

He fished his new ID out of his back pocket, hating the thought of himself on disability. Mallory had hers in hand. Curious, Gabe tried to peek at her picture, and she quickly hid it from view. "Oh, no," she warned. "It's gross. I was eleven."

"Let me see it." He tried his persuasive voice on her.

She gave him a look with her eyebrow raised.

It made him laugh out loud. "I'll see it sooner or later," he reasoned. "Might as well show it to me now."

She thrust it in front of his face. "Fine. There it is. Try not to vomit on my feet. Thank you." She whipped the ID away and shoved it into her shorts pocket.

Gabe grinned. At eleven, she'd looked like a boy.

They both turned toward the gym. But then Gabe thought better of it. "Let's not interrupt Mom's class," he said. "Let's go this way." He pointed toward the weight room.

In the weight room, he laid several mats on the floor. Mallory watched inquisitively.

"Now I'm going to teach you how to defend yourself," he said, rubbing his hands together.

"Mom already taught me," she replied.

Somehow, he wasn't surprised. "She did, huh? Well, let's see what she taught you. Maybe I can add on."

Mallory looked him up and down. "Most boys aren't as big as you," she pointed out, frowning.

Boys? Mallory was on to him already. "Are you kidding? I'm scrawny right now," he retorted. "Suppose I just walk right up to you—come up onto the mat—and I grab your shoulders like this. What do you do?"

"I can do lots of things. I can break your nose." She showed him how. "Kick you in the groin, in the knee. Elbow you. If you were shorter I could make your eardrums explode."

Wow. "Okay, different approach. Suppose you think of me as a friend. We're lying on the beach, looking at the stars." He gestured for her to lie on the mat beside him. "Suppose I all of a sudden roll over and pin you flat. Now what?"

He'd thrown a heavy leg over hers and pinned her shoulders to the mat. Mallory was helpless. She gazed up at him, frowning.

Tut, tut, Helen. You forgot the old slickeroo.

"One of your hands is free, right?" he pointed out. "You go for the eyes. Don't do it now, obviously, but if you ever have to do it, do it hard. Then get the heck out of there and start running."

Mallory gave him the tiniest of smiles.

"Now roll over," he instructed. "Suppose some creep pushes you facedown in the sand and he's about to jump on top of you."

"I roll out of the way?" she guessed.

"Too hard. You just got the air knocked out of you. Scrunch up on your right side and kick with your left foot."

Mal gave it a try.

"Lead with the heel," Gabe instructed. "Now do it again."

They worked their way through several more drills. Then Gabe began stringing them together.

Helen pushed her way into the weight room just in time to see Mallory kick Gabe in the knee, tug him to the mat, land a karate chop to the neck, and scramble out of harm's way.

They both spotted Helen at the same time.

"What are you doing?" she demanded, directing the question at Gabe.

His thoughts had scattered the moment he laid eyes on her. He sat up, using the edge of his T-shirt to wipe the sweat out of his eyes. She was wearing a skintight violet outfit with a high neckline, but despite the concealer she'd used to tone them down, the bruises on her neck were still obvious.

"He's teaching me some safety moves," Mallory answered for him.

"I already taught you those," Helen replied, an impatient glimmer in her eyes.

"Not everything," Mal protested. "Hey, what happened to your neck?"

"You might accidentally hurt her," Helen added, ignoring the question.

Mallory's eyes widened. "Did you hurt Mom's neck?" she asked in disbelief.

"It was a mistake, honey. I woke him up from a bad dream," Helen answered on Gabe's behalf. "What are you two doing here?" she finally demanded.

"I wanted to show Dad where you work," Mallory explained.

"Oh." Helen frowned as if the thought had never occurred to her. "You want a tour?" she asked.

"Sure." They both scrambled to their feet.

"Mal's not allowed in this room until she's sixteen, by the way," Helen added, turning toward the door.

"Ah," said Gabe.

"I could pass for sixteen," said Mallory airily.

"Come on. I'll show you the cardio room."

Gabe remembered the gym well enough: a weight room, two basketball courts, and an indoor pool. But the cardio room was new. He wandered in and looked around, impressed with the equipment. Several people were taking an early lunch hour and getting in a run on the treadmills. He didn't recognize a soul.

"Why do you have to be sixteen to run?" Mallory asked plaintively.

At the sound of her voice, a woman on the treadmill turned her head and nearly went flying off the machine. "Gabe!" she cried in surprise, catching herself. She powered off the treadmill and rushed him. "Oh, my God, you're alive!"

Gabe suffered her embrace and bemusedly met Helen's eyes over the woman's shoulder. The look in his wife's eyes made him blink. *She didn't think . . . ?*

"Look at you!" the woman fawned, holding him at arm's distance. "You look great. I mean, you're thin, but you're alive, so who cares?" Her smile faded as she realized she was getting no response. She cut her gaze to Helen and released Gabe abruptly, apparently just noticing his family. "Hi, Helen," she said, her smile turning brittle. "Well, it's good to see you. Er, Luther and the others should be back any day now. I'll tell him to drop by."

Luther. Yeah, Luther Lindstrom, the ensign on his SEAL team—no, wait, he was a lieutenant now. "I'd like that," Gabe said as the pieces fell into place. This was the flirtatious secretary, Veronica, who worked in Spec Ops. She must be dating Luther now. He glanced at her left hand, dismayed to see a diamond winking there. What was the man thinking?

Veronica gave him a parting smile and sashayed back to the treadmill. Instead of resuming her workout, she gathered up her things, showing her backside to its best advantage.

Gabe looked at Helen, wary of her silence. "I think you need to leave now," she told him, her expression shuttered.

She couldn't be thinking what he thought she was thinking. Veronica wasn't an old flame of his, was she? He was beset by an image of her perched on the corner of his desk, her skirt raised high enough to reveal a pair of black garters.

Uncomfortable with the memory, Gabe turned away. "Thanks for showing us around," he muttered, aware that he hadn't even apologized for last night. Fuck it, he could do nothing right!

He pushed his way out of the cardio room, depression ambushing him again. At this rate, he'd never convince Helen he was worth keeping. He'd nearly killed her last night. Now she seemed to be accusing him of something.

Halfway down the hall, Gabe realized Mallory wasn't behind him. He paused at the water fountain and waited.

Still she didn't come. Helen stalked out of the cardio room alone, her expression tense.

"Where's Mal?" he asked, forgetting his own confusion for the moment.

"I let her out of the emergency exit. She said she didn't want to be with you right now."

She was definitely accusing him. Gabe blocked her path as she tried to move past him. "You let her go?" he asked.

"What was I supposed to do, force her to be with you?" The light of battle was back in her eyes.

"What the hell did you say to her?" he wanted to know.

"I didn't have to say anything. It was written all over your face."

"What was?" When she didn't answer, he demanded, "Are you saying I cheated on you?"

"Didn't you?"

"How the hell am I supposed to know?"

With a sound of disgust, she pushed past him.

He caught her before she could take two steps. In fluid movement, he backed her against the wall. He felt the tension in every muscle of her body. "I suppose you're going to tell me now that you're not jealous," he prodded, pulling gently on her ponytail. He could feel Helen's breasts, full and firm, against his chest. *Ah, yes.*

To his consternation, her eyes grew bright with tears. She tried to turn her head to one side, but he tugged harder on her hair, keeping her immobile. "Helen, look at me," he demanded. "I didn't cheat on you."

She shook her head, biting her lower lip.

Her obvious hurt tore at him like shrapnel. "Baby, don't," he pleaded, pulling her to him with sudden remorse. "Don't be upset. I would never have done that," he said with sudden certainty.

She pushed against him with surprising strength. "Let me go."

"No, I want you to believe me. I want you to forgive me for last night."

She twisted frantically away from him. "Stop manhandling me!" she ground out.

In his desperation to be forgiven, he realized he was doing just that. He released her at once. Before he could think of what else to say, she twisted free and stalked down the hall, her ponytail swinging.

Gabe wanted to put a fist through the wall, only the wall was cinder block. Not a good idea. He took a shuddering breath and cursed a blue streak. What the fuck had gone wrong here? He'd been well on his way to forging a bond with Mallory, and then something out of his past—or rather, someone—leapt out of the shadows to throw him off course. Bringing him right back to where he was several days ago.

Mallory. He needed to find the kid and explain.

Explain what? That Veronica flirted with all the guys, that

he'd never cheated on Helen? Could he honestly be sure, when he couldn't remember his last two years at Dam Neck?

Yes. No way in hell would he have betrayed his wife. Veronica was good-looking, but she didn't hold a candle to Helen.

He rubbed his face vigorously. Exhaustion stole over him without warning, making him want to lie down on the mats in the weight room and go to sleep. What the hell? The medication was supposed to keep him awake.

But now his eyes were threatening to cross. His muscles felt sapped of strength. The long walk home was suddenly more than he could handle right now. No way could he catch up with Mallory, especially if she was running. He needed a car.

He thought about that for a minute.

He *had* a car. The Jaguar was his. He'd bought it back in California. Helen usually drove the Jeep, only the battery was dead, she'd told him. If the spare key to the Jaguar was in the magnetic box where he'd hid it long ago, then he was good to go.

Yeah, yeah, the doctor had told him not to drive, but he wasn't going to kill himself going twenty-five miles an hour. He'd return to pick up Helen later, and then she could drive him to his appointment with Dr. Terrien at four.

But first he needed to find Mal and explain. And then he needed a power nap.

He left the gym and spotted the Jaguar in the parking lot. Letting himself in with the spare key, he eased behind the driver's seat and gave a growl of contentment. This was the best welcome yet. The engine throbbed with quiet power as he pointed the car toward home.

Mallory wasn't anywhere on the jogging trail. By the time Gabe drove through the back gate and parked in his driveway, he was more than worried. Where had Mallory gone? She'd been upset, thinking the worst. And though she pretended to be tough, he knew she was a softy inside. He didn't like the thought of her hurting.

Using the house key Helen had left for him, he let himself in. Priscilla barked happily to see him.

"Mal?" he called.

No answer.

He went to the kitchen and chugged down a glass of water. God, he was tired. But he needed to make a phone call. Ask Helen if she knew where Mallory might be.

He looked up the number to the gym and asked for her.

"This is Helen." Her scratchy voice sounded worse coming through a wire.

"It's Gabe," he said.

Startled silence on the other end.

"I'm looking for Mallory. Do you know where she might've gone?"

"Where are you?"

"I'm at the house."

"How'd you get home so fast?"

"I borrowed the Jaguar. I'll pick you up at fifteen-thirty, but I want to know where Mallory is."

"You're not supposed to drive," she said, sounding frustrated. "Why are you looking for Mallory?"

Why? "She's a teenager," he supplied. "She's angry. Christ, Helen, do the math."

Her silence this time was reflective. "She's probably playing foosball at the Rec Center."

"Will you check for me, please?"

"All right," she answered, sounding bemused. "If you don't hear from me, then that's where she is."

"Thanks," he said. He rubbed his right eye. "I have to . . .

I have to sleep for a few minutes. See you . . . at fifteen-thirty. 'Kay?"

"Go," she said. "You sound like a zombie."

"Mmmm. 'Bye."

He dropped the phone in its cradle and made a beeline for the living-room sofa, where he crashed facedown on the cushions, managing to kick off his tennis shoes before falling asleep. The phone rang several minutes later, but he didn't hear it.

An hour later, Mallory spied Gabe asleep on the couch and hushed the dog into silence. The fact that he hadn't stirred at her entrance worried her.

"Good girl. Shhh," she said to the dog, patting Priscilla's head. "I'll walk you in a minute." She approached Gabe as silently as possible, her eyes wide with trepidation. She'd never known him to sleep like the dead. He lay facing the room, and he hadn't even cracked an eye.

A foot away, she stopped and listened. He was a silent sleeper, but she could hear him breathing now. She sank onto the carpet, relieved to know he was alive. Dead would be worse.

The dog threatened to lick her, so she looped an arm around its neck, never once removing her gaze from Gabe's face. Remembering what had happened in the cardio room, how that woman had thrown herself at him, she took a sharp breath. The pain of betrayal lanced her heart anew. *Imagine how Mom feels,* she told herself.

How could Dad have done that to her? To them?

She stared at his face, memorizing it. He had a great face. All the girls in middle school had had a crush on him. Mal knew he was handsome. But she liked his face more now, because she'd seen expressions on it that she'd never seen before. Humor, sorrow, wonder . . . *desire.*

He didn't want that woman at the gym, she assured herself. It was Mom he wanted. She remembered the fire in his eyes last night before they'd read together. He'd wanted to grab Mom right there and take her to the bedroom.

He'd stolen a kiss from her.

Mallory felt a little better thinking about that. But then there was Mom to contend with. Her mother hadn't said it in so many words, but it was obvious things had changed. She hadn't welcomed Gabe into their lives as her long-lost husband. She'd put him in the study to sleep, explaining lamely that he might be dangerous after what he'd been through. She used to be the one pulling Dad out of his shell, vying for his attention. Now her mother was ignoring her father, and everything was backward.

She didn't have to be a genius to read the writing on the wall. Her mother didn't want to be married anymore.

Now Mallory knew why. On top of never being home and working all the time, Dad had cheated. No wonder he'd stopped kissing her mother, stopped paying her attention. He'd been giving all his love to someone else.

Whenever he did come home, he'd been preoccupied and short-tempered. The only time he seemed to notice Mallory was when she'd left a chore undone or transgressed in some other way. He'd brought her to the edge of tears sometimes because he never seemed to notice when she tried her best, only when she failed.

Then the Navy told them that Gabe was missing—presumed dead—and Mallory had tried to see his absence in a positive light. He hadn't been around much anyway. She didn't have to stand on her head to get his attention.

But it hadn't felt right. It'd felt empty without him. There had been that awful sense of waiting, of feeling like she'd lost something very special.

She hadn't wanted him dead.

And she didn't want him leaving now, either. Especially not now.

But how was she going to keep him at home, when Mom wouldn't forgive him, or love him again?

She blinked back the tears that threatened.

Daddy, don't go, she pleaded silently. The word echoed in her heart, filling the empty places. *Daddy. Daddy.*

He looked so vulnerable sprawled out on the couch. He'd never been vulnerable before. The tears she refused to cry made her throat ache.

If he left them for good this time, she'd have no one but Reggie. That thought was depressing enough to push a tear out the corner of her eye. It slid warmly down her cheek.

Reggie was smart and funny. But Reggie was unpredictable, like a tornado changing course and swerving all over the place. She didn't want to be sucked up in his confusion. But if Gabe wasn't going to stay, what difference did it make?

Angry with herself, she dashed the wet streak from her cheek and scrambled to her feet. Bawling never did any good. *Just suck it up,* Dad used to say. *Life stinks. Deal with it.* He'd taught her lots of sayings, and she'd memorized them all.

She patted her thigh, gesturing for the dog to follow her to the door. Snapping Priscilla's leash on, Mallory slipped from the house to walk her. After that, she'd head over to Reggie's place.

Reggie's parents had split up three years ago, and he'd survived. She supposed she would survive too.

Chapter Seven

He caught hell for taking the Jaguar.

"Next time, just ask me for a ride," Helen scolded as they sped toward Oceana Naval Air Base—late, because Gabe had slept clear to three forty-five. "What if you'd fallen asleep or driven into a tree? You know, sometimes rules do apply to you, Gabriel. This is the only car that's working right now, and I can't afford to have it in the shop."

Apparently she only called him Gabriel when she was pissed at him. He accepted her lecture because it gave the illusion that she actually cared about him. Besides, she was absolutely right. Breaking the rules was what he did best. It was his job to get his men around insurmountable obstacles, and he was damn good at it. But right now he wasn't a SEAL. He was nothing but a washed-up warrior with an ache behind his right eye that wouldn't go away.

And after what he'd done to Helen last night, he deserved to be chewed up one side and down the other. Anger beat the hell out of apathy, he reasoned. So he kept his mouth shut and took the verbal lashing.

At the same time, he kept his eyes open and refamiliarized himself with the area. The road they flew along bisected a field of open farmland, but Virginia Beach was growing at such an alarming rate that what was left of open land would soon be subdivided into neighborhoods like the rest of the area.

"Where's Mallory?" he asked when Helen had finally finished her tirade.

She threw him a troubled look. "I called to tell you she wasn't at the Rec Center, but you didn't answer."

Concern reared its grisly head. "I didn't hear the phone ring," he said. Christ, he'd never be on active duty again with his senses so dulled! He shook his head in disgust.

"She's probably at her friend's house," Helen guessed. "Can you hand me my cell phone? It's in my purse."

He didn't know she had a cell phone. She hit a speed-dial button, keeping her eyes on the road. "No answer," she finally said, slapping the phone shut.

Behind her violet-tinted sunglasses, he saw her eyebrows flex with concern. Since he'd last seen her, she'd showered and changed into a sand-colored top and white shorts. She looked cool and comfortable. Her legs were tanned to a golden brown. He wanted very much to run a hand up her silky-looking thigh.

As if sensing his gaze, Helen shifted uncomfortably.

They drove another five minutes in silence, and it was clear to Gabe she was finished with her lecture, finished with talking to him, period.

The longer he studied her, the whiter her knuckles shone against the steering wheel. "You know what they say about riptides?" he added, philosophizing out loud.

She made a sound of disinterest, giving all her focus to the road.

"It's better to let the current carry you out than it is to fight it. You can drown trying to fight it," he pointed out.

"You always were full of trite, little sayings," she tossed back.

He'd thought his metaphor was clever. "Mallory needs me," he said, laying down his trump card.

She whipped her head around, her temper roused. "Well, when did this revelation occur to you?" she asked sarcastically.

He took her question seriously and thought about it. "I don't know," he finally answered.

She shook her head as if regretting her question.

"I think she's neat, Helen," he felt compelled to add. "She's smart, *really* smart. And she's got great intuition. She could be anything she wants to be."

Looking puzzled, Helen divided her attention between him and the road.

"You don't agree?" he asked.

"Of course I agree. Yes, she could be anything she wants to be. Why didn't you tell her that a year ago? Two years ago? The only time you noticed her was when she screwed up! I swear, I think she started misbehaving just so she could have a piece of you."

He cringed inwardly. "Fuck," he muttered, looking out at the fields. He thought about the holes in Mallory's left ear. "I'll make it up to her," he promised.

Helen was so quiet he looked at her to gauge what she was thinking. She was worrying her bottom lip, oblivious to the traffic thickening around them. "That'll be good for her," she finally said.

The implication was clear: he could make it up to Mallory, but he'd never be able to make it up to her.

"Look," he said, rubbing his throbbing right eye, "maybe

you could cut me a little slack here. Whatever I was like in the past, I'm sorry. I'm very sorry. I'd like to be given a second chance." He opened his eyes and found her gripping the steering wheel, her whole body tense.

"It's not that simple," she told him.

"What's not simple about it?"

"There's a whole history, here, okay?" she shot back with a note of panic in her voice. "You can't just wish it away."

"If you're talking about Veronica, I didn't sleep with her. I swear to God."

"Then how come you used to stay late at the Spec Ops Building when she was the only one there?"

"How the hell am I supposed to remember?" God, his eye hurt. "Jesus, Helen, she's engaged to Luther, now, if that diamond on her left hand means anything. Can we just leave it in the past?"

They paused at the gates of Oceana Naval Air Base, their conversation on hold as Helen flashed her military ID. "Look, I'm sorry you can't remember," she said as she drove them toward the hospital complex. "But even if I could forget, it doesn't change anything for me. I like my life the way it is. I don't want to go backward with the hope that it'll be different this time."

He recognized that it had taken a lot of courage for her to say those words, which was probably why she'd said them so quickly. At the same time, frustration pounded inside him, beating in time to the tattoo behind his right eye.

Why was she being so stubborn about her independence? It wasn't going to kill her to give him a second chance, damn it. He stared at her hard, wondering how to break through the barrier she'd erected.

It was the firm line of her lower lip that gave him an answer. He thought of their wedding photograph in which they'd been kissing, and he had a sudden, overpowering urge to soften that lower lip, to part it from the upper one and plunder the sweet cavity between. She was afraid to touch him, he realized with a flash of insight—not because she thought he would hurt her, but because she just might give in to him.

It was his last resort.

Helen had just pulled the Jaguar into a parking space in front of the psychiatric offices. She took off her glasses and slid them into the compartment on her visor. He didn't give her the chance to take the key from the ignition. Twisting in the seat, he reached for her, fitting his hand against the side of her face.

Her eyes flared with alarm.

"I'm going to kiss you," he warned her "Maybe I'm not the one who needs to remember. Maybe you are." With that, he leaned swiftly forward, at the same time pulling her mouth to his and kissing her hard.

She gave a cry of surprise or denial, he didn't know which. He was too enthralled with the soft texture of her rose-petal lips to let up now. Her scent, wildflowers and woman, filled his head, and he felt himself sinking into her. Jesus, she tasted even better than she looked! His tongue delved deeper. His hands burrowed into the silky mass of her hair, slid over her satiny skin. Holy hell, she even *felt* better than she looked.

Helen tried to steel herself. *Don't feel the rush!* But the kiss stormed her senses, cascading over her like a powerful waterfall, soaking her instantly, dragging her into its current.

It had been way, way too long since Gabe had worked his magic on her. She craved his taste, his texture, his single-minded intent. The desire she'd tried so hard to resist exploded inside her. She threw an arm around his neck, pulling him closer, breasts aching for his touch, even as her conscience demanded that she let him go.

Without severing the kiss, Gabe somehow found the lever that adjusted her seat. She sank smoothly backward. To her private gratification, he threw a leg onto her side of the car, coming up and over her, fitting his wonderfully hard body against her softer one, a denim-clad thigh between her legs.

"You taste so good," he muttered, devouring her mouth.

She gave a helpless moan, struggling to keep her eyes open. She felt the palm of his hand skim her torso, searing through the fabric of her shirt. As it inched higher, she arched with need, heart thumping in expectation of his palm on her breast.

This is crazy, she thought. *We can't have sex in the front of the Jaguar in broad daylight.* But then his hand settled on her breast, and the heat of his palm burned that thought away. He stroked his thumb over the taut peak, and grenades of pleasure exploded all around her. She quivered, wanting more. A year of celibacy had done nothing for her restraint.

The sudden blare of a car alarm jarred their passionate haze. Gabe lifted his head, his eyes clearing as he realized where they were. With a look of regret, he withdrew to his own seat.

Helen fought to get a handle on her disappointment. *That was a low move,* she thought, straightening her rumpled shirt.

"Gotta go," he said, glancing at the car's digital clock. Without another word, he pushed open his door, and he was gone.

She sat there, reeling from his touch. *Bastard,* she thought, replaying the kiss instant by instant. In less than ten seconds, the man had made her mindless with desire. She'd known he was dangerous to her equilibrium, but she'd had no idea just how dangerous.

A year of sexual deprivation wasn't helping any, either. Her nerve endings screamed for a continuation of that kiss. God help her, she knew what he could give her, and she wanted it. This wasn't good. If Gabe got his claws into her that way, it would be twice as hard to walk away from their marriage.

She needed help. Groping in her purse for her cell phone, she dialed her best friend's number with fingers that trembled. Leila would talk sense into her again, remind her of all the reasons she didn't need Gabe in her life.

Fortunately for Helen, Leila, who owned a ballet studio, was between dance classes and could take her call.

"He kissed me," Helen said in lieu of a greeting.

Leila heard everything Helen meant to convey in that single sentence. "He just kissed you, nothing else?" she asked.

"We were in the car in front of his doctor's office, but if we'd been anywhere else, it wouldn't have stopped at a kiss. He's still got the touch," she added, her voice tinged with longing.

Leila sighed, clearly understanding what that meant, though as far as Helen knew she hadn't been intimate with a man since her husband walked out years ago. "Well, obviously, the solution is never to find yourself in a place where he could take it to the next level. The car is safe."

"He's got me thinking seriously about the next level," Helen admitted.

"Don't do it," Leila cautioned. "The minute you sleep with him, you're going to want to recommit. You know I'm right."

"You're right. But he said the sweetest things about Mallory on the way here."

"You're at the doctor's now?"

"Yes. He said Mal was neat and smart, and she could be anything she wanted to be."

"Maybe he's using her to get to you. You know he's sharp, Helen. If he wants to stay married—"

"He asked me to give him a second chance."

"Well, there you go. He's figured out your two weaknesses, Mallory and your attraction to him, and he's exploiting both to get what he wants. You need to remember what it is that you want. It's always been about him; now it's about you."

By the time Helen severed the call, a half hour had elapsed and the air conditioner was blowing warm air. With her shirt sticking to her back, she got out of the car and entered the doctor's office, feeling considerably more in control with Leila's pep talk fresh in her head.

She hadn't been two minutes in the waiting room before Gabe wandered in with Dr. Terrien in his wake.

"He wants to talk to you," Gabe said, taking a seat opposite hers. He stretched out his long legs and folded his arms across his chest.

Helen hid her dismay behind a polite smile. The doctor greeted her warmly and gestured for her to precede him down the hall. She glanced back once at Gabe and found him watching her. The vulnerable look in his eyes tugged at her.

"Gabriel tells me," Dr. Terrien said, after they'd taken their seats, "that he's starting to remember pieces of his past. He remembers part of his captivity." The doctor paused. "And he remembers making love to you."

Helen flushed. It was all she could do to appear disinterested.

"He recalls how hard he worked to keep his emotions under control. His fear was that caring for someone might affect his actions as a SEAL, might make him less effective."

"Why are you telling me this?" Helen asked, cutting him off. She didn't want to hear Gabe's reasons. They only undermined her determination.

"I'm wondering if you've noticed changes in your husband," the doctor admitted somberly, "and if so, how has he changed?"

Helen took a deep breath. She'd just been through all this with Leila, who'd pointed out that the changes for the better were probably temporary. "Well, you know, he doesn't have any job to distract him. He's more attentive, more interested in Mallory. I guess he just has so much time on his hands, now." She shrugged, not quite satisfied with her conclusions.

"He mentions your daughter quite a bit," Dr. Terrien agreed with a smile.

Helen mentally rolled her eyes. She didn't want to believe what Leila was telling her—that Gabe was just using Mallory to get to her.

"What about you? Does he treat you differently?"

Locking her hands together, Helen considered how to answer. "He's more like he was when we first met," she admitted, "but not really. There's something different about him, something more reflective, calmer, if you know what I mean."

The doctor nodded encouragingly.

"He seems . . . sad, I think. I catch him just staring into space and I wonder if he's remembering something. He also holds my gaze more than he used to. I know that sounds weird." She looked down at her interlaced fingers, feeling awkward.

"Is he asking something of you?" the doctor inquired.

"Like what?" The first thing that came to mind was sex, but that was her own subconscious talking.

"I don't know. What do you think?"

She pictured Gabe's eyes, his gold-green eyes, looking vaguely sad, pleading for something. "My support?" she guessed.

He nodded once, profoundly. "He used that exact word in here just a little while ago. He said he needed your support."

Helen felt as if a vise had closed around her chest and was starting to squeeze. "I can't," she said faintly. *Besides, Leila would kill me.*

"He said you didn't look through the albums with him. That Mallory was sent to do the job."

Helen swallowed down her guilt.

"What are you afraid of?" Dr. Terrien gently asked. "Do you think he'll hurt you, as he did last night?" He nodded at the bruise on her neck.

Helen shook her head. The vise around her chest squeezed harder. "No," she said. "That was a case of mistaken identity. I know he didn't mean to. It's . . . it's something else."

"Yes?" he prompted.

It was time to be frank with Dr. Terrien. The man was astute enough to guess the truth eventually. "Our relationship is temporary," she said baldly. "We're going to separate when Gabe gets his memory back."

"Ah," said the doctor, looking pained.

Helen didn't know what else to say. She suffered a strong urge to defend her decision and sat there convincing herself she didn't owe him any explanation. This was her life, after all.

The doctor placed his palms together as if meditating. "Well, then, your support may also speed you in that direction. The sooner Gabriel heals, the sooner you can release him."

Those words struck a melancholy chord within her. Yet they also made sense. There was some risk in getting involved, yes, but if the ultimate goal could be attained more quickly that way, perhaps she ought to do it. Besides, Gabe really needed her help right now; she'd never seen him looking lost, as he had lately. "What do I do?" she asked, accepting her fate.

"Spend time with him. Go through the albums together. Take walks. Go places you've gone before. Concentrate on the way things smell. The olfactory senses are often the door through which the memory reenters."

Helen drew her lower lip through her teeth. All that meant spending time with Gabe, leaving herself vulnerable to his virility, his new, appealing ways.

"I can see that you've made your decision, Mrs. Renault—Helen," he amended kindly. "But you may find that Gabe is a different man than he was before. Life-threatening experiences tend to change people. If you find he hasn't changed, then you can at least walk away with a clearer conscience for having helped him."

Helen felt as if a weight were slowly lifting from her shoulders. That was it. She'd been battling her guilt for days. The doctor's words made the reason clear. She hadn't given Gabe the chance that he deserved.

"You're right," she said, thinking Leila was going to have a cow.

Dr. Terrien gave her a considering look. "Has Gabriel ever talked with you about his childhood?" he asked her out of the blue.

Helen cocked her head to one side. "He's told me about his parents, who are dead, but not much. I've always sensed a reluctance to talk about the past, so I don't go there."

Dr. Terrien was quiet for a moment. "What do you suppose a man thinks about during a year of torture and isolation?"

It was a provocative question, though definitely a rhetorical one. Helen stared back at him, her mind churning.

"Why don't you ask your husband about his past?" he recommended.

She gave him a quizzical look. "He's not exactly open about it."

"Give it a try," the doctor encouraged. "He's been quite candid with me. Perhaps if you discuss the past with Gabe you'll understand why he committed himself to the SEALs the way he did. Why he ignored you."

Startled by the doctor's accurate assessment of their problems, Helen nodded. "Okay," she agreed, though she couldn't imagine Gabe opening up to her that way.

"He's pretty hard on himself," the psychiatrist added. "It would help if you could forgive him for what happened last night." His gaze slid once more to her bruised neck.

She touched the sore spot self-consciously.

"He might have killed you," Dr. Terrien admitted, lifting his bushy eyebrows. "But he didn't. Something in his subconscious mind recognized you, Helen. I believe you're safe with him. Still, make sure he's awake next time you surprise him," he added with a twinkle in his eye. "The dreams will come more often now. If you feel the need to wake him, call his name and identify yourself. Let him know he's dreaming. Soothe him in whatever way works."

Erotic visions flickered through her mind. She held the doctor's gaze with difficulty.

"Well, time's up." Dr. Terrien stood up abruptly. He stretched out a hand. "We're making good progress," he informed her heartily. "I'm going to stay here and take care of some paperwork. I'll see Gabriel tomorrow."

Helen murmured her thanks and made her way back to the waiting room. Gabe was sitting in the same chair, his legs stretched before him, arms still crossed over his chest. "I'm worried about Mallory," he said, giving her a searching look.

Helen was starting to worry also. "I'll check the message machine at home," she suggested.

She pulled her cell phone from her purse and dialed the house, accessing the remote messaging system. The only message was from her father. At his irate tone, she flinched, holding the receiver away from her ear.

"Why the hell didn't you call us and let us know?" he railed. *"We want to see Gabe at the first opportunity. In fact, we're thinking about coming down for a visit. Give us a call. Tell Renault, welcome home."*

Helen disconnected the call and slapped the cell phone shut.

"Who was that?" Gabe asked.

"My father. Admiral Johansen just told him you're back." She hadn't called her parents herself. Dealing with them and Gabe at the same time was more than she could handle.

"No message from Mallory," he deduced, coming smoothly to his feet.

"I'm sure she's fine," Helen said, reassuring both of them as she led the way out of the office. "She spends a lot of time with her friend Reggie. He lives right down the street."

"A guy?" Gabe sounded alarmed.

"Don't worry. He's half her size. He's barely an adolescent." She stuck the key in the car door.

He sent her a narrow-eyed look over the top of the car. "I don't care if he's Pee Wee Herman. He's a guy."

Helen glared at him. "Mal and Reggie have been best friends for three years. You try and tell her she can't hang out with him anymore."

He put his hands up in the air. "Just show me where he lives," he said.

Fair enough.

They drove in silence for a while. Traffic was thick with everyone racing home from work. Helen took a secluded back road and they finally made some progress. Dr. Terrien's advice prompted her to say something.

"I think my throat's almost healed," she said casually, keeping her eye on the road.

Gabe said nothing in return. She sensed the tension building in him.

"Dr. Terrien says your subconscious recognizes who I am. So you don't have to beat yourself up anymore," she added. "I'm safe with you."

Hah! Leila would have a good laugh over that one!

"That might be an exaggeration," Gabe drawled.

She glanced at him sharply and found him gazing at her thighs.

Oh, my. His look made her skin feel prickly. How was she going to resist him? How could she keep him from sinking his claws into her now that she could no longer avoid him?

She leaned forward and snapped on the radio, letting the smooth voice of Garth Brooks come between them.

Gabe hated country music. She played it just to irk him; after all, her days of pleasing Gabe were over.

Moments later, she glanced his way to find him listening contentedly. He caught her eye and smiled. "I think I like country music," he said without any affectation whatsoever. "It's more peaceful than I remember."

Oh, God. If he did one more thing right, she was going to grab him and kiss him again.

"Eddie?" Noel Terrien didn't have to identify himself. He was doubtless the only person who ever called the man on the other end Eddie. But they'd gone to elementary school together, and the habit was just too old to shake.

"Noel," said the other man, sounding surprised. "You have an update for me?"

"The patient's memories are returning," Noel admitted. He didn't like violating his patient's privacy, but the military world wasn't like the civilian one. With rank came power and the ability to bend the rules. Besides, Noel owed Eddie a favor for securing him this job. His year at the Detox Center had made it hard to find work in the civilian sector.

In the background he heard Eddie's desk chair creak. "What, already?" He sounded disbelieving.

"I'm pleased with his progress," Noel admitted, wishing he could take the credit. "I wouldn't be surprised if he recovers all his memories within a month."

A startled pause followed this announcement. "What about the damage to his frontal lobe? Any sign that it's affecting him adversely?"

"Not that I can tell, but it's really too soon to give you a definitive answer."

"Has he remembered his last mission?"

"Oh, no. I've been focusing on the two years prior. No reason to reawaken unpleasant memories until the earlier ones are reestablished."

"Right."

"But he is remembering his captivity. Just bits and pieces, too fragmented to put together yet. He remembers the name of the man who interrogated him—let me see." Noel consulted his notes. "Seung-Ki was his name."

"Did he reveal any military secrets?"

"We're not at that point yet. The patient seals up like a clam when I try to drag the details out of him."

Thoughtful silence on the other end. "I appreciate you keeping me informed."

"Hmmm," said Noel. He couldn't honestly say that it pleased him, too, but beggars couldn't be choosy. Besides, if the patient's memories affected national security, Eddie had a right to know.

"Keep me posted," said his old friend.

"Will do," Noel replied, adopting the lingo Eddie used with such ease now. He lowered the receiver back into its cradle, slipping Gabe Renault's file into the drawer. He wished he could dismiss the twinge of his conscience as easily.

Mallory regarded the miniature cigar with trepidation. "Where'd you get it?" she asked her friend.

Reggie's freckles were so prominent they could not be disguised by mere shadow. They sat in the gloomy basement that he'd transformed into a hangout. The old checkered couch was musty with mildew, and it had a few loose springs that got your attention if you sat down in the wrong place.

"Some guy at the beach gave it to me for free," he boasted. He put it to his lips and flicked the lighter with his thumb.

"Wait a minute," Mallory protested. "This is what they warned us about in health class. You can get addicted to this stuff."

"No way," he argued. "They were talking about the hard stuff. All the kids in high school smoke marijuana. It's harmless." The lighter flared, and he stuck the end of the joint into the flame.

Mallory watched uncertainly. She knew Reggie was reckless, but this was taking things too far. The flame illumined his bright red hair and made his blue eyes shine. Then it was gone, leaving a line of smoke that went straight up in a vertical line.

It smelled funny. Mallory leaned away, watching Reggie's reaction. He took a deep drag on it, then gave a series of hacking coughs. He laughed at himself, his eyes watering. "Lemme try that again," he said.

This time he managed to inhale without his lungs convulsing. He held his breath just like they'd seen in the movies. Mallory held her breath, too.

Reggie glanced her way and laughed, expelling the smoke in her direction. "Wow, I can feel it already," he said. "It's like I'm flying. Cool!"

A spurt of curiosity overcame her repugnance.

"Wanna try it?" he said, extending the butt to her.

"Not yet," she said. She imagined her parents' reaction if they found out, and she quailed.

Reggie didn't have to worry about that. His dad was long gone and his mom was at work.

"Wooeeh," he said, taking another hit. "Man, this is so relaxing," he said, flinging himself down on two adjacent cushions. He winced, no doubt encountering a spring.

Mallory knew a moment's envy. She could use some relaxation herself. She was stretched as tight as a drum. The lid was bound to blow off the top of her world, and she didn't know how to stop it.

But she had a gut feeling that sucking on a marijuana cigarette wasn't the answer.

Reggie's dog went crazy upstairs. Reggie didn't seem to notice.

"Someone's here," Mallory guessed, shaking his knee.

"'Sprobably the postman," he replied, unperturbed.

The spitz upstairs continued to yap. Mallory stood up,

feeling uneasy. "I'm going to go check it out," she said, heading for the steps.

The doorbell rang. She hurried toward the front of the house and peered out the window. At the sight of the Jaguar, she shrank back into the shadow. "Oh, *shit!*" she breathed.

She heard them talking. Ohmigod, what should she do? Open the door and pretend everything was good? She had to. Her bike was out front. They knew she was here.

She scooped up the growling spitz with one hand and gripped the doorknob hard with the other. "Hi, guys," she said, pulling the door open. "Looking for me?"

Her mother gave her a friendly smile. "Hi, honey. We were just wondering where you went."

"I'm right here," Mal said, sensing something dangerous in Gabe's taut form as he stood there silently, looking straight into her face.

"Where's Reggie?" he asked.

Mallory gripped the doorknob harder. "Down in the basement," she said. Her heart thudded now in earnest.

"I'd like to meet him," her Dad said.

No, no! "You've met him before," she stalled, striving to sound casual.

"I don't remember," he said succinctly.

It was time for a serious distraction. "Really? Like you didn't remember that woman at the gym?" It took all her courage to throw that one out, because this Gabe she recognized. This was the Gabe who kicked butt, and he was going to kick hers if she wasn't careful.

"Mallory!" Mom gasped.

Gabe's gaze moved past her challenging expression into the darkened house. He took a slow deep breath and she knew with gripping fear that he could smell it. The marijuana smoke.

She was dead.

"Nice try, kid," he said very calmly. "Let me in."

Mom smelled it, too. A look of horrified surprise crossed her face.

Mallory felt suddenly sick to her stomach. She wanted to slam the door in their noses, but that wasn't likely to stop Gabe. She stepped back and opened the door wider. "He's down in the basement," she heard herself say. "I told him not to do it."

Chapter Eight

What'd you do to him?" Mallory demanded the moment Gabe reappeared at the front door. He'd made her stay with her mother, even though she was dying to save Reggie from the thrashing he was bound to receive.

"Watch your tone," Helen warned, drawing her closer.

Gabe paused before the pair of them, his expression calm. "We just had a talk that's all," he said mildly. He gave Mallory a once-over, his eyes dark with disappointment.

"I didn't try any," she said, ignoring her mother's warning squeeze.

"I didn't think you did," Gabe retorted. "From now on, you two will hang out at our house. We need to sand the deck," he said shortly. And then he strode past them toward the car.

Mallory gaped after him, dismayed by the thought of hard labor but immensely relieved not to have been forbidden to see Reggie again.

"Hop on your bike and come home now," Mom said, releasing her arm. "It's almost time to eat." She followed Gabe to the car.

Mallory stared after her parents, dazed. For the first time ever, they seemed to be on the same team. *Wow,* she thought, her spirits rising from turmoil. *Dad is being totally cool about Reggie's experimentation. Or is he?*

She cast a worried glance at the basement door. Was Reggie down there bleeding to death? She'd have to find out later. Gabe was giving her *The Look* out the window of the car. She started for her bike.

The Jaguar pulled out of Reggie's driveway.

"Hey, Mal!"

She had just begun to pedal after the car when Reggie stuck his head out the living-room window, the spitz's grinning face beside him. She braked hard. No signs of a beating.

"I have to work at your house tomorrow," he said, sounding stunned.

"You're lucky he didn't kill you!" she called back.

"He said he'd kill me if I did it again."

"Then you better not."

Reggie shrugged as if to say her father's threats didn't faze him, but he looked pretty shaken.

"See you tomorrow," she said. "What time are you coming over?"

"He said I had to be there at eight o'clock—oh eight hundred," Reggie mimicked, rolling his eyes.

Mallory heaved a groan and started pedaling. She didn't want to get up early tomorrow, but the alternative—a lengthy grounding of the type Gabe used to favor—was even worse.

Considering all that, she pedaled toward home with a curiously light heart.

*   *   *

Goddamn it, he couldn't sleep. Not with the bastards jabbering in the room across the hall. He hoped they weren't planning to come for him again. *Not tonight,* he prayed. *Jesus, God, not tonight.* He was still sore from last night.

Some new guy had wanted a turn with him. Given his slight stature, the guy packed an incredible wallop. It made Gabe wonder if all North Koreans weren't experts in tae kwon do. Every inch of Gabe's torso was beaten and bruised. Of course, he hadn't said a word to dishonor himself, even though he knew everything there was to know about coastal security in the Chesapeake Bay.

Just leave me the hell alone, he thought wearily. He shifted on the stone ledge, trying to get comfortable. He'd give his eyeteeth for a couple of Ibuprofen.

Cancel that. He didn't want any of his teeth pulled.

Well, shit, now he was wide-awake. There wasn't any going back to sleep with such a ruckus going on. Slowly, painstakingly, he slid to the far right side of his ledge, pausing to rise above the crushing pain in his ribs. At last his shoulder hit the cinder-block wall.

From here, he could see through the peephole of his cell into the room across the hall. It never ceased to amaze him how much technology was crammed into that little space. Computers, printers, scanners, monitors, zip drives, and routers covered every square inch of tabletop. His captors had every technological gadget known to mankind.

Five years ago, the scenario would have been thought impossible. Today it still seemed like something out of a bad movie. Gabe and his captors were in the desolate mountains of North Korea, miles from the capital city of Pyongyang where his SEAL team had inserted to evacuate the missiles. Yet, even in this remote, windswept region, in a bunker overlooking nothing but bare mountains, they had Internet access, and they weren't using it to order Christmas gifts online.

It was just the sort of thing that had prompted the creation of the Department of Cyberspace Security a while back.

Gabe's captors preferred to work at night. From what Gabe had gleaned thus far, they nosed around in U.S. municipal and state Web sites, looking for information on local energy infrastructures, water reservoirs, dams, highly enriched uranium storage sites, nuclear and gas facilities. When they discovered vulnerabilities or information worth selling, Gabe suspected they offered it to more renowned terrorist groups in exchange for money.

The same was true of their captive. They'd worked him over for whatever information they could get. He suspected they intended to pass it along to other hostiles in exchange for a fee. Only, he hadn't told them anything yet that wasn't a bald-faced lie.

As was his habit, Gabe tuned his ear to their quickly spoken Korean. He'd grown accustomed to their dialect, somewhat different from the Korean he'd studied in language school. Their sentences were punctuated with English computer terms, giving him an added advantage.

If he ever escaped his cell, he'd take something with him—that was for damn sure. After all, they'd taken nearly a year of his life and a couple of fingernails. A man couldn't put a price on that.

He considered the questioning he'd endured thus far. Fortunately, he knew very little about the Navy-Marine Corps Intranet, or he'd be hurting a lot more than he was right now. They had the wrong SEAL for that kind of information. Luther Lindstrom would have been a better catch.

But the questions about coastal security were wearing him down. They'd discovered a discrepancy in his lies and they were getting ruthless on a quest for the truth. His left hand still throbbed where pins had been thrust beneath his nails. Now they'd taken to depriving him of water. He hoped they wouldn't go for his teeth.

Sitting up nights listening to their conversation wasn't the most consoling form of vengeance. But Gabe swore to himself he'd have his day, providing they didn't kill him first. He thrust that grim possibility from his mind and stilled his thoughts to listen.

Strange. Normally he could make out his captors' voices clearly, but tonight they seemed far away and garbled. He couldn't translate a damn thing.

Probably a result of dehydration, he guessed. Or had they slipped a Mickey into the rice he'd had for dinner? He pushed himself off his ledge, shuffling toward the door to better hear them. His toe encountered something hard and wide blocking his path.

What the hell?

He squinted at the object, making out a leather chair, a desk, and a computer monitor. It looked just like his desk at home.

He blinked and peered about more closely. Wait a minute, this *was* his home. He was standing in the middle of the study with just a hint of hazy moonlight slipping under lowered blinds. Jesus Christ, he was sleepwalking!

With the feeling that he'd just traveled through time and space, at warp speed, Gabe groped for the chair. His stomach heaved, threatening to upend itself. Just like the last dream, it had seemed so real. His body ached as if it had been pummeled only yesterday. If he hadn't woken up . . .

No, Dr. Terrien didn't think he would hurt Helen again. But there was always a possibility he'd do something without realizing it. He'd never forgive himself if he did.

He teetered back to the couch and collapsed on it. He was grateful for the memories, really he was. But the recollections of his torture replayed themselves over and over, making him sick to his stomach. He forced himself to review each one. He had to know whether he'd betrayed his country. What had he said in a moment of agony?

By the time his memories played out, he was thoroughly nauseated and shivering with aftershock, but he was comforted to know that he hadn't jeopardized anyone's safety. He hadn't let his team down.

It comforted him to know why his captors had been ruthless in their quest for information. He thought of the news he'd heard on television the other night. With so many North Koreans starving to death and no financial aid forthcoming, they were selling information for money. It wasn't anything personal; they were simply trying to keep from starving to death.

Cursing quietly, Gabe glanced at the digital clock. Three forty-two. The sleeping pill's effects had obviously worn off. There was no way he would fall back asleep, now. Not with his thoughts so disturbed,

His gaze was drawn to the computer monitor, and a chill went through him. They were probably still out there, on the other end of cable fibers. Maybe there was some way to track them down—he didn't know. Luther was the man to talk to about that, and according to his fiancée, he wasn't even home yet.

Still, he felt drawn to the computer. It was linked, in some way, to his past. He moved from the couch to the leather chair, and his heart began to thump with expectation. *What?* He pondered his strange reaction.

Reaching under the desk, he powered on the computer and sat back as it booted up.

The "You've Got Mail" icon flashed onto the screen, and Gabe jumped like he'd been hit with a defibrillator.

What the hell is wrong with me?"

The sense of déjà vu was inescapable—this had happened to him before. He'd sat down in front of a computer and . . . and, *shit!* He couldn't remember! With shaking fingers he clicked the button, only to open Mallory's inbox.

It was filled with messages from Reggie, most of them forwarded jokes. Nothing pertained to him or to his situation.

Disgusted with himself, Gabe closed the mail and performed a search for a reputable newspaper. A hell of a lot had happened in the world this past year. As the newspaper's home page popped up on screen, he went immediately to the electronic archives. He'd never be a SEAL again if he didn't do his homework and learn what he'd missed.

On her way to the kitchen for breakfast, Helen paused outside the study door. Was Gabe awake? She was certain she heard a tapping sound, as if he were busy at the keyboard.

Though pricked with curiosity, she continued past his door, refusing to knock. Catching him alone at the crack of dawn was not a good idea. After that scalding encounter in the car yesterday, she was too susceptible to find herself alone with him. Nor could she afford to be late for work when she was still playing catch-up.

She tiptoed into the kitchen, pausing to grab a muffin out of the fridge. Eating it standing up, she strained her ears for sounds signaling his activities. Her gaze strayed out the window, where the sky glimmered a predawn silver. It promised to be another hot, dry day. Her wildflowers could use some rain.

The potted plant on the windowsill caught her attention.

She stepped closer, enjoying the crunch of walnuts in her banana nut muffin. It was the cactus Gabe had brought home from the hospital, she realized with surprise. He'd planted it in a ceramic pot Mallory had made for him in middle school, a simple pot with handles on both sides and a lapis lazuli glaze.

Gabe must have found it in the cupboard and resurrected it. Had he remembered that Mallory made it for him? She doubted it; it was probably just the right size. The chubby little cactus appeared to be thriving. Looking at it put a funny feeling in Helen's chest.

"You're up early."

A nut went down the wrong pipe as she gasped and whirled. "God! I told you not to sneak up on me!" She coughed to clear her lungs.

"Sorry." He looked especially contrite with a lock of hair falling over his forehead. "You going to work already?" He looked her up and down, his gaze alight with undisguised interest. She doubted she looked at all appealing in a pair of navy sweatpants, but his look told her otherwise.

"I'm still trying to catch up," she explained. She gave him a quick once-over. He looked like he'd been up most of the night. His hair was a mess and his eyelids looked heavy—a surprisingly appealing combination.

Stepping away, she poured herself a glass of orange juice. As she chugged it down, she tried not to think about why he was standing there, staring at her.

The seconds ticked by, and her awareness grew exponentially. He was stalking her, she realized, like the giant cat he was named for. When he was hungry enough, he would pounce—he always had. Yet he continued to stand there, eyeing her with that unnerving stare.

Don't touch me. She sent him a kinetic message. *If you*

touch me, I will melt in your arms like butter and I'll never forgive myself.

He didn't reach for her. She didn't know whether to be grateful or disappointed.

"Well, gotta go," she said, using the same words he'd used yesterday. Leaving her glass in the sink, she headed toward her bedroom to brush her teeth. The Gabe she knew would follow in her shadow and ravish her on her king-sized bed. Her legs felt rubbery as she cruised down the hall.

Once in the bathroom, she realized he wasn't behind her. She scrubbed her teeth, staring at her reflection and the stark disappointment in her eyes.

Was he waiting for *her* to go to him? It wasn't going to happen, she told herself. The minute she succumbed to him, she would feel things she was better off not feeling. Feelings that would make it so much harder to cut the strings between them.

Leila had suggested that he might use sex to get what he wanted, and he wasn't. Thank God he wasn't. It was better this way.

Teeth gleaming and hair combed, she left her room and headed swiftly to the door, determined not to be waylaid again. The study door was closed, and all was quiet within.

Why, she wondered, did she feel so terribly let down?

Gabe lengthened his stride. There was nothing like an early-morning run to perk up the senses and take one's mind off sleeping with his wife.

His jog with Mallory had taught him a humbling lesson: If he wanted to get back on the team, he needed to get in shape again. It wasn't anything unusual for a SEAL to run several miles in a single night, weighted down with equipment. At one time, he could have done that and scarcely broken a sweat. Yesterday, he could hardly run one mile, wearing nothing but a lightweight T-shirt and shorts.

He grunted in disgust. At least he felt good this morning—a little sore from yesterday's run, but not at all tired from his sleepless night. He left the house in advance of Helen—not trusting himself another second in her presence. He'd left Mallory to sleep in until seven-thirty, when he would roust her from bed to begin a long day's work on the deck.

The early-morning air filled his lungs. It wafted off the ocean, bearing the salty bite of the Atlantic, the scent of dew on sand. The sun was beginning to peek over the watery horizon. As he ran, pumping his arms and legs in an easy rhythm beneath him, Gabe watched the sky brighten from silver to yellow to peach.

God damn, I've missed the sunrises! With a catch in his throat, he acknowledged that truth. Though he couldn't recall for certain that he hadn't seen them, simple instinct told him that he'd been deprived of mornings like this: relishing his physical freedom, the light on his face, air streaming over his limbs to cool the sweat that came from healthy exertion. No, he hadn't done this in over a year.

Thank you, God! he thought, closing his eyes briefly in profoundest gratitude. *Thanks for this second chance!*

Not just a second chance to be free again, but a chance to connect with his wife and stepdaughter. He'd kept himself aloof from them before. Given his obsession for his work, that hardly came as a surprise. What surprised him now was his willingness to feel what he'd once been afraid of—love so overpowering that it snatched his breath away. Not that he wasn't still frightened of giving his heart away. He was terrified, especially with Helen threatening to reject him. But since his captivity, or perhaps because of it, he'd changed. He wanted to take the emotional risk of loving, truly loving someone.

Looking at Helen this morning, seeing how devoted she was to her career, how determined she was to be strong and independent, his chest had swelled with admiration. Regardless of her resistance, he owed it to her to give what he ought to have given her before: his unconditional commitment.

Aware that his lungs were straining, Gabe slowed to a pace he could maintain. Sandfiddler Drive was deserted this morning, with the vacationers sleeping in. Just one or two locals were up, lights shining in their kitchen windows. It was peaceful; it was perfect.

He wanted to be able to run like this whenever he could, taking pleasure from the sound of the surf, the beauty of the sunrises, the security of knowing his family was safe and well protected. Protected by men like him—peacekeepers, guardians.

Yet the reality of his life failed to jibe with his idealized vision. His family might soon be an ex-wife and a forgotten stepchild if he didn't tread carefully. And he was more of a burden on the taxpayer than he was a peacekeeper.

With his thoughts taking a nosedive, Gabe began to feel the aches and twinges in his unaccustomed muscles. Hearing a vehicle approach behind, he moved off the road and quickened his stride, not wanting to look like the sorry spectacle that he was.

A glance over his shoulder revealed a police car, making its early-morning rounds. Gabe held his head higher. Here was a fellow peacekeeper doing his job, keeping the beachfront safe from thieves and miscreants. Probably the night shift heading in after a long night's patrol.

Hoo-yah, he thought. It was a good thing there were men

and women willing to defend the home front. He'd be one of them again, soon, he swore.

He realized, with a sudden leaping of his heart, that the car was right behind him. He could hear its engine rumbling, hear the sand churning under its right tires as it veered off the shoulder.

Gabe glanced back, thinking the driver hadn't seen him or was playing some sort of joke. To his horror the engine gunned, and the vehicle slammed into the back of his thighs.

Gabe had had just enough warning to spring off the balls of his feet, sending him up and over the hood of the car, rather than underneath it. He rolled, making the briefest eye contact with the driver, a man with a hard jaw and steely eyes. His shoulder struck the mirror on the passenger side, and he was somersaulting through the air.

By some miracle, he managed to land on his feet. He staggered backward, hitting an electric box. While his mind struggled to reason through what had just happened, his instincts prompted him to turn tail and run.

The car was slowing to a stop. Gabe tried to tell himself that the driver would jump out and profess with great concern that he hadn't seen him. But the passenger pushing open his door bore an object in his hand that looked remarkably like a gun.

Gabe wasn't going to stick around and ask questions. He broke into a zigzag run, cutting between two houses. A shot rang out, and a bullet whizzed past, narrowly missing him. *Holy shit!* The wisest thing he could do was to get out of the open.

Aches and pains forgotten, Gabe darted into the crawl space beneath a cinder-block home, only there wasn't any need to crawl, with the first floor well above his head.

Adrenaline flowed through him, making him feel more

alive than he had in weeks. He concealed himself behind a thick pillar, ears straining for sounds of his pursuer over the thumping of his heart.

He hoped the man would follow him into the dark. In the dark, Gabe had the advantage.

It wasn't long before he heard the telltale sound of sand compressed beneath stealthy footfalls. He held very still, willing the man to come closer. A dot of red flickered along the cinder-block columns to his right and left. The man had a visible laser-sight designator. He obviously meant business.

"Manning." From a distance Gabe heard a whispered call.

The red dot disappeared. Footsteps receded. "I lost him. He got away."

"Next time. It's getting too light out here."

Gabe waited for their car doors to slam shut, waited for the cop car to pull away before he came out of his hiding place. Belated rage made his nerve endings tingle as he watched the taillights of the sedan swing around a corner and disappear.

What the hell had almost happened? Why would the local police be out gunning for him?

God damn it, they'd left him reeling with questions and with a definite foreboding about the future. *Next time,* they'd said. Hell no, there wasn't going to be a next time, not if he could help it. He'd talk to the chief of police himself and get this situation straight.

Breathing hard, he glanced down the street in the direction of his home. *Mallory.* He'd left her sleeping in the house alone. Assuming they knew where he lived, his assailants might return to his house to wait for him there.

He started to sprint in the direction of home, then pulled himself up short. Master Chief's house was closer. He'd go there, tell Sebastian what had happened, even though it made no sense. Master Chief would give him a ride back home, make sure the area was secure, give him backup.

Avoiding the road, Gabe darted between houses. He ducked under clotheslines heavy with towels, skirted hedges, and steered clear of barking dogs. Minutes later, he was climbing the steps to Sebastian's A-frame, ocean-front cottage.

He'd barely even knocked when Master Chief yanked open the door. "Jaguar," he said in surprise. Dressed in battle-dress uniform with a mug of coffee in his hand, he was clearly on his way to work.

Gabe sucked in air, trying to calm his racing heart. "Need to use the phone," he gasped.

Sebastian stepped wordlessly aside, and Gabe made a beeline for the phone in the kitchen. After five rings a sleepy voice answered, "Hello?"

"Mal, it's Dad." He took a deep breath, striving for a normal tone. "I went jogging. Do me a favor and lock the front door. Don't answer it for anyone. I'll be there in a minute."

A puzzled silence followed his request. "'Kay," she said.

"Do it," he urged. He hung up and turned toward Sebastian, who stood there, eyeing him steadily. "Master Chief," he said, "why would the cops be trying to kill me?"

Sebastian put his mug down on the counter. "I think you'd better start at the beginning," he suggested evenly.

"Give me a ride to my house. I'll tell you on the way there."

Sebastian lifted the keys to his 1960 Ford Falcon off a peg on the wall. "Let's go."

Thankful for his friend's calming influence, Gabe followed him outside, sweeping the area for any sign of the cruiser. Once within the steel hull of Sebastian's car, he poured forth the details while Sebastian listened intently.

They pulled into Gabe's driveway a minute later. Gabe waited for Sebastian's reaction. The master chief wasn't one to make hasty judgments. Gabe knew his story sounded ludicrous but his relationship with the master chief was based on trust. If anyone was going to believe him, it'd be he.

"What do I do, Sebastian?" Gabe prompted as the car continued to idle and Master Chief kept silent.

Bright morning sunlight lit the lower half of the noncommissioned officer's face, leaving his espresso-colored eyes in shadow. "You don't think I made this up?" Gabe added with a prickle of frustration.

"No," said his friend quickly and quietly. "But I don't think you should tell anyone else. Let me look into it."

"It sounds like a fucking hallucination," Gabe agreed.

Sebastian pursed his lips and shrugged. "Maybe it's supposed to."

"What do you mean?"

The NCO shook his head, his expression thoughtful. "I don't know. Maybe this has something to do with your disappearance. When the warehouse exploded, there were unanswered questions—an official inquiry with no definitive results."

Gabe's heart beat faster. A memory flickered through him, too quick to catch a fix on. "Jesus, are you saying I was left behind or that someone made a careless error?"

Master Chief stared at him as if the answer were branded on Gabe's forehead. "That you were left behind," he answered, very seriously.

Gabe was startled into momentary silence. "Who the hell would do that?" he asked.

"I don't know. But let's suppose this incident is related. If you make a complaint against the station and they deny it, it could ruin your chances of returning to the team."

Gabe took a sharp breath. "I'll sound paranoid," he agreed. A SEAL couldn't afford to suffer imaginary fears; there were enough real fears to contend with.

"Let me look into it," Sebastian repeated. "I know a former SEAL who joined the force. He can make a few subtle inquiries. No one will know."

"Manning," Gabe recalled. "The cop with the weapon was Manning. I heard the other guy call his name."

Sebastian nodded. "I'll start with that. In the meantime, I'll set a watch on your house if you like."

"There's no need for that." Gabe turned the offer down abruptly. Shame ate away at his insides. "I can protect my own house," he muttered.

"*Bueno,*" Sebastian said soothingly. "Call me if anything else comes up. Echo Platoon will pull into port any day now. As soon as they do, we'll get together and brainstorm."

Gabe rubbed his temple with sudden doubt. "It makes no sense," he admitted, viewing the situation from Sebastian's perspective. "Maybe it didn't happen. Maybe I fucking imagined it."

Sebastian regarded him wordlessly for a moment. "How do you feel after being hit?" he inquired.

Gabe tried to rotate the shoulder that had struck the mirror. "Shoulder hurts like hell."

"Then it happened," said Sebastian. "Go inside and check the place out. Give me a thumbs-up if it looks clear."

"Thank you," Gabe said. He pushed the heavy door ajar and met his friend's eyes, wondering at the worry he saw in them.

Chapter Nine

G abe put the sander down, spat a fleck of sawdust from his mouth, and admitted defeat. The sun shone hot upon his back. The sweat dripping from his forehead made his eyes sting. His shoulder throbbed with every beat of his heart. And even though he'd popped an extra Dexamphetamine to keep him awake, he was numb with exhaustion.

"Guys," he said, turning to eye Mallory and Reggie who were toting the deck furniture to one end of the deck. "Listen, we're going to have to finish this tomorrow."

Mallory's look of astonishment would have been comical if he had the energy to laugh.

"Reg, you're going to have to go home. I'll see you tomorrow morning, same time," Gabe informed him, winding up the cord on the electric sander.

Pleased by the unexpected reprieve, Reggie shot Mallory a grin and shrugged. "See ya," he said, loping toward the stairs.

Gabe left the sander under the picnic bench and headed

inside. Mallory followed close behind. "What am I supposed to do?" she asked.

"Read your book," he suggested wearily. "I don't care. Just stay inside and keep away from the windows. Wake me up if anyone drops by."

He caught a glimpse of her puzzled expression as he marched into the bathroom and shut the door.

She thinks I'm losing it, he thought with disgust. He peeled off his clothes and prepared to step into the shower. A backward look in the mirror revealed a swelling contusion by his left shoulder. He was glad to see physical proof of the unlikely incident this morning.

Five minutes later, he emerged from a hot shower, dried himself off, and realized he'd forgotten a change of clothing. He secured the towel around his hips and stepped into the hall, running straight into Mallory who seemed to be standing there, waiting for him.

It was too late to cover his naked chest. Gabe compressed his mouth with regret and watched Mallory's eyes flare with horror, gaze flickering from one ghastly scar to another. He watched her take mental count of them—one, two, three— and those were just the ones on his chest. His back was in worse shape. He kept his back to the door so she couldn't see it.

To his surprise, she raised her eyes, giving him a level look. "Are you all right?" she wanted to know.

"Yeah, sure," he said, edging his way toward the study.

"You seem kind of . . . off balance," she added, frowning at him with motherly concern.

"My shoulder hurts," he said, seizing the first excuse to come to mind.

"What'd you do to your shoulder?" she instantly demanded.

He rolled it unconsciously, feeling its stiffness. "I fell when I was running this morning. No big deal."

But she was already circling around him to get a better view. "Oh, my God!" she cried.

He didn't know if it was his recent bruise that prompted the exclamation or the sight of his mutilated back.

"What were you doing? Running backward?" she asked, laying a gentle hand on the swollen area. She gave him a searching look.

He knew an urge to grin. Damn, she was smart—too smart to be fooled by his lame excuse. "Don't worry about it," he repeated. "It's fine. Just a little stiff. I need to sleep," he added. "Go read." He pointed down the hall toward her bedroom, putting on his sternest face.

"I'm going," she said, still obviously concerned. At the last instant, she rose on tiptoe and kissed his cheek. "Sleep tight," she added, breezing down the hall and out of sight.

Gabe lay on his couch a short while later, reflecting on Mallory's reaction to his scars. Behind eyelids that felt they'd been sealed together with superglue, he saw her horror and sympathy.

She hadn't found his scars too terribly repulsive. In fact, she seemed to accept them, maybe even respected him more for the hell he'd gone through. She'd even given him a kiss.

What would Helen do if she knew what this last year had cost him? Maybe she'd be merciful like her daughter.

It was his last thought before he tumbled off a cliff into oblivion.

He was late for his appointment again. Helen had gently shaken him awake, saying, "Gabe, it's Helen. Time to wake up." Their progress out the door was further delayed by her insistence that he put ice on his shoulder. Mallory hadn't wasted a minute informing her mother of his injury.

"How'd that happen?" Helen wanted to know as he took the ice pack from her hands. To his disappointment, she didn't sound nearly as sympathetic as Mallory had. She certainly didn't kiss him to make it better.

"Stupid accident," he muttered. His tongue felt strangely uncooperative, so he kept his responses to a minimum, staring out the car window as they sped toward Oceana.

The fact that she accepted his explanation without further questioning depressed him.

His session with Dr. Terrien wasn't any better. With Sebastian's suggestion for discretion in mind, Gabe had very little to say. He was basically still asleep, even though his eyes were open.

"Is there something bothering you, Gabriel?" the doctor inquired. "I felt we were making good progress yesterday. Today you have nothing to tell me."

Gabe rubbed his gritty eyes. "I'm tired, Doc. The sleeping pills run out of steam by three in the morning. During the day, I want to sleep. The Dexamphetamine doesn't seem to help."

Dr. Terrien rubbed his palms together. "Go ahead and take three sleeping pills at night," he suggested. "As for the Dexamphetamine, it won't be effective if your body is exhausted. Give the medication time."

Opening his bleary eyes, Gabe experienced a simmering of resentment. If he had to talk to get their session over with, then so be it. "You want me to tell you something? I'll tell you. Last night I dreamed about my prison cell. It was in a bunker on the top of a hill overlooking rocky wasteland. There was a window, a long narrow one, way up by the ceiling and a ledge that I slept on. Through a square in my door,

I could see another room across the hall. My keepers stayed up all night in that room surfing the Internet."

"The Internet?" Dr. Terrien interrupted on a note of disbelief.

"That's right. They cruised the Net looking for sites susceptible to terrorism: local energy infrastructures, water reservoirs, dams, nuclear and gas facilities, stuff like that. When they found what they perceived to be a vulnerability, they sold the information to the Big Boys, al-Qaeda, Hamas, you name it."

Dr. Terrien eyed him closely as if trying to determine whether Gabe was pulling his leg.

"No remarks?" Gabe prompted.

"Well"—the doctor shifted uncomfortably in his chair— "I don't know much about international concerns, Gabriel. I'm sure this information would be of interest to the DIA or the FBI, who will be glad to hear it when they debrief you. But they won't do that until you have your memory back. For now, I don't think it's wise to dwell on memories that are so . . . volatile in nature."

Gabe could barely contain a disbelieving snort. "You want me to forget what I've remembered?" he rephrased, struck by the absurdity of it.

Dr. Terrien gave him a look that was equal parts concern and reprimand. "I want you to leave the trauma of your captivity at rest for as long as possible. There are other, more healing memories to recover first. You'll need them in order to cope with the rest."

Gabe stared at the doctor in disbelief. From the point of view of security, Dr. Terrien's advice was ludicrous. "But I remember now. I can't just file this shit away and pretend it isn't important. Christ!"

The doctor heaved a sigh and rubbed his chin. "There is

something you should know, Gabriel," he said after a reflective moment. "I didn't mention it before, because I thought you had enough to deal with."

Gabe's spine stiffened and the muscles in his back clamped down. "What?" he demanded.

"A common side effect of PTSD is paranoia," the doctor said gently. "Even after the trauma, a victim continues to perceive a threat. The body and the mind have been conditioned to do this. It's perfectly natural. In this case, you may simply be imagining that your attackers pose a threat to your country. The threat may not be real."

Gabe refused to digest what the man was telling him. "You think I'm making this up," he concluded. His temple began to throb again, close to his right eye.

"No, no," the other man was quick to assure him. "Some of your recollections are real, there's no question," Dr. Terrien comforted. "But your projections about the future and the intentions of your captors may be fabrications of your mind. You can't be sure, my friend."

Gabe clamped his jaw shut. He was too pissed off to respond with anything remotely civil. The silence grew taut as it stretched between them.

"How about this," Dr. Terrien finally proposed. "Why don't you take notes on your dreams, and next week we'll review them. We'll separate your memories from your projections and take action if you still want to. Believe me, Gabriel, you don't want to carry these feelings with you forever. You can trust me on this one."

Gabe gave a humorless laugh and rubbed his throbbing temple. Could he? Dr. Terrien was asking him to ignore his training as a warrior, as a protector of the people. On the other hand, the advice made awful sense in light of what had happened this morning.

Maybe he hadn't been hit by a cop car. Maybe a tourist had nicked him by accident and he'd imagined the rest. Policemen trying to run him down—how unlikely was that? North Koreans selling cyberspace technology to terrorists—maybe. Both stories sounded like fabrications. What if he'd made them up?

Christ, he was glad he hadn't mentioned the incident this morning. Next thing he knew, he'd be locked in a padded cell.

As much as he didn't want to admit it, the doctor had a point. Perhaps he ought to consider his memories with skepticism. If they were just a figment of his imagination, he could sure as hell breathe easier. He wouldn't have to fret about his country's vulnerabilities, wouldn't have to glance over his shoulder thinking someone was after him. He'd know it was just his mind playing tricks on him.

But, Jesus, if he was in that bad a shape, he'd never be a SEAL again. He tugged his hair until his scalp hurt, wondering how he would ever discern between truth and fiction.

"Why don't we call it a day," the doctor gently suggested. "I've given you plenty to think about. I don't want you to worry, Gabriel. Paranoia is a normal part of PTSD. As you regain your memories, the paranoia will fade. Take each day as it comes, and don't let your memories distress you. Call me over the weekend if you feel you need to," he added kindly.

Mumbling his thanks, Gabe shook the doctor's hand and stumbled back into the waiting room, where Helen sat jotting notes to herself. She looked from him to the doctor, her brow puckering with concern.

"Helen, my dear, could I borrow you for a minute?" Dr. Terrien inquired.

Gabe repressed a groan and threw himself into a soft chair. Great. Now the doctor was going to tell his wife he was a fucking paranoid.

He watched Helen trail the doctor back into his office. She tossed a worried glance over her shoulder.

Gabe grappled with the urge to pick up the coffee table and throw it. Helen would come out thinking he belonged in a psycho ward. She'd never trust her heart with him now.

At eight o'clock, shortly after choking down a dinner of dried chicken and peas, Gabe got the call he'd been dreading.

"It's me, sir," Sebastian said. His dampening tone told Gabe everything he needed to know.

"Go ahead," he said, bracing himself for the final blow.

A subtle pause on the other end. "According to the local police, there were no officers on patrol in this area at six in the morning," Sebastian said quickly.

It wasn't like the information was unexpected. Nonetheless, it lodged uncomfortably in Gabe's mind. "What about the name Manning?" he asked in a strangled voice.

He could picture Sebastian shaking his head on the other end. "They have no officers by that name," he said without inflection.

Gabe blinked several times. He had pretty much a photographic memory. And he could picture the Chrysler with perfect clarity, its shiny paint, the glinting chrome. It was hard to believe he could have invented such detail.

"Here's the deal, Master Chief," he forced himself to say. "The PTSD makes me paranoid. My doctor said so. I appreciate you looking into the matter for me. I don't think it happened."

Sebastian kept quiet for a long time, no doubt processing

what it meant for his lieutenant to be paranoid. It meant he wouldn't be a SEAL again anytime soon. "How did you hurt your shoulder then?" he asked.

Gabe shook his head. "I don't know. Something happened; I just don't know what. Maybe I blacked out and fell on something."

"*Dios,*" the NCO muttered. A lengthy pause followed as he hunted for the right words to say. "Call me if something similar happens," he invited.

"Will do." Gabe glanced up at his family. Helen was scrubbing dishes at the sink. Mallory dried and put them away. Both pretended they weren't listening. For their sakes, he hoped he wouldn't have to call the NCO again. "Sebastian," he added, a bitter taste in his mouth, "don't tell anyone about this."

"No, sir. The platoon will be back tomorrow. First squad will get together soon."

The compassion in Sebastian's voice made Gabe want to crawl under the carpet and die. "You bet," he said, clinging to his dignity. "Thanks for your help."

"Anytime."

When he put the phone down, he noticed his fingers were shaking. He looked up and found both Helen and Mallory eyeing him inquiringly.

"Was that the master chief?" Helen asked, drying her hands on her apron.

"Yeah." Gabe shoved his hands into the rear pocket of his jeans. "He, uh, he says the guys'll be in tomorrow. They'll be wanting to get together."

"Oh, great." She gave him an uncertain smile. "Maybe we can have a gathering on our deck."

He gave a brisk nod. "Sure, as soon as I finish sanding it." He cleared his throat. He needed to be alone, to brood over the horrifying fact that his mind was playing tricks on him. "I'm going to tuck in early tonight." He glanced at Mallory, whose face fell.

"But I wanted us to walk on the beach together," she cried.

Gabe glanced at Helen, who remained notably quiet. The urge to bury his head in a pillow conflicted with the equally powerful yearning to walk on the beach, maybe reach for his wife's hand . . .

But then he pictured a sniper setting up his weapon in the dunes. With a long-range, infrared laser scope, he could take Gabe out in an instant—maybe even his wife and kid, too.

The threat was as unlikely as it was ridiculous, he knew. His paranoia was getting the better of him. "It's getting dark," he said, his gaze darting out the window at the mauve sky. "I don't want you walking the dog in the dark."

They gave him identical looks of incredulity.

"Well, then, come with us," Mallory reasoned aloud.

Gabe fought his illogical fear. There was no sniper. He knew that. At the same time, he was certain he hadn't blacked out while taking a jog. He remembered every second of the incident with perfect clarity. In that case, someone really *was* after him. If so, he was more of a liability to his family than a shield. They'd been walking the dog alone for a year now without incident. But if he were the target for some faceless enemy, he'd be jeopardizing their lives by joining them.

"Forget it," he said, turning away from them with self-directed anger. "Go without me. I need some sleep."

As he stalked toward the sanctuary of the study, he overheard Mallory's whispered comment. "Something is going on with Dad."

Damn right, something was going on with him. He was

losing his fucking mind. And unless his memories resurfaced soon, he'd turn into one of those pathetic Vietnam vets that never got his life back on track.

He'd be a burden on taxpayers indefinitely.

Helen laid her purchase on the counter at Expressions, Leila's dance studio, and dug in her purse for her checkbook.

"I knew you'd like this green one," Leila said, ringing up the spandex halter top and slipping it into a bag. "You're one of the few people I know who looks good in lettuce green," she added, giving Helen a searching look. "How are things going?" she asked, darting a look at the only other customer, a woman browsing through the racks of leotards.

Helen made a face and shrugged. "In some ways . . . great," she admitted. "Having him home—it's nothing like I expected."

One of Leila's dark eyebrows arched.

"Gabe's so different now," Helen elaborated. "He used to hate being home. He couldn't wait to get back to work. Even when he took leave, he used to pore over paperwork." She shook her head, unable to reconcile the differences.

"He's not like that now?" Leila prompted, sounding skeptical.

"Not at all. He seems content to be with us. He's got all these home projects that he's working on. Sanding the deck, doing the laundry. He's even training the dog to behave."

"Doesn't he seem, you know, depressed?" Leila queried, pitching her voice discreetly.

Helen considered how he'd looked this morning when she'd found him on the deck, just sitting there gazing out at the ocean. "Sometimes," she admitted. "Not depressed, exactly, just thoughtful. I think he's coming to terms with the memories that are returning. He was tortured pretty badly," she added, her heart constricting with pity.

"You don't think that makes him dangerous."

Helen considered the night he'd nearly strangled her to death. "Not really," she answered, unwilling to share what had transpired then. "What's the total?"

Leila pushed a key on the register and named a price.

"His psychiatrist says I'm safe," Helen added, scribbling the sum into her checkbook. "But he does think that Gabe is suffering paranoid delusions because of the trauma. I didn't believe him, at first, but then last night, Gabe seemed afraid to leave the house."

"Afraid?" Leila scoffed. "Gabe's never been afraid of anything in his life."

"I know it's—" Helen ripped out the check and handed it to her friend. "It's weird."

"Doesn't that concern you? I mean, it sounds like he spends a lot of time alone with Mallory."

Helen took offense to the warning while soothing herself that Leila was only looking out for their best interests. "I'm not worried about him and Mallory. He's been great with her. Right now he's got Mallory and Reggie helping him sand the deck. Mal enjoys the heck out of it, but she's picked up on Gabe's disquiet."

"Maybe he needs to get out more," Leila suggested, "so he can see that he's safe now. Why don't you take him to dinner?"

"I can't believe you're telling me to do that," Helen replied.

"For his well-being," Leila corrected. "He has to get his bearings again, that's all."

"That's what his doctor says." She took the bag Leila handed her. "I think I will."

Leila grabbed her hand and clung to it a moment. "Be careful, Helen," she said. "I know he seems different now but . . . you don't know that he's going to stay that way. You don't know he's not dangerous, either to you or to your heart."

"I hear you," Helen said, thankful for her friend's concern. "It's just that . . ." She hesitated, wondering how to put into words the feelings Gabe was stirring in her lately, feelings of concern and compassion and genuine amity. Added to the physical attraction she'd always felt for him, those feelings were eroding her determination to live without him. "He's getting to me, you know?" she admitted, imploring Leila to understand. "It's like he really wants to connect with me, to be the husband he's never been. I find myself thinking it would be so nice to let him hold me. I mean, it's obvious he wants to."

Leila put her elbows on the counter and studied her face. "What you're saying is you want to sleep with him," she interpreted.

"Well, he *is* my husband," Helen defended herself. "And when he looks at me now, it's not in that predatory way that he used to look at me. It's like he's waiting patiently for me to come to him."

"You'll regret it," Leila predicted. "He'll suck you in and spit you out. How many times has he done that in the past? Helen, you've got to protect yourself."

"I know." It was true. Every time Gabe had showered her with attention, Helen had reported the heartwarming news to Leila, only to turn to Leila again when Gabe receded, eager to leave on his next mission. "But I miss the intimacy. I just want to be touched again," she admitted as yearning grew in her. "Do you know how long it's been?"

Leila's face reflected sympathy. "Yes," she said. "I do. And I know exactly how you feel."

That was said on such a heartfelt note, that Helen cocked her head suspiciously. "You could have any man you want," she pointed out, giving her friend a quick inspection. Leila was a work of art—fine-boned, high-breasted, with long, elegant legs, a headful of coal-black hair, thanks to her Turkish heritage, and the face of a supermodel.

"Well, thanks"—Leila gave her a tight smile—"but when you've had the best, it's hard to settle for less."

Helen's eyes widened. "You never said Altul was that good."

Leila choked out a laugh and waved a dismissing hand. "Not Altul," she corrected, referring to her husband, the one who'd abandoned her.

Intrigued, Helen gave her friend a probing look. "Who?" she demanded, her curiosity roused.

Leila shrugged her shoulders and avoided eye contact. "It doesn't matter."

"Tell me," Helen wheedled. An incredulous smile seized her. Was it possible that Leila, Queen of Bitter Hearts, was actually infatuated?

"I can't," Leila said quickly. "You know him."

Helen gasped with surprise. "I know him?" she breathed. "Is he military?" She assumed so, since all the men she knew were Navy.

Leila pursed her lips together and considered Helen through her lashes. "Okay," she decided. "I'll tell you, but you have to promise not to tell anyone, especially Gabe."

Why would she tell Gabe . . . unless . . .

"It's someone he works with," Leila admitted. "Sebastian León."

Helen straightened abruptly. "Oh, my God!" she cried. "He's perfect for you."

"What?" Leila scoffed. "No way. He was a one-night deal. I'd be crazy to want anything more."

"What are you talking about?" Helen argued. "He's handsome, single—"

"Stop," Leila commanded. "There are several reasons I won't see him again." She ticked them off on her scarlet-tipped fingers. "One, he's a SEAL. SEALs get up and leave whenever they're called, and they might never come back."

With a pang of understanding, Helen realized just how much that would devastate Leila, who'd been abandoned once already.

"Two, he's Mexican and therefore as chauvinistic and macho as Altul was."

Leila's ex-husband had been Turkish and dominated every aspect of his wife's life.

"And three," Leila added, "he's been a bachelor all his life, and he isn't interested in commitment."

Helen considered the cons as objectively as possible. Leila was right. She didn't need a repeat performance of her disastrous marriage to Altul. "But you'd look so good together," she lamented, picturing the striking pair.

"Oh, we're good together, all right," Leila said, fanning her cheeks and looking suddenly flushed.

Helen let out a laugh at the absurdity of it all. "Look at us," she said, shaking her head. "We're pathetic. We can't live with them and we can't live without them. You're going to have to tell me more about this one-night stand," she warned. "Right now, I've got to get going."

"Go," said Leila, waving her away. "Get those old folks up and moving," she said, smiling her rare smile.

Helen waved good-bye and pushed open the door, setting

off an electric chime. She was off to the local nursing home to lead the geriatrics through stimulating exercises. Normally, she looked forward to her volunteer work on Saturdays, but today, she drove to the nursing home preoccupied by thoughts of Gabe. She'd avoided spending time with him all week, and now she felt guilty about it. Dr. Terrien had convinced her it was time to offer Gabe her unconditional support, if only to get him out of her life more quickly. One thing she couldn't stand was to see Gabe looking confused and wary of his own shadow.

It would do him good, she decided, to take him out tonight—with Mallory acting as escort.

When the old Gabe reemerged, she would know that she had done her job, and then she would release him, exactly as planned. But maybe she should let him love her one last time. A powerful yearning overtook her, forcing her to acknowledge that she still desired him; that he wielded the same tremendous power over her senses as he always had. Leila was right to have warned her.

If she was going to let Gabe claim her body, she'd better be prepared to face the consequences. Her heart would yearn for reciprocity, and if Gabe did again what he'd done in the past, transferring his focus to the team, it would surely kill her.

Hearing a car engine over the whine of his sander, Gabe snapped it off and set it on the deck rail, assessing the dark blue sedan as it approached the house. He peered through the tinted window at the driver, a cold sweat breaking out under his T-shirt.

It wasn't the steely-eyed cop that had tried to mow him down, assuming the man was even real. It was an older, heavyset man in a suit, reading house numbers as he drove by.

Gabe glanced at Mallory and Reggie, who were working on the rails at the rear of the deck with squares of sandpaper. He looked back at the sedan, not at all surprised to see it pulling into his driveway. "Mallory," he called.

"Yeah, Dad?"

"Come here a sec."

She dropped her sandpaper and joined him quickly.

"You see a car in our driveway?" he asked, hating to inquire about the obvious, but it never hurt to have a witness.

"Who is it?" Mallory asked.

As the driver emerged from the car, Gabe realized he could answer the question. It was Ernest Forrester, the Defense Intelligence officer who had grilled him at the hospital, the man who'd sent him into an anxiety attack last week. He could feel a case of heartburn coming on right now.

"Someone from the government," Gabe said vaguely. "Listen, if anything weird happens, get inside and call my master chief. I put his number on speed dial, number three."

"Okay," she said, giving him an uncertain look.

Not wanting to see the doubt in her eyes, Gabe trotted down the steps to greet his visitor.

"Mr. Forrester," he said, encountering the man at the bottom of the stairs. He extended a hand.

Forrester mopped his brow with a handkerchief while returning Gabe's handshake. "You remember me," he said, his handshake brief but sturdy. "You look a lot better."

Gabe gave him a tight smile. "What brings you here?" he asked, aware that he was being rude. He ought to offer the man a glass of ice water at the very least, especially if he'd driven all the way from northern Virginia to pay him a visit.

"I've come to see if you remember anything yet," Forrester said, squinting through fleshy eyelids.

Gabe's spine stiffened. He hated the fact that his memories were everyone's business. "I remember a little," he admitted reluctantly. "It's coming back to me piecemeal, mostly in my dreams."

"Care to tell me what you know?" the man invited, polite but unrelenting. He glanced longingly at the house.

Gabe noted the man's dark suit and decided to have mercy on him. "Why don't you come in?" he said.

Minutes later, Forrester was settled on the floral couch, a glass of water in his hand. "You were telling me what you remembered," he prompted, taking a sip of his drink.

Gabe felt a cinching sensation in his stomach. The instinct to guard his memories warred with the belief that Uncle Sam had his best interest at heart—or at least the best interest of his country. Here was a chance to warn the government of North Korea's quest for information—providing he hadn't invented that particular threat.

"All right," he said, occupying a seat opposite the officer. He related in detail what he'd told Dr. Terrien yesterday, explaining that the North Koreans fed information to terrorists worldwide in exchange for money. "They're desperate for food," he finished. He sat there, aware that his hands were curled into fists. He hoped Forrester wouldn't notice his inexplicable tension.

The officer's deep-set eyes probed Gabe's expression. "It's no less than we've suspected," the man admitted, putting down his drink, "but I appreciate the specifics." He whipped out a notepad and asked Gabe to repeat the types of sites that had been scrutinized.

"Their leader's name was Seung-Ki," Gabe added, when he was done.

Forrester looked at him sharply. "Tell me about Seung-Ki," he invited.

Gabe's throat grew tight. Images flashed through his mind, accompanied by ruthless recollections of pain. He took a deep breath, searching for his voice that seemed suddenly to have deserted him.

"What kinds of questions did he ask you?" the officer inquired gently. He seemed to understand that Gabe was locked in an emotional struggle.

Gabe swallowed down the bile bubbling up his throat. "They wanted to know about the Navy-Marine Corps Intranet," he rasped. "Configurations, passwords, firewalls—stuff I couldn't tell them even if they broke me. They grilled me on coastal security." He slid his tongue to the hole where his upper right cuspid had been, and doubt tugged at him anew. "I don't think I told them anything real. I made up a lot of lies." He looked down at his fisted hands.

"Did they catch you lying?" The man was relentless.

"Once or twice," Gabe admitted.

Forrester surprised him by giving him a commiserating look. "Don't beat yourself up about it," he advised, even as a bead of sweat rolled from his temple to his jaw. "The fact that you made it out alive says a hell of a lot for you."

"Thanks," Gabe choked.

"What about the mission?" the man added, all-business once again. "You have no recollection of falling into enemy hands?"

Gabe averted his gaze to look out the window at the endless ocean. SEAL missions were strictly confidential. He wasn't at liberty to discuss that memory, even if he did remember.

"You were sent to intercept the transport of four surface-to-air missiles," Forrester prompted, making it clear he already knew the objective. "Three of the SAMs were recovered. The fourth one presumably exploded, taking your life with it."

Gabe looked at him again, keeping quiet.

"You're alive, Lieutenant," the man pointed out on a note that made Gabe's scalp prickle. "My job is to find out if that fourth missile still exists. Ring any bells?"

"Bells" wasn't the right word. Sirens started screaming in Gabe's head, causing him to grip the arms of the chair. A vision streaked through his mind—that of brilliant lights piercing his eyes, of a noise so explosive it threatened to burst his eardrums. He sucked in a breath, searching past the noisy blast for a tangible memory. But all he saw was black.

"Lieutenant?" Forrester's face swam closer. "Are you all right?"

"I'm okay," Gabe replied, shaking from the top of his head to the toes of his tennis shoes. "I don't remember anything right now."

"You sure? You look upset, like something returned to you."

"Maybe it did. I don't know." Christ, he felt dizzy. He rubbed his eyes with a trembling hand.

"Tell me what you saw," the man implored, refusing to give up. It was this very tenacity that had sent Gabe into a nervous attack once before.

Gabe was determined to get this man out of his hair for good. He dared another peek into the past, and relived the blinding light, the deafening crash, then nothing, silence. "I think I remember an explosion, but nothing before or after," he replied, giving him a challenging glare.

Forrester nodded as if accepting that he'd pushed Gabe far enough. "Okay, here's what you do," he said, with gravity. "The minute you remember more, you give me a call. No one

else, you got that, Lieutenant? I'm the only one you talk to."
He handed Gabe another of his business cards.

Gabe looked at the card, then up at his visitor. "Why?" he
demanded. "What's this about?" The officer's tone had sent
a cold shiver up his spine.

Forrester gave him an inscrutable look. "Just trying to pin
down the fourth missile, that's all."

But that wasn't all—Gabe could tell there was more. The
officer only confirmed Gabe's instinct by adding, "If you recall more of the mission, Lieutenant, kindly don't discuss it
with anyone—not with your command, not even your psychologist. Give me a call immediately." He lowered his
voice, adding conspiratorially, "We have reason to suspect an
insider." He straightened to his feet, tugging down his wrin-
kled jacket. "So keep in touch," he added, sticking out a
hand.

"Wait a minute." Gabe ignored the man's hand as he came
to his own feet. "What are you saying to me?" he demanded.

Ernest Forrester sighed, fingering the notepad in his
breast pocket. "You may know something about that fourth
missile that someone out there doesn't want you remembering."

The blood slipped slowly from Gabe's face. "Jesus
Christ," he whispered, feeling suddenly light-headed.

Forrester gave him an uncertain look. "You all right, Renault?"

Gabe turned away, pacing to the breakfast bar and back
again. "What would you say if I said someone tried to kill me
the other day?" he asked.

To his relief, Forrester didn't scoff at him. "When was
this?" he wanted to know, pulling out his little notepad again.

Gabe related what had happened. Forrester jotted down
the information. Glancing at the man's notes, Gabe saw that

they were written in code. "My psychologist says I imagined it," he added. "He says paranoia is a side effect of PTSD."

Forrester pocketed his notepad and shrugged. "That may be," he admitted. "I'm not a doctor; I'm just an analyst. But if you ask me," he added, giving Gabe a dark look, "I wouldn't dismiss the incident as a delusion. There's too much here that doesn't add up."

With a shudder, Gabe recalled Sebastian's intimation that he'd been left behind. What if someone had wanted him to perish in the exploding warehouse? That same person wouldn't want him remembering now.

"You take care of yourself, Lieutenant," the officer added, intently. "Wouldn't hurt to get some of your friends to watch your back."

"Right," Gabe said, thinking of his platoon members.

"Well, better get going. I'd like to beat the rush-hour traffic," he explained, extending his hand a second time.

Gabe shook it and escorted him to his car.

Long after the sedan pulled away and disappeared from view, he stood at the bottom of the steps staring after it. Goose bumps moved across his skin in waves. Mixed feelings roiled within him. But the emotion that came across most strongly was relief.

He wasn't paranoid.

He hadn't imagined the attempt on his life.

On the heels of that startling revelation came the sudden urge to flush out his attacker and discover the motive for eliminating him. If Sebastian was right and he'd been left behind at the warehouse in Pyongyang, then his faceless enemy had been after him for some time.

Jesus, who the hell was it? Someone on the inside, Forrester had said. Someone on the team? The idea was inconceivable. Every SEAL he knew was a true-blue patriot like him, willing to die for his team members, never to betray them.

Locked in Gabe's memory was the answer to the question. He slapped himself on the forehead, wanting to dislodge the secret.

With a string of muttered oaths, he turned toward the stairs, taking them two at a time. He could feel his self-identity solidifying anew, prompted by the stubborn determination to seek out his foe and destroy him before he himself was destroyed.

"Everything okay, Dad?" Mallory met him at the top of the stairs. Seeing the look on his face, she took a wary step back.

"Yeah, great," he said, welcoming the flood of adrenaline in his bloodstream. "Let's finish this project." He stripped off his T-shirt, no longer wanting to hide the scars that marred his flesh. He'd earned them, by God. He was going to catch the sorry son of a bitch who'd put him through hell this last year and make him suffer for what he'd done.

Mallory stared at him in consternation. "Okay," she said, moving to the far side of the deck, where Reggie was taking a break. The two of them had nearly finished sanding the picnic table.

Gabe snatched up the sander and resumed his work, pushing it over the railings with firm, determined strokes. A car went by on the street below and Gabe snatched his head up, jumpy as a squirrel on a high-voltage wire.

Obviously, his imprisonment had affected his nervous system. He'd better calm down and refocus or he'd never be a SEAL again. The time had come to pull the mother of all crabs from its burrow.

Chapter Ten

Helen could see the trio up on the deck, still hard at work. It was three-fifteen in the afternoon and the sun glared down at them from a cloudless sky. Mallory would be sunburned by now if she hadn't used sunscreen. Helen shook her head and sighed. Why, oh, why, didn't fathers think of these things?

She caught herself in the middle of that question. Gabe isn't really Mallory's father, she reminded herself. He'd never gone to the trouble to adopt Mallory legally. She killed the engine and scrambled out of the car, wearing the lettuce-green halter top she'd bought at Leila's studio.

Up on the deck, a radio played softly, masking the sound of her ascent. She peeked around the corner, anticipating the sight of teenagers hard at work.

They hadn't heard her. All three of them were rubbing the wooden deck furniture with sandpaper, a sound that made her molars clench. Her gaze slid from Reggie's flame-red curls to Mallory's sunburned skin to Gabe's bare back, glistening with sweat.

And then she saw them. Scars puckering the skin of his magnificent torso. A gasp filled her lungs. Each scar was different: one still purple and healing, others faint and pale. She couldn't imagine what on earth would have caused such marks, but the force and the malice behind each one of them was painfully apparent. Her heart seemed to twist and fold over on itself. *Oh, Gabriel, what did they do to you?*

He straightened abruptly and swiveled, catching the look of horror on her face before she had a chance to recover. With a frown, he averted his gaze.

Oh, no, he'd misinterpreted her dismay.

Prompted to reassure him, she marched straight up to him, forcing him to make eye contact. He squinted down at her, his hair windblown and sweat glistening on the hard lines of his jaw. She offered him a smile that made his brow clear.

"You're hard at work," she said brightly, glancing at the smooth wood around her.

His gaze dropped to her mouth, and her heart beat faster to know that he was thinking of kissing her.

"We're almost done," he said. "Did you have a good time with the old folks?"

His interest took her aback. He'd seemed truly proud of her this morning when she announced where she was going. "Yes, thank you."

"I like that top," he added, flustering her further as his gaze lingered on her chest.

"I bought it from Leila's shop this morning." At his confused look, she added, "Leila Eser, my friend who owns a ballet studio?"

He shook his head minimally, letting her know that he didn't remember.

"Well, listen, since you guys are almost done, I thought you might want to go out for dinner or something."

"We're done now," Mallory declared. She threw down her square of sandpaper and snatched up a pitcher, turning it upside down to shake the last drop of fruit punch from it.

Reggie collapsed in a deck chair and groaned.

Helen winced. He looked painfully pink, especially about the ears. "Er . . . next time you guys work outside you'd better wear sunscreen," she couldn't help but point out. "You look like lobsters."

Oops. She saw the dismay on Gabe's face as he took in the pink glow to Reggie's and Mallory's skin. "Oh, crap," he muttered. "All right, guys. You heard the lady. Sunscreen tomorrow when we work in the front yard."

"What!" Mallory cried, dabbing at the stain she'd just put on her shirt. "Oh, come on," she groaned. "We worked all day today!"

Helen watched with bemusement as Gabe gave Mallory a frown and crooked a finger at her. There was something different about him this afternoon. Working on the deck had revived him somehow. He leaned down and whispered in her daughter's ear.

Taking advantage of his distraction, Helen darted a look at the taut plane of his abdomen. He'd put on some badly needed weight since his homecoming, but every sinew and muscle of his tortoiseshell stomach was still in evidence. The line of dark hair that arrowed from his navel to the waistline of his shorts had the same effect as it always had. She reached for the back of a chair, stricken with desire.

Lifting her gaze, she intercepted the little smile on Mallory's face as her daughter bent down to gather up scraps of sandpaper.

"What?" Helen asked, sensing that something had just gotten past her.

"What do you mean, 'what'?" Gabe retorted, winding up

the cord on the electric sander. "We still have to stain the deck," he said, switching topics on her abruptly, "but now you can go barefoot and not get a splinter."

Helen took in the smooth lines of the deck with a rush of appreciation. "I love it," she said honestly. "Thank you so much."

Gabe offered her a steady look. "You don't have to thank me. I live here, too."

Tension squeezed back inside her. She shouldn't let him get away with that kind of comment. He made it sound so permanent, and she'd already told him he was going to leave when his memory returned.

But now was not the time to press the issue. Healing Gabe's mind was her first priority. Besides, she had no issues with the Gabe before her. This Gabe was amazing. He kept her daughter safe from temptations. And even with the scars on his chest, he looked like a god in his low-slung shorts.

Yes, it was risky business, putting off their inevitable separation. But she refused to be so heartless that she would cast out a man plagued with irrational fears and stripped of his memories. When the old Gabe manifested himself, she would know her work was done.

It was a thankless job, no doubt. But Gabe had been a proud and independent male, a true patriot, and a tremendous asset to the military. She owed it to the world to restore him to his former glory, even if it meant that he would take back the warmth she now basked in.

"So," she suggested, "why don't you guys clean up? Reggie, you want to come to dinner with us?"

As Reggie debated with Mallory over the severity of his sunburn, Gabe took a step closer to Helen. He smelled like sweat and Mallory's Berry Bouquet body wash, and she found herself wanting to fill her senses with him, wishing she could touch him and not worry that he would wind up breaking her heart.

"Thanks," he said, his gaze searching.

It was obvious he sought a reason for her willingness to spend time with him. "It was Dr. Terrien's idea," she admitted, unwilling to give him false encouragement. "He wants me to take you places we've been before."

"Ah." The light in his eyes abruptly dimmed. He gave her a bittersweet smile and walked past her without another word, heading down the steps to put his tools away.

She wished suddenly that she could take her words back, if only to banish that disillusioned smile.

She should have gotten a virgin margarita.

Helen had reasoned that a good strong drink would numb her to Gabe's virility. Wrong. It made her think reckless thoughts as she gazed at his neck, so tan and strong above his crewneck collar; at the hard line of his jaw, the sensual curve of his lower lip. All she could think about was how desperately she wanted him to kiss her again.

It wasn't entirely the tequila's doing, though. It was Gabe's fault, too. In contrast to last night, when he'd seemed leery of stepping foot outside the house, he struck her as indestructible now.

He'd selected a booth near the rear of the restaurant and put his back to the wall, where he scanned the room with a patient watchfulness that made Helen shiver and think about sex.

At the same time, he managed to make pleasant conversation, the way he used to do when he was courting her. She found herself mesmerized by his clever thoughts, his slightly sarcastic sense of humor, his insight into just about every subject that existed.

No wonder she'd fallen in love with him! She caught herself in that thought. Oh, no, she was doing exactly what she swore she'd never do! She was letting down her guard; letting Gabe lure her back to him, when she knew—*she just knew*—he would freeze her out again. As soon as his memory returned, as soon as he became a SEAL once more, he would turn his back on her and disappear, shrugging off her love as if it meant nothing to him.

Sitting immediately beside him, Mallory looked as flushed as Helen felt, her eyes bright and shiny, her mouth tipped in a perpetual smile as she chattered on about her school schedule that had come in the mail that day.

And Mallory was only drinking root beer. Which, in Helen's opinion, didn't go with Mexican, but who could account for teenage tastes?

The food arrived, still sizzling, a perfect complement to the wooden booths, exposed beams, and whitewashed walls. Helen watched Gabe bite into his fajita-style pizza. "This is good," he muttered, momentarily distracted from his vigilance.

She knew he would like the food. They'd come to this restaurant before, about two years ago. In contrast to this pleasant interlude, that had been a disappointing family outing, with Gabe thinking of his next assignment. Memories of that night were supposed to keep Helen focused, to remind her that she was only helping him along his way. This was not a prelude to reconciliation.

Yet the past seemed to be fading before her very eyes. Gabe took a swig of his drink, smiled at her, and pointed at her chicken taco salad with his fork. "How is it?" he inquired.

"Great," she said. "Good." It wasn't half so delicious as the way he smelled, but she didn't say that. He'd dredged up the bottle of cologne she'd given him their last Christmas together. She would have sworn he'd never used it before. She definitely would have remembered.

"This is the best food I've ever had," he added, taking another hearty bite.

"Is that your way of putting down my cooking?" She fixed him with a stern eye, hoping to whip up some vestige of her resentment. She felt awfully vulnerable without it.

"No," he said, wiping his mouth with a napkin, his forehead creased with apology. "No, your cooking is great."

A laugh of disbelief escaped her. "Okay, now that's doing it a little rare," she said. "I know my cooking is pathetic."

"All right, it is pathetic," he agreed, a teasing light in his eyes, "but that just makes moments like these more special, don't you think?"

She did. In fact, this moment was becoming way too special. She was drowning in bliss, savoring every minute of being the perfect family unit, wishing it could always be this way, knowing it wouldn't. The old Gabe would eventually come back, and then what?

The arrival of more salsa saved her from having to answer him. As the waiter moved away Mallory piped up, "So, did you, like, eat rice for a year, Dad?" She gave him a pitying, sidelong look.

Helen held her breath. She'd avoided the topic of Gabe's captivity for two reasons. One, it seemed taboo to discuss it. Two, how was he supposed to answer if he couldn't remember?

As Gabe glanced at Mallory, a faraway look entered his eyes. "Yeah, I think so," he replied, tipping back his beer.

Clearly encouraged, Mallory pressed on. "Are you starting to remember stuff?"

"Yeah," he said shortly, a sign that the conversation was disturbing him.

"We're supposed to be remembering what happened before Dad left," Helen interrupted, giving her daughter a meaningful look.

"Do you remember eating here before?" Mallory wasted no time in firing this question off to Gabe.

He looked up rather surprised, his gaze flickering around a room he clearly did not recognize. "No," he said.

"You were all stressed out about going somewhere dangerous, and I spilled my Sprite by mistake and you yelled at me."

Gabe looked from Mallory to Helen with dismay. "I'm sorry," he said.

"Honey, let's not talk about bad things," Helen encouraged. "Let's just have fun tonight."

Have fun? Heavens, where did that thought come from? But Gabe's grateful look assured her she'd said the right thing. She took a bite of her salad and chewed, searching for an appropriate subject to bring up. So much about their prior relationship screamed *keep off.*

Then she remembered Dr. Terrien's suggestion that she ask Gabe about his past. "So, who were your role models when you were a kid, Gabe?"

He gave her a funny look, pizza suspended halfway to his mouth. "Er . . ." He searched his memory. "I guess Bruce Springsteen doesn't count?" Squinting, he searched his mind for a moment. "Senior Chief Black, who told me I could be an officer. Oh, and Sergeant O'Mally," he said definitely.

"Who was he?" Mallory asked.

Gabe paused. "I never told you about Sergeant O'Mally?" Mother and daughter shook their heads simultaneously.

"Really? Wow. Well, he was a cop who cruised Acushnet

Street when I was a kid. He had this big, black Harley with a siren on the front."

"And?" Helen prompted, intrigued by his unexpected answer.

"And he was kind of like my dad back then. I was sort of screwed up as a kid," Gabe admitted with a shadow of a smile. "No one gave a damn if I skipped school or broke the law, so I got into trouble fairly often. Whenever I did, there was Officer O'Mally getting off his Harley. He'd dust me off and tell me to straighten up my act. He kept me out of jail for the most part, till I stole a car."

"You stole a car!" Mallory gasped, her mouth falling open.

Gabe glanced at Helen as if worried that he'd said the wrong thing. Clearly he assumed she already knew the story, but she didn't. Gabe had never admitted to any past indiscretions. As far as she'd known, he'd had a normal if somewhat lonely childhood, with no brothers or sisters, just a grandmother who raised him when his parents died. She returned his look without expression.

Shrugging, Gabe forged ahead. "Well, not to make excuses or anything, but my grandmother was too . . . old to keep an eye on me. I didn't have a mom or dad like you do," he added meaningfully. "Anyway, Sergeant O'Mally paid my bail so I could get out of jail. He testified for me in court and somehow got me acquitted, provided I joined the military."

Helen was amazed to see a blush creeping over Gabe's cheekbones. It was obvious he wasn't too proud of who he'd been back then, but he'd told the truth, regardless. Obviously, as Dr. Terrien had implied, he'd come to terms with his past during the long months of his captivity. She'd had no idea his childhood was so troubled.

The truth made him strangely more appealing to her.

He was human, after all, not the perfect male machine that executed his moves flawlessly and made others feel inferior.

Mallory's curiosity had been thoroughly roused. "How old were you when your parents died?" she asked Gabe.

"Honey, eat your dinner before it gets cold," Helen interrupted, shielding Gabe from having to answer.

His brow puckered with confusion. "My mom died when I was six. Didn't I tell you this before?"

"No," said Mallory, answering for her mother.

"She died in a car crash."

Helen had heard that much, but it had been both parents the last time.

"What about your dad?" Mallory pressed.

Gabe lined up the leftover crusts on his plate. "I never knew my dad," he said matter-of-factly. Helen's jaw grew slack. "He was a fisherman that pulled into port and got my mother pregnant. My grandmother tracked him down to try and get support from him, but he disappeared again."

He'd lied to her. The old Gabe had lied to her.

Astonished, Helen could only stare at him, her heart trampled. He'd never once told her that he didn't know his dad, that he was the product of a seaport dalliance. Her heart trembled with emotion. She wasn't half as sorry for herself that Gabe had lied to her as she was for the boy he'd been and then the man, who'd felt he had to lie to keep from being stigmatized. Certainly her own father would have thought twice about introducing her to Gabe had he known of Gabe's illegitimacy. Her father was old-fashioned like that. He'd had a hard enough time dealing with Mallory's conception.

At last Gabe had told the truth. But why? Why let her glimpse that part of him now? There was once a time when she'd longed for him to share a piece of himself. Unexpected tears pricked Helen's eyes.

He pushed his beer away abruptly, shaking his head as if to clear it. "Man, I don't have any tolerance for alcohol anymore," he commented, drawing her from her introspection.

"It's your medication," Helen said, suddenly worried. "I told you not to have any beer."

He made a face. "You go for a year without a beer and see how you like it," he answered, smothering a burp.

Mallory was regarding his profile with a solemn look, her burritos forgotten. "We're both bastards," she blurted, out of the blue.

Silence fell over the table. Helen's breath caught. *Oh, my baby!* Mallory seldom mentioned her illegitimacy; it was her own private burden.

"Tha'sright," said Gabe, and Helen was startled to hear his words slur together. She was even more astonished when he threw an arm around Mallory's shoulder and pulled her against his side, squeezing her tight. Mallory buried her nose against Gabe's chest, and a vise closed around Helen's heart.

Why had he waited till now to show Mallory such affection?

He's drunk! she thought, seizing that excuse. Not technically drunk, but his medication was interacting with his beer. She wondered with sudden consternation if she would have to help Gabe get to the car.

With his arm still around Mallory's shoulder, and his head resting against the back of the booth, he no longer looked like a predatory cat, but a big, sleepy one. His slightly unfocused gaze settled on Helen's cleavage, cunningly revealed by the neckline of her orange sundress.

"Mom looks good tonight," he whispered to Mallory, loud enough for Helen to hear him.

Mallory turned her head to see.

Helen fought to appear unaffected by Gabe's rough-toned praise. He wasn't thinking clearly. "You're definitely inebriated," she said in a cool voice that disguised the liquid warmth spreading through her.

She looked away under the pretext of hailing the waitress. To her dismay, her gaze collided with that of the last man on earth she wanted to see tonight: the executive officer of SEAL Team Twelve, Lieutenant Commander Jason Miller.

Crap, not him! Tension whipped through her, making her spine stiffen. Not only was Gabe in no condition to reunite with his XO right now, but Helen herself had been avoiding the man like the plague. Over the past twelve months, he'd tried repeatedly to insinuate himself in her life, taking for granted that his George Hamilton looks would make him irresistible.

She hadn't appreciated his sly offers of comfort when first hearing the news of Gabe's disappearance. It had been increasingly difficult to extricate herself from his groping hands while clinging to politeness and protocol.

Oh, dear Lord, he's coming over to our table! She kicked Gabe under the table. "Sit up!" she hissed.

Bless Gabe for jerking to attention. A second later Miller drifted up alongside them. For a second he took in the cozy scene before his dark gaze came to rest on Gabe. His mouth assumed a smile.

"Renault," he said, "this is incredible. We never thought we'd see you again."

Gabe, stuck in the booth, struggled to stand while saluting. "Commander Miller," he answered, syllables slurring together.

Miller's gaze narrowed a fraction, telling Helen he'd noticed Gabe's inebriation. "At ease, Lieutenant," he said, waving Gabe down. "I was planning to swing by your place tonight and welcome you back properly." His onyx eyes slid to Helen, dipping toward her bosom. "We just got in."

He gave her a look she couldn't interpret. Loathing? Disapproval? His black-as-ink eyes glowed with it.

For his part, Gabe was staring at the man, as if he were struggling to remember something.

An awkward silence fell over the quartet. Miller's gaze rested briefly on the bottle of beer near Gabe's hand. "You don't have much to say, Renault," he commented with false friendliness. "Are you drunk?"

Gabe's steady gaze had never looked more sober. "No, sir. Just stunned to see you after all this time."

The XO nodded, avoiding Gabe's gaze. "Well, I understand you're having some problems remembering." It sounded more like a question than a statement.

Helen took a sharp breath at the tactless reminder.

"It's coming back," Gabe said smoothly.

For some reason Gabe's reply seemed to discomfit his senior officer. He stuck his hands into his pockets. "Glad to hear it," he said, not sounding glad at all. "You all enjoy yourselves. Helen." He scorched her with that same look before wandering back to the woman who waited for him by the bar.

"What a jerk," Mallory commented a little too loudly.

Helen barely caught herself from seconding the opinion.

For his part, Gabe said nothing. The mellow expression he'd worn moments earlier was gone, replaced by a mask that she recognized as belonging to the old Gabe. He withdrew his arm from around Mallory's shoulder. "Let's go," he said.

"I'm waiting for the bill," Helen pointed out, crushed that their lovely evening had come to such an abrupt end.

She gave the waitress her credit card and signed the slip—

all without protest from Gabe, who'd always insisted on paying in the past. Odd, now that she thought of it, he hadn't even brought up the issue of money since his return.

"Thanks for dinner," he said, striding before them as they left the restaurant and headed down the busy sidewalk toward their car.

"You're welcome. Are you sure you don't want to walk on the boardwalk?" It was a beautiful night, with the sun just beginning its golden descent toward the shore. Teenagers were everywhere, cruising down Atlantic Avenue, windows open, music pounding. The city exuded scents of the ocean, grilled seafood, and suntan oil. Mallory looked crestfallen that they were heading home so soon.

Gabe stared straight ahead, carving a path for them through the crowd with no lingering trace of inebriation. "I'm sure," he said shortly.

He tried to hide it, but Helen could hear preoccupation in his voice. She and Mallory followed in his wake, tensely aware that he was acting like he used to—coldly withdrawn. The encounter with his XO had gotten to him. Was it just because Miller had needled him for losing his memories, or was there something more?

They rode home in absolute silence, mother and daughter both disheartened by Gabe's detachment. As he stared out the car window, the shadows of trees flickered over his face, creating the same effect as camouflage paint.

As the minutes ticked by, Helen found herself wanting to comfort Gabe, even at the risk of being rejected. Her husband had been through so much lately. It wouldn't cost her much to reach for his hand and squeeze it. She wrestled for the courage to do it.

Finally, turning left onto their street, she laid her hand over his. His fingers folded, clamping over hers like a trap.

She could feel the desperation in his grip. He needed her. More than that, the heat of his palm was dredging up memories of them lying skin to skin, bodies touching from head to toe, merging, straining to get closer.

She pulled into their driveway with no recollection of the road she'd just traversed.

Mallory hopped out of the car. Gabe did not let go. Helen sat there, unable to turn off the ignition with her hand trapped in his. Neither could she settle the thrumming of her blood. He shifted his body and looked at her. The heat in his eyes scorched her bare shoulders. His look promised such intense physical pleasure, she was speechless.

Feeling the inevitability of it, she slid toward him, lifting her lips to his. For a moment, he let her kiss him, not moving a millimeter to encourage or dissuade her. But then something in him snapped, and he was kissing her with barely controlled intensity, ravishing her mouth in a way that made her think some very explicit thoughts.

With a groan, Helen forgot that she hadn't come to a full decision regarding Gabe. All she knew was that she wanted him so badly she couldn't think anymore; she wanted him *tonight*. She completely forgot that Mallory was up on the deck waiting for them. Gabe's tongue was causing so much friction that her body was going up in flames.

He brushed a hand over her breast, abrading the nipple. He kissed the line of her jaw and swirled his tongue behind her ear.

"Oh, God," she panted, with no control over the frantic words tumbling out of her mouth. "I need you. I need you."

He lifted his head abruptly and looked at her, searching her gaze as if looking for something. "That's not enough," he replied, shocking her with his words and even more with his actions as he thrust the car door open and got out. He was marching up the steps to let Mallory in before it even registered in her sluggish brain that he was gone.

Abandoned, Helen could only stare after him, her mouth agape. He didn't look back once but let himself and Mallory into the house, shutting the door behind them.

Helen realized the car was still running. She cut the engine with a quick twist of her wrist and covered her eyes with regret. What had she done? She'd told Gabe they were through, and there she was kissing him feverishly and telling him she needed him.

And what was his response? To demand more of her, of course. It wasn't enough for him that she wanted him. Oh no, he would have nothing short of her complete capitulation.

The bastard.

It was so like him to pull the plug, just when she was feeling her most vulnerable. It came to her that he wasn't using sex to get what he wanted; he was withholding it! Yes, his plan was to drive her crazy with desire and then maybe—just maybe—he'd give her what she wanted, provided she told him she loved him first.

As dreadful as it seemed, that had to be it. Gabe was an incredible tactician, as anyone in SEAL Team Twelve could attest to. He never went without a COA, a course of action. What if Leila was right to warn her? What if everything he'd done up to now, all the apparent changes in him, was an act to call up her feelings for him?

She didn't trust him enough to be sure that it wasn't. In the face of his new sincerity, she'd let her guard down. Big mistake. And here she was, half in love with him again. Hadn't she learned her lesson enough times already? How many times did Gabe have to hurt her before she realized that loving him was harmful to her health? Did she really want to get up tomorrow to find that she was Jaguar's woman again, a possession acknowledged when it suited him; a wife he otherwise ignored?

"Wake up, Helen!" she hissed at herself, thrusting open her door with more force than necessary. And no, it wasn't just sexual frustration that made her slam it shut behind her. It was rage. Rage that she'd actually believed he'd changed.

She should have listened to Leila, who had her best interest at heart.

Chapter Eleven

Gabe stared at the fragments of light that moved from opposite sides of his ceiling and came into a starburst at the center. A car was passing along the street below him—the eleventh car that night. He held his breath until the sound of the motor faded into the distance. It was just another car, not a would-be assassin coming to hunt him down.

He hadn't slept a wink as yet. In a fit of rebellion he'd ground up his sleeping pills—symbols of his ineptitude—in the kitchen disposal. Christ, he couldn't even sleep when he wanted to! Next he would have trouble pissing on demand.

He punched up his pillow and shifted onto his side. If he didn't have so many thoughts ricocheting through his brain, he'd sleep just fine, he assured himself. His reunion with the XO tonight had set off all kinds of strange memories. They flitted through his mind, shadowy images accompanied by shards of remembered pain. None of it made any sense.

Or did it? Maybe Miller had had something to do with his supposed death in the warehouse a year ago. That would explain the dark foreboding that had risen up in him at the sight of his XO. That would explain Miller's nervousness. Or was there another reason Miller had been less than thrilled to see him?

Gabe hadn't missed the downward sweep of the man's eyes as he ogled Helen's cleavage. Nor was he immune to the tension that had arced between the XO and his wife.

Had Helen and Miller started something? Were they having an affair? If so, then it had definitely gone sour, given the veiled dislike in Helen's eyes. But Miller was clearly still intrigued. Had he wanted Helen badly enough to eliminate his own teammate?

Gabe ground the heel of his palm into his aching right eye and willed his blood pressure to subside. It wouldn't do him any good to lie here simmering. He'd confront Helen in the morning, let her explain that burning look in Miller's eyes.

At least his men were in port. That meant he could contact them tomorrow, arrange for a meeting. Then he'd get their insights about the night he disappeared.

God damn it, he couldn't stand so many loose ends, trailing into dark, mysterious corners! If he could only recollect that night, then he would know whether someone had turned on him.

With a whispered curse, Gabe swung his feet to the floor. He wasn't going to fall asleep, not with such weighty thoughts circuiting his brain.

The only thing that would comfort him now was Helen.

He gave a groan, dropping his face into his hands. She would be lying in her bed right now, her limbs soft and pliant with sleep. All he had to do was to cruise down the hall and slip into her bed. He had reason to guess he would encounter a minimum of resistance. *I need you. I need you,* she'd whispered in the car.

And while those words had filled him with triumph,

they'd left him yearning for more. He'd wondered if it was really him she wanted or the warrior in the picture in his top drawer? *That* man wasn't pocked with ugly scars or cursed with a mind devoid of memories. *That* man didn't suffer illogical fears that someone was out to get him.

It'd almost killed him to do it, but he'd severed the kiss, admitting to her that it wasn't enough. He wanted his wife to open her heart to him the way Mallory had. So far, Helen hadn't given the slightest indication that she'd changed her mind about their future together. In fact, she'd made a point to tell him that spending time with him was Dr. Terrien's idea, not hers.

Her kisses tonight had been hot enough to sear his soul, but what he wanted even more was the promise of tomorrow. He wanted forever, and as far as he could tell, Helen was still thinking along the lines of one more time, for old times' sake.

Still, he couldn't fault her for withholding her heart. From what he could gather, he'd strung her along in the past, encouraging her love when he needed it, ignoring her otherwise. It would take time for her to realize that her heart was safe with him this time. He just hoped he had the willpower to cling to his resolve. His desire for Helen was eating him alive.

He lifted his head from his hands, and the computer monitor winked at him coyly.

It seemed to be taunting him, harboring some sort of secret. But what? He'd spent the other night discovering that the world was as much of a mess as it had always been. The computer hadn't told him anything he didn't already know.

A dull thud brought his head around. Gabe froze, waiting to identify the noise outside before dismissing it.

Nothing. Other than the distant pounding of the surf, it

was utterly quiet. So quiet, in fact, that even the insects were mute on this mid-August evening. It was the kind of quiet Gabe held in suspicion.

A scuffling sound reached his ears—the sound of someone running across sand.

He rose and crossed to the window, flattening himself against the wall. A peek through the blinds revealed a figure melting into black.

Someone was out there.

My nemesis, he thought, wondering at the same time if he was just hallucinating. After all, every car that had gone by earlier had been an ordinary car.

By why take the risk with his wife and daughter sleeping in the rooms next door?

Feeling faintly foolish, Gabe moved to his dresser to don a black T-shirt and jeans, clothing meant to disguise him in the dark. He slipped out of the study and drifted down the pitch-black hallway, the hair at his nape prickling.

He missed the weight of his Heckler and Koch MP5 submachine gun, sitting heavy in the crook of his arm. What the hell had happened to it? he wondered.

A faint creaking noise propelled him toward the great room, where bars of moonlight slanted over the lumpy furniture. Given the wraparound deck and many windows, this room was most vulnerable to penetration.

He went down on hands and knees and crept through the shadows. Anyone peering through the horizontal blinds would have difficulty seeing him, but he'd see them at once, silhouetted by the moonlight.

He ran straight into the wet nose of his yellow Lab. Priscilla popped up from her doggy throw, completely oblivious to the noises outside. She thumped her tail at Gabe, ready to play even at this late hour.

"Stay," he said firmly, praying she'd recall the command from their daily training sessions. "No barking!"

Eager to please, Priscilla held as still as her quivering body allowed.

"Good dog." Patting her head, he repeated the command and crept to the window behind the couch, his exit portal. Coming to his feet, he eased open the latches. The window slid upward with a squeak that was muffled by the roar of the sea. He unhooked the screen and placed it by his feet. Then he stuck his head out.

The balcony at the back of the house seemed deserted. He couldn't hear anything over the crashing surf. He suffered the dampening suspicion that he was crazy.

Gesturing to the dog one more time, he eased his torso out of the window. In two fluid movements, he stepped onto the balcony rail and up onto the roof, praying the shingles held. Praying the dog wouldn't start barking.

The rough tar gripped his bare feet, giving him good traction despite the buffeting wind. As he followed the edge of the overhang around the back of the house, crawling like a crab, the moon slipped behind a sheet of clouds, so that he had to feel his way.

Whispers. Gabe froze, his ears pricked to the sounds directly below him. His heart beat faster. At least he wasn't crazy. There were two men under the overhang, maybe three. Cautiously, he eased himself onto his stomach and peered over the edge.

Roger. Two tangos, dressed in desert camouflage. There was just enough light upon their shoulders for Gabe to make out the weapons they carried: MP5s, .45-caliber pistols, and a Gerber blade. One of them wore a radio headpiece. He tapped on the mike once—a signal to go ahead.

Who the hell? Gabe wondered. The men were obviously professionals. They carried American weapons.

A third man melted out of the shadows of the front deck to join them, and Gabe's adrenaline surged. How many more were there? Even with the element of surprise, he'd have trouble taking on three trained fighters.

The third man cradled a box in his arms. He set it down and opened it. *Explosives,* was Gabe's first thought.

Sure enough, the man straightened with a roll in his hand—electrical tape most likely. He moved closer to the house, underneath Gabe and out of his line of vision. But Gabe could hear him, stringing something along the length of the wall.

His mind worked at full speed, calculating his odds. So much depended on whether there were others. Should he jump these guys or wait for them to leave? Maybe they'd be content with rigging the house and then they'd split.

But what if the explosives were set to go off right away? Would he have time to disarm them or just grab Mallory and Helen and get the hell out?

The second and third man moved to help the first. They bent down by the box, then went to work on the rails Gabe had recently sanded. With quick, precise movements, the men unrolled their tape. Or was it really tape? It fluttered in the wind like party ribbons.

Just then, the moon sailed out of its hiding place, and Gabe recognized the hawklike profile of Vincent DeInnocentis, junior enlisted man in his platoon.

Reality burst over him, evaporating his crazy suspicions like the hot sun drying a damp sidewalk. "Oh, fuck me," he groaned, putting his forehead to a tar-covered shingle. He couldn't believe he'd been so badly taken. His buddies were back, and they were papering his house in welcome. That was all. No skulking terrorists. No explosives. Jesus, to think what was going on in his mind!

He shook his head at how mental he was. At the same time, gratitude swelled in his chest for the men who'd come to welcome him home. He knelt there a moment, bathed in the warm glow of their commitment. Then he decided he might as well have a little fun with them. Anticipation licked over him as he scooted to the roof's edge and positioned himself to drop.

Wait. Wait. Now.

He leapt silently off the roof and took Vinny down with a thud. The two other SEALs whirled, weapons flashing in the darkness. Inside the house, the dog barked once.

Gabe had Vinny pinned to the ground with Vinny's own Gerber blade pressed to his throat.

"It's Jaguar!" the second SEAL said, grabbing his companion before he could leap on top of the pair.

Gabe grinned up at them. "You guys make sorry-assed tangos," he chided, coming to his feet. He handed Vinny back his blade and extended him a hand. "You forgot to secure the roof," he added, pulling up his victim.

"Son of a bitch," DeInnocentis cursed, shoving him in reprisal. Glowering, he looked like a young Al Pacino. "Welcome home, asshole sir," he amended, throwing an arm around Gabe in a hug.

The others stepped forward to do the same. Gabe recognized them both: Teddy "Bear" Brewbaker and the former professional football player, John Luther Lindstrom, known affectionately as Little John. Glimpsing the unabashed tears in both men's eyes, Gabe's relief was so profound that he returned their fierce hugs with all the strength that was in him.

These men were his family. They'd been through hell and

back together, more times than he could count. There must have been moments this last year when he thought he'd never see them again. Damn it, his eyes were swimming with tears.

Bear spoke into his headpiece. "Come on up, guys. Jaguar surprised us." Groans of disgust were audible on the other end.

As Luther released him, Gabe took note of the camouflage paint and the rather odiferous BDUs. "You guys came straight from the boat?" he asked in disbelief.

"Yes, sir. We docked this afternoon, but the XO gave us a bunch of last-minute checks to run. We sent Vinny out to rustle up some party streamers and balloons. We didn't even get to blow them up!" Luther sounded like a kid who'd been denied a treat.

"I'll get over it," Gabe promised. He sensed rather than heard three more SEALs jog up the deck stairs. Westy McCaffrey took the lead, followed by a young SEAL Gabe didn't recognize and then Sebastian at the rear.

Westy was the first to reach him. He was the only one who'd found time to trade his camouflage in for a pair of jeans and a white T-shirt. With his hair in a ponytail and tattoo exposed, he looked nothing like the other SEALs, but that was due to his undercover counterterrorist work.

Westy threw his arms around Gabe and rocked him like a baby. "Shit, sir, it's good to see you," he exclaimed. He set Gabe at arm's distance, giving him a once-over with laser-blue eyes that could see straight into a man's heart. What he saw there made him squeeze Gabe's arms in silent sympathy.

In danger of bursting into tears, Gabe focused on Sebastian, who was hanging back, giving the men a moment to reunite. Gabe longed to tell him what he'd learned from

Forrester yesterday. In fact, all the men had a right to know. Several of them had witnessed the warehouse exploding. Maybe they could shed insight as to what had happened.

A moment of silence settled over the squad as they stood there looking at each other. "This is our new man, PO3 Rodriguez," Westy spoke up, introducing a cautious, young man of Hispanic origin. "He's our weapons specialist."

"Honored to meet you, sir." Rodriguez gave him a smart salute.

"Thanks, PO3."

The men fell silent again, eying Gabe expectantly, waiting for him to say something. "I saw the XO tonight," he admitted, watching their faces closely.

They shared quick looks. "He came by to see you?" Sebastian took a step forward, closing the circle.

"Not exactly. I was having dinner with my family, and he happened to be at the restaurant."

His news was met with an uncomfortable pause. "Yeah, he, uh, he said he had a heavy date and he'd catch up with you tomorrow," Westy volunteered.

The man couldn't lie to save his life. Gabe gave them all a stern look. "Don't bullshit me, guys," he warned. He turned to the man with the authority to speak for the others. "Master Chief, does the XO have a problem with me being home?"

Sebastian's expression gave nothing away. "The XO's been hard to work with this last year," he said vaguely. "He has difficulty leading without your help. I'm sure he'll be glad to have you back."

He didn't sound too sure.

Gabe raked his gaze across the men's faces. "We need to discuss what went wrong," he said finally. No one asked what he meant. It was obvious he was referring to the op-gone-bad, the night he was taken.

"Did they treat you all right, sir?" asked Luther with gentle concern.

While marveling that a man could be a SEAL and still retain the qualities of a Boy Scout, Gabe couldn't bring himself to tell the worst of it. "I've got a few marks on me," he admitted. "I'm working on remembering now—guess I blocked some shit out."

He wanted to add that he hadn't betrayed his country, only his tongue wouldn't form the words.

"We don't think you said anything you shouldn't have, sir." It was Vinny speaking up on behalf of the platoon.

"Not you, sir," seconded Teddy, the only black man on the team.

Their absolute faith in him made it suddenly necessary to take a deep breath. Gabe held it until the high emotion in him subsided. "Thanks, guys," he said gruffly. "So is it just that the XO thinks I screwed up or is there something more?"

No one wanted to say anything, but Gabe could tell by their long faces that there was definitely more. He turned to the master chief. "I want to get together," he said. "Soon."

Sebastian nodded. "How about tomorrow evening? Does anyone have prior plans?"

"Works for me," Westy replied.

"I'm in."

"We can meet at my house," Luther volunteered, "say sixteen hundred hours?"

"Great," said Gabe, looking forward to the reunion. "Listen, I'd love to invite you all in, but my wife might have something to say about it. Besides, you guys are ripe."

They chuckled with satisfaction.

"Training op?" he asked, eager to hear what they'd been up to.

"Just work, sir," Westy answered, sounding bored.

Work was the term they used to describe their routine of patrolling the coast. The men looked forward to the special operations that broke up the monotony. Their boat, a coastal patrol craft called the USS *Nor'easter*, defended the coast ten miles out from Tangier down to the Outer Banks. The very reason Gabe knew so much about the bay's security was that he'd lived and breathed it day to day.

"So no major changes," Gabe deduced.

"Same old thing, Lieutenant," Luther reassured him.

A memory stitched through Gabe's mind, as quick as a needle, before receding. He ran his fingers through his hair, frustrated by the elusiveness of his thoughts.

Gazing at his men, it dawned on him that they looked exhausted. "Hey, thanks for coming, guys," he said, freeing them to seek their beds.

He pumped hands and clapped shoulders and watched them wander toward the stairs. The urge to weep made his chest feel full and tight. Not even the dog heard them leave. There were no more barks coming from inside.

As they faded into black, Gabe was left with the hope that one of them would have an answer to the mystery that plagued him.

All around him, party ribbons ruffled gently in the midnight breeze.

Helen pushed her way into the kitchen, pleasantly winded from a morning run. She drew up short to see Gabe on the other side of the great room, staring out the rear window at the ocean. She'd caught him in similar reflection a number of times, his thoughts so profound that he didn't seem to notice her entrance at all. It wasn't a good sign for a man in his line of business.

She regarded him a moment, noting the way the sunlight gilded his mussed hair, lightening the tips to create a shaggy halo. Something about his posture tugged at her heartstrings. She could read the weight of his thoughts by the slouch of his shoulders. The military bearing that had so attracted her when they'd met was nowhere in evidence. Why was it, then, that she found him more appealing than ever?

Immediately she chided herself for her ongoing obsession with him. Her cheeks flamed anew as she recalled her humiliation last night. She shut the door loudly behind her, causing him to pivot with a start. If he was waiting for her to give her heart, he could wait till hell froze over. She wasn't as foolish as she used to be.

Stalking into the kitchen, she took note of the circles under his eyes, the glint of stubble on his jaw. He looked like he hadn't slept all night.

"Morning," he said, moving in her direction. "How was the run?"

"Good." She turned to the water dispenser for a chilled glass of water. "You're up early." She filled the glass, painfully aware of his steady gaze.

"I heard you leave the house," he said.

"Sorry. I tried to be quiet."

"Have a seat. I'll make us breakfast," he offered unexpectedly.

She cut him a quick, uncertain look. He'd often made breakfast on Sundays—when he was home, at any rate. Had he suddenly remembered that, or was there something he wanted to discuss?

He moved directly beside her, brushing her shoulder as he

reached for a mug from the cabinet. Alarmed by his proximity, she scuttled toward a stool and perched upon it.

She tried to get a feel for his state of mind. Following their encounter last night, he'd disappeared into his study, and she hadn't seen him since. If he'd been up all night, he'd had plenty of time to think about her hasty words. *I want you. I want you!* She cringed just to think about it.

She hoped he wouldn't press her about that now. Either she wanted him in her life or not, he would point out. Which was it?

He paused by the coffeemaker, staring at the mug he just poured. "How do you take it again?"

"Cream and sugar." He was actually pouring her a cup of coffee. How sweet was that?

He handed her the brew, prepared the way she liked it. Helen sipped and waited.

"Did you hear the dog bark last night?" he asked.

She cocked her head at the question. "N——o," she said, thinking back.

A smile touched the corners of his mouth. "My men dropped by to see me. They were planning to paper the deck with party streamers, only I heard them coming and foiled their plan," he added, his smile widening to a grin.

Ah, a reunion with his SEAL buddies. Was that what he wanted to talk about?

Nothing made Gabe happier than spending time with his platoon, first squad. A cynical smile curled her upper lip. He'd preferred their company to hers so many times she'd been jealous of them.

"They used to stop by after your disappearance," she recalled. "They wanted to make sure I was keeping my spirits up."

In actuality, it was she who ended up comforting his men,

but Gabe didn't need to know that. They'd mourned his absence daily. It had been achingly clear that he'd saved his best for them and given her the leftovers.

Gabe nodded, obviously expecting that they would do that much. "What about Miller? Did he come, too?" His gaze sharpened perceptibly.

Now she understood the point of this conversation. Astute as he was, Gabe had noticed the tension between her and the XO, and he wanted an explanation. She knew a perverse urge to rouse his jealousy—not that doing so made any sense given her renewed pledge to resist him.

"Yes," she heard herself say. "He visited often, but never with the men."

He went as rigid as a pole, gratifying her illogical desire to goad him. "He came alone?"

"Uh huh." She left it to him to fill in the gaps, wary at the same time of misleading him.

He turned toward the refrigerator and opened it, staring at the contents. "Scrambled eggs?" he asked.

"Oh, sure."

He took the eggs and a bag of bread out of the fridge and laid them on the counter. "So what did you and Miller used to talk about?" he asked mildly.

His tone could not disguise a hint of jealousy. Satisfaction coursed in Helen's veins, making her heady for more.

He started opening cabinets, hunting for a bowl to break the eggs in.

"Second cabinet to your right," she directed him. She needed to tread carefully. On the one hand, she didn't want to ruin Gabe's ability to work with Miller in the future. At the same time, she longed to toy with him as he'd toyed with her in the car last night. "He expressed concern, is all. He wondered if I had enough money. Did I need a shoulder to cry on? That kind of thing." She shrugged, letting her words imply what they would.

Gabe turned and met her gaze. "Did he tell you any details about my last operation?"

Her expectations spiraled downward. "No, nothing," she recalled. "Why? You think your XO had something to do with your disappearance?" The thought appalled her, but she wouldn't put it past the sneaky bastard.

Gabe picked up an egg and cracked it neatly on the bowl's edge. "Speculation," he muttered. He repeated the process with four more eggs and started whipping the yolks. It was impossible to tell from his austere profile what he was thinking.

He poured the eggs into a hot pan and swiveled in her direction. "Did you cry on his shoulder?" he asked, a banked fire in his eyes.

Delicious heat stole through her. He *was* jealous! Why that pleased her so immensely, she couldn't say, especially when she'd sworn up and down that their future together was over. And now that she'd incited Gabe's jealousy, she needed to downplay Miller's part. "No," she said, "I didn't."

"Never?"

"Never."

"But he hit on you," Gabe insisted.

She shrugged. "He always had a reason for showing up— some document I had to sign, or to hand me a pamphlet on grief. Eventually he asked me out, and I turned him down. That's it."

Except that it took a half-dozen rejections for her to get her point across.

Gabe turned toward the stove. "You'd tell me if you and he had a thing going," he said, a note of uncertainty in his voice.

The Gabe she'd married had never suffered a moment's doubt about her faithfulness. He'd been that confident of his sexual prowess and his desirability. "I'd tell you," she found herself assuring him. Immediately she asked herself why she was protecting Gabe's feelings. In the end, she was going to leave him anyway.

But first she'd drag him to her parents', if only to prove to herself that he could flip the switch and turn into the old Gabe without warning.

She'd come up with the idea last night, while lying in bed simmering with shame and frustration. "How would you like to go to Annapolis tomorrow?" she queried, putting her decision into words.

He seemed distracted by the question. "What for?"

"My parents have been dying to see you." She watched him fluff the eggs with a deft hand. "They're threatening to come down here, but maybe you'd like to get away for a while."

He was quiet so long she rolled her eyes. Jeez, it wasn't like the man had a packed schedule!

"Tomorrow's Monday," he stalled. "Don't you have to go to work?"

"I can afford a few days off." Not really, but desperate means called for desperate measures. Besides, she wanted to get this over and done with.

Her father had a gift for transforming Gabe into the quintessential SEAL. Something about his commanding presence called up Gabe the Machine, a coldly detached individual obsessed with national security and international concerns. If she needed proof that that Gabe still existed, she had only to place him in her father's presence. He would forget all about Helen and Mallory and his new life with them.

Gabe transferred the eggs onto two plates, plopped toast

beside them, and deposited the plates on the breakfast bar. "Okay," he agreed, handing her a fork. "Mal and I are busy today, though. And I'm meeting with my squad tonight."

"I hope you're not meeting over here," Helen said, casting a glance at the untidy living room.

"No, Luther volunteered his place."

She pictured Veronica's effusive welcome, and her appetite dwindled.

"It was his idea," Gabe assured her, settling on the stool next to her, his long legs planted firmly on either side.

"What are you and Mallory doing today?" she asked. "Staining the deck?"

"Nope." He took a huge bite out of his toast.

Helen eyed him steadily. "Well, what then?"

"Can't tell," he said, pretending to zip his mouth shut.

A secret. Helen's heart fluttered. He was doing it again, making himself irresistible.

"You're going to fix my Jeep," she guessed, telling herself he was just manipulating her. He'd reel her in till she was his, and then he'd treat her as he had before.

"Not yet. Don't you have somewhere to go today?"

"It's Sunday," she pointed out.

"Maybe you could go to church. Take Leila with you."

She let out a disbelieving laugh. "Leila is Muslim, Gabe. Look, if you want me out of the house, just say so. What time do I need to be gone?"

He glanced at the clock on the wall. "Before eight-thirty?"

Shaking her head in bemusement, Helen finished her meal. "Thank you for breakfast," she said, crossing to the sink to rinse her plate. She could feel Gabe eyeing her backside, where her spandex shorts hugged her thighs. It was only six-fifteen in the morning. Mallory would sleep for at least another hour. *Plenty of time to indulge in some satisfying sex,* came the wistful thought.

She shut off the water with an impatient gesture. The man was testing her restraint. One minute she vowed to have him out of her life forever; the next she was wishing he'd make love to her. She abandoned the sink and strode deliberately down the hall.

Chapter Twelve

Pulling into the driveway several hours later, Helen found Gabe and Mallory stacking stones in the alcove between the zigzagging stairs. As she stepped out of the car, Gabe glanced up, sending her a look of hopeful expectation.

Helen hesitated. That was definitely not a look she'd seen before.

She stepped from the car and approached the pair warily. A mound of irregularly shaped rocks obstructed the driveway. It wasn't gravel or fill, but beautiful river rocks of various hues: rose, violet, amber, and orange.

"We're making a rock garden!" Mallory blurted, taking in her mother's look of confusion.

A rock garden. Like the one she'd torn from the magazine in Dr. Terrien's office. How on earth had Gabe guessed that she wanted a rock garden?

He answered her question by holding up the crinkled article that had inspired her. It must have fallen out of her purse at some point. "Do you want it to look just like this?" he asked, indicating the picture. "We can do it any way you want," he added, full of enthusiasm.

"This is fine," she replied, unnerved that he'd picked up on her unspoken desires, let alone acted on them. Leila, whom she'd just had lunch with, had to be right. No one would go to such great lengths unless he was trying to win a war. Gabe was used to winning. He'd do anything to earn himself a permanent place in her life.

We'll see, she thought, eyeing their arrangement dazedly. She wasn't as naive as she once was.

And yet, another side of her watched with burgeoning hope as Gabe picked up two rocks and set them at angles to each other, eyeing the picture to be certain that he'd got the angle right. There wasn't any hint of guile in his earnest expression. Sweat rolled from his shaggy hairline over the curve of his jaw. His yellow T-shirt clung to him.

She pictured the scars hidden under the damp fabric. How could the abuse he'd suffered at the hands of the enemy made him more generous? If it had been she who'd endured such horror, it would have left her disillusioned, bitter, angry with the world.

These changes in Gabe had to be temporary at best. Once he recalled his nightmare in its entirety, he would surely grow angry and embittered. He would focus his energies on seeking revenge and, in the process, forget about his family.

It was inevitable. She needed to brace herself. Falling in love with this half-finished version of Gabe would be a serious mistake.

Keeping notably silent, she stepped past the working pair and up the stairs, guilt chasing her the entire way.

Six of the eight men in first squad, Echo Platoon, crowded around the kitchen table in Luther Lindstrom's kitchen. Among those absent were Lieutenant Commander Jason Miller, uninvited, and PO3 Rodriguez, the newest member, who was otherwise occupied.

Luther's fiancée flitted around the men, clearly in her element as she placed aromatic cookies before them and filled their glasses with milk, beer, or Coke. The men muttered their thanks, ignoring her as much as it was possible to ignore a pair of lush breasts thrust in their faces or her silky dark hair brushing their shoulders.

Teddy "Bear" Brewbaker broke the ice by bringing up a common complaint: Miller's penchant for penny-pinching. "He calls it wasting ammo," he groused, setting down his beer with a thud. "What's a kill house for if we're not going to shoot it up? Christ, all he worries about is what it'll cost to replace the thing."

The men shook their heads in unanimous disgust and added in their two cents. Then they all looked expectantly at Gabe, who had requested this get-together.

Gabe gave Luther a meaningful look and tipped his head in Veronica's direction.

"Ronnie, we're going to need some privacy," Luther called rather hesitantly. SEAL business was strictly confidential.

She clucked her tongue in annoyance and abandoned a cookie sheet in the sink, wiping her hands on her apron as she flounced out of the room.

Gabe took a deep breath, keenly aware of the silence that had fallen over the table. "Er, I don't know how much the master chief has told you guys . . ."

One look at their blank expressions and it was clear that the answer was *nothing*. Sebastian was the soul of discretion.

"All right, here's the deal," he continued, pitching his

voice low. "I want to know about the night I disappeared. I want to know what the hell went wrong."

Westy McCaffrey shared a look with Teddy, before fixing his laser-blue eyes on Gabe and taking it upon himself to answer the question. "There were just four of us on the mission, sir—you, me, Teddy, and the XO. We had to lift four SAMs from a warehouse in Pyongyang. It was a perfect setup. Dark as Hades, no activity in the port. We took an SDV into the harbor," he added, making reference to the SEAL Delivery Vehicle, a miniature wet sub too small to be picked up by radar, "and swam ashore. We'd carted off three of the SAMs when we started taking on fire. There were shooters in the catwalks overhead—how they got there, we don't know. They started shooting up the place, and either they were lousy shots or they only wanted to scare us off. No one took a hit, but Miller ordered a retreat."

Gabe held up his hand for a moment to assimilate what he'd heard. Visions flickered through his mind, dimming before he had a chance to view them clearly. "Hold up a minute. Who were the shooters?" he wanted to know.

Westy and Teddy shook their heads. "Don't know, sir," Teddy said. "We never got a good look at them. They were all hidden, which makes us think they were there before we arrived—that's what freaks me out."

"So what made them wait to start shooting?"

The men shook their heads, no one the wiser.

"I have a theory," Sebastian spoke up suddenly, and the men turned expectant gazes his way. "At the time of this mission," he reminded them, "weapons were disappearing faster than we could get to them. And it wasn't just Echo Platoon or SEAL Team Twelve who came up empty-handed. It happened to other operations, too. SEALs inserted to interdict weapons shipments and the weapons were already gone. Someone was beating us to the punch."

Thoughtful silence followed the master chief's observation.

Gabe swung his attention back to Westy. "What happened once the shooting started?" he wanted to know.

Westy looked like Satan himself when he frowned, a trait that made him a natural for infiltrating terrorists. "We pulled back under Miller's orders and were dropping into the water when I noticed you weren't on the XO's buddy line," he continued. "I signed to him—*Where's LT?* He motioned for me to keep moving. Once we got to the SDV, Miller said you wanted to stay with the missile. That sounded like something you'd do, sir, especially given the situation Master Chief just described. Strange thing is neither Teddy nor I heard you say it over our headsets."

Teddy nodded to corroborate Westy's story. All the men looked at Gabe, wondering if he'd volunteered to stay behind or if Miller had somehow ditched him and why?

"We tried to make radio contact with you but we couldn't. All of a sudden, kaboom! The whole fucking warehouse went up in a ball of fire," Westy finished, glowering.

"We couldn't believe it," Teddy added, shock still lingering in his dark eyes even after a year's time.

"Teddy thinks it was detonated," Westy added, pinning his blue gaze on the explosives specialist.

"Talk to me, Bear," Gabe pressed, wiping clammy palms on his blue jeans. His heart was thudding fast. He'd been there, damn it. He ought to recall what had happened.

"It's just my opinion, sir," the black man admitted. "Yes, there was oil all over the place and bullets being fired, and that alone could have caused a fire. But the explosion that took out the building looked rigged to me. It went *boom,*

boom, boom in a perfect line, like the place was rigged with C-4, two pounds of it at least."

A thoughtful silence descended over the group as each man pondered the growing list of questions: who were the other men in the warehouse? Not the native population, surely, who wouldn't have sacrificed their own warehouse or the goods inside it. It had to have been outsiders like themselves, men determined to cover up clandestine activities.

Gabe threw out the million-dollar question. "What happened to the fourth missile?" he wanted to know.

"Disappeared," said Teddy.

"No trace of it when we reconned the next night," Vinny added, letting Gabe know that the others had been called in at that point. "There was nothing there."

They all gazed solemnly at Gabe, and he could just imagine the gut-wrenching despair they'd experienced thinking their mission had gone awry, believing they'd lost one of their own.

"Fuck, sir, we had to sift through the ashes to look for you," Westy recalled, his voice raw with remembered agony. "Wait a minute, we did find something. We found your tooth!" he added, clearly just remembering. "Master Chief, what happened to the tooth?"

Sebastian León sat forward. "It was used to ID Jaguar," he replied, a glimmer of speculation in his dark eyes.

Gabe slid his tongue into the empty slot at the side of his mouth. Relief tickled his lungs, prompting him to throw back his head and laugh. His men got a clear glimpse of where his tooth had once been. "Oh, Jesus," Gabe sighed, wiping a tear of mirth from the corner of his eye. He didn't reveal to them how he'd agonized over the loss of that tooth. "Someone must have knocked me out and maybe dragged my ass out of there before the place blew," he conjectured.

The men muttered their thoughts out loud until Master Chief held up a hand for silence. "Listen up," he said, causing the table to fall quiet. "No one talks about this with anyone," he advised, meeting each of their gazes, one by one.

Gabe looked away, suddenly self-conscious. Sebastian was repeating the caution that Forrester had relayed to Gabe and Gabe, in turn, had shared with his master chief before their meeting today. The men would follow Sebastian's orders without question and without need for explanation.

"What we need to discover," the master chief continued, "is whether Miller had anything to do with Jaguar's disappearance. Keep your ears to the ground and your eyes open. Report anything unusual to me or to Jaguar."

He paused a thoughtful moment before adding, "Someone may be trying to terminate him before his memory comes back." To the dumbstruck squad members, he relayed the story of Gabe's close encounter with the police car.

Gabe bore their startled looks as stoically as possible. A part of him still fretted that he'd made the whole thing up. Not a single patrol car at the Sandbridge Police Station had shown any damage done to the passenger's side mirror.

"We weren't satisfied at the hearing a year ago," Sebastian recalled. "Jaguar should not have disappeared on us. I don't like it when history repeats itself. We learn from our mistakes. We protect our own."

"Hear, hear," muttered Westy.

Sebastian spent the next few minutes outlining the need for caution. The men would take turns guarding Gabe's back, sitting in a parked car outside the house at night, playing sentinel on his deck by day.

Gabe's stomach burned with secret shame. He wanted to insist that he could protect his family, but could he? More than once now, Helen had sneaked up on him without him even noticing. He'd been too caught up in dealing with the memories coming back to him. "Hold up, Master Chief," he interrupted. "We're going out of town tomorrow," he recalled. "I'll call you when I get back."

Sebastian gave him a considering look. Reaching under his pantleg, he released the Velcro strap of a gun holster and handed both the holster and the gun to Gabe. "Take this with you," he implored.

In the holster was a Glock 23, a semiautomatic, registered in Sebastian's name, no doubt. Master Chief was going out on a limb to give it to him. Gabe accepted the offering, noting the weight of the weapon with a feeling of premonition. He nodded gratefully and strapped the weapon to his own calf.

With Gabe's situation tentatively resolved, the men passed the next half hour reminiscing. To Gabe's gratification, he recalled most of the episodes rehashed, including various missions during Operation Iraqi Freedom.

"When was that?" Gabe asked with a tingle of excitement.

" 'Bout two years ago."

"No, it was like eighteen months."

"I remember it," he marveled, relief rushing through him. Piece by piece, his past was coming back to him. If only the most important links would fall into place!

A half hour later, they tramped toward the door. Gabe was last in line. To his astonishment, Veronica slipped out of the darkened corridor and coiled her arms around his waist. "Welcome home, Jaguar," she murmured, her tone intimate.

He froze, shocked by the feel of her breasts against his back. At that same instant, Luther ducked through the doorway. He drew up short to see his fiancée's arms around Gabe's midsection. "Veronica!" he said sharply, his tone reflecting shock.

Her arms fell away. Sending a wary look at the hulking

junior lieutenant, Gabe continued wordlessly out the door, his thoughts tripping over themselves. The feel of Veronica's breasts, firm with the implants she touted, had prompted a memory he wished he could forget. He'd been with Veronica. But that was before Helen, he was certain of it. It'd been a long time ago, when he first came to Dam Neck.

Luther escorted him all the way to Sebastian's car. Wary of his silence, Gabe darted him a look. Thankfully the younger man didn't look jealous, only thoughtful. Knowing how smart Luther was, surely it was only a matter of time before he called off his engagement.

The setting sun painted Sebastian's primer-covered Ford a rusty orange. As Gabe reached for the door handle, Luther put a hand on his shoulder, startling him. "Glad to have you back, sir," he said with sincerity. "Can't wait to have you on the team again."

"Thanks, Luther," said Gabe. He felt the need to say more, to offer the younger man advice, but the words stuck in his throat.

As he slipped into Sebastian's car, he let out a breath of relief.

Sebastian cut him a curious look.

"How long has Luther been engaged?" Gabe wanted to know.

"Two months." Sebastian backed the car up. "I'm praying his vision clears before he screws his life up."

"Amen to that," said Gabe. Marriage was tough enough, even with a partner who was faithful. He was doing everything within his power to illustrate his devotion to Helen, and still she'd given him no hope that she'd changed her mind about separating.

But he wasn't throwing in the towel just yet.

*　　*　　*

Helen prepared to set the table, giving only half her attention to her mother's soliloquy. Ingrid Troy required a minimum of feedback to keep a conversation flowing. So far, Helen's lack of response had gone unnoticed.

"We heard from Pandora yesterday," Ingrid added, sticking her head into the oven to read the meat thermometer. "She and Derek are coming for Thanksgiving with the kids. I told her you and Gabe would be here, too. Another half hour on this ham," she determined, closing the oven and straightening to her full height.

Whether from the heat in the kitchen or the pure ecstasy of seeing Gabe again, Ingrid's Scandinavian skin glowed. Taller than her daughter, the statuesque Swede looked nowhere close to her sixty-three years. Seeing Gabe alive after believing him dead had led her to prepare an elaborate celebratory feast.

Helen hesitated over the silverware she was pulling from the drawer. Would she even be with Gabe at Thanksgiving? Her heart grew heavy at the thought. It all depended on whether his memories returned and how much he changed as a result. Her parents would be crushed, of course. She heaved a sigh. What the hell. The only time she'd ever met their expectations was when she'd married Gabe.

"What's Pandora up to these days?" she asked, not having spoken to her perfect, older sister in a couple of weeks. Conversations with Pandora, who had married a lawyer and begotten two beautiful children, left Helen achingly aware of her shortcomings.

It was ridiculous at her age to feel inferior. She'd done well for herself, despite her rough start. She was the Fitness Coordinator at Dam Neck, for heaven's sake! Even if her marriage to Gabe suffered the ending she predicted, she had nothing to apologize for.

Moving to the connecting dining room, Helen laid the sterling silver about the china plates. They were eating in the formal dining room. The cherry-wood table gleamed in the sunlight coming through the front windows. A bouquet of long-stemmed roses made Helen think about her wedding day.

If only Gabe could forget his memories permanently. If only he could stay the way he was, she'd be willing to take a chance on him.

Coming to the end of the table, she raised her eyes to gaze across the living area. Gabe sat with her father in the glassed-in sunroom at the end of the house. Through the large panes beyond them, the immaculate lawn of the Georgian home swept down to the Potomac River. In a mirror's reflection, she could see his face as he followed her father's words. By now she had expected he would assume what she thought of as his military demeanor—a narrow-eyed, thin-lipped look her father never failed to inspire in him.

But Gabe wasn't wearing that look just yet. The expression on his face was one of solemn respect. As her father droned on and on, Gabe's gaze strayed toward Mallory, who sat in the living room, staring glumly at the television.

A frown depressed Gabe's forehead as he pondered the reason for Mallory's long face. Helen already knew that Mallory hated coming here. Her grandfather's strictness kept her on pins and needles. There were no other teens in the area to play with.

From where he was seated, Gabe hadn't even noticed Helen's regard. His concern for Mallory was as genuine as she'd already guessed. And given the way he looked at Helen, he probably loved her too.

She took a sharp breath at the realization. What would happen to his feelings when his memories returned? Could he remain pure of heart while recalling the atrocities perpetrated on him? Could he think of anything beyond a blinding need to seek revenge? Even memories of their life before his mission were sure to have a negative impact. It was futile to hope that his memories wouldn't change him.

She turned away, wishing he could stay this way forever.

Gabe discovered the commander to be well informed about the North Korean situation. In the same oratory style Gabe recalled from his years at the Academy, Commander Troy brought Gabe up-to-date on U.S. foreign policy with that country.

The decision to curtail humanitarian aid, Oliver Troy explained, was instigated by an international trade scandal—millions of yen belonging to a Japanese-based company had disappeared during a computer transaction. All fingers pointed to North Korea as the culprit. Soon after, the U.S. caught wind of shipments of arms to Malaysia and the Middle East, to countries well known for their support of terrorism.

"It's a damn shame," the commander added. "The country is too cold and rocky to grow their own produce. Without humanitarian aid, the population will starve to death. The one thing they do have is technology, and they're using it to eke out a living, ferreting out vulnerabilities on the Web and selling their information to terrorist groups worldwide."

And didn't Gabe know it. Without realizing it, Oliver Troy had summarized Gabe's personal experience. His captors had been ruthless in their quest for information, working him over thoroughly to try to get what they wanted. He rubbed his right temple, wondering what exactly had prompted that side of his head to ache again.

"What happened to you, Gabriel?" the commander suddenly inquired. "Your base commander, Admiral Johansen, told me personally that he believed you were dead. Yet here you are, sitting in front of me. I'm more than amazed. I'm astounded."

Meeting the man's blue eyes, Gabe shook his head, wishing that he had an answer. "I don't remember, sir."

"They blamed your death on faulty equipment. Your headset wasn't working, or some such thing."

Gabe caught himself lifting a hand to his ear, prompted by a vague memory.

Oliver Troy narrowed his gaze at him. "I wouldn't be surprised if the committee takes another look into the matter, now that you're alive. Too many loose ends," he added, shaking his head.

Gabe shifted uncomfortably at the thought. He'd have to *remember* first, if he was going to testify, and the thought of remembering still made his palms sweat.

The commander hitched up a pant leg and leaned closer. "I've always wondered if your disappearance didn't have to do with the weapons being stolen," he admitted sotto voce.

Gabe eyed the commander closely. "What do you know about that?" he asked. Jesus, did the whole world know what SEALs were up to these days?

Troy lifted his silvery eyebrows. "Everyone knows someone was beating the SEALs to the interdiction sites. You, yourself, were furious about it," he added. "Before your disappearance, you told me you were going to cast some nets. Next thing I knew you'd disappeared."

Goose bumps scrambled up Gabe's arms and stabbed at his scalp. Maybe he'd stumbled on the identity of the weapons' thief, and he'd confronted him! He sat, riveted by the sudden certainty that he had. Somewhere, then, in his repressed memories was the name of the culprit, the mother of all crabs.

"Suppose you confronted him," the commander proposed, giving voice to Gabe's thoughts. "Suppose you scared him enough to do something."

Adrenaline stormed Gabe's system, making him want to jump out of the chair and prowl about the room. "Then I was targeted," he said quietly. Sebastian and Forrester had already intimated as much. Confirmation from this man was all he needed to be convinced.

Troy nodded deeply, his mouth firming with the gravity of Gabe's situation.

Gabe sucked in a deep breath He knew who the traitor was—someone on his own team, possibly. Jason Miller sprang to mind. The man would have access to the necessary information, and yet . . . he was a coward, a follower. He lacked the backbone to instigate his own operation.

Who, then?

"Son of a bitch," Gabe muttered, overcome by an uneasiness that had him scanning the trees beyond the large-paned windows. There could be a sniper out there right now, ready to take him out. "Are shipments still disappearing?" he wanted to know as he assessed potential hiding places. No assassin in sight, yet the Glock 23 was strapped to his calf, loaded and ready, just in case.

"Johansen admitted to me that we lost a nuke last week," the commander admitted. "It was being transported via tanker to Yemen. When the SEALs from Team Two interdicted in the Indian Ocean, all they found was a torn-up cargo hold."

Gabe swallowed uneasily. A nuke—dear God! What would the traitor in their midst be doing with a nuke? Selling it on the black market, where it could fall into terrorist hands? Did he have no brains, no common sense? The last thing this volatile world needed was weapons of mass destruction up for sale!

"You always were a lucky son of a bitch," the commander commented out of the blue. "You were meant to make it out of that warehouse alive, son. Just as you're meant to catch this wild card and eliminate him before he does any lasting harm."

Ah, the call to duty! Gabe smiled, remembering Troy's remarkable ability to motivate the seamen in his classes, filling their minds with future glory and ambition.

The man had changed Gabe's life. He remembered it well. But he couldn't remember escaping from the warehouse. Or could he?

In that instant, a memory crystallized, providing him with a crisp image of what had happened to him. His arms and legs were bound. His head felt like it'd been crushed. He was tossed into the bed of a pickup truck. A brilliant light flashed before his eyes, blinding him. At the same time a deafening crash shook the metal bed beneath him and drove a spike into his head.

Dazed by the unexpected memory, Gabe fought to hold it in place, searching through the smoke and noise for a face. Two small men shut the tailgate at his feet and leapt into the cab, carting him quickly away. "Some of the locals found me," Gabe admitted hoarsely. "They got me out of there right before the place blew."

The commander frowned at him. "Did you just remember that?"

"Yes, sir," Gabe admitted. A film of sweat dampened his back, making his shirt cling.

"Keep it to yourself awhile," the man advised, frowning.

"Wait until you remember everything. Then nail the son of a bitch that sold you out."

Gabe nodded, his brain seething with possibilities. He was starting to remember; it wouldn't be long now. There was no more denying what his instincts were telling him: he'd been targeted that night in Pyongyang. If not for the locals who'd pulled him from the burning warehouse, he wouldn't be alive today.

"Hey!" the commander shouted, startling Gabe from his heavy thoughts. He realized that the man was addressing Mallory, who snatched her hand from the chessboard on the coffee table. "How many times have I told you not to touch that?" he berated.

Noting Mallory's chagrin, Gabe rallied to her defense. "Excuse me, sir. Do you mind if I play a game with her?"

Troy colored faintly beneath his weathered complexion. "Not at all," he blustered. "Go ahead." He waved Gabe toward the living room.

"You know how to play, Mal?" Gabe inquired, stepping across the threshold into the living room. A game of chess would be just the thing to take his mind off his preoccupations.

Mal's eyes sparkled with relief. "Sure," she said.

He settled on the sofa across from her, pausing to take note of the commander's glowering expression. "Care to join us, sir?" he called. "This has the potential to get ugly. Mallory has inherited her grandfather's genius."

To his satisfaction, Oliver Troy rolled to his feet, looking mollified. "Don't mind if I do," he muttered.

Half an hour later, with Mallory's queen poised for a checkmate, Helen ventured into the living room to announce that lunch was ready. The announcement stuck in her throat as she beheld her daughter on the brink of toppling her grandfather's miniature kingdom.

"Checkmate," Mallory said with commendable humility.

"By God, I don't believe it!" Oliver Troy thundered in appreciation. "She's a chip off the old block. Did you see that, Ingrid?" he asked as his wife also peered into the living room, startled by the noise. "Your granddaughter just bested me at chess."

"Well, well," Ingrid exclaimed, surprise etched on her lovely face. "It's time for lunch now," she announced. "Kindly wash up and head to the table."

"Aye, aye," the commander replied.

Mallory quirked a smile at him and received an answering grin.

From the other side of the coffee table, Gabe met Helen's gaze with a small, satisfied smile of his own. Somehow he'd conquered the generation gap that kept Mallory and her grandparents on formal terms. To Helen's complete disorientation, he followed the smile with a slow, suggestive wink.

It was the wink that did it. With a curious sense of relief, Helen accepted that her plan to bring out the old Gabe wasn't working. Hope beat like the wings of a fledgling leaping from the nest. *Just let him stay this way,* she found herself praying. *Please don't let his memories take him away.*

Chapter Thirteen

At ten o'clock that night, Helen faced the inevitable. She was going to have to share a bed with Gabe. The situation was entirely of her own making. She'd given her parents no indication that she and Gabe didn't sleep together. God knew it was nobody's business but hers. She had planned to slip into Mallory's bed the moment her parents retired, only no one had warned her that Mallory's bedroom had been transformed into an office.

Her daughter was sleeping on the sofa in the living room. Helen could hardly join her there. There was no way around it; she would have to share the double bed, half the size of her bed at home, with Gabe.

She dawdled in the shower, wondering how to get around this hurdle. Her body tingled with traitorous anticipation. As she lathered every inch of her skin with scented soap, she berated herself for her ritual preparations. Nothing was going to happen if she could help it. She simply wasn't ready to take that leap of faith.

It was one thing to entertain the thought of Gabe forever

in her life. It was entirely another to let him in her bed and in her heart.

They'd gone jogging in downtown Annapolis earlier this evening. Gabe, whose stamina was usually far greater than hers, lasted about as long as she did. They'd run four miles and called it quits. He'd showered before her and was presumably waiting for her beneath the sheets.

Helen took the time to dry her hair, brushing it so that it fell in silky layers down her back. She scrubbed her teeth until they sparkled. *Enough already,* she told her image firmly. *You're sharing a bed, that's all. You are not going to have sex with him.*

Flushed with anticipation, her body had other ideas.

She donned her silken pajamas and put her ear to the door. Absolute silence came from the adjoining room. Still, she could picture Gabe in his boxers, sitting in the middle of the bed, back against the headboard, hands clasped behind his head, in an attitude of supreme confidence.

Where on earth would she find the will to deny him? With a quiver of anticipation, she flipped off the light and stepped into the guest room. Expectancy took a nosedive. Gabe wasn't waiting on the bed.

Her unaccustomed eyes scanned the room. There he was: lying spread-eagled on the floor, half-covered by a blanket, his pillow askew, dead to the world.

More disappointed than she cared to admit, Helen knelt beside him and shook him gently. He didn't budge. In the faint glow of the bathroom nightlight, she studied his precise features, the dark fringe of his eyelashes.

His mouth looked particularly vulnerable in sleep. She felt a tug of compassion for him. Poor man, would he ever get enough rest to compensate for his deprivation?

Pulling the blanket over his shoulders, she resisted the

urge to brush the hair off his forehead. He could sleep on the floor if that was what he wanted. Evidently, he had the willpower to keep his distance.

Which was more than she could say for herself, at this point.

With a sigh, she headed for the bed and slipped beneath the sheets. The bed felt cold and lonely. She scooted to the edge of the mattress and studied her husband from a distance.

He struck her as a stranger who was yet somehow familiar. He wasn't the Gabe she'd married. That man had been clever, self-sufficient, and ruthless. His strength and intelligence had fascinated her. But, in the end, his emotional detachment had chilled her love until it grew brittle and died.

This Gabe seemed to have a heart where the other had none. Confessing his lonely childhood, he'd laid himself bare. He'd sacrificed his pride by begging for a second chance. He devoted himself to Mallory, the daughter he'd never had time for. Just imagine what it could be like, Helen marveled, if she allowed him to be devoted to his wife.

She marveled at the possibilities. Life could be *good* with this man, if only his memories didn't steal him back. With a wistful sigh, she closed her eyes. Ignoring the yearnings of her body, she told herself to go to sleep. There was always tomorrow. And for the first time in a very long time, tomorrow looked promising.

Gabe rolled over on the cement ledge and found himself staring up at the familiar face of his youngest cell keeper, Jun Yeup. The young man's smile was nowhere in evidence this afternoon. Sunlight slanted through the narrow window to illuminate a broad face, pinched with worry, eyes dark with concern.

Gabe lurched to his elbows. The weight of Jun Yeup's

silver cross settled warmly on his own bare chest. "What is it?" he asked in English, never having revealed to his captors that he spoke their language. At the same time, he listened for the usual noises—the sound of his guards in the room next door, the din of activity in the compound outside. It was strangely quiet.

"Today is Festival of Rice," Jun Yeup whispered, speaking in broken English, his gaze darting to the door. "Everyone go to temple that way." He pointed toward the eastern portion of the compound.

Caught by something in the boy's tone, Gabe searched his gaze. What was Jun Yeup telling him?

He felt an object being pressed into his palm. His fingers closed around it. He could tell without looking that he was holding a key.

A key! His blood pressure soared. Jesus, God! What he thought was happening couldn't be happening.

"Wait when sun sets," Jun Yeup advised, fear now evident in his whisper. "Then go. Go quick. Go into sun." He gestured. "You see small water. Go with water. Go quick."

Gabe could only gape at his young savior. He'd always known Jun Yeup was different. It wasn't just the cross hanging from his neck, it was the sympathy in his eyes, the gentleness of his touch. Ironically, he was Seung-Ki's nephew, and Seung-Ki was Gabe's chief nemesis. Jun Yeup would pay with his life for letting Gabe escape.

"What about you?" he asked, gripping the boy's sleeve. "You can't stay here. Your uncle will kill you."

Jun Yeup's eyes burned with hope. "I go with you," he seemed to decide with sudden bravado. "To South Korea."

Ah, shit. Gabe pulled the boy's forehead down to his in a modified embrace. "You can't come, Juni," he said, using his pet name far him. "It's too dangerous." He looked deep into

Jun Yeup's dark eyes, needing to convey the truth of his words.

"I go to grandfather," Jun Yeup amended, with a weak smile.

"Good," said Gabe, his throat clogged with sudden emotion. He gripped the key in his fist until the blunt edges gouged his palm. He couldn't believe this was happening. Christ Almighty, he'd been hoping for a break forever!

"Look," Jun Yeup added. With a coy grin, he reached over and lifted a pair of scruffy tennis shoes off the floor.

Glancing at the shoes, Gabe smiled his thanks. They were at least three sizes too small, but they would beat the hell out of bare feet.

Laughter in the compound made them freeze like thieves. Jun Yeup shot across the room to stow the shoes behind the door, out of sight to anyone peering in. With the sound of voices approaching, he lifted a hand in farewell, his eyes blazing with righteousness. "God will see you," he said. He slipped from the cell as silently as he'd entered.

Gabe stared at the closed door, missing the kid already. *God watch over you, too,* he thought, a lump riding high in his throat.

The hours until sunset passed as if in a dream. Gabe plotted his escape, summoning maps and charts from his memory. He weighed the odds of penetrating the DMZ proper or circumventing it. He donned the tennis shoes, wishing he had a knife to cut the ends off and relieve his bunched toes. All too soon, the sky in the ventilation slit began to mellow.

He waited until the compound itself fell silent, until the last tread of footsteps wandered off in the direction of the temple. With a whispered prayer for safety, Gabe rose, key in hand, and let himself out of the cell he'd dwelled in for three hundred and sixty-one interminable days.

Just before closing the door, he paused to look back. The room had been a chamber of hunger, thirst, and physical torment. In that time, he'd relived every moment of his life. It had been a purgatory on earth, a place to review his sins and seek forgiveness. The sudden swelling of nostalgia in his chest surprised him. Surely, he wouldn't miss this hell on earth.

Yet it was there, on that cement ledge where he'd caught only snatches of sleep, that he'd come to terms with his past. He'd reviewed his childhood—years he'd thought he'd forgotten. He recalled how it had felt to be a boy who lost his mother. He remembered how he'd wept for her until it felt that there were no more tears—in fact, no heart at all inside him. He'd recalled his teenage years, understanding for the first time the anger and the despair that had driven him. He'd felt so different from the other kids, so cheated of life's pleasures. Retaliating, he'd lashed out, hurting himself more than anyone.

Thank God for men like Sergeant O'Mally, Master Chief Black, and Commander Troy, men who'd believed in a better part of him, men who'd sparked his desire to rise from the ashes.

Yet, at the same time, none of them had taught Gabe what this cell had taught him—this shrine of penitence and reflection. It had taught him that his true purpose in life was just not to beat back terrorists and keep the world from seething with madness—that was one goal, certainly. But the other, equally important, was to connect with others in ways that were profound and elemental. It was that connection that made life sweeter, gave it purpose, dignity, and power.

Since the loss of his mother, Gabe had refused to connect with anyone. Connection meant potential pain, potential weakness. Given his line of work and the dangers involved, he didn't want emotions to govern him. He'd run from them, putting in extra hours at work, taking part in every mission possible, just to keep from loving Helen. And whenever they'd made love, he'd kept his eyes tightly closed, refusing to feel more than physical pleasure, holding in the love that swelled inside him, freezing her out.

Despite his efforts to isolate himself, he'd failed. He'd discovered in his incarceration that love existed in him, regardless, and thank God. What he'd feared would be a weakness had, in fact, made him stronger. His connection with Helen had kept him alive. Because the one thing he valued more than anything—more than pride, more than patriotism, more than his own body—was his wife. He was determined to see her again, if only to tell her how very much she meant to him.

How many times had he lain on that ledge and prayed for the chance to make amends?

With pressure on his chest and with the recognition that this was it, his chance to make good on a private promise, he shut his cell door quietly behind him.

Then he turned and eyed the room across the hall. Reaching for the latch, he jiggled it and found it locked. No problem. He'd seen more than one of his captors use the key on the lintel above. He helped himself, needing only half an hour or so to avenge his yearlong captivity.

The room was air-conditioned, a luxury afforded to the computers, but not to him. He shivered at the cold and made a beeline for the computer that was booted up and running. Heart thumping, he eased onto an incongruous wicker chair and summoned the basic hacking skills he'd learned in a course offered to SEAL officers a while back.

Entering Microsoft Office through DOS wasn't the easiest trick in the book. It took him more than fifteen minutes before he made any progress. At last he found himself going through folders, hunting for information that could be used against his captors. His skill with Korean font was minimal, but there was still plenty to catch his eye.

Holy shit! Blueprints to weapons compounds.

Inventories of weapons arsenals.

Experimental weapons.

A list of buyers, including Nigeria and Iraq—no surprise there.

He lumped the information together in a zip file. Put in responsible hands, this kind of intelligence would put a dent in terrorist groups everywhere. The compounds in North Korea could be targeted and destroyed. The buyers dealt with.

But how to warn his country? He didn't have time to print the files. Paper got wet, was easily destroyed.

E-mail. He'd send e-mail to someone stateside and attach the files!

With sweat trickling down his bare back, Gabe opened the e-mail. He sat there a moment, struggling to recall the address of his commander. *Think. Think. Think.*

He was aware that he'd lost some memories from the concussion he'd arrived with, but this was downright annoying. He and Lovitt had communicated via e-mail on a daily basis. What the hell was his address?

Drawing a blank, Gabe aimed higher. He'd mail this stuff to the FBI, to the Department of Cyberspace Security. But a hunt on the Internet failed to supply him with any specific e-mail address. He settled on the "Contact us" address, adding a explanatory note explaining who he was and what he'd found. Then he fired off the message, praying it would fall into conscientious hands.

A glance at the computer clock warned him that it was getting late. He was pushing his luck, but first things first.

Ducking under the desk, he pulled out the computer case, removed the side cover, and ripped out the motherboard and CPU, smashing them into pieces. In less than ten minutes, he'd debilitated all the computers in the room the same way.

Every instinct screamed for him to leave. He could hear shouts of laughter in the distance. If they caught him now, they'd kill him for what he'd done.

He stuck his head into the hall. He could hear men approaching the back door of the bunker. He raced toward the front, running down the bare hall, naked light bulbs swinging overhead. Pushing through the metal door, he crept up the cement steps that brought him up to ground level.

There were several tangos at his seven o'clock, meandering toward the bunker in a drunken knot. Otherwise, it was a clear shot to the chain-link fence.

Go! With speed he'd forgotten he possessed, Gabe sprinted toward the fence, expecting shouts to arise at any moment. Adrenaline coursed through his veins, giving him added speed. His lungs felt in danger of bursting. He hit the fence with enough momentum to get him over the top. He slid under the first row of barbed wire. Sharp prongs raked his back and buttocks, but he scarcely felt the sting. He was acutely aware, however, of the voice crying out in Korean, "The American is escaping!"

On the other side of the fence, Gabe set off again, grateful for the too-tight tennis shoes for absorbing the rocky terrain as he slipped and scrambled down the hillside, heading directly toward the golden glow in the sky that marked the sun's descent, due west.

He felt like he'd run for miles when he hit the stream. The gurgling of the water was scarcely audible over the sawing of his breath. He slipped on the muddy bank. Water rushed into his shoes. And then he heard the sound he'd been dreading: the barking of dogs.

He floundered into the water, frustrated that it could be so shallow and so rocky at the same time, coming scarcely to his knees. It felt as viscous as glue, slowing him down when he wanted to run like hell.

Over his shoulder, he caught sight of flashlights, strafing the darkening hillside as the tangos searched for him, dogs straining on leashes as they led the way. Wary of being seen, Gabe crouched lower and moved apelike over the rocky streambed.

Go, go, go! He pushed himself to move faster, fingers taking a beating as he felt his way.

But the dogs were closing in. They led their masters directly toward him, cutting a hypotenuse across the open land. At this rate, they would intercept his position in minutes.

He was tempted to abandon the stream and race up the hill to his right, but ultimately a move like that would get him caught. Better to stay by the water where he was certain of his direction, where his scent would be washed away.

The howling of the dogs was like fingernails over a chalkboard. It filled Gabe's head with paralyzing visions of what the future would be like for him if he were caught again.

Suddenly the streambed deepened, immersing him to his waist in frigid water. *Thank you, God!* With a deep breath, he looped under the surface, swimming as fast and furiously as he could, the current like wings, speeding him on his way.

Suddenly, two hands closed over his shoulders, yanking him up and out of the water.

No! he raged, throwing off his assailant. With a loud thump—*Thump?*—the attacker flew off him, making contact with an object that threatened to topple over.

Disoriented, Gabe twisted into an upright position and

found himself on the floor of Commander Troy's guest bedroom. Helen lay in a heap not far away. In the faint glow of the bathroom nightlight, he could see her rubbing the top of her head, a painful grimace contorting her beautiful face.

God damn him, he'd done it again!

Ow, ow, ow! Helen rubbed the top of her head with her palm and kept an eye trained warily on Gabe. He sprang toward her and she flinched, but then the lamp over her head snapped on, and she saw that he was staring down at her with horror in his eyes.

"Talk to me," he demanded, his voice gruff with confusion. He peeled her fingers from her head and peered down at the throbbing spot.

"Did I break the skin?" She didn't want to drip blood on her mother's carpet.

"No," he said, running a finger lightly over the welt. "Just a red mark. Son of a bitch!" he exploded, lurching to his feet. He wheeled away from her and paced to the door, before turning abruptly back.

"I'm sorry," she apologized, anxious to dispel his temper. "I shouldn't have awakened you so abruptly."

"Don't apologize," he retorted, dragging his fingers through his hair. "Fuck!"

"I thought you were dreaming. You were breathing really hard," she rushed to explain. "Then all of a sudden you stopped. I couldn't hear anything, and I was afraid you were going to die—"

His gaze went through her, as if he were seeing something else. "I was holding my breath," he said.

"Holding your breath? What do you mean—you were dreaming?"

He tucked his hands under his armpits, his T-shirt straining over his chest muscles. He thought for a moment. "I was escaping," he admitted, his voice pitched low, his gaze turned inward. "I had to swim down a stream. They had dogs after me." He paused for a split second. "I need to use the phone," he said, turning unexpectedly toward the door.

"Wait!" she called, scrambling to her feet. "At this time of night?" She pushed her way past him and blocked the exit. "You can't go out there, Gabe. You'll wake up Mallory." Besides, he wasn't in the right frame of mind to talk to anyone right now. "Talk to me first," she invited, propelling him toward the bed. "Tell me what you remember."

To her relief, he allowed her to move him. He sat on the edge of the mattress, as tense as a trapdoor.

The shock in his eyes seemed to be clearing. "Before I left the compound I found some files on my captor's computers," he explained, "and I e-mailed them to the FBI. I need to know if someone found them."

"What kinds of files?"

"Intelligence stuff. You're better off not knowing. I need to call," he said again.

"Can't it wait till morning? Who'll be in the office at this time of night?"

A glance at the clock confirmed what she was saying. He heaved a sigh, releasing his intentions for the moment. He looked back at her, his thoughts clearly shifting, given the look in his eyes. "Helen," he whispered, capturing her face between his hands. "I made it back."

"Yes," she marveled, amazed to see a sheen of tears in his eyes.

"You kept me alive the whole time I was there," he added unexpectedly. "It was you who gave me the strength to stand up to them."

She stared at him, absorbing the implication of his words.

"You remember everything now?" she asked, finding his memories safer to discuss than his feelings for her.

He hesitated, closing his eyes. A look of concentration came across his face. "No," he determined flatly. "Damn it!" He banged his fist against his forehead. "I still can't remember the mission!"

Tension rushed back into him, and Helen stroked his chest, finding it a relief and a pleasure to touch him. "Hush," she soothed, "it'll come back just like the rest. Focus on the positive."

He nodded, letting his shoulders relax. His arms stole around her, pulling her closer. She was highly conscious of the fact that he wore nothing more than a pair of boxers and a T-shirt. She'd forgotten just how warm he always was. "You really remember us together?" she asked, not quite able to believe it.

"Yes," he said, his tone reflective. He held her gently, his hands straying as if comparing how she felt now to what he recalled of her.

"So you remember when my father introduced us? You remember meeting Mallory for the first time?"

"You were the most beautiful woman I'd ever seen," he admitted, his tone reflective. "Mallory was cute but she scared the hell out of me."

"Really?" She'd had no idea. The old Gabe had seemed so fearless.

"I knew I'd make a lousy father," he added.

Helen trembled. This moment had come so unexpectedly. Now that he remembered their history together, past and present were merging right in front of her. Surely the weight of the past would drown their newfound happiness. "You're a good father now," she pointed out, hearing regret in her voice.

"I'm trying," he said earnestly. "I know I have a lot to make up for, a whole hell of a lot."

She gazed up at him, unable to stanch the hope gathering inside her. His memories were back, but he still sounded like the new Gabe.

"I went through hell this last year," he reflected, his voice roughening as tears once again glimmered in his eyes. "I thought I'd never get out of there alive. But something kept me going." He took her hand, laying it over the center of his chest and held it there. "Something right here," he said, "had you inside it." His gaze searched her face as he hunted for the right words. "I was such an idiot, Helen," he said, a crease appearing between his eyebrows. "I thought that loving you would make me weak, make me less of a SEAL." He broke off with a laugh of incredulity. "But instead, it made me strong. You—loving you—gave me the determination to come back."

She wasn't aware of when her own tears started falling. All she knew was that her cheeks were wet and her heart had expanded to ten times its normal size, making it hard to breathe. Not in her wildest dreams had she ever imagined Gabe confessing such words to her—*loving you*. They defied her expectations. They left her stunned. They changed everything.

She could only stare at him, reconciling what she'd heard to what she knew of him. As the seconds stretched to minutes, Gabe looked away, his hands falling to his sides. "I understand if you still don't want me," he said on a heartbreaking note. "I know what I look like. I know what my captors did to me."

With a cry of denial, she grabbed him firmly, keeping him from stepping back. "Stop it," she scolded. "Don't ever think that, Gabe," she told him. "You know I want you. I told you that just the other night."

"Forever?" he asked, pressing her for commitment.

She wanted to say yes. On the surface, it appeared that Gabe's captivity hadn't changed him at all. If anything, it had given him time to accept the death-defying power of love. But she'd learned her lesson once before about putting her faith in happily-ever-after. She would wait to see if this new Gabe had sticking power before she gave her heart to him again. "Maybe," she replied. It was the best she could do.

He considered her answer for a solemn moment. "Maybe is enough," he decided. He pulled her closer, breathing her scent as if it were life-sustaining oxygen.

Helen thrilled as proof of his desire prodded her hip.

"Let me love you, Helen," he rasped in her ear. "I dreamed about it all the time—how I'd love you again, when I got you in my arms."

She trembled with desire so overwhelming she could barely get an answer out. "Yes," she breathed, standing on tiptoe to offer him her lips.

His kisses were deep and unbearably sweet. He took his time, reacquainting himself with every corner of her mouth, drawing on her lips and tongue as if savoring their taste and texture.

Slowly, agonizingly, he parted the buttons of her pajama top. He swept a hand up her back, around the indent of her waist and up to capture a breast. Tenderly, he stroked his thumb over her nipple and her knees wobbled.

With a hum of satisfaction, he swung her onto the bed and laid her on her back. For a moment, he regarded her in the lamplight, studying her face, her moist lips, her breasts peeking through the parted halves of her pajama top. "You know what my biggest fear was?" he asked.

"What?"

"Not seeing you again."

His words put pressure on her chest. She felt terribly guilty for not feeling the same way.

Shadows filled his eyes. "You didn't miss me," he realized.

She wanted to deny it; to say that she'd wept oceans of tears for him, only she hadn't. "I grieved for you when you were still with us," she replied, choosing her words carefully. "You were there, physically, but never emotionally."

He gave her a sad, sad smile. "That won't happen again," he swore.

It won't? She longed to believe him. The promise that he would connect with her on a deeper level was almost too good to be true.

"Will you do something for me?" he asked her, stroking the side of her face.

"What's that?"

"When we make love," he said, "I want you to keep your eyes open."

She smiled at him quizzically. "Why?"

"So you can see how much I love you."

There it was again: the L-word. A word he'd said so seldom in the past, she'd doubted it was even in his vocabulary. Yet this was the second time he'd said it in just minutes. "Okay," she said with trepidation. He was asking her to take risks, risks she'd taken before and regretted.

He peeled back the lapels of her pajama top, exposing both breasts. Bending his head, he worshiped her till she was breathless. The palm of his hand, rough from working on the deck, skimmed her torso, moving lower.

He slipped his fingers under the elastic band of her pajama pants. At the same time, he looked deep into her eyes.

His fingers crept beneath the lace barrier of her panties. Heat flooded Helen's cheeks. Her eyes fluttered shut.

"Look at me," he insisted gently.

She obeyed, at the same time feeling his fingers comb through her pubic hair. Twin torches of desire burned in his eyes, turning her shyness to shamelessness. With sudden carnal craving, she parted her legs for him, giving him access to a part of her that melted like wax beneath a steady flame.

He touched her deliberately, tenderly, reverently. As in the past, he knew exactly how to arouse her. She couldn't hold back the moan of surrender that escaped her. She fought to keep her eyes open as stark, unprecedented pleasure stormed her senses. Gabe watched every nuance of her expression, gauging his next move by the look in her eyes.

"Please," she heard herself beg as she clutched his shoulders with need. She didn't want to be alone in this. She wanted him with her.

It was obvious he'd been waiting for that one word. In a fluid movement, he stripped her clothes from her, pausing to take in her glorious nakedness. Reaching for his own shirt, he hesitated. "Do you want me to leave it on?" he asked.

His question summoned immediate contrition. "No," she firmly replied. She helped him out of the shirt, her fingers going straight to his scars. They were part of him now. If she was going to assume the risk of loving him again, that meant accepting all of him.

Still, she had to swallow a gasp of dismay. His once-smooth torso was ridged with lines and bumps. There was even an indentation under his arm where a piece of flesh had been torn from him. She measured the hollow with silent horror, aware all the while that Gabe was watching her.

Her fingers found a scar that went from his collarbone to a dusky male nipple. "What was this?" she asked, tracing it lightly, her heart in her throat. Anger burned in her for the men who'd treated him so ruthlessly.

He shook his head minimally. "Later. Not now."

She understood. Now was not the time. Her emotions were already jumbled. With the need to assure him of his appeal, she placed her lips against the scar and traced it with her tongue. His intake of breath made her realize this was exactly what he needed.

She was going to kiss every mark on his body before the night was through.

Pushing him back against the pillows, she came up over him, and bent her head again to reverence the wounds on his chest. "Roll over," she said when she was done.

Acquiescent, he complied. There were far more marks on his back. It took ten minutes to find and kiss them all, her hair drifting over him like a silken shawl. He held perfectly still, enduring her caresses in silence. At last, when she was done, she saw that he'd covered his face with one hand to hide the torment she'd unwittingly called up.

"I'm sorry," she apologized, struck with remorse.

He pulled his hand away and looked at her, a small smile curving his lips. "I'm not."

With those surprising words, he rolled over, swept her into his arms, and rolled over again, pressing her into the mattress. He kissed her with his whole heart in the kiss. As heat leapt between them, all thoughts of the past evaporated.

He shucked his boxers with an expedient tug. And then they were lying skin to skin. She found him warm and achingly familiar. He kissed her neck, her shoulders, her breasts and lower, with those same scandalous, openmouthed kisses she'd mourned. He paused at last between her thighs, wreaking succulent havoc, just as he had in the past.

Oh, heavens. She buried her fingers into the silky short

strands of his hair and clung to him. Again, he brought her to the edge of desire. She refused to go over the top without him. She wanted to look into his eyes when that happened, to see what Gabe had been hiding from her all this time.

As though attuned to her desires, he broke away and covered her. His slow, inexorable possession was all the satisfaction she could possibly want. But the look on his face made it twice as exhilarating. His cheeks were flushed with passion; his jaw set at an angle that betrayed pleasure. The burning look in his eyes let her know she was the only woman in the world he loved, and that he loved her absolutely. The fact that he'd survived unspeakable horror just to come home to her said it all.

It was the look, more than anything, that did it. With a ragged cry, Helen surrendered to the exquisite sensations coursing through her. Through slitted eyes, she watched him, watching her. His look of satisfaction added an unbelievable element to her orgasm, making it unlike anything she'd ever experienced.

She knew the exact moment that his own pleasure spiked. He kissed her at the same time, groaning into her mouth, his eyes closed at last under the power of his release.

He collapsed on top of her, muttering an exclamation that made her smile. A moment later he lifted his head to look at her. "You're beautiful," he said, kissing her again.

Gabe had always been the first to leave the bed, never pausing to relish the feeling they'd shared. She held her breath to see what he would do now. Sure enough, he turned, but he took her with him as he rolled onto his back. She lay sprawled across his larger frame, her body still joined to his.

He put his arms around her, heaved a deep sigh, and closed his eyes. Helen found the perfect place to lay her head. This pose made her feel impossibly close to him, as if she were his blanket, protecting him from the cold, cruel world.

"Gabe?" she whispered, wanting to talk more, thinking he just might convince her to give her heart to him completely if they talked a little longer.

No answer. Peering up at him, she found his eyes closed. His breathing was slow and even, and she realized with amazement and some chagrin that he'd fallen asleep. Just like that.

Stretching out a hand, she managed to snap off the light. He hadn't withdrawn intentionally, she told herself, but the effect was still the same. He was too tired to bask in the afterglow of their lovemaking. The past had left its mark on him, after all.

To think that Gabe's captivity had only wrought good things in him was simply naive. There were plenty of negative consequences—like this sudden exhaustion, for instance. And when the novelty of his return wore off; when the SEALs called him back into service, who was to say he wouldn't fall back into his old habits?

No, she was right to be cautious. Endings this good only happened in fairy tales.

Chapter Fourteen

Helen sat on a bench outside the lecture hall watching the activity in Annapolis Harbor. Mallory, pretending to stalk the pigeons along the walkway, was checking out the plebes, newly arrived at the academy, who passed between the dorms and cafeteria in a tight-knit group.

Helen stretched her bare legs out before her, wishing that the sun would pierce the heavy cloud cover so she could at least work on her tan. The flapping of sails and the clanging of chains blended with the cries of seagulls. The scent of an impending storm mingled with the mouth-watering aromas of the restaurants in town.

Helen closed her eyes. Despite the less-than-perfect weather, she smiled with satisfaction at the memory of this morning's romp in bed. Gabe had proven himself very much awake and more than willing to lie in bed all day, if her mother hadn't called them down to breakfast.

The jangling of Helen's cell phone pulled her from her reverie. She frowned a second at her purse, then pulled out her phone and opened it. "Hello?" she said.

A significant pause followed her greeting. "Helen, this is Jason," said a voice she'd rather forget.

Jason Miller, Gabe's XO.

"Oh, hi," she answered coolly, recalling Gabe's suspicions that Miller had been involved in his disappearance. Jason had insisted she buy this cell phone soon after. She wished she'd had the forethought to change her number. What could he possibly want from her now?

"I'm calling on Commander Lovitt's behest," he said unexpectedly. "He'd like to see Renault in his office this weekend if possible. He's out of town this week."

Helen sat up straighter. "What's this about?" she asked, though most likely Jason wouldn't tell her. SEAL business was always confidential.

He hesitated, as if measuring how much to say. "Lovitt just heard from the FBI. Apparently your husband sent some files to them from the PDRK, identifying himself as a member of SEAL Team Twelve. Lovitt wants to commend him, that's all. How's he doing with his memories, by the way?"

Thrilled by Jason's news, Helen turned her head toward the lecture hall, hopeful of Gabe's reappearance. The FBI had found his files! Wouldn't he be thrilled to hear it! "Great," she said without thinking. "He's remembered pretty much everything."

The startled silence on the other end recaptured her attention. "Well, not everything," she amended. "He can't remember the last mission."

"I see," said Jason, who sounded alarmed just the same. "But he has memories prior to that?"

"Yes," she said, wondering what he'd done that would make him so nervous.

A ragged breath sounded in her ear. "You know, Helen,"

Miller added, his tone tense and high-pitched, "he'll never make you happy."

Helen made a face at the phone. Jason's inference was even more unwelcome now than it had been before. "That may be true," she acknowledged, disliking him intensely, "but then, neither will you. I'll pass along your message from the commander. Bye." She slapped the phone shut. "What a nerd!"

"Who was that?"

Gabe's quiet question startled her into dropping the phone. It clattered onto the bench and fell between the slats. "Lieutenant Commander Miller," she admitted, ducking down to get it. "Do you always sneak up on people?"

"I saw you looking for me a second ago," he said, rounding the bench. He stood in front of her with his arms crossed, his held cocked suspiciously to one side.

"I was," she said. "Jason called to convey a message from your commander. Get this: the FBI found the stuff you e-mailed from North Korea!" She put her phone into her purse and smiled up at him, expecting him to be thrilled. "Lovitt wants to see you this coming weekend," she added. "He's out of town right now. Maybe he'll want you back on the team now, especially with your memories returning."

To her consternation, Gabe flinched instead of smiling. He startled Helen by abruptly sitting down beside her, a hand clasped over his right eye.

"Honey, are you okay?" she asked with concern. He'd sat so quickly, it was almost like he thought he might faint.

Gabe peeked at her from under his hand and cast her a wry smile. "Honey?" he retorted. "I'm a honey now?" He chuckled with satisfaction and then groaned. "God, what is it about that man that gives me a headache?"

"Who, Lovitt?"

"Miller."

"Oh, him. Yeah, he gives me a headache, too," she admitted.

"Why does he have your number?" Gabe asked, rubbing his temple as he gazed at her through his lashes.

Helen sighed. "It was his idea that I get a cell phone in the first place. Something about Mallory needing to get hold of me."

"Yeah, right." Gabe flinched again. "Damn it!"

"Are you going to be okay? I think I have some aspirin in my purse." She started riffling through it.

"We need to head home," Gabe told her, his tone harsher than the situation merited.

"Okay," Helen agreed, truly worried for him. Was he starting to freak out on her or did his head just hurt? "We've stayed long enough. Did you get to see some of your old instructors?"

"Yes," he said, grimacing.

"Mallory!" Helen called her daughter from the end of the boardwalk. "Time to go!"

"Easy," Gabe implored.

"Sorry." She tried to help him to his feet, but he shook her off. To make amends, he grabbed her hand and held it tightly all the way to the car. Fortunately, they'd packed their bags this morning and stowed them in the trunk.

She would call her mother and tell them not to expect them for lunch.

They drove straight into a rainstorm. Gabe stared through the blurred windshield at the highway ahead. The lines dividing the lanes of Interstate 95 seemed to bleed one into the next, into the next, creating a streaming effect, though it was probably his vision playing tricks on him. He seemed caught between sleep and wakefulness, unable to commit to either one as Helen drove them home.

What was wrong with him? News that the FBI had found his files ought to have made him ecstatic. His yearlong captivity in hell hadn't been for nothing. He'd made himself look good, not only for escaping, but for bringing back enough intelligence to put a dent into North Korea's terrorist-driven activities.

Lovitt wanted to talk to him this weekend. Like Helen said, with his memories returning, it couldn't be long before he was put on active duty again.

So why had just the mention of Miller's name given him this pounding headache? He'd taken his daily dose of Dexamphetamine rather than Helen's aspirin to help combat it, but it only seemed to dull his senses. Given Commander Troy's misgivings, on top of Sebastian's and Ernest Forrester's, he couldn't afford to walk around like a zombie. He needed to stay sharp in the event that he was still being targeted.

He'd felt sharp as a razor yesterday—why not today?

The answer came to him with burst of clarity: *Because he'd forgotten the Dexamphetamine, that was why.*

Not only had he felt better without it, he'd recovered years of his life in one night. He remembered nearly everything, with the exception of the mission-gone-wrong. The most crucial piece of his memory eluded him, still.

Struggling to reason clearly, Gabe stared at Helen's slim fingers, coiled so trustingly in his. She cast him a worried glance, no doubt wondering at his continued depression. He dredged up a smile for her, then reached into his right pocket and pulled out the narrow pillbox to give the Dexamphetamine a considering look.

"Stuff makes me sleepy," he commented out loud.

She slanted him a frown. "It's supposed to keep you awake."

He jammed the pills back into his pocket. "Doesn't work," he said, dropping his head limply against the headrest.

"Close your eyes and take a nap," she encouraged. "We'll be home in a couple hours." She peeked over her shoulder at Mallory who was engrossed in the novel Gabe had started with her last week.

Gabe turned his head also, giving Mallory a quick look of approval. His gaze went past her, out the rear window. There, an unmarked police car, same model as the Chrysler that had nearly run him down, was tailgating them.

Gabe straightened in his seat, shaking off his drugged haze. "How long has that car been behind us?" he asked, his heart beating faster.

Helen glanced into the rearview mirror. "I'm not sure," she said, studying it. "Is it a cop? I'm not speeding."

He stared hard at the driver, but the wet weather and the windshield wipers kept the man's face indiscernible. Still, Gabe didn't like the situation. "Pull off at the next rest stop," he advised. He reached down and withdrew the Glock 23 from the holster strapped to his calf.

Helen gasped at the sight of his weapon. "What are you doing?" she asked sharply, her hands gripping the steering wheel. "Where did you get that?"

"Calm down." He gave her a steady look. "It's just a precaution. There's some unsettled business going on, that's all. I don't want you involved in it."

He saw the color drain from her face. "What are you talking about, 'unfinished business'?" she asked.

He checked the ammunition magazine and slipped the weapon out of sight again, deliberating how much to tell her.

He didn't want Helen worried about him, but at the same time, it was in her best interest to be informed. She had Mallory to think of, after all.

He positioned himself against the door, so he could see out the back and the front of the car at the same time. "Someone tried to get rid of me in Pyongyang," he explained, as casually as possible so as not to overwhelm Mallory, who was staring at him, not blinking. "They've tried again more recently, and I don't think they've given up yet."

Mallory slipped lower in the seat, so that her head was below the window.

"Stay there," Gabe said with a nod.

"Okay."

"Stop scaring her," Helen said, on a sharper note. He looked at her, surprised.

"You're telling me that someone has tried to kill you and they're going to try again," she repeated.

She didn't have to put it quite that melodramatically. "It has to do with weapons that were disappearing before the teams could get to them," he explained. "I might have realized who it was and confronted them. They're afraid I'll remember now."

She divided her attention between him and the highway. The angle of her eyebrows made it clear she didn't believe him.

Great, his wife thought he was paranoid, too. "You can ask your dad," he said with some annoyance. "He's the one who put the theory together."

She shook her head as if to clear it. "Okay," she said, with an intonation that meant, *Now you've really lost your mind.* A second later she added, "There's a rest stop in two miles."

He'd already seen the sign. "Pull off. We'll see if this guy follows us."

The next two miles took an eternity. The only sound in their vehicle was that of the rain and the slapping of the windshield wipers as they tried and failed to clear the glass. Helen had stopped asking questions, but her gaze flicked repeatedly to the rearview mirror.

"He's following," she said as she pulled onto the ramp.

"Go ahead and park the car," he said, infusing reassurance into his tone. "Right up front with everyone else."

She did as he said, pulling into a slot between an empty economy car and a pickup truck with a dog in the back. With the engine still running, they watched the navy Chrysler creep past and nose into a parking place farther down.

"Stay in the car," Gabe said, easing open the passenger door. If he was going to be targeted in public, he wasn't going to jeopardize his family in the process. He slipped into the warm rain, pulling the Glock free of his pant leg at the same time and tucking it under his shirt, which he hastily tugged loose.

With long, purposeful strides and keeping one eye trained on the motionless Chrysler, he crossed a grassy area devoid of bystanders. He stepped behind a tree and waited, watching the vehicle for any sign of movement.

He was not afraid. If anything, he was in attack mode, ready to take down his opponent and force some answers to his questions, to discover once and for all who his enemy was. Even his head had stopped pounding.

At last, the door of the Chrysler opened. A leg appeared, clad in navy slacks. Then a silvery head, a frail hand. Gabe could not have been more surprised when an older gentleman unfolded from the car, fumbling to open an umbrella.

The adrenaline drained out of him, leaving him faintly nauseated. He glanced toward his own vehicle and saw, even through the blurry window, Helen's look of relief. She shook her head and rolled her eyes.

With chagrin, Gabe knelt and stowed away his weapon in a movement too quick for the casual eye to see. Then he marched toward the public rest room, irritated with himself, angry for putting Helen and Mallory through unnecessary turmoil.

Standing at the sink a moment later, he eyed the Dexamphetamine pills one last time before upending them. They slid one by one down the drain and out of sight. He felt better for watching them go.

There was nothing wrong with him—nothing that time wouldn't heal, at any rate. He sure as hell didn't need those pills making him sleepy and messing with his mind.

He lifted his gaze and caught his reflection in the mirror. The grave-eyed warrior looking back at him seemed to be telling him something.

The driver of the Chrysler hadn't been a hit man—true enough. But he could have been. In his gut, Gabe knew it was only a matter of time before he was targeted again. There were too many loose strings, as Commander Troy had said.

What if the enemy *had* come after him? What if he'd decided to take Gabe's family out for convenience sake? On a lonely stretch of highway, all it would take was a sudden sideswipe to send their vehicle plummeting toward the trees. Helen didn't have the training needed to keep the car on the road. And Gabe wasn't supposed to drive.

He shuddered, picturing the tangle of steel, the bloody result of a high-speed impact.

As long as he was with them, Helen and Mallory weren't safe.

Gabe nodded at his reflection, acknowledging the unspoken message. Yes, he needed to remove himself from their lives for the time being. The possibility that they might become involved in this vendetta was too awful to accept.

Helen wouldn't like it—especially after last night. Hell, *he* wouldn't like it. He recalled her hesitant acceptance of him with a pang so powerful it took his breath. He relived the moment of her surrender with a groan. Nothing had been more satisfying than waking up with Helen in his arms this morning, making love to her again, as soft morning sunlight stole across their bed.

He would have to give it all up—at least for a while. The thought was nearly intolerable, but the alternative was worse.

He loved them too much to put them in harm's way.

"What are you doing?" Helen asked, pausing at the study door. She watched with a cramp in her stomach as Gabe pulled clothing from his dresser and dropped it into a duffel bag. "We can just roll your chest back into the bedroom," she suggested, hearing uncertainty in her voice. He looked like he was planning to go somewhere.

Gabe dropped the half-filled bag to the floor. "I need to talk to you, Helen," he said, his expression somber. He gestured for her to take a seat on the sofa.

She inched into the room, her feet suddenly leaden. Ever since the incident on the highway this morning, she'd been struggling with her doubts. Just as she'd suspected, Gabe's trauma had taken a worse toll on him than he admitted. His ordeal at the hands of terrorists had left a deep streak of paranoia coursing through him. Not that she blamed him one bit. But the reality of his mental state put a damper on the wonderful new beginning they had made last night.

She sat tensely on the couch, her hands clasped in her lap. He eased down beside her, his jaw muscles flexing. "I'm going to stay with Master Chief," he told her. "Just for a while; till this thing blows over."

She tried to think over the pain that crashed through her. "What thing?" she demanded. "The killer at the rest stop was just an old man. Why do you think someone's after you?"

"I'm not the only one who thinks it," he said deliberately. "An agent at the DIA, the master chief, and your father all believe the same thing. Somewhere in my head is the name of the person stealing weapons ahead of the SEALs. That person left me in Pyongyang to die. He wants me dead now."

Helen heaved a sigh of confusion. She didn't know what to believe; it sounded so far-fetched. But if her father thought it was true, then perhaps it was. "I don't see how leaving here will make any difference," she insisted. "If you're worried, just get your men to protect you."

Gabe shook his head. "I'm not worried about me, Helen," he told her. "I can take care of myself."

This was said with confidence so like the old Gabe's that she had to smile.

"It's you and Mallory I'm worried about. As long as I'm close to you, your lives are in danger. You've been fine without me this past year. It's not you that's being targeted, it's me. I need to remove myself."

"But what if the threat's just in your head?" she suggested gently. "Dr. Terrien says that—"

"Dr. Terrien doesn't know *shit*," Gabe interrupted. He pushed to his feet, crossing to his bureau. "He has tried to convince me—and he's clearly convinced *you* that I am freaking paranoid. I know what I remember, Helen, and I know when something isn't right. You can believe it or not, it really doesn't matter."

Helen was startled to hear his voice crack. Obviously, it did matter. He wanted her to believe him. She stood and crossed over to him, putting her arms around his stiff shoulders. She wanted to believe him, yet at the same time, she didn't. The possibility that someone wanted Gabe dead conflicted with the hopefulness of their reunion; it competed with the possibility of newfound intimacy.

But when Gabe made his mind up, Helen knew it was useless to try to change it. Tears of regret pushed into her eyes as she held him. "I just wanted us to be a normal family," she admitted.

He sighed, squeezing her as if to absorb her sorrow. "I'm sorry," he lamented. "This isn't what I want, either. But this is how it's going to be until I'm sure I'm not a liability."

He released her suddenly and crossed to the window, bending one of the blinds to peer outside. Helen heard a car go by. She watched him regard it with suspicion, and her heart ached for him. How could he not be paranoid when he exhibited this type of behavior? Tears of pity rushed into her eyes. The past had been cruel enough to him already. Why couldn't it just let him be!

He turned, catching sight of her tears. "Please don't cry," he begged. He crossed to his dresser, yanking out T-shirts and socks and stuffing them in the bag with haste. "I have to go."

"How will you get to your appointment tomorrow?" she asked, thinking that maybe Dr. Terrien could help him.

"I'll take a taxi." By his curt reply, it didn't even sound like he intended to see his psychiatrist.

"You'll be reprimanded if you don't go." The military was persnickety when it came to mandatory medical appointments.

He gave her a ghastly smile. "They've taken my job. What the hell else can they do to me?"

With that, he zipped shut the duffel bag and slung it over

his shoulder. "I *will* be back," he promised. He took two steps forward and planted a searing kiss on her lips.

She was too disheartened to respond.

He turned his back on her and left.

Helen heard the front door close. She supposed she ought to offer him a ride to Sebastian's house. The man lived on the side of Sandbridge. But no, she wouldn't be party to his leaving. Mallory would think it was her idea.

Oh, Mallory! Helen shook her head, letting the tears fall. What was she going to tell her daughter?

Mallory dried Priscilla's paws with the towel that hung in the laundry room. Hearing the front door open and close, she rehung the towel and urged the dog up the steps, through the drizzle. Gabe appeared on the landing where the steps turned. He had a big, Navy-issue duffel bag slung across one shoulder. Mallory took one look at the bag and froze.

He descended the remaining steps, his footfalls silent. The look in his eyes as he bore down on her confirmed her worst fears.

She could tell he was leaving.

"Mal," he said, pausing before her. He reached for her shoulders but she wrenched them away. *No!* She didn't want him telling her the bad news.

"I have to go away for a while," he said, dropping his hands to his sides. "I want you to be good for Mom. I'll call often and check up on you."

"Where are you going?" she asked, amazed that her voice could sound so steady.

"I'm going to stay with Master Chief," he replied. "That way you and Mom are safe."

"Safe from whom?" she scoffed, hiding her pain behind anger. "An old man?"

He just looked at her, his gaze shadowed. "I want you to finish the book we started," he told her, changing subjects. "And read the other ones before school starts."

School wouldn't start for another two weeks. "How long will you be gone?" she asked, fighting an undertow of despair.

"I don't know," he said. "Now promise me you'll look out for your mother. And don't do anything stupid. You know what I mean."

She ignored him as he put his hand on her damp hair and kissed her forehead. Then he turned to negotiate the last few steps.

At the last instant, Mallory whirled and threw herself against his back, latching her arms around him.

Her heart slung itself against her ribs. She wanted to beg him to come back soon. But pain had a death grip on her vocal cords and she couldn't say a word.

He placed his hands over hers and squeezed them. "Take care," he said gruffly. Then he pried himself loose and without a backward glance, stepped off the stairs and started for the street.

Eyes burning, Mallory watched him walk away, his long strides taking him toward the bend in the road. He stepped into puddles as if he didn't see them. The showers had let up, but the sky was still an ominous gray. Anvil clouds surged in from the ocean, promising still more rain.

Helen had walked to the far end of the beach before realizing she'd walked clear to the master chief's cottage.

She stopped abruptly, ignoring Priscilla's tug on the leash. The sun sank lower, turning the water to pearl gray and oyster pink. The sand locked her into place at the surf's edge. This was as far as she would go.

Priscilla whined, wanting to join the family playing Frisbee a short distance away. Helen gazed up at the dark windows of Sebastian's A-frame home and wondered if Gabe could see her, if it would make any difference to him if he did. Two days had never seemed so endless.

She was glad now that she hadn't promised him forever. If she had, his decision to leave would feel twice as awful. She tried not to think about herself. It was Gabe who was suffering. His scars ran deeper than the surface scars she'd kissed. His captivity had infected his mind, making him blind to what was real; causing him to invent imagined fears, imagined foes.

At least that was Dr. Terrien's assessment. She'd called him yesterday to warn him that Gabe would likely miss his appointment. When she'd explained why, the doctor's response was to reassure her. *He lived with more horror than you or I can imagine, Helen. His mind is accustomed to constant threat. Just give him time.*

Time she could give. Her heart was another story.

It still troubled her that Gabe seemed so certain someone had reason to kill him. What if he was right? What if his life really was in danger?

She'd called her father to get his opinion.

He's left you? Oliver Troy inquired in alarm.

He thinks his life's in danger, Dad. I want to know what you think.

Her father had hesitated. *This isn't the kind of thing one discusses over an insecure phone line. If your husband suspects a threat, then the threat is real.*

It couldn't be. She'd hung up the phone more uncertain than ever. Gabe had to be imagining things. The alternative was too terrible to imagine: her husband hunted down by a ruthless killer?

God, if something happened to him a second time . . . it would devastate her!

She'd considered calling the master chief and asking his advice; after all, Gabe was staying with him. But every time she went to do just that, she hesitated, fearing she would say something that jeopardized Gabe's chances of returning to the team.

His career meant more to him than anything. How ironic, she thought, mired ankle-deep in the sand, that Gabe's career continued to steal him away from her—this time for the mental toll that it had taken. Still, she never wanted to see him struck from the team, not for any reason. Being a SEAL was his reason for being; it was what he did best. She refused to imagine anything less for him.

Rousing from her thoughts, Helen was startled to find that the sun had dropped behind the rooftops, casting irregular shadows onto the shore.

"Come on, Pris," she called, urging the dog to head home.

Only it wasn't really home now, was it? Mallory was there, of course, as quiet and unsmiling as she used to be. Poor Mallory, she hadn't guarded her heart as Helen had. In her naiveté, she'd still believed in happily-ever-after.

Chapter Fifteen

A sharp rapping at the door wrenched Gabe's gaze from the morning paper. The knock seemed to echo off the exposed timbers of Master Chief's pointed ceiling. It was charged with purpose.

Gabe picked the semiautomatic off the table and slipped it into the waistline of his jeans. Master Chief was out back, cutting through the surf in his morning swim. It was 7 A.M., a little early for visitors. Gabe went to answer the door.

Helen? he wondered, his heart beating faster at the possibility. At the same time, he didn't want her stopping by. He'd put them both through the wringer by leaving, and one parting, filled with misunderstandings, was enough.

A peek through the eyehole revealed a beautiful, dark-haired woman. A friend of Master Chief's, maybe? Gabe cautiously opened the door.

It took him a moment to recognize her. Dancer-slim, the woman wore her long black hair in a ponytail. She was dressed in a vivid orange leotard, and a matching tie-dye skirt. He blinked at the canary brightness of her. No, she was definitely not a friend of Master Chief's. He'd never go for such a colorful woman. She was Leila Eser, Helen's best friend and proprietress of a ballet studio.

"Hi," he said, curious to know why she was here. Had Helen sent her?

The woman ran her dark, exotically tilted eyes over his rumpled shirt. He hadn't shaved that morning. "Do you remember me?" she asked, one elegant eyebrow rising over the other.

"Leila Eser," he said. "You're Helen's friend."

"That's right." Her gaze went beyond him, into the house.

"Would you like to come in?" Gabe asked, since she seemed to expect it. As she swept into the austerely furnished living room, he couldn't help but notice how out of place she looked, like a colorful canary in a drab, wooden cage.

She seemed to have similar thoughts. With an ill-at-ease expression on her face, she darted a look about the place.

"Can I offer you some coffee?" he asked, tamping down his curiosity long enough to be civil.

"Please," she said, and he moved toward the wall of custom cabinets to pour her a mug of Starbucks. Master Chief was particular about his coffee. "Black is fine," she added, before he could ask.

Accepting the mug from him, she took a hesitant sip. Her eyebrows rose in approval of the brew, and then she fixed her dark-as-night eyes on him, and he knew he was in trouble.

"Helen doesn't know I'm here," she began, giving him an uncomfortably direct look.

"How'd you know where to find me?" he cut in.

"I know Sebastian," she retorted coolly.

She knew Master Chief? By his first name? Thrown off balance by her answer, he resolved to shut up and listen.

She moved gracefully around the clunky furniture and

chose a perch on Master Chief's favorite armchair. Gabe followed suit, sitting across from her on the couch.

"Let me be frank by telling you straight off that I never liked you."

Her candid admission struck him dumb. He blinked in surprise, harboring no such feelings for her. In fact, he'd always admired Leila for her unswerving devotion to his wife.

"Helen tells me you've changed," Leila continued, assessing him through the steam of her coffee.

"I hope so," he said fervently.

"Then why are you hurting her?" the woman demanded. "I've never seen her this unhappy."

Oh, hell. Gabe rubbed his stubbled jaw with agitation. "I'm not doing this to hurt her," he said through his teeth.

She gave him a look that was nearly sympathetic. "Then you need to keep your appointments with the doctor," she advised. "You're sending the wrong message by not going."

A bitter smile seized his lips. Apparently, he hadn't convinced Helen that his precautions were necessary. She still thought he was making up threats; that he was paranoid. "Tell her I'll go to my appointment today," he said. Anything to make Helen happy.

Leila was putting down her coffee cup when the glass door beside them slid open. Master Chief froze at the threshold, his lean, muscled body rimmed with sunshine, water still glinting on his tanned skin. He wore a pair of tiny swim trunks, a towel around his neck, and a look of utter stupefaction.

Gabe had *never* seen that look on Master Chief's face before. The man stepped into the house and softly slid the door shut. Not a word had come from him yet. He put out a hand as if to keep Leila Eser from flying off her perch. "Don't move," he said, corroborating Gabe's guess.

His eyes, darker than Leila's, but every bit as mysterious, never left her. He tugged the towel off his shoulders and wrapped it hurriedly around his waist, his movements uncharacteristically clumsy.

Leila ignored the man's orders and rose to her feet. She approached Sebastian with feline grace and handed him her mug. As he reached out and took it, the towel at his hips slipped to the floor.

Leila whirled, perfuming the air with some exotic scent. She walked straight to the door, ponytail twitching enticingly. "Have a good morning, gentlemen. I'll see myself out."

Master Chief exploded into action, but it was already too late. The door had shut behind her. He reached for the doorknob.

"Sebastian!" Gabe called him back. "You don't want to go outside like that." It was all he could do not to break into great gales of laughter.

Sebastian looked down at himself. He'd be the laughingstock of the neighborhood venturing forth this way. He hit the door hard with the heel of his hand. "How do you know her?" he demanded, turning flashing dark eyes at Gabe.

Gabe had never been more entertained in his life. "She's a friend of my wife's." He was getting cramps in his cheeks from trying not to smile.

Master Chief strode back into the living room and snatched up his towel. "What's her name?" he asked, fastening it around his hips.

"You don't even know her name?" The grin that threatened to split Gabe's face got the better of him. "She knows yours."

"Just tell me her name, sir!" Sebastian snarled.

This was priceless. Master Chief was crazy in love with Leila Eser.

Gabe told him her name, first and last, and watched his senior enlisted officer whisper it like an incantation—not once, not twice, but three times.

"Where does she live? What does she do?" demanded the man. His black eyes gleamed like hot burning coals.

Gabe had always sensed that Master Chief had this kind of intensity in him. Yet up until this moment, the man had been control personified. He never raised his voice above a murmur. He could think calmly in the deadliest of situations. It was clear, however, that he'd gone completely ape-shit over Leila Eser.

"Wait a minute," said Gabe, holding up his hands in a time-out gesture. "My turn. How come Leila knows your name and you don't even know hers?"

"I know her," Master Chief insisted. He seethed with energy, prowling about his home like a big, black cat.

"What, like in the biblical sense?"

Master Chief didn't comment. "I've been looking for her," he admitted, running a palm over the seat she'd been sitting in.

"Let me guess. You had some sort of rendezvous with her and she took off after that?" He had to bite the insides of his cheeks to keep from howling.

Master Chief took scathing notice of Gabe's amusement. "You think this is funny?" he asked with dangerous calm.

Gabe had to turn around to hide the tears in his eyes. "Funny? Hell, no." It was hilarious. They were perfect for each other, intense and fearless. Yet at the same time they were nothing alike. Master Chief preferred muted colors and drove broken-down classics, never having the time to restore them properly. If Leila Eser owned a car, Gabe would bet his savings that it was new, fast, and cherry red.

"You know where she works?" Master Chief asked with determination.

"Sure. If you drive me to my appointment today, I'll show you her studio," Gabe bargained. "You can visit her while I chat with my psychologist." Recalling Dr. Terrien's opinion of him, some of Gabe's good humor fled. But he would go to his appointment today because Helen wanted him to.

First things first, however. This morning he was planning to pick up the phone and chat with Ernest Forrester, a man whose investigations might shed some light on Gabe's situation. Forrester had been out of town for the past two days and was due back in the office this morning.

Gabe glanced at his watch. It was nearing 8 A.M.

"Call," said Sebastian, guessing Gabe's intent. They'd discussed their next move over coffee.

The subject of Leila Eser was put on hold for the moment.

Gabe lifted the phone and tapped out the number he'd memorized. On the other end, the phone rang and rang. Just as he was about to end the call, a woman answered. "Hannah Geary," she said, sounding stressed.

"Geary, this is Lieutenant Renault, U.S. Navy. Is Ernest Forrester in the office yet?"

A lengthy pause answered his request. "Lieutenant, I'm sorry to be the bearer of bad news," the woman said in a strangled voice, "but Ernie was killed in a car accident while he was out of town. It was a hit-and-run. No one's been charged yet."

The woman's distress was the first thing that penetrated Gabe's consciousness. Then the actual finality of Forrester's life. Then the implication of a hit-and-run. Gabe sucked in a breath. Was it possible Forrester's death—if it had been intentional—had something to do with Gabe's own situation?

"I'm sorry," he said, meaning it. It was hard to wrap his mind around the sudden tragedy. Christ, he'd spoken to Forrester just last Saturday! "Did you work closely with him?"

"We were very close," she admitted, her voice cracking. "I know about your case," she added.

She did? "Do you think Ernie's work might have had something to do with the accident?" he gently probed.

She lowered her voice to a conspiring whisper. "Let me put it this way. No sooner did we hear about his death than a bunch of suits came in and emptied out his files. They even pulled the hard drive from his computer."

That did sound suspicious.

"I want you to know I intend to pick up where my partner left off," she added with feisty determination.

That didn't make Gabe feel any better. If Forrester had been eliminated for getting too close to the weapons-nabber, Gabe didn't want the same thing happening to his partner. She sounded all of twenty-something. "Look, I think you should let it go and lay low for a while."

His advice prompted a bristling silence, but Gabe wasn't about to recall it. Ernie Forrester was dead. The timing was too suspicious given the man's determination to unravel the mystery behind Gabe's disappearance.

Jesus, this whole affair would be over if he could just remember!

"If you need any help," he continued, "or if something else comes up, I want you to call me." He relayed Sebastian's home number. "You might want to call from a neutral location," he added.

"Got it." *I'm not an idiot,* her tone implied.

Admiring her tenacity, Gabe hung up and lifted his gaze

to Master Chief's frown. "Forrester's been killed in a hit-and-run," he said grimly. "That was his partner, some kid who smells a rat and wants to go after it. I hope she's smart enough to leave well enough alone."

"Worry about yourself," Sebastian advised.

"Why worry? I've got the Sandman covering my six."

Sandman was Sebastian's code name, for the simple reason that he put tangos fast asleep—permanently.

"What time is your appointment?" the master chief asked, switching subjects.

"Four o'clock." Gabe dragged a hand over his jaw. Should he talk to his psychologist? Forrester had warned him against it, and now Forrester was dead.

Did the affable Dr. Terrien have Gabe's best interest at heart? Or was he a conveyor of information, a hound sent to sniff out what the patient remembered?

He pictured the doctor reporting his most intimate thoughts to a third party. Nah, Terrien didn't have the look of a conscienceless traitor. Besides, it was chiefly due to him that Helen had given him a second chance.

Shrugging inwardly, Gabe consigned himself to another counseling session. After all, he hadn't recovered all of his memories yet. And his personal life was in shambles.

Sebastian pushed open the glass door of Expressions: A Dance Studio, and promptly set off an electronic chime that played a refrain from *The Nutcracker*.

To his relief, the first room was empty of people, giving him a moment to steady his erratically beating heart and wipe the sweat from his palms. The room was painted turquoise and decorated in dancewear, leaping, prancing, and pirouetting along the walls. Each leotard was a shade of neon green, ultraviolet, or canary yellow. Feeling dazed, Sebastian took it all in, in a slow turn.

The first thing he heard when the chime stopped ringing was her husky voice counting out steps over piano music. He whirled toward it and found himself peering down a hallway toward a partially opened door.

"And one, and two, and three and turn! And one, and two, and three and bend! Now stop. Shoulders back. Eyes here. Curtsy. Where are your smiles? Much better!"

A smattering of applause followed these instructions. Leila's voice melded into the sea of excited chatter. The door flew open and out poured a wave of little girls, eyes bright with accomplishment, cheeks pink from exertion.

Tiny legs in leotards, ballet slippers, and tutus. To Sebastian, they looked like fairies, an entirely unfamiliar species, whimsical and otherworldly. As they skipped out of the studio, one of them raised her gray-green eyes at him and offered him the sweetest smile he'd ever seen.

He was still reeling from that smile when he glanced up and found Leila poised at the door, eyes flashing, mouth pursed in disapproval that he should dare interrupt her afternoon routine.

"I don't have time to talk," she informed him. "I have a group of teenagers coming in at four-thirty." She spun on her toes and disappeared behind the door.

Sebastian went after her. He hadn't expected this to be easy.

He found her sweeping the hardwood floor with a soft-bristled broom. She wore a form-fitting leotard with a gossamer skirt around her hips that did nothing to conceal the slender length of her thighs. He wanted to throw a towel over her.

"Why did you come here?" she demanded, seeing him at the door. She swept the length of the room, pushing the broom as she went.

He walked directly into her path. "You used me," he growled, not letting her get by him.

"I have work to do. Kindly step aside."

He snatched the broom from her grasp, instead. "I'll do the work," he said. "You can do the explaining." He stalked away from her, pushing the broom as he went. "For three months I have looked for you," he berated. "You left without explanation. Without even telling me your name!" He pivoted expertly and bore down on her again, not a speck of dirt lost in the process.

She stood in the same spot with her arms akimbo and her chin in the air. She looked so striking that he wanted to toss aside the broom and grab her. He wanted to punish her with a kiss that would leave her shaking and trembling the way she'd left him that perfect May night.

He'd cherished the memory for months, now. A cool breeze, a full moon glinting on the ocean's waves, and a mysterious woman, dancing in his arms on the terrace of the Shifting Sands nightclub. All seduction and smoldering glances, he had fallen over his feet to get to her first. To his amazement, she'd accepted his advances. He'd swept her to his home where he had spent all night putting out her fire.

Apparently, he'd done his job too well. Toward the wee hours of dawn, she'd slipped away while he slept. And she hadn't even left a note.

That night had changed him forever. Gone was the fear of what he would do when he retired from the SEALs. He was going to have a wife and kids, a vision he'd never pictured for himself. It was a revelation. Yes, he'd have a wife exactly like his dream lover and a little girl, like the one who'd smiled at him in the hallway.

He stopped less than a foot from Leila's tense form, devouring her with his gaze but not touching.

She was breathing hard, he noticed. Clearly she was not as immune to him as she would have him believe. "What's your excuse, *bonita*?" he inquired, returning to his lecture. "Or do you always use men so callously?"

"It's no more than men do to women every day," she countered, her black eyes glittering.

"Not all men," he corrected softly. "You know what I think? I think you are a coward. Only cowards do not give their names."

He was goading her and he knew it. Yet he wanted to wound her with his words, because she had done worse to him. She had made him crazy with lust and then she'd disappeared.

"You're afraid of intimacy," he added, moving close enough to smell her jasmine-scented skin. He took a long deep breath, unsettling her enough to make her take a step back.

"And what do you know of intimacy?" she hissed. "Have you ever been married?"

That shut him up. No, he hadn't. He'd been married to his job. It wouldn't have been right to give his best to the SEALs and expect a wife to make do with leftovers. "No," he admitted.

"Have you ever had your heart ripped out by the one person you trusted most?"

She was trembling now, reminding him of a butterfly, and he knew with a sudden pang that she'd been married to the wrong man entirely, someone who had not seen what he saw in her right now. Longing to comfort her, he looped an arm around her and pulled her against him. He gripped the broom in his other hand, a link to sanity. She had a gift for making him lose his mind.

He couldn't tell which was stiffer, the broom handle or the woman, but at least she wasn't resisting him.

"*Ah, querida*, I didn't know," he said soothingly. "I am sorry." Bit by bit she relaxed against him, her body conforming to his, softening with the heat that grew between them. He put his nose to her hair and gave an inward groan. Her fragrance recalled that magical night so vividly!

She had a perfect shell of an ear, one that begged to be ravaged by his tongue. Her breasts were flattened against his chest, the way they'd been when they made love. The woman was exquisite. She was also vulnerable, delicate. He would take his time with her this time.

"Will you have dinner with me tonight?" he asked.

She struggled to free herself, but he held her fast. "I'm working tonight," she said quickly.

"Tomorrow then," he insisted, loving the feel of her small hands against his chest.

"I work tomorrow as well."

He kept a lid on his frustrations. "I am only asking for dinner," he assured her. "I promise I won't touch you."

"How can I believe that?" she scoffed. "You're holding me against my will right now!"

"Against your will?" he asked with disbelief.

"Yes!"

"Then you wouldn't want me to put my lips on yours and kiss you until your legs give out?" he asked, looking her straight in the eye.

"No," she answered faintly. Yet her knees seemed to wobble, and a pulse beat frantically in that tender spot at the base of her neck.

"Very well." It cost him a great deal, but he released her, mollified to see her waver on her feet. "Pick a night," he demanded inexorably.

Leila wrung her hands. "Just dinner?" she queried, her gaze dropping regretfully to his mouth.

"Just dinner. I give you my word."

Out in the hallway the chime went off, and the sounds of teenage laughter heralded the next batch of students. Leila glanced, distracted, toward the door. "I'm free on Friday," she told him.

"Friday, then," he said, taking the offer and running with it. "Seven o'clock? Where should I pick you up?"

"Right here," she said. "I have to ask you to leave now. I need to get ready for the next lesson." She held her hand out for the broom, and he relinquished it, giving no indication of the triumph that blazed in his chest.

"Until then, *querida*." He let his gaze drift over her scantily clad figure. Then he turned away, trying not to strut as he walked to the door.

The teenaged girls in the front room fell silent as he strode past them en route to the exit. They gaped at his lean, dark looks.

Not bad for a man of forty, he thought, pushing his way out into the heat.

The sight of his Ford Falcon still covered in primer with a crooked front fender, drew him up short. He couldn't begin to picture Leila in the passenger seat. He would have to come up with alternate wheels. His car wasn't good enough for her.

Maybe Westy would lend him his sapphire-blue 300ZX. A hot, little sports car suited Leila Eser far better. Yes, yes.

Just thinking of her in Westy's car made him as horny as a toad.

But he'd meant what he said. It might kill him to do it, but he was going to treat Leila like an icon of the Virgin Mary on Friday night. They were going to enter into this relationship slowly. Because as heavenly as Leila was, she'd once been devastated by love. And if he intended to make her his bride, he had to first put her heart back together.

From his usual straight-back chair, Gabe studied Dr. Terrien's expression for any sign of duplicity. The man had greeted him with affable delight and trailed him down the hall to their meeting room.

"Tell me everything," the doctor invited, looking straight into Gabe's eyes. "Your wife says you recovered most of your memories earlier this week."

With a stab of betrayal, Gabe imagined the doctor and Helen chatting behind his back. "That's right," he confirmed. "We went to Annapolis to visit her parents, and the dream I had there must have switched a trigger or something. I remembered everything, actually." He decided at the last second to stretch the truth as a sort of experiment. Let the doctor believe he knew *everything*, then wait for the consequences. If someone came after him immediately, Gabe's suspicions would be justified.

Dr. Terrien regarded him with his shaggy eyebrows raised. "Well, wonderful!" he exclaimed. He seemed sincere in his praise. "It's only been, what, a couple weeks. That's tremendous! Tell me all about it. Start with the mission. What do you remember there?"

Gabe assumed a reflective posture. It was curious that the doc would suddenly want to talk about the mission-gone-wrong. Or was that just a sensible place to start?

He concocted a story based on what he could recall of the explosion, viewed from the back of a truck. "I was keeping an eye on the fourth missile," he related, "hunkered down behind a pallet of barrels, when suddenly I looked up and this tango was standing over me."

"Tango?" the doctor interrupted, betraying his civilian background.

"Terrorist. He knocked me in the face with the butt of a rifle"—like Gabe would ever be caught unaware like that—"and it must have rendered me unconscious. I was bound with electrical tape and dumped into the back of a pickup. Next thing I heard was the warehouse exploding. I have no idea what caused it."

"Fascinating," Dr. Terrien murmured, shaking his head sympathetically.

Gabe then recounted his stay at the mountaintop compound. He highlighted his friendship with Jun Yeup and explained how the young man had aided his escape. He mentioned helping himself to the information in the computer room and forwarding the intelligence to the FBI. He added that his efforts had convinced Lovitt to meet with him the day after tomorrow.

"So what do you think?" Gabe added. He watched for the smallest nuance that might betray the doctor's thoughts.

"I think you're a hero," Dr. Terrien replied, admiration shining in his eyes. "You deserve the highest commendation for everything you've been through. You really are an incredible man, Gabriel." The light in his eyes dimmed with consternation. "Your wife tells me that you think your life is in danger," he added.

Gabe's heart felt like it was folding over on itself. Why didn't Helen believe him? Were his convictions that farfetched or was the truth simply too awful to imagine?

"Someone tried to kill me in Pyongyang," Gabe said baldly. "I have reason to believe they'll try it again."

"But you said it was a terrorist who tried to kill you," the doctor reminded him.

He'd been caught in a lie already. "All right," he admitted, shifting in his seat. "The truth is I still can't remember the mission. But what if it wasn't a tango?" He thought of Forrester, killed in a hit-and-run. "What if it was someone I knew, someone I'd dug up some dirt about and he didn't want me ratting on him. Suppose he decided to eliminate me, only it didn't work. I survived, thanks to a couple of locals who dragged my ass out of the warehouse before it exploded. What then? Wouldn't this person want me dead?"

Dr. Terrien regarded him dubiously. "Gabriel," he said, "I want to believe you—well, you know what I mean; of course I wouldn't want any harm to befall you. But you need to realize that your nervous system is so accustomed to threat that, perhaps, you've invented this situation in order to justify the way you feel. It takes time for the mind to grasp that the danger is over."

Oh, Christ, not this again. Gabe bit his tongue and forced himself to hear the doctor out. The man still thought he was paranoid.

"Have you called the police about this?" the doctor asked, looking worried.

Gabe thought of the police car that had tried to mow him down. If he said the police were in on the scheme to kill him, the doctor would definitely think him crazy. "No," he said succinctly. "But I can tell you that an agent from the DIA, the one looking in to my disappearance is dead, killed in a hit-and-run."

That news gave the doctor pause. He rubbed his chin with his fingertips, his brow puckered with concern.

"Let me ask you a question, Doc," Gabe added, driving his point home.

"Go ahead," the man invited generously.

"Is there, by any chance, someone else who's been following my progress?"

It was impossible to tell if the flicker in the doctor's blue-gray eyes was guilt, surprise, or consternation. "Well, of course," he said. "Your commander wants to know the moment you're completely recovered. He can't wait to have you back on the team."

Commander Lovitt. "You've talked to him about my progress?"

Dr. Terrien cleared his throat uncomfortably. "Well, yes, in a manner of speaking. I'm required to give him updates."

So much for confidentiality, Gabe thought with a sneer. He should have heeded Forrester's advice and said nothing to his psychiatrist—not that Lovitt was in any way involved in the conspiracy to kill Gabe. But if Gabe hadn't shared his paranoid thoughts with the doctor, he'd have stood a better chance of returning to active duty. God damn him for an idiot!

"You know what," Gabe said, standing up abruptly. "Thanks for hearing me out. I'm sure these sessions helped my memory to return, but I think I'm wasting my time now."

With a curt farewell, he strode from the room and out of the office suite, only to stand on the curb outside, waiting for Sebastian to pick him up.

Chapter Sixteen

Mallory regarded her reflection in the bathroom mirror through critical eyes. The dye was coming out of her hair so that it was now a charcoal gray instead of black. Her nose was too big for her face and covered with freckles. Her mouth was too wide. She hated the way she looked.

Maybe she should dye her hair another color or put some earrings in those empty holes in her ears. Mom and Dad would have a cow if she did that. The thought of them having a cow intrigued her. They'd have to talk about what they were going to do to her for defying them. She reached for the jewelry box on the counter and fished out a couple of sterling silver studs.

Putting earrings into the holes that were almost completely closed was pretty painful. It took her mind off Gabe's absence. The house echoed with silence during the long hours that her mother worked, but Mallory couldn't stand to go outside. Every father in America was vacationing with his kids. It made Mallory sick at heart to watch them rollicking in the surf and souvenir shopping.

She'd been so sure that things would work out with Gabe coming back into their lives. He was everything a dad should be. He was fun but strict at the same time. He was nice, too, making faces at her and casting her warm looks that made her feel good about herself.

The best part was that her mother liked him, too. She'd held his hand all the way home from Annapolis, right up to when Gabe thought the car behind was following them and he'd pulled a gun out from under his pant leg. *A gun!*

That was when everything got weird. Dad had started talking about someone trying to kill him. Mom had turned tense and quiet. Mallory's blissful happiness had started to crack apart and splinter, just as it had years ago when her new dad had gone out of his way to avoid her.

Holding her ear still with one hand, Mallory pushed four studs through the narrow holes with the other, biting her lip for bravery. God, that hurt! Slipping the back onto the posts, she regarded her handiwork.

Four silver studs in her left ear didn't make her any prettier, she realized, disappointed.

The doorbell rang, startling her from her bleak thoughts. Who would that be? Reggie wasn't allowed to come over while Mom was at work. The dog started barking shrilly. Mallory stepped from the bathroom to investigate.

Peeking through the narrow window by the door, she was surprised to find a policeman standing outside. Her mother had warned her many times not to open the door for strangers, but this was a policeman. By the look on his face, he had something important to share with her. What if Gabe had been hurt or . . . or killed, Mallory thought, reaching for the lock. She grabbed the dog's collar, holding Priscilla as she cracked the door.

"Mallory Troy?" the officer asked, his eyes obscured by dark sunglasses.

"Yes?"

"I'm Officer Clemens," he introduced himself. "You need to come with me."

At her hip, Priscilla growled. "Why?" Mallory asked. "Is there something wrong?"

The officer frowned at her impertinence. "I think you know," he said with disapproval. "Are you going to walk out of here or do I need to cuff you?"

The blood slipped from Mallory's face. Somehow the cops had found out about Reggie and the marijuana. God, she was in for it now! "Are you going to call my mom?" she asked, frightened in a way she'd never been before.

"Absolutely. Let's go."

Mallory glanced down at the dog, who continued to growl at the officer, her fur bristling. "I'll walk you later, Pris," she promised, giving the dog a farewell pat. With that, she let herself out, locked the door behind her, and followed the officer stoically down the steps toward his waiting vehicle.

"Hello?" Gabe reached for Master Chief's telephone, thinking that it might be Hannah Geary.

"Gabe, it's Helen."

Just the sound of her voice caused his heart to leap from despondency, but then her urgency registered. He'd just been thinking about her, wondering if he shouldn't call and check up on his family. "What's wrong?" he asked, sitting up straighter.

"It's Mallory. I haven't seen her since this morning when I went to work."

Gabe looked around Master Chief's empty house as if he might find Mallory lurking behind the heavy furniture. There was only Petty Officer Rodriguez, sitting across from him engrossed in a *National Geographic*. "Have you tried Reggie's?" Gabe asked.

"He says he called her around four and no one answered the phone. Something's wrong, Gabe. The dog had an accident in the house which means she hadn't been walked. Mallory's never forgotten to walk the dog."

The petty officer lowered his magazine to look at Gabe inquiringly. Sebastian had ordered him to babysit while he was out taking Leila on a date.

"How about the Rec Center on base?"

"No, I called there, too. No one's seen her." Her voice seemed to rise on a wave of panic.

"Okay, listen," Gabe soothed, getting up and pacing to the kitchen where Rodriguez wasn't as likely to overhear his private conversation. "She's probably just having a rebellious moment. She's been pretty glum over the phone."

"Yeah, no kidding."

"Maybe she's just acting out. It's my fault." He shook his head. "I should have talked to her some more, made her realize this was about me and not about her at all."

"What do I do?"

She sounded so distraught he wanted to leap through the phone line and pull her close. If Rodriguez had a vehicle, he could borrow it and be over there in a flash. Then he thought of Master Chief's Falcon, sitting in the carport outside. Sebastian was borrowing Westy's car to take Leila on a date.

"I'll be right over," he promised.

"Are you sure? I could come pick you up."

"No, you need to stay by the phone. I'll be fine."

"Okay," she agreed and hung up.

Gabe scoured the house for Sebastian's keys, but he couldn't find them.

"Sir, you're not supposed to go anywhere," Rodriguez reminded him, barring the exit.

"Step aside, PO3," Gabe snapped impatiently. "My wife needs me."

"Then I'll go with you," the young man offered. "I have the keys to Master Chief's car." He dug into his pocket and produced them.

Gabe snatched the keys out of the young man's hands. "No, thanks. This is family business. I'll deal with it." He pushed past the younger man, who trailed him to the door.

"But Master Chief said I needed to stay with you!"

Gabe raced outside and jumped into Sebastian's old car, locking it before Rodriguez could claim shotgun. The last thing he needed was some young SEAL spreading rumors about Jaguar's personal life. With nearly all his memories intact, the chance to return to active duty was fast approaching. He couldn't afford family-related issues to slow him down.

At the same time, family came first, not the team. He berated himself for not predicting Mallory's reaction to his absence. He should have made it clear that no matter what his state of mind, he'd always be her father. As a matter of fact, he'd initiated the process just this morning to have her legally adopted. Wouldn't it be the most awful irony if something happened to her before he could make that dream come true?

Sebastian despised the dress Leila was wearing. He would have thought it the dead-last item she would own, let alone wear, on a first date.

Sitting in the passenger seat beside him, she looked like a nun cloistered in a habit. The black dress went from her ankles to her neck, disguising every inch of her slim, elegant body, except for her arms. It was sleeveless. He supposed he ought to be grateful for that small consolation, but right now her arms were folded across her torso like a shield, which he did not take to be a good sign.

She wore her hair up. Silver earrings shimmered on her earlobes and at least ten assorted silver bracelets jangled on her wrists. She wore slim black sandals that failed to disguise the scarlet toenail polish on her elegant, little toes. Over all, she looked ready to attend a formal cocktail party.

Boy, was she in for a surprise.

His navy Bermuda shirt and light slacks ought to have tipped her off. She made no comment, however, as he pointed Westy's car toward the ocean, driving it just over the speed limit. It was a gorgeous evening, just cool enough to hint of the fall weather to come, but warm enough to sit on the beach and watch the sun go down.

When he pulled into Back Bay Wildlife Refuge, Leila still said nothing, though a quick peek at her revealed a puzzled slant to her eyebrows.

"We're here," he said, flashing her a grin as he zipped into one of the many parking spaces. The refuge was rarely advertised to tourists. Its goal was to offer a sanctuary to sea grasses, wild ponies, and rare birds, not to take in the revenue brought to the beach by its annual visitors. In fact, the only other cars in the parking lot were a Park Ranger SUV and a police car.

Sebastian rounded the vehicle to do his gentlemanly duties, but Leila had already pushed open the door and was stepping out under her own steam.

He turned toward the back of the car to retrieve the picnic paraphernalia he'd packed, while beseeching the Virgin Mary to warm the blood in Leila's veins.

She was his future after retirement. He had to convince her of that; otherwise, what was the point of retiring?

She took the blanket out of his arms without being asked.

"I can carry it," he protested. He had the loaded basket in his other hand and he still needed to close the hatch on the ZX.

"Don't be a chauvinist," she said, her black eyes goading him.

He slammed the car shut with more force than necessary. But he abstained from rising to her taunts, because he sensed that they would fight the same way that they made love—heatedly. And he didn't want to fight with her tonight. No, tonight he would give her no excuse to deny him her heart.

They walked toward the beach in silence. The wind molded Leila's ridiculous dress to her body, making it seem less of a sackcloth than it had first appeared. Sebastian caught a glimpse of bright red silk through one of the dress's armholes. The vision threw his thoughts into a spin. *Madre de Dios*, was she wearing a scarlet bra and matching panties?

His palms, suddenly sweaty, caused his grip on the basket to slip. In that instant, his goal for the evening shifted from convincing Leila to risk her heart to him—although that was still the long-range plan—to convincing Leila to take off that hideous dress.

They would need to talk, first. He would need to be soft-spoken and unthreatening to attain his goal. "Let's go into the dunes," he said, pointing inland.

She complied with surprising acquiescence. He realized the wind was playing havoc with her silky black hair.

They came up on a pristine valley surrounded by mounds of white sand and sea grass, which kept the wind at bay. The unblemished bowl felt soft beneath Sebastian's loafers. He kicked his shoes off and turned to take the blanket from Leila's hands, brushing his fingers over hers intentionally. She jerked away from his touch. He took it for a good sign.

With the enormous blanket quilting their nest, he set the basket down in the center and gestured for Leila to sit. He sat beside her, the basket at their knees. He could see her reluctant curiosity as he lifted the lid.

The bottle of wine was the first thing to come out. To his gratification, it was still chilled. Corkscrew and glasses followed. Not plastic cups, mind, but genuine crystal inherited from his grandmother. That was what had made the basket so heavy.

Leila fingered the heavy goblet he passed to her, her eyes reflecting wonder. He filled her glass nearly to the rim.

Let her drink until her blood warms, he thought.

He opened a Tupperware of sliced celery and carrots, complete with dip, and set it between them. Then he lay back on one elbow and sipped his wine, content to gaze at the object of his desire while she nibbled daintily on a celery stalk.

Crunch. Her sharp little teeth bit into the stick and she chewed, repeating the action until the celery was gone. She took a sip of the wine, and her eyes widened. Her gaze flew to his, and she sniffed the aroma just to be sure.

"This is Columbia Crest Chardonnay," she exclaimed.

It was the second thing she'd said to him all evening, other than calling him a chauvinist.

"Yes," Sebastian said, immensely relieved that she'd spoken again—and impressed that she knew her wines.

"You like good coffee, too," she added, bringing up the other morning.

Recalling his embarrassment that day, he felt himself blush and was grateful to his Mexican ancestors for his swarthy skin. "I do," he said evenly. "I am particular about my food."

Leila frowned. "Me too," she admitted, taking another sip.

He saw his opening and jumped straight in. "Then we have something in common," he replied.

"You think so?" Her tone was suddenly as chilly as the glass in his hand.

"How can you deny it?" He took a pull on his drink, needing its courage quickly. The subject of their future together had come up faster than he was ready: "You know we are good together." Jesus, the men would die laughing if they heard him.

Leila narrowed her eyes at him. "You promised we would eat dinner together, nothing more."

"Ah, you're hungry," he said, glad for the reprieve.

He set his glass and hers securely in the sand, and then he began pulling out their dinner: grilled chicken breasts, potato salad, and barbecued baked beans. Leila was subtly inspecting the fare. "You made this yourself?" she asked, coming to the correct conclusion.

"I like to cook," he said with a shrug. "And you?"

She shrugged as if to pretend she could take it or leave it, but he suspected the former. With a smug smile, Sebastian reached for the food and began dishing out the meal.

"Was your husband a chauvinist?" he asked, still rankling from her earlier accusation.

She picked up her plate and stabbed a fork at her potato salad. "He was Turkish," she said abruptly. "The culture is male-centered."

"But you're Turkish, too," he pointed out. "So you knew what to expect."

Her eyes flashed at him. "I'm an American," she said. "I was born and raised in Virginia."

"I'm Mexican," he added, raising a spoonful of beans to his mouth. "I was born and raised in Puerto Vallarta."

"That's another male-centered culture," Leila muttered.

Sebastian shrugged, not the least offended. "My father died when I was twelve. My mother raised all eight of us alone after that. It wasn't easy for her. A man can be a partner in life."

She put her fork down slowly. "I'm sorry your father died," she said, proving she did have a heart after all. Long lashes hid her eyes as she toyed with her chicken.

"And your parents?" he asked. "Where do they live?"

"They went back to their homeland, to the clear waters of the Mediterranean."

"Any siblings?" he prodded.

"I have a brother who lives in California. I see him once a year."

Her answer drove home the depth of her isolation. While he didn't live near his brothers and sisters, all of whom lived in Texas, he made a point to visit them and call them often, provided he was not at sea or on a mission.

He wanted to ask about her husband, who had apparently abandoned her, but he sensed that subject was still taboo, given the limited time they'd known each other.

"Listen," she suddenly said, confirming his speculations. "I didn't come out with you tonight to get to know you better."

He gave her a grim little smile. "Why did you come out with me?" he asked, playing along.

"To apologize." She took a quick sip of her wine. "I had no right to withhold my name from you that . . . that night." Her olive complexion could not quite disguise the pretty pink color that suffused her face. "Even though men do it all the time, that doesn't make it right. I ought to have told you my name."

He'd asked her. Plenty of times. *Call me whatever you*

like, she'd said in her throaty voice. It had turned him on at first that she could be anything he wanted. He'd surmised for a while that she was a hooker. Why else would she be reluctant to give her name? But later that night, when he'd found her surprisingly self-conscious, he'd known she wasn't a woman of the night. She was a good girl going off the deep end. And then he'd been desperate to know her name, only she wouldn't give it to him.

"Apology accepted," he said, even though it still irked him that he'd spent months trying to track her down. He'd questioned people who had been at the Shifting Sands. He'd even asked the guards at the gate. Tracing her license plate number, he'd discovered that she'd used a rental car that evening, and the rental agency wouldn't give him her real name. In all, she'd been so effective in covering her trail, he'd wondered for three long months if he'd been duped by a spy.

"Just tell me why you did it," he demanded, even though he suspected he knew. She was lonely. She was needy. She was terrified of a relationship.

His question clearly unsettled her. She clasped her hands together, bracelets jangling. "I needed . . . I needed to do it," she said, shrugging one shoulder. "Please don't ask me."

"For yourself?" He wanted clarification. "Or for someone else?"

She looked at him not understanding. "What do you mean?"

"Did someone put you up to it?"

"Of course not." Speculation turned to humor. "What, do you think I'm an agent or something?" She laughed then, surprising him.

Laughter transformed her face from merely lovely to breathtaking. Sebastian sucked in a breath. *There she was!*

The woman who'd smiled up at him as he held her in his arms, dancing them slowly about the patio of the club, the moon luminous overhead, the ocean purring in their ears.

"Leila," he muttered, giving up pretending that his passion for her was subdued. "You are the most beautiful woman I have ever met. Please do not push me away. I must get to know you better."

"No!" she said, her smile fleeing. She shifted away from him, as if fearful that he might leap on top of her and leave her no choice.

He was seriously tempted. But honor squashed the impulse. If she ever invited his touch again, he wanted it to be with the same warmth she'd shown him three months ago.

His frustration grew. "I'm not going to touch you," he said, seeing that she was about to bolt from him. "I just want to hear your reasons. Given how good we are together, it makes no sense that you don't want to be with me now."

He was upsetting her. He could see the turmoil in her eyes. She was a complicated woman. He liked that about her, though her pride frustrated him.

"All right," she said, having struggled with herself. "I suppose I owe you an explanation." She took a shuddering breath. Her food and drink sat on the blanket, forgotten. He'd never get her drunk enough to take off the dress at this point.

"My marriage was short and stormy," she began. "I was not the kind of wife my husband expected, though I tried. God knows I tried. One day, I went home and found my house empty. Altul had taken everything but my clothes. I never saw him again. He went to Turkey," she added miserably. "He'd threatened to do it, to find a wife who knew how to care for him better . . ." She trailed off, a hitch in her voice. "He left me with a lot of debt," she added bitterly.

And a broken heart, Sebastian thought. He wished fervently that he could find that bastard and teach him a lesson. He'd trampled Leila's untamed spirit by making her feel less than what she was. "I know people who could help you to find him," he offered, thinking he just might pay the man a social call.

"No," she retorted. "I want nothing from him." She lifted her chin and looked at Sebastian proudly. "I repaid the debts, and I filed for divorce. It was complicated without his consent, but I managed just fine."

Her bravery stirred a powerful emotion in him. "Your story touches my heart, *bonita*," he admitted, like a true red-blooded Mexican.

"Don't do that," she begged, looking away. "Sadness is a waste of time and energy. I should know. I've wept an ocean full of tears, and it changes nothing. Besides, I'm not finished. You won't be half as sympathetic when I've told you the rest."

"Told me what?" he asked, intrigued.

"The reason I picked you up that night."

The air in his lungs evaporated as he waited for the other shoe to drop.

"I was hoping to get pregnant," she said in a rush. "I want to have a baby. Before it's too late." She looked down at the pattern on the blanket. "I just don't want the father of that baby, or any man for that matter, in my life."

Glaring insight lit the romantic shadows of Sebastian's memories. Here he'd thought she'd picked him up because she found him irresistible. He'd dazzled her with the admission that he was a SEAL, one of the few elite warriors in the world. She'd seemed so hot for him, so eager to climb into his bed, when all she'd really wanted from him was his sperm.

Well, *pendejo!* If that didn't bring a man down a peg or

two he didn't know what would. What had been a night of heated passion for him was no more than a frenzy on her part to conceive!

Still, he managed to put a positive spin on this revelation. If she'd been so desperate for his sperm three months ago, then perhaps she was still desperate for it. He had plenty to go 'round. An endless supply, actually.

"It's understandable you would want a child," he said, measuring his words carefully. "Someone to love . . . who loves you back unconditionally."

She searched his face, clearly suspicious of his easy acceptance. "Aren't you furious that I was using you?" She shook her head, her color deepening. "I am mortified that I was so bold about it. But time is running out for me. I . . . I had just turned thirty-eight."

He quirked an eyebrow at her. "You mean, it was your birthday?" What a hell of a way to celebrate.

"Yes," she admitted, looking away.

"Well, well," he murmured, satisfied that he'd given her something special that night. "That makes you, what, a Gemini?"

"Taurus," she replied. "I'm right on the cusp."

He smiled at her slowly. Ah, yes, the bull. He should have realized, given her stubborn nature.

"That night was so out of character for me," she insisted. "I couldn't face you again and explain. I knew I would, eventually. Just . . . not then."

"But you came to my house, to speak with Jaguar. You must have known you'd run into me."

"It was time," she said softly. "I am so sorry," she added, wringing her hands.

Sebastian didn't want her remembering that night and

cringing. He wanted her to think of it as he did: as an epiphany, an encounter that had changed their lives forever.

"Stop apologizing," he demanded. "I don't want your mortification. I don't want your explanations."

She fell silent on him, and he realized he'd spoken too harshly. "Do you still want a child?" he asked, snatching up his only ace and playing it.

She raised startled eyes at him. "Why?"

"Sleep with me again," he offered. "And again until it happens."

Of course, he was offering her much more than his DNA. He was offering marriage, a house, a future for the two of them and their unborn children—in the plural. Only he sensed she would run the other way if he even hinted at any of that.

She was looking at him like he'd lost his mind. "Are you serious?" she asked.

Hell, yes. "Yes," he said.

"Why would you do that, after the way I used you?"

Was she kidding? "I'm a very magnanimous person," he answered with a straight face. He ruined it by laughing. "You want the truth? The truth is, that night with you was the best experience in my life, *querida*. I would do anything to relive it."

"You would agree to give me a baby," she said slowly, "with no strings attached?"

She was eyeing him so hopefully he couldn't bring himself to stipulate the offer. "I would," he said. Of course, he had no intention of letting it end that way. If he planned it right, she would fall in love with him and marry him. And then she would see that not all men made lousy husbands.

"I need to think about it," she said, sounding stunned.

He shrugged. "Fair enough. Care to go for a swim in the

meantime?" The first step in his seduction was getting that dress off.

"I didn't bring my swimsuit," she said, looking him up and down.

"So?" He unbuttoned his shirt and tossed it aside, along with his sleeveless undershirt. When he reached for his belt, Leila's gaze skittered away. "I'm going to wear my boxers," he said. "You can wear your underwear. It's no less than a bikini." He came to his feet and let his pants drop. He saw her take a peek at his light blue boxers.

"Aren't the sharks feeding at this time?" she asked.

"I'll keep you safe," he promised, giving her an encouraging smile.

She looked tempted, she truly did. Her eyes strayed to his naked chest and lingered on his flat abdomen. "I don't know," she said, wavering. "You go first. I'll think about it."

That was enough for him. Relishing the future, Sebastian took off running to the waves, his feet scarcely touching the sand. Spanish had the perfect expression for this feeling— *Qué maravilla la vida!* Wasn't life just grand?

Chapter Seventeen

Gabe wasn't at his home for more than five minutes when the phone rang. He was holding Helen in his arms, asking himself what the hell he'd been doing, staying away from her. She pushed herself away from him at the first ring and snatched up the receiver.

"Hello?" Two seconds elapsed. "Yes, it is." Another two seconds. "Oh, my God."

The color leached out of her face. As her gaze locked on to Gabe, he experienced a sick lurching in his gut that went hand in hand with receiving bad news.

"Yes, he's here. I'll bring him," she said. Then she turned and hung up the phone.

"Who was it?" He dreaded asking.

"Security at Back Bay. Mal's okay," she said, clutching the counter for support. "But she's in trouble. She was caught smoking pot on the beach there. We have to go pick her up and pay a fine, apparently."

Relief made him weak. At the same time, anger swamped

him, rocking him on his feet. "What the hell was she doing smoking pot? I thought we'd been through this before!"

Helen went rigid. "Well, maybe the stress was just too much for her!" she shot back, color reappearing in her cheeks.

He acknowledged her accusation with a nod. "You're right," he muttered. "I just thought Mallory was smarter than that. How much is the fee?"

Helen blinked at him. "They didn't say."

He found that odd. "Really."

"We need to go." She headed for her purse. "She must be terrified."

She'd better be, Gabe thought grimly. He couldn't believe Mallory would defy them both so openly—smoking marijuana on a nature reserve, for God's sake. The fine was probably huge.

But if she'd actually been smoking the stuff, then it was obvious he'd screwed her up with his decision to leave. Maybe he ought to have stuck around. Maybe Helen and Mallory were better off with him than without him. He cursed under his breath, confused.

Helen led the way outside. Gabe paused to retrieve his gun from Master Chief's car, ignoring Helen's look of dismay. To her credit, she didn't say anything about him being paranoid or crazy. He took the keys from her fingers and drove the Jaguar himself, pointing it toward Back Bay.

It took less than five minutes to arrive at the entrance. The gate was already down, signifying that the reserve was closed for the night. The sun was still setting, however, shedding a crimson glow over the sand dunes. Gabe leapt out and manually raised the bar, which wasn't locked.

Driving into the deserted reserve, he glanced sidelong at Helen and found her rigid in the seat, looking as tense as he felt. As she turned her head to look at him, he saw the shadowed worry in her gold-brown eyes, and he knew what she was thinking. Poor Mallory was out here all alone with the park security. She must be feeling very intimidated, very scared.

Gabe wanted to reassure his wife. But he didn't like the cold feeling in his stomach. Something didn't feel right. As he guided the car toward the parking lot, he reviewed what Helen had told him earlier. It wasn't like Mallory to abandon her dog. Nor had she ever mentioned Back Bay Wildlife Refuge as a place for teens to hang out.

He coasted into a parking space, surprised to see Westy's 300ZX parked on the side closest to the beach. It was the only civilian car in the parking lot.

"That's your chief's car," Helen said, recognizing it also.

"Master Chief borrowed it for his date with Leila. They must be out here, somewhere."

She perked right up. "Leila's on a date with Master Chief?"

Gabe chuckled. "I think he's been bit by the love bug."

A Park Ranger SUV and a police car were the only other vehicles present, both parked near the information office. Gabe did a double take. The police car was a carbon copy of the one that had nearly run him over.

Helen was out of the Jaguar and heading toward the office, a wooden bungalow painted in driftwood gray.

"Wait a minute," Gabe called, hurrying to catch up with her. "I don't like this," he admitted, considering their options. Suddenly he wished he hadn't been so quick to leave Rodriguez behind.

"Come on, Gabe," she urged, reaching for his hand. "Mal's got to be scared to death!"

Maybe. Maybe it was paranoia, playing tricks on him. Maybe it wasn't. What if his faceless opponent had taken desperate measures to pull Gabe away from his men? What if he'd kidnapped Mallory to lure him to this remote area?

He had to think fast. At this point, all he could do was to keep alert. At the first sign of trouble, he'd react. "Stay behind me," he said, pulling Helen back.

With a look of annoyance, she stepped behind him.

They approached the bungalow cautiously. Other than the crash of the ocean and the whistling of wind through the sea grasses, the place was eerily quiet. Their footsteps sounded loud on the wooden stoop. Just as they reached the solid wood door, it opened, propelled by the arm of a big man in a policeman's uniform. "Evening," he said curtly.

Even with the sun sucking daylight from the sky, the man wore suspiciously dark sunglasses. But it was the jaw Gabe recognized. Without so much as a second's hesitation, he grabbed the man by his hair and hauled him forward, planting a knee in his midriff and landing a double-handed chop to the back of his neck. The cop collapsed face first on the wooden porch, out for the count.

Helen looked up from the still figure, dumbstruck.

"Go," Gabe instructed her, pulling the pistol from his waistband. "Run down the beach and get Master Chief. Hurry!"

"But . . ." She didn't understand what was happening.

"Now! That way!" He propelled her in the direction that Master Chief and Leila had most likely taken, and when he was satisfied that she was safely out of range of the bungalow, he slipped around the nearest corner, calling on his training to keep his panic subdued.

He'd rescued too many hostages to count, but not once had the hostage been a member of his family. He hoped to God Mallory wasn't hurt. He strained his ears for any sounds coming from within the building, but all was quiet.

Drifting in the shadows on the dark side of the building, he longed to take a peek inside. Maybe Mal wasn't even in there. Maybe they were keeping her somewhere else.

But then he heard it, a muffled cry followed by an ugly thump.

Jesus! Shit! That was Mallory's voice he'd just heard! No doubt she'd been trying to warn him, and her bravery had just been met with a ruthless countermeasure.

Helen would never forgive him if something happened to her daughter. He refused to believe they would kill the kid. It was him they were after. He allowed himself a moment of dread-filled relief. At least he knew for sure he wasn't paranoid.

He crept toward the rear window. The blinds were pulled. He put his eyeball to the screen and caught sight of a figure slumped low in a chair. *Mallory,* he realized with a shudder of rage. She'd been gagged. Her entire body looked limp, telling him she'd slumped into a faint.

Son of a bitch! He was going to kill the bastard that hurt her. His gaze scanned the room and discerned the outline of a man standing by the door—the one named Manning, who'd come after him that morning with a laser sight. He, too, was dressed like a cop.

The fact that he wasn't pacing made Gabe uneasy. The man was standing perfectly still, listening. Suddenly he cut his gaze to the window, looking directly at him.

Gabe ducked out of sight. The single light inside went out, further proof that the man inside was an expert. Who but a professional would be sent to take out a SEAL?

Gabe backed up quickly, careful not to make a sound, desperate to get himself out of the open.

The sound of breaking glass encouraged him to run.

Floop! A bullet hit the sand directly in front of him, fired by a gun with a silencer—a suppressed Heckler and Koch by the sound of it. *Floop!* The man discharged another bullet, this one narrowly missing Gabe's heel.

It was pure luck that the land dipped downward at that point. Gabe dived into the natural trench, maneuvering himself to face the bungalow while pulling the Glock 23 from his shin strap. He peeked between two clumps of sea grass and took aim at the building. His attacker ducked out of sight.

Gabe didn't want his bullet striking Mallory. He refused to consider that she might be dead already.

Were these the same men that had killed Ernest Forrester? The question streaked through his mind, intersecting with thoughts about his current situation.

He needed to think of a plan before his opponent threatened to use Mallory as a shield. God, he should have let Rodriguez tag along. His only hope was for Helen to find Sebastian. He would need the Sandman to take this bastard out without jeopardizing the kid's life.

The temptation was too much.

With her feet buried in the still-warm sand, Leila could see Sebastian in the indigo shadows that followed sunset. He looped under the waves like a porpoise, hair sleeked back, skin glimmering. He'd offered to give her a baby.

A baby! An infant to cradle against her breast and cherish. Their child would have black hair like the two of them, golden brown skin, and dark, liquid eyes. She would be exquisite! Intelligent like the master chief of SEAL Team Twelve. Delicate, like her mother.

Oh, but it wasn't really the baby she was thinking of as Sebastian shot up out of the water, shaking droplets from his hair. Standing in the sea, he looked like a lean Poseidon. He hiked his sagging boxers higher on his hips, and she knew a raw urge to march up to him and tug them off.

Desire pooled in her belly. She wanted to feel him pressed against her. All she had to do was join him in the sea. He'd left the decision up to her. She gnawed on her lower lip, pride battling temptation.

Yes, she wanted it badly enough to sacrifice her dignity. Gathering the material of her dress, she pulled it over her head. Wind caressed her torso and thighs, stirring downy hairs and rousing her to exquisite sensitivity. She abandoned the protection of the dunes and approached the waves.

Sebastian had caught sight of her undressing. He stood just before the breakers as if locked in place, water seething about his thighs as he regarded her approach. The closer she came, the more she could feel the heat of his gaze scorching her. He made her feel so alluring, so wanton.

Self-consciously, she stepped into the surf. The warm water lapped about her ankles, her calves, and higher as she waded toward him.

He held out his arms, and she slipped into them on a sigh of surrender. Their mouths came together in the next instant, hot and wet, merging.

Leila lost her orientation. Behind her closed eyes, the world seemed to spin, the sky and sea commingling in dizzy shades of cobalt, blue, and black. She surrendered herself to the euphoria, the same exhilaration she'd felt in Sebastian's arms three long months ago.

Allah, but the man knew how to kiss! His tongue devoured her, worshiped her, tasted corners of her mouth she'd never given a thought to before. And all she could do was cling to him and moan, and let him have his way.

It was impossible to overlook the fact that he was as eager

for her as she was for him. His hands roamed her freely, heightening her awareness. He spanned her narrow waist; slid one hand up and over her breast, dampening her bra. With his other hand, he cupped her bottom, rocking her against him.

Leila crowded closer to keep from melting into the sea and sand. Without warning, he scooped her into his arms and began to stride toward the dunes. She clung to him, licking the salt off his neck with shameful greed, running her hands over his powerful shoulders, raking her nails lightly over his back. How good it felt to abandon her rigid code of ethics. She should have done so earlier.

He growled deep in his throat. "You make me the happiest man alive," he admitted.

His declaration warmed her, for she sensed the words were true.

He lowered her onto the center of the blanket. There was just enough light left to make out every detail of his silhouette: his sculpted torso; a hawklike face with a mouth curved into a sensual half smile; and eyes gleaming with such desire that her toes curled inward.

Her bra fastened in the front. With a sound of approval, he unhooked the clasp with dexterous fingers, peeling back the sodden fabric. She arched unconsciously, craving the heat of his mouth on her. He answered her silent plea with inexorable nips and licks, making her want to sob for mercy.

Then his mouth moved lower. As he hovered over the flat plane of her abdomen, his kisses grew tender, and she wondered with a stab of emotion if he were thinking of the baby he'd promised to give her. For the first time ever, it occurred to her that he would have feelings for his child.

Suddenly their agreement seemed too complex. Sebastian

wouldn't just impregnate her and leave it at that. Oh, what had she agreed to? She couldn't . . .

He was pulling her panties down, inch by inch, causing her thoughts to fly away like dried leaves. His lips followed his fingers. She didn't dare look to see what he was doing or else she'd climax embarrassingly early. It was enough to *feel* him, fingers brushing the inside of her thighs, his tongue leaving damp traces at it roused her to unbearable sensitivity.

The small portion of her brain that was still functioning registered that this seduction was completely irrelevant to their agreement. Babies weren't made with oral sex. But, oh, she couldn't make him stop. Not when the firm tip of his tongue finally slipped into the place where she wanted it most.

Allah and all the prophets! She writhed beneath the tender lashing, fisting the blanket to keep herself from grabbing his hair and locking him there shamelessly. He knew exactly how to please a woman, his timing flawless. She felt a flash of jealousy for all the women who had enjoyed his generous skill. Sebastian was hers alone!

The crazy thought penetrated her brain in the same instant that she climaxed. It caused her orgasm to be intense, both emotionally and physically. *He is mine! All mine! Oh, yes!*

She lay in its wake, utterly drained and at the same time terrified. What had she done? Hadn't the experience three months ago taught her anything? Didn't she know how vulnerable her heart was to love? For now she wanted more than just a baby. She wanted Sebastian to love her mindlessly, completely, forever!

One orgasm, and already she was dreaming of a future. Yet Sebastian León was a SEAL, married to his job. Those were his very words, words he'd told her three months ago to explain why he'd never married. She was setting herself up for disaster.

She had to say something. He was shucking his boxer shorts with one hand, holding all his weight on the opposite elbow. If his eyes glowed with desire earlier, they glittered with lust now. With his underwear still on his thighs, he positioned himself over her, probing her entrance with his hot insistence.

"Wait!" she cried, pushing against his shoulder. Yet at the same time, her body betrayed her and she lifted her hips in welcome.

He slid into her tightness with such single-minded intent that she gasped in further protests. It wouldn't be fair of her to call a halt to this now. Besides, he was filling her so completely, it was impossible to ask him to stop. Urgent feelings stormed her senses.

If he only knew how many times she'd lain in bed aching for a repeat of that tempestuous May night!

And then he began to move and the past was gone. There was only the present and the future. The agonizing glory of Sebastian sliding in and out of her; the salty taste of his tongue moving in tandem with his body as he kissed her; the feel of his callused palm against her bare buttocks, lifting her to him. Her thighs straining, another climax lifting her higher and higher.

Why had she resisted him so long? This was the epitome of fulfillment. This was paradise.

But then she remembered. Oh, yes, there was a serpent in paradise.

Just as she was about to explode a second time, a cry penetrated her sensual haze and Sebastian froze. The cry came again, it was a woman yelling, *"Master Chief!"*

Sebastian pulled out of Leila so quickly and was scrambling over the sand dunes, tugging his boxer shorts up before Leila had even determined who the woman was calling for.

She lay there befuddled, achingly unfulfilled and disoriented, regretting already the bargain she'd struck to make a baby.

Chapter Eighteen

I t took Sebastian a moment to calm Helen down to where her disjointed message made any sense. And then it clicked. Their suspicion that someone might come after Jaguar was being realized. He'd been lured into a net, where Mallory, his stepdaughter, was being used as bait. So, where the hell was Rodriguez, who was supposed to be guarding Gabe's back?

"He told me to come get you," Helen added out of breath. "Hurry!" She tugged at his bare arm, apparently not even realizing that he only wore his boxer shorts. Of course it was nearly pitch-black now that the sun had sunk out of sight.

Sebastian sent a distracted look over his shoulder. He could make out Leila's head and shoulders as she peered over the dunes at them. *Mierda,* he thought. "Just a minute." He sprinted back toward the dunes, not wanting to shout.

"I'll be back, Leila," he said, reaching for her slim shadow. Her skin felt so soft beneath his touch he was consumed with regret. "There's trouble. Don't leave this place, whatever you do. Stay down and out of sight."

"What—"

He cut off her question with a quick kiss. Snatching up his slacks, he hightailed it back to Helen, who was literally pulling her hair out.

"Where are they?" he asked her as he stepped into his pants.

"At the information center. Hurry!" She started running.

"Wait, I'll go alone," he told her. "Stay there in the dunes with Leila. It'll be safer that way."

"I can't!" she cried. "They have my daughter!"

He put a heavy hand on both her shoulders. "I need you to stay here," he said in his best no-nonsense voice. "We can't afford to be distracted."

Even in the dark, he could see her eyes fill with helpless tears. "Go," he said, nudging her toward the dunes. "Stay with Leila until we return for you."

As she trudged reluctantly to higher ground, Sebastian took off at his fastest run. Minutes later, with the silhouette of the bungalow in sight, he gave a low bird whistle, a signal to Gabe that he was present. An answering call came from a swale to his left.

Sebastian dropped to the sand and elbow-crawled through the prickly grasses, taking care to remain behind a barrier at all times. A good pair of night-vision goggles would expose him, otherwise. Inch by inch, he worked his way through the valleys of sand to where Gabe was lying in wait.

"Glad to see you, Sebastian," Gabe whispered, keeping his head low. "There's one man inside and another lying on the front stoop, unconscious."

"Where's Rodriguez?" Sebastian inquired, peeved that a simple order hadn't been followed.

"Not his fault," Jaguar said. "I left him at your place. I had no idea this was a setup."

Thank God he just happened to be here with Leila. "Weapons?" he inquired, making a sign of the cross, as was his habit before engaging the enemy.

"He's got a hushpuppy . . . I've got the Glock you gave me."

"Can he see?"

"Roger. I caught a reflection of his NVGs when a plane went by. My daughter's in there," Jaguar added, his whisper sounding strained. "He knocked her out or something."

"Points of entry?" Sebastian asked, taking note but keeping his focus.

"Two—the front door which is probably bolted. And the window on this side, broken pane. I've been thinking," he added. "Remember the hostage situation in Yemen back in oh one?"

Sebastian smiled grimly and nodded. "We'll play it exactly the same. You go in to negotiate. I'll take the window."

"I'll need to keep my weapon," Gabe added with a frown. "He knows I'm carrying."

The tango wouldn't likely give up Mallory unless Gabe handed over his weapon. "I'll have to take him by surprise," Sebastian concluded. "Keep it simple, stupid," he added, an adage that had served SEALs well over the years.

"Thanks," Gabe said, patting his shoulder before slithering past.

"You're going to owe me when this is done," Sebastian muttered. He couldn't forget the ecstasy he was feeling mere minutes ago. He hoped to God this situation wouldn't cause Leila to change her mind about sleeping with him.

Gabe dropped out of sight. Sebastian knew he would come around the building shortly and knock on the front door. He waited with a familiar chill around his heart.

The knock came seconds later. Gabe's voice, raised unnaturally loud for the benefit of his master chief, sounded over the pounding surf. "Give up the girl!" he shouted. "I'm turning myself in."

Sebastian dared a peek over the dunes. A shadow moved at the window, telling him the tango had turned toward the door. Breaking out from his hiding place, Sebastian sprinted toward the building, staying upwind of the window, so that the patter of his footsteps would be carried away.

"Where's your wife?" he heard the man call out.

"I don't know. I told her to run. She's up the beach somewhere. Just take me," Gabe demanded. "I'm the one you want. Leave my wife and kid out of this."

Hugging the rough planks of the bungalow, Sebastian crept closer. He didn't look forward to cutting himself on broken glass, but without the tough fabric of a Kevlar vest or a blanket to throw over the ledge, that was pretty much inevitable.

"I'll unlock the door," the man inside was saying. "I want you to toss your weapon in first."

"I don't have a weapon."

"You're lying. Toss in the goddamn weapon or I'll break your daughter's fucking neck."

"Fine. You don't have to touch her."

There came the sound of a bolt sliding open. That was Sebastian's signal to reach for the windowsill and start climbing in. A weapon skittered across the floor, the sound of which muffled the tinkling of broken glass beneath his grip. With a shard cutting into his palm, he pulled himself upward and hooked his right foot over the ledge. Bits of glass slid beneath his ankle, making his purchase tentative.

He clung like a cat in a tree, staring into the shadows, wishing he had vision as good as Jaguar's. To get into the window unheard, he would have to wait for a distraction. He could feel blood pooling warmly beneath his right hand. *Maricon,* that little piece of glass hurt like hell!

He stared into the room, ignoring his own pain. The tango was over by the door. He held the submachine gun in one arm and gripped Gabe's pistol with the other. Moving behind the chair, he pointed the Glock at the slumped figure sitting there. Sebastian's hold on the windowsill became instantly more secure. Mallory's life depended on him leaping through the window at the right time. What kind of sick son of a bitch would aim a gun at a child?

"All right," the man called out, his calm, clipped messages betraying a military background. The fact that he hadn't turned the lights on—that he preferred to operate in the dark was also telling. It worried the hell out of Sebastian. "Come in with your hands on your head. One funny move and I'll put a bullet in your daughter's skull. Step on it."

Mallory roused to the sound of that threat. The throbbing in her head made her stomach heave, but she remembered in an instant where she was. She sensed her assailant behind her, and she stilled. The worst thing she could do now was betray that she'd come to. She remained in a slouch, feigning unconsciousness, her heart threatening to jump out of her throat, blood roaring in her ears.

The room was dark. At the creaking of the door, she dared a peek between her lashes. Gabe's silhouette appeared in the doorway, ringed by a single light from the parking lot. His elbows were up in the air, his hands on his head. He was the most welcoming sight she'd ever seen in her life, until she felt the cold barrel of a gun pressed against the back of her head.

Oh, shit!

This couldn't be happening. But it was. She'd realized within ten minutes of the cop's arrival at her house that the police could care less about Reggie getting marijuana from some dealer. The cop had locked her into the back of his sedan and driven right past the police station. She'd banged on the glass partition between them, but he'd ignored her. That was when the cold truth hit her square in the face. This so-called arrest had nothing to do with her. It had something to do with what Gabe had tried to tell them on the way home from Annapolis: that someone was trying to kill him. With horror that made her shake, Mallory realized she was being used as bait, to lure Gabe to his death.

The cop drove her to Back Bay Wildlife Refuge, where another man in uniform waited for him. Their brief conversation only confirmed what Mallory had already concluded. They intended to kill Gabe, take his body out into the ocean and dump it.

It was all she could do not to throw up. She'd vowed to herself instead that she would do whatever it took to keep Gabe alive.

"That's close enough," said Manning. She recognized him by his voice.

Gabe froze.

Mallory glanced surreptitiously around the room. Where was Clemens? Oh, yeah, Dad had knocked him out already. How had he known? she wondered, grateful for his sixth sense. She'd tried to warn him that there was still another one. The jerk must have knocked her senseless——she had a headache from hell to prove it. Despite her warning, he now had the upper hand. Not only was Gabe surrendering, but there was a gun pressed to her head.

"Put these on," the bad cop commanded, tossing something in her father's direction.

Even in the dark, Gabe caught it midair. Mallory heard the now-familiar clink of handcuffs. Her own wrists were bound behind her back, cutting into her tender skin. Her feet were taped to the legs of the chair. She was helpless to interfere . . . or was she?

While teaching her self-defense, Gabe had instructed her to use any weapon at her disposal, and right now, the legs of the chair she was sitting on were the closest weapons at hand. She had to act—now—if she was going to save him.

With fear clamping down on her shoulders, Mallory threw her weight forward, pushed to her feet, and rammed the back of the chair against her assailant's knees as hard as she could. His weapon discharged, causing her ears to ring and filling her nose with the acrid stench of cordite. She cringed, half expecting to feel a bullet tearing through her flesh.

She never saw Gabe move. One minute he was standing before her, the next he was pulling both her and the chair out of the bungalow. There came the sound of thrashing from inside. Gabe tugged at the tape that kept her tied to the chair.

"Run!" he said, the minute she was free.

But she hadn't taken a step before the thrashing subsided, and a tall, dark figure staggered into the door frame. A strangled scream died in Mallory's throat. She thought it was the other cop coming after them, but it wasn't. She recognized this man as her stepfather's master chief.

"I had to break his neck," Sebastian panted. "He fought like a demon."

Gabe was looking around like he'd lost something. "Son of a bitch," he cursed quietly. "Where'd the other one go?"

The other cop, Mallory realized. With her hands still locked behind her back, she huddled against the building, scanning the dark oceanfront for any sign of Clemens. Pinpricks of fright stabbed at her legs and arms.

"He must have run," Sebastian guessed. The area around the bungalow was quiet.

"Take Mallory inside," Gabe instructed, thrusting her at his colleague. "Dial 911. I'm going to find Helen. Where'd you leave her?"

Mom! Mallory was suddenly terrified for her mother.

"We're right here," called a voice on the wind. Helen leapt up the porch steps at a run, her friend, Leila, immediately behind. Throwing her arms around Mallory, she held her tight. "My baby," she cried, "are you all right?"

Mallory swayed against her mother, never more relieved to cling to her sweet scent and soothing embrace. "My head hurts," she admitted.

"It's okay now," Helen crooned. "Daddy and Sebastian saved you."

"Let's get back inside," Gabe said, clearly concerned about the bad guy on the loose.

"We saw a man run into the water," Leila volunteered, still out of breath. "Then we heard a gunshot. Is everyone all right?"

"Almost everyone," Sebastian answered dryly.

It was clear what he meant as Helen helped Mallory back into the building. Even in the dark information office, the body of the second man was hard to overlook, sprawled as he was in the middle of the floor, his head cocked at an unnatural angle.

"Close your eyes," Helen said, turning her daughter away from the body. "Leila, can you find the keys that go to these handcuffs?"

Leila stepped gingerly over the dead man and produced a ring of keys. Seconds later, Mallory rubbed the feeling back into her freed hands.

"Sebastian, make that call," she heard Gabe say.

Master Chief put down the receiver. "I can't, sir. The line's been cut."

"I've got my cell phone," Helen offered. Mallory felt her fumble inside her purse. "The signal is weak," she added, handing it to Gabe.

Gabe took the phone from her and pushed three buttons. A reedy voice filled the silence. "Nine-one-one. Do you have an emergency?"

In a matter-of-fact voice, Gabe summarized the bizarre events that had just unfurled. As they replayed in Mallory's mind, all her strength seemed to leak out of her legs. She was going to drag her mother to the floor if she didn't find a place to sit, *now*. The dark walls of the room were reeling, and she was going to throw up.

Thankfully, Gabe must have had one eye on her, because he ditched the cell phone and grabbed her right as she fell.

Her knees never even hit the floor.

You can go home, Commander Shafer had told them an hour ago. But Gabe and Helen were still at the Portsmouth Naval Medical Center, hovering over Mallory who'd been allowed to sleep at last.

In the dim lighting, the bleached white bandage on her head gave her a rakish look, a look heightened by the four silver studs in her left ear, which everyone forbore to comment on. Other than a mild concussion, she was unharmed— at least in a physical sense.

Smoothing Mallory's sheets, Helen was excruciatingly aware of Gabe, who sat on the other side of the bed, his back to the window, where the curtains were drawn. She could only imagine what he was feeling, having been the apparent cause for Mallory's false "arrest."

How strange that only weeks ago, Gabe had been the one

lying in a hospital bed, and she and Mallory had come reluctantly to claim him. Even the doctor on duty was the same. Commander Shafer had congratulated Gabe on his amazing recovery. He'd treated Mallory with fatherly concern.

Tonight Gabe looked exhausted, his face haggard and drawn. She knew he blamed himself for what had nearly happened. And yet, it wasn't his fault. It was hers, for not believing him. He'd tried to warn her of a conspiracy against him. She ought to have believed him, but the truth was, she hadn't wanted to. She hadn't wanted to face the most terrifying scenario imaginable.

Now her sweet, innocent daughter lay injured and traumatized all because Helen had refused to believe what Gabe was telling her. And the worst part was that it wasn't over yet. The bad guys were still out there, still on a mission to hunt Gabe down and bury his memories permanently.

With a chill in her spine that wouldn't go away, Helen rounded the bed and approached the chair Gabe was sitting in, both to seek and to offer comfort. His gaze rose to hers, and before she knew what he was doing, he'd tugged her into his lap. She stifled a sob as he wrapped his arms around her and buried his face in her hair.

With a shake of her head, Helen recalled a time when Gabe would die before admitting to any kind of uncertainty. It both shook and touched her that he would bare his doubts to her now. Yet, as they clung to each other, she was struck with the certainty that, together, she and Gabe could get through anything. *Just let those bastards try again,* she thought fiercely.

"Jesus, Helen. I almost got her killed," he whispered, so as not to waken Mallory.

She feathered her fingers through his newly trimmed hair. "Oh, honey, it wasn't your fault," she reassured him. "It was mine for not believing you. You're a hero. You managed to rescue Mallory and save yourself at the same time."

"Because Master Chief happened to be there."

"That's okay. Everyone can use a little help. No one is invincible."

He was quiet a moment, searching her face with eyes that glimmered in the dark. "I can't believe I underestimated the enemy. I should have realized they would use my family to get to me."

"Hush." She tugged on the locks of hair she'd just soothed. "You're not a psychic. Besides, who could have guessed they'd be so ruthless as to use a child, dressing as cops and telling her she'd done something wrong?"

They'd talked about this earlier, when the real police had escorted them to the hospital, hounding them with questions. Gabe hadn't mentioned a thing about someone wanting to kill him. Respecting his reasons—whatever they were— Helen, too, had kept silent. The fact that the dead man had passed himself off as a cop and was driving a sedan marked with the Sandbridge Police logo had thrown the police into a frenzy of speculation. They'd eventually left the hospital, scratching their heads as they departed.

"Why can't I remember?" Gabe lamented, shaking his head against her shoulder. "If I could just recall that night and why I was left behind . . ."

"Shhh. Don't think about it," she advised. "You're trying too hard."

"How can I not think about it?" he demanded, glancing at Mallory.

Helen made up her mind. "I'll help you forget," she promised, her resolve strong and steady. "Come home with me tonight." She'd made her decision in that instant: she was going to risk everything to hold her marriage together—her heart and even her life, if necessary. Gabe had suffered alone too long. The least she could do, as his wife and as the woman who loved him, was to defend him from those who wanted him dead.

He lifted his head and looked at her, his eyes gleaming like a cat's in the shadows. "I'm dangerous to know," he warned her.

A warm shiver stole over her. "So I've realized," she admitted. "But there are some things worth fighting for, Gabe. And our love is definitely one of them."

His arms tightened around her. "I needed to hear that," he said with wrenching gratitude. He pulled her forward and kissed her thoroughly. Their lips merged in a perfect, sensual caress. Desire flared between them, somehow heightened by the events of the evening and the threat that still lingered.

In the kiss, Helen tried to convey her newfound commitment. Tonight and every night, whether Gabe regained his memories or not; whether he became an active-duty SEAL again or remained permanently disabled, she would stand by him. He'd proven that despite the horror he'd endured, he was capable of tremendous generosity and devotion. She'd be a fool to ever let him go.

"You win," Gabe announced, breaking off the kiss. He rose to his feet, easing her intentionally against him as her feet approached the floor.

Helen stepped over to Mallory's bed, reluctant to leave her.

"Hey, Dad?" Mallory murmured, surprising them both by proving herself to be awake.

"Yeah, kiddo." Gabe was right there, looking anxious.

"Are you coming home?" she asked.

He hesitated, clearly still reluctant to involve his family in the vendetta against him. "There's nowhere in the world I'd rather be," he answered honestly. Leaning over the bed rail, he kissed Mallory on the cheek. "You're the greatest, you know that?" he told her. "Your warning saved my life."

Her green eyes slitted open and she smiled. "I couldn't let 'em kill you," she replied.

"You did good," he said. "A couple of my men are going to stand outside, and we'll be back here in the morning. Are you okay with that, or do you want me to stay?"

"You can go," she said, closing her eyes as if it hurt to keep them open. "You need to rest."

Her thoughtfulness struck him mute. He glanced up at Helen with tears in his eyes.

"Good night, sweetheart," she said, kissing Mallory's other cheek. "We'll be back first thing in the morning."

"'Kay," Mallory said peacefully.

Stepping from Mallory's room into the hallway, Helen blinked furiously to keep her tears subdued. In contrast to the hospital room, the hallway was bright with recessed lights and crowded with people.

Taking stock of them, she realized Gabe's eight-man squad was present, minus Jason Miller, whose absence was certainly conspicuous. Some of Gabe's men had taken up residence along the benches. Others lounged against the wall. Master Chief was off to one side in earnest conversation with Leila, who stared over his shoulder with a blank expression. Catching sight of Helen, she broke away from him while he was still in midsentence.

"How is she?" Leila wanted to know.

Helen still couldn't get over Leila's long black dress. "She'll be fine," she assured her friend. "I'm just sorry we had to ruin your date," she added, sending a questioning look at the master chief.

The man's eyes blazed with emotion—something Helen

had never before witnessed. He looked capable of picking up the potted plant beside him and throwing it. *Easy, boy.* Helen looked back at Leila, noticing for the first time the lines of strain around her friend's lovely eyes. "Are you okay?"

Leila shrugged. "I'm fine, just worried about you and Mallory."

Helen gave her a searching look. "We'll talk later," she promised.

"There's nothing to talk about," Leila said.

Oh, sure. Given the fury glittering in Master Chief's eyes, there was plenty to talk about. "I'll call you tomorrow," she insisted. Maybe after a good night's sleep, Leila would view her evening with a fresh perspective.

A murder on the first date wasn't the best way to start.

Helen turned toward Gabe and found him sharing words with Chief Westy McCaffrey. The Counterterrorist SEAL never failed to rattle Helen's sensibilities. She was used to SEALs being clean-cut military issue, but since Westy had to infiltrate terrorist regimes, he was allowed to grow his hair long. He wore a pair of jeans and a white T-shirt that failed to disguise the fearsome tattoo on his left arm. He wore a total of three hoops in his ears and a grim expression that made him look like Lucifer himself.

"I'll follow your car," Helen heard him say, letting her know that Westy intended to keep watch over their home. "Vinny and Bear have permission to park their butts here in the hall."

"Thanks, Chief," said Gabe, clapping the man on his shoulder. "But you're not going to sit in your car. No need to get harassed by the police, who'll be stepping up security outside my door."

"Whatever you want, sir." Westy caught Helen's eye and

winked at her, putting her at ease. The guy wasn't as scary as he looked.

Gabe bid good night to his squad. He approached his master chief to thank him again for his help.

With an unaccustomed frown, Sebastian was nonetheless civil. "Good night," he said, putting a fatherly hand on Gabe's shoulder. He nodded at Helen and sent another scalding look at Leila, before stalking toward the rear elevator, preferring his own company as he left the hospital.

Helen and Gabe trailed Leila toward the main elevators. Westy following behind them like a guardian angel from hell. Gabe surprised Helen by reaching for her hand in plain sight of his men.

Despite Westy's added protection, Helen felt an icy finger of fear rake her spine as they exited the hospital doors en route toward the parking garage.

Someone wanted Gabe dead, and the police seemed more outraged over civilians impersonating law enforcement officers than they were over Mallory's abduction.

With renewed trepidation, she clung to Gabe's hand. She wasn't the only one scanning the shadows for potential assassins.

Chapter Nineteen

Gabe found a message from his commander on the answering machine at home. *"I heard you had a rough evening, Lieutenant, and that your daughter is still at the hospital. Sorry to hear that. You'll have to tell me what the hell's going on when we meet on Sunday. I'm out of town for the rest of the week; otherwise, I would have been there to show my support. Take care of yourself and your family, and I'll see you at our appointment. Out."*

Gabe deleted the message.

"Sounds like the CO wants you back on active duty," Westy noted.

"I hope so," Gabe replied. "Can I get you anything to eat or drink, Chief?"

"No, sir, I'm fine."

"Let me show you where you're sleeping." Gabe led the way down the hall toward the study.

It gave him tremendous satisfaction to hand off the room he'd slept in, alone, for weeks. Helen had made it clear that she expected him to sleep with her, in their bedroom, for the rest of their lives. "The couch is a little lumpy," he apologized.

"Not a problem," Westy replied, testing the softness of the plaid cushion. "I won't be sleeping anyway."

The chief was going to keep watch, with his SIG Sauer P226 across his lap, so his lieutenant could relax. What a guy.

"Yeah, well, don't panic if you hear strange noises coming from the bedroom," Gabe warned him, dryly. Westy flashed him a grin that made Gabe feel incredibly good about himself. "Chase," he added, calling Westy by his real name.

"Sir?" The man's blue gaze invited confidence.

"Whoever's responsible for what happened tonight isn't going to stop until he's caught or I'm killed. If that happens, I want you guys to watch over Helen like you did before."

Determination hardened the lines of Westy's jaw. "We're not going to let you die again, sir. We took our eyes off you last time. We're not going to make the same mistake twice."

Gratitude swamped Gabe. "Thank you," he said roughly. "Good night." He turned toward his bedroom and his waiting wife.

Helen was naked. Gabe savored the view of her curled up on her side, fast asleep. One corner of the blanket was pulled over her torso, leaving her tanned thighs and silken shoulders bare. He could just make out the tops of her breasts. Her hair spilled over the pillow like spun gold.

Lying there like that, she took his breath away.

It took all his discipline to turn away and take a shower. He emerged in record time and dimmed the lights, so that the only light remaining was a soft pink tulip bulb beside the bed. With a towel around his hips, he eased onto the mattress and peeled back the blanket covering her. *Exquisite.*

She stirred and unfolded, her limbs lithe and firm and nicely tanned, except in some very private places. Offering him a sleepy smile, she raised her arms over her head, so that her breasts rose invitingly. Growling with anticipation, he caught her by the waist and fastened his mouth on them, suckling with intent.

She'd given herself to him in Annapolis, but that had only been a maybe. Tonight was different. In Helen's amber eyes was an unqualified invitation to forever.

He promised himself she would never, *ever* look back on this night and regret giving him a second chance. He knew he was a lucky man. Some might disagree, considering what he'd gone through in North Korea. But the truth was he'd been given the opportunity to review who he was and what he'd done with his life. He'd done well as a SEAL, carving a reputation for himself as a dedicated leader, selflessly serving his country. But as a father and a husband, he'd failed miserably. Only when he'd been captured and tortured had he come to understand that it was love that gave him the strength to defy his captors; it was family that gave him a reason to survive.

And so, tonight was more than an opportunity to make love to his gorgeous wife. Tonight was a reaffirmation, a new beginning. Desire crackled between them, as palpable as ever, drawing them together with urgency. Pushing himself deep inside her, Gabe gazed into Helen's radiant eyes. His fingers threaded through hers as she convulsed delicately around him. In her pupils he saw the reflection of his own face. "I'm sorry I didn't believe you, Gabe," she apologized.

He kissed her, not wanting to be reminded of the events that brought him here. Sliding a hand between their bodies, he touched her in a way that made speech impossible for her. He wanted tonight to be a cherished memory for years to come.

But she managed to speak anyway. "I love you, Gabe!" she gasped, climaxing with gratifying force.

Her confession short-circuited his intent to make love to her for hours. Scalding pleasure burst through him, rocketing him to the stars and back again, proving that he might be Navy SEAL but he was still only human.

Leila pushed her sunglasses back up her slippery nose and realigned her body on the poolside lounge chair so that the slats didn't gouge her hip bones. The book she was reading failed to capture her imagination, and she found herself reflecting on the previous evening.

It had been a date like no other—that much was certain. She'd gone out with Sebastian, swearing a private oath that she wouldn't sleep with him. To guard herself, she'd pulled out her ugliest black dress—one that Altul had bought her, if only to remind her how a man could break a woman's heart.

It had taken Sebastian less than an hour to convince her to take it off.

Stupid! she seethed, jamming the errant glasses up on her nose again. She was so easily led astray where Sebastian León was concerned. He'd probably laugh if he knew she'd been a virgin on her wedding night. To him, she must look like an easy conquest. All he had to do was to dangle a carrot in front of her and she'd strip for him!

Bastard!

Of course, it was a very big carrot, one that no man of her acquaintance had ever offered her: a baby. No strings attached.

No visible strings anyway.

She'd come to her senses mere seconds after climaxing. She'd realized the truth the minute he'd pulled out of her and disappeared to help a frantic Helen.

The strings were in her heart.

She was incapable of letting Sebastian make love to her without falling in love. In that crystalline moment, when he was buried deep inside her and she was drowning in bliss, she had caught herself doing it: falling in love with him. Just as she had last May, when she'd seduced him.

The realization was sufficiently terrifying to make her change her mind. She didn't want to fall in love with a SEAL. Because every time he left to go on a mission, she would feel as if he were leaving her. Leila had seen what that lifestyle had done to Helen and Gabe's marriage!—although, now they seemed to have reconciled. Time would tell the truth in that situation.

In Leila's experience, the future was always worse than anyone suspected. With a troubled sigh, she blinked down at the book she was reading and tried once more to involve herself in the heavy text. A shadow fell across the pages, distracting her. She refused to look up, knowing it had to be George, the annoying Greek man who lived in the condo next to hers.

"Go away," she said. Her waspish tongue had, unfortunately, not deterred George yet. Nor did it deter him now.

With her nerves already taut, Leila whipped off her sunglasses and glared up at the interloper. "I am not in the mood . . ." Her voice trailed away as she beheld not George the Greek, but Sebastian the SEAL, looking very appealing in a short-sleeved knit shirt that was impossibly white and navy shorts that looked like they'd been ironed.

He sat, uninvited, on the lounge chair next to hers. "I'm afraid you have no choice," he said, icily polite.

Leila winced, hearing determination and a strong dose of wounded ego in his tone. She'd tried to tell him last night at the hospital that she'd changed her mind about their agreement.

"Actually, I do," she insisted, flipping over onto her back and sitting up.

Sebastian's gaze slid down her oiled body then back up again. He seemed confused by her answer.

"Have a choice," she clarified.

His jaw hardened. A glint came into his eyes that let her know she was in for a long, tough battle.

"You can't just cancel an agreement," he growled, his voice pitched low, so as not to draw the attention of the other sun worshipers. The pool was well attended on this sultry August afternoon.

"I'm sorry," she said, mindful of the frustration in his voice this time. "I am. I should never have agreed to it in the first place. I only went out with you to apologize. I didn't even intend to have sex with you." She whispered the last sentence.

"In case you missed it, we didn't exactly have sex," he articulated through his teeth.

"Look, I understand that you're frustrated. I didn't mean to tease you—"

"You think this is just because I'm frustrated?" His magnificent eyes flashed with anger. "This is more than that. Frustration is easy. I can take care of that myself."

Okay—too much information. Leila rubbed her bleary eyes. She hadn't gotten much sleep last night, what with all the excitement, and Sebastian killing a man—dear God, she hadn't even begun to digest that detail! "I don't think this is the time to talk," she said, keeping a lid on her temper. "I'll call you in a couple of weeks—"

"No." His reply was unequivocal.

She looked at him again, taking note of the mulish set to his chin. "I see you're used to getting your way," she noted.

"Leila," he begged in a low voice. "Whatever I did wrong, please allow me to make up for it. I was wrong to press you, I admit it. Please don't push me away like this. I need you so much!"

She was taken off guard by his impassioned plea, by the throbbing desperation in his tone. She felt herself weaken. Desire tugged at her, further undermining her defenses. She thought about his delicious kisses, about the pleasure he'd given her, and her decision to avoid him seemed suddenly extreme.

"I can't," she wavered, aware that her breasts were tingling beneath the tiny triangles of her bikini top.

"Please," he said again. "We can do this entirely by your rules. Whatever you want, I will give it to you."

Oh, God, he was making this impossible! She closed her eyes, swallowing against the dryness in her mouth. What she wanted was to drag him into her cool condominium and strip his clothes off and have mind-blowing sex with him. But if she did that, then she'd fall in love with him and he would leave her, to do what SEALs did.

She didn't want to face that kind of heartache.

"I can't," she repeated. She stood up suddenly and took the two steps that sent her plunging into the pool. He'd come to the pool fully dressed. He couldn't follow her into the water. This was the only place she was safe—the only place she could cool down.

He watched from his seat on the lounge chair for half an hour. Leila did laps, pushing herself farther than she'd ever pushed herself, all to keep from getting out of the pool and facing temptation again.

Finishing off a backstroke, she turned at the far end, her

gaze sliding helplessly toward Sebastian. The lounge chair was empty. Her gaze swept the pool area.

He was gone.

Her disappointment was so heavy, she nearly sank. She gripped the edge of the pool, wondering what conclusion he'd come to. Had he given up on her then? The weight on her heart told her she didn't want him to give up so easily.

She dragged herself out of the pool and sat on the ledge, feeling miserable. She'd done the right thing, she told herself. She'd protected her heart. Loving a SEAL wasn't worth the risk of a broken heart.

Not even if he gave her a baby.

So why did she feel that she'd let something precious slip away?

The call came at two o'clock in the afternoon. Gabe picked it up in the kitchen. Sweaty and hungry, he and Helen had just put the crowning touches on the rock garden.

"Hello?"

"Gabe Renault?"

"Yes."

"This is Sheriff Dunton, Sandbridge Police Department. We've identified the man who abducted your daughter. I thought you might want to know, he was a former SEAL. It took some time to find his records. He's been officially dead for three years."

What the hell? Gabe mopped his forehead with a kitchen towel, his thoughts in a tailspin.

"Seeing as how he was already legally dead, I see no reason to press charges against the man that killed him, Sebastian León," the man continued, shuffling papers in the background. "But I'd sure like to know what this is all about.

Why don't you come down to the station and we'll go over it again."

Gabe heaved an inward sigh. He turned to eye Helen as she entered the kitchen door. She looked as hot and sweaty as he felt from working in her wildflower garden. The tank top she wore clung to her damply, making it amply clear that she wore no bra underneath. "Uh, maybe this afternoon," he hedged, admiring Helen's backside as she bent over the sink and washed her face. "I'm busy this morning."

He hung up abruptly and took the two steps needed to grab his wife by the waist and pull her back against him. Her warm chuckle only aroused him more. "Mallory might wake up," she reminded him, nonetheless squirming against his zipper.

He lifted her off her feet and dragged her into the walk-in pantry. Shutting them into the small dark space, he released the button on her shorts and pushed them over her hips.

"What about Westy?" she panted, grabbing a shelf for support.

"Catching a nap," Gabe managed, freeing himself from his jeans. He slipped a hand under her tank top, cupping a breast as he pushed himself inside her, finding her wonderfully wet and warm.

Love was a powerful aphrodisiac, he realized. The way he figured it, having been gone for three hundred and sixty-eight days total, he could make love to Helen every day for the rest of their lives and never make up for his deprivation.

"Still love me?" he rasped, every nerve in his body humming with pleasure. Helen's scent blended with that of cooking spices and filled his senses.

"Forever," she replied.

Chapter Twenty

G abe and Rodriguez had just left the house for a meeting with Commander Lovitt when the telephone rang. Helen stretched beneath the cool sheets and reached for it. "Hello?" she said, hoping to hear from Leila.

"Helen, this is Noel Terrien," said a familiar, doleful voice.

She came up on one elbow. Casting an eye at the clock, she wondered why the doctor would be calling on a Sunday. "Hi, how are you?" she asked, a question in her voice.

"Is your husband there?" the doctor asked on a tense note.

"No, I'm afraid not. Is something wrong?"

Dr. Terrien hesitated. "Helen, I haven't been completely honest with Gabriel about certain matters, and the situation is beginning to weigh on me. I'd like to come clean with him."

An unpleasant feeling twisted through her. "What do you mean?" she asked.

The doctor sighed. "Gabriel's commander, Eddie Lovitt, is a friend of mine. I owed him a favor, so when he asked me to take on your husband's case, I agreed. The other day, Gabriel wanted to know if someone was following his recovery. I admitted that his CO was keeping tabs on him. I thought Eddie was eager to have him back on the team. Now I'm not so sure. I just called the Naval Medical Center to see if Gabriel's prescription had been renewed, if he was taking his medication—"

"It made him sleepy," Helen interrupted. "I don't think he takes it anymore."

"I know," the doctor sighed. "I learned with the call that someone had altered his prescription without my approval. He hasn't been on Dexamphetamine at all, but a memory inhibitor."

Stunned, Helen grappled with the implication. "I don't understand. Are you saying his CO had something to do with that?"

"Only someone with the right kind of contacts could have altered my initial prescription. It dawned on me that Eddie seems more afraid of Gabriel's memories than he is interested in having him back on the team."

"Oh, my God," Helen said, horrified that Gabe's superior, whom he admired and served with loyalty, would dare to meddle in her husband's treatment.

"I didn't realize I was steering Gabriel in the wrong direction," Dr. Terrien continued, clearly upset by his role in the subterfuge. "All this time I've been insisting that his fears are illusions, but they may not be. I just don't understand why Eddie would want to repress Gabe's memories, unless he did something wrong that he doesn't want your husband remembering."

"Gabe is visiting his commander this morning," Helen admitted. Every bone in her body had turned brittle. Outside her bedroom window thunder rumbled.

"I'm sorry for my part in this," the doctor lamented.

"That's okay," Helen reassured him. "I'm just grateful that you told me." She hung up the phone and lay in her bed, paralyzed for the moment. If Lovitt had purposefully tried to repress Gabe's memories, could he also be the one trying to kill him? No, surely not. Commanders in the Navy weren't ruthless killers with hidden agendas.

Still, Gabe deserved to be warned about Lovitt's possible involvement. She sat up and called the Spec Ops Building, but no one answered. Where were the duty personnel? Surely someone else was at the office.

Giving up, she went in search of Vinny, who had taken Westy's place in guarding over them.

On a Sunday morning, Sebastian would normally have gone to church and enjoyed the brunch at the Shifting Sands. He'd have dressed himself in his best suit, one of three that he'd owned for years and took meticulous care of.

This morning, he was not dressed for church. He was scarcely dressed at all, sitting in his living room wearing boxer shorts and watching reruns of *Gilligan's Island*. He hadn't even bothered to make fresh coffee.

It was not a good sign.

But why expend the energy of showering, shaving, and dressing with no one in his life to appreciate the results? Leila had turned him down. It was over between them.

He closed his eyes, letting his misery overtake him for the moment. Soon he would think of a plan—something guaranteed to make Leila change her mind. But for the moment, he would wallow in self-pity. This was not a side of him his men ever saw. Sebastian the SEAL was not ruled by his emotions. But Sebastian the man had no choice. He was a Latino, after all. And Latinos were fools for women.

Oh, but what a woman! Just thinking of Leila, the beautiful, complicated package that she was, caused his heart to yearn for her. He'd been born to shelter her, to stand loyally by her side, to father the child she yearned to hold.

Still, she'd failed to grasp the depths of his devotion. Perhaps he ought to have been more explicit.

The phone rang shrilly, startling him. Thinking it might be Leila or a member of the team, he lunged for it. "León."

Hesitation on the other end. "This is Hannah Geary. May I speak with Lieutenant Renault?"

Disappointment made him short. "He's not here."

Thoughtful silence now, and grave. "Can you tell me where he is?"

Sebastian glanced at the watch that never left his wrist. "He had an appointment with the commander at Spec Ops this morning."

"Commander Lovitt?"

Hearing dismay in her tone, he sat up straighter. "What's this about?" he demanded.

"Who are you?" she countered.

"Master Chief León. I work with Lieutenant Renault."

She seemed to consider whether to confide in him or not. "I don't think it's a good idea for him to visit the commander alone," she told him vaguely.

Why not? "The XO should be there and other duty personnel. Why don't you tell me what this is about?"

His confiding tone got the results he wanted—it usually did. "Very well," she relented. "You know my partner who was killed, Ernest Forrester?"

"Yes."

"Lovitt's the one he was investigating."

Stunned, it took Sebastian a moment to find his voice. "For what?" he asked, though he feared he knew.

"Trafficking weapons."

Impossible! Sebastian cast his eyes to the window and the ominous ocean. Yet, it made terrible sense. Lovitt had insider information. He could time his interdictions to take place before the team's scheduled arrivals. He had necessary contacts to hire a band of former SEALs to do his dirty work, like the one Sebastian had killed the other night.

"How do you know this?" Sebastian demanded. She'd told Jaguar that Forrester's files had been cleared out, his hard drive removed.

"Ernie's notebook was discovered in the wreck. One of my colleagues must have slipped it into my mailbox. His notes were encrypted, but I cracked the code. Ernie's been investigating Lovitt for some time. I think there's enough evidence in the notebook to lock him up."

Sebastian reeled. This was red-hot information, the kind of traitorous activity the Navy abhorred. And yet, Lovitt had been getting away with it for how long? Had he grown leery of Forrester's suspicions and arranged to have him killed?

It hit Sebastian square on the chin that Geary herself was in danger. "Where are you calling from?" he asked, suddenly concerned.

"From my brother's house," she admitted.

"Do you have the notebook?"

She hesitated slightly. "I do."

"Does anyone else know about this?"

She hesitated, telling him that her next words were a lie. "No, no one."

Sebastian rubbed his forehead, thinking swiftly. "Do not assume you're safe," he warned her. "You're probably being watched right now."

"That's why I'm here," she told him.

"Where's the nearest naval installation in your area?" he asked.

"Annapolis."

"Are you familiar with it?"

"Not really. I did my training at Quantico. And forgive my cynicism, but I don't trust naval authorities not to make this notebook disappear. Someone is protecting Lovitt or Ernie's office wouldn't have been cleaned out."

Good point. "Quantico, then," he agreed. Quantico was mostly Marines. They could be trusted to see to Geary's safety while handling the evidence with care. "Go there right now and surrender the notebook to the military police. Ask them to place you in a witness protection program. I'll call ahead and alert them of your arrival."

She considered his course of action in silence. "Sounds doable," she said, severing the call with efficiency that made Sebastian's eyebrows go up. He hoped to meet Hannah Geary one day. She followed orders like a SEAL.

He sat in his chair, too shocked to think clearly. His own commander had been stealing weapons right under their noses and they'd been none the wiser! Seeing the receiver still in his hand, he put it down. The first order was to get in touch with the MPs at Quantico. He did that at once, alerting them to the analyst's imminent arrival. They promised to keep close watch on the notebook and protect her security.

As for Jaguar's situation, there was little benefit to alerting the military police at Dam Neck. Until the notebook was in Sebastian's hands, the authorities would scoff at such allegations.

Thank God PO3 Rodriguez was guarding the lieutenant's back this morning. Surely Lovitt wouldn't do something so drastic as to try to kill Jaguar right there on base. Yet if Geary's suspicions were correct, then it was the CO who'd planned the incident at Back Bay Wildlife Refuge. But why? Jaguar must have stumbled on something a year ago that made him a liability to Lovitt's operation. Lovitt may have ordered Miller to leave Jaguar behind in the warehouse—a warehouse Lovitt's workers had set to blow the moment they absconded with the fourth missile, a missile that could have profited Lovitt hundreds of thousand of dollars on the black market.

Appalled to think that he'd worked so closely with Lovitt and never once suspected his perfidy, Sebastian scraped a hand over his bristles. He snatched up the phone a third time and called the Special Operations Building. To his dismay, no one answered. Where the hell were the duty personnel?

Cursing, he severed the call and punched in the numbers to Vinny's pager. The petty officer second class was keeping watch over Helen and Mallory.

Sebastian then raced up the stairs to his loft and threw his clothes on. His phone rang as he scrubbed his teeth. "Vinny!" he barked, expecting the petty officer on the other end.

"No," a woman said in uncertain tones.

Sebastian's heart stopped dead. It was Leila. *Madre de Dios*, her timing could not be worse. "Leila," he replied, trying not to speak with gunfire urgency. "I'm sorry but I can't talk right now. Can you drive over to Helen's and stay with her and Mallory? The Sandbridge Police have posted a watch, but I need to pull Vinny away, and I'd feel more comfortable if Helen had someone with her."

Leila answered his call to duty immediately. "Okay," she agreed. "Is something wrong?"

"We have a situation. I can't explain. Please, just get there as fast as possible. I'll call you later," he added, glad for an excuse to keep the lines of communication open.

Severing the call, he tossed the phone onto his bed,

jammed his feet into his boots, and laced them up in record time.

His cell phone started ringing as he switched the ignition in his Falcon and fired her up.

"I tried your house but your phone was busy," Vinny informed him.

Sebastian was speeding, kicking up sand in his haste to get to the back gate. Fortunately, the streets were relatively empty on this overcast morning. The skies looked like they would open up at any moment. "Is Rodriguez with Jaguar?" he rapped out.

"Yes," Vinny answered. "What's the news?"

"Lovitt is behind the missing arms shipments." He swerved to miss a trash can that had rolled into the street. "I want you to contact every member of the squad. Tell them we're meeting at Spec Ops in ten minutes. Leila's on her way to stay with Helen and Mallory."

Despite the implication that they were going to challenge their own commander—a violation of the Uniform Code of Military Justice—Vinny answered with a clear affirmative. "Yes, Master Chief. I need to tell you that Jaguar's psychiatrist called. Someone switched Jaguar's prescription, so that he's been taking memory inhibitors. The psychiatrist thinks it was Lovitt—that the CO's worried that Jaguar will remember something."

It was all the confirmation Sebastian needed. "Roger," he said grimly. "Meet you in ten minutes."

Sebastian dropped his cell phone and gave the road his undivided attention. At that precise minute, rain began to pelt the car, pounding on the windshield, distorting his vision before his wipers kicked into action. Thunder rumbled overhead, causing the old beater to vibrate.

Sebastian muttered under his breath, cursing his self-absorption and his blindness for not realizing that Lovitt was the villain all this time. They'd suspected only Miller, but Miller was too spineless to have effected such an undertaking.

Hopefully Lovitt had no idea now how close to exposure he really was. Maybe he and his lieutenant were enjoying a civil repartee in which Jaguar was discussing the information he'd forwarded to the FBI. Lovitt would then commend him for passing on such valuable intelligence, and Jaguar would walk out of there, safe and sound.

But the circumstances two nights ago spoke of desperation on the CO's part. He knew his clandestine operation had a potential leak in the form of Gabriel Renault. He was afraid the lieutenant remembered more than he admitted.

Last time Lovitt had sent his renegades to take out Jaguar. This time he would want to finish the job himself.

Overhearing Vinny's hasty phone calls, Helen knew something was terribly wrong. He'd contacted all the members of first squad, asking them to report to the Spec Ops Building ASAP. If that was all he'd said, it wouldn't worry Helen that Gabe was at Spec Ops himself. What worried her was the news that Lovitt had been stealing weapons abroad. It didn't take a rocket scientist to realize that he was the one trying to kill Gabe all this time. Her husband must have come across something last year that could have exposed Lovitt, and Lovitt had been taking measures to prevent that ever since.

Now Gabe was alone with him—well, not completely alone. He had Rodriguez to guard his back. But he'd left his gun at home, knowing he'd have to pass through security at Spec Ops and not wanting to cause Sebastian trouble for lending it to him.

With a cold feeling of fatality, Helen thought about the gun, tucked in the drawer of her bedside table.

As if sensing urgency in the air, Mallory wandered out of her bedroom to stand by her mother. Helen saw with a glance that the studs in her ear were gone.

"What's going on?" Mallory asked, taking in Vinny's tense expression as he hung up the phone for the last time.

"Leila's coming to stay with you," he said, checking the pockets of his battle-dress uniform, as if taking inventory of his weapons. "There's still a cop outside if something comes up."

"We're coming with you," Helen decided, adrenaline surging through her system. She couldn't just sit back and wait, dreading another call that said her husband hadn't made it.

"No, ma'am," said the SEAL. "You need to stay here."

"I am not staying here," Helen insisted. "Gabe is my husband. I lost him once before. I have no intention of losing him again!"

Vinny gestured toward Mallory. "What about your daughter? She's still recovering from a head wound."

Torn, Helen glanced at Mallory, whose face still bore marks of the assault two nights ago.

"I need to go," the SEAL said, slipping out the door. He had shut it and was gone before Helen could make up her mind.

"Damn it!" she cursed, stamping a foot in frustration.

"I feel fine, Mom," Mallory said. She turned toward the closet to rummage for her shoes. "Let's go after Dad."

Helen regarded her with admiration. "No, Mal. Vinny's right. We should let Gabe's men handle this. We'd probably just get in the way." She thought again about the gun. Her father had taught her to peg a can at fifty paces. If Gabe's life was the least bit in danger and she had the opportunity to save it, she would kill to protect him. "We don't have a car," she added, torn by the need to do something.

Mallory straightened, pushing the hair out of her eyes. "Leila's here," she said, hurrying toward the door. "We can take her car."

There'd be trouble getting Leila's car on the base, but it was worth a try. "Hold on just a sec," Helen said, racing down the hallway. She went straight to her bedside table and pulled Gabe's gun from the drawer. It felt cold and heavy in her hand. Double-checking the safety, she shoved it into her waistband.

Leila was waiting at the front door, her hair wet with rain.

"We're going after Gabe," Helen explained succinctly.

"Yes," said Leila, taking one look at the determined gleam in her friend's eyes.

The door slammed behind them as they hurried to Leila's car, ignoring the policeman who frowned out his car window over the newspaper he was reading.

Back in the house, the bud on Gabe's cactus unfurled in a bloodred bloom.

Miller was on his way out, Commander Lovitt explained, casting Gabe a somber gaze across the glossy surface of his desk. The man was just too incompetent. He should never have let Gabe stay behind on the night of the mission-gone-wrong. "Do you remember that night, Lieutenant?" Lovitt added, fixing him with his silvery eyes.

Gabe wrestled with just how much to say. "Not fully, sir," he admitted. "I'm told I was knocked unconscious at one point. I may never remember it."

Lovitt narrowed his gaze at him in a considering manner. "I can't give you back a year of your life, Lieutenant," he said matter-of-factly, "but I can promote you to Lieutenant Commander. Given the intelligence you hunted up, you certainly deserve a promotion." He patted the information the FBI had edited and forwarded. "How'd you like to take the patrol craft out for a little spin, get your feet wet again?"

Gabe considered the offer with enthusiasm. "Are you saying I'll be back on the team soon, sir?"

"Absolutely. As soon as I process the paperwork. In the meantime, we've got a few new gadgets aboard the PC you'll need to familiarize yourself with. Have you got an hour or so?"

"Yes, sir! Er, would PO3 Rodriguez be able to accompany us?" he asked, leery of leaving behind his bodyguard a second time.

"I don't see why not. How about filling me in on your daughter's abduction as we drive over to Little Creek."

As they stepped into the parking lot a few minutes later, the rain came pouring down. "We'll take my car," the CO offered.

The coastal patrol craft was docked at Little Creek Amphibious Base, just a short trek from Dam Neck. Gabe sat in the passenger seat, as the commander drove them at a breakneck pace down the slick boulevard.

Rodriguez sat in the back, his MP5 submachine gun close at hand. Considering the company he was in, Gabe wondered at the prickling of his scalp.

Despite the CO's reckless driving, they arrived at the Amphibious Base intact. Gabe stepped into the rain, relieved. Cool rivers of water soaked his fatigues as he ran a satisfied gaze along the waterfront.

God, he'd missed his job! Missed the formidable appearance of the gray-hulled battleships and amphibious craft. Missed the smell of the tar and the sea brine, even the antics of the seabirds, hunkered now in the parking lot to avoid the bad weather.

Because it was Sunday, there were few personnel on-site, just a couple of guards who saluted them as they marched along the cement jetty, past the other water craft and toward their own boat: the USS *Nor'easter.*

The sailor standing watch let out the standard whistle as the CO preceded Gabe up the gangplank. Gabe returned the sailor's salute, not recognizing him. A crew of twenty-five regular Navy kept the ship up and running. Being a member of the eight-man SEAL squad, he didn't always know their names. Still, he was left with an uneasy feeling not to see a single familiar face.

Not even the skipper of the ship was around this rainy Sunday morning. In fact, other than the sailor on watch, the boat appeared deserted. The hairs on Gabe's neck rose slowly to attention. He was just recognizing that he'd walked into a trap, when Rodriguez lodged the barrel of his submachine gun against Gabe's ribs and urged him to step inside the bridge.

Adrenaline rocketed through him. God damn him for a blind idiot! It wasn't Miller whose incompetence had nearly gotten him killed a year ago! Miller had only been following Lovitt's orders, as was PO3 Rodriguez, now. Christ Jesus, it was his own CO who was trying to kill him! But why?

As Gabe stared, confounded, at his commanding officer, Lovitt swaggered toward the controls and started flipping switches. "You should always remember how to steer a boat, Lieutenant," he drawled with a smirk. "You never know when the skill might come in handy." He picked up the ship's loudspeaker and called out, "All hands prepare the ship for leaving port. The Officer of the Deck is shifting the watch

from the starboard quarterdeck to the bridge. Away all lines."
He released the handset to add, "I've always enjoyed saying
that."

Gabe's gaze flew out the rain-speckled window to the
deck below. Two more men in Navy jumpsuits had appeared
to help the first man haul in lines and take them out for storage below. With a sinking feeling, Gabe noted the men
weren't built like average sailors. They were more renegade
SEALs in Lovitt's employ.

"Under way. Shift colors," the commander added, and the
PC began to back out of its berth.

Gabe cursed himself for not making the connection earlier! *Shit!* He should shoot himself for his own incompetence
but he doubted that would be necessary. There wasn't any
question, given the other night, that Lovitt was taking him
out to sea to execute him. He shuddered with indignation,
sweat bathing his pores.

His only hope now was to reason with the man. "If something happens to me, sir, an investigation will certainly expose you," he threatened through his teeth.

It took all of Lovitt's focus to negotiate the narrow chan-
nel that took them out into a bay. "There won't be an investigation, Renault," he replied, his poise unruffled. "The Navy
will be satisfied with my statement."

"And what will that statement be?" Gabe pressed, ignoring the prodding of Rodriguez's gun.

Lovitt glanced over his shoulder. "That you went ballistic
on me—a side effect of your PTSD, apparently. Then you
shot yourself in the head"—he clicked his tongue in mock
regret—"overcome with guilt for betraying your country,
apparently."

"Betraying my country! You slimy son of a bi–ugh!"

Rodriguez shut him up, jamming the butt of his weapon between Gabe's shoulder blades.

Gabe staggered forward, taking firm rein on his temper. Outnumbered five men to one, with no weapon of his own, he needed to keep his cool and think. The only thing he had going for him was his brain.

The PC continued to speed forward, smashing into swells, sending up white spumes on either side of the boat. But, hell, if he thought too long, he'd have all five men to contend with at once. Better to deal with these two first, seize the radio, and call for help.

Gabe twisted without warning, grabbed the barrel of Rodriguez's gun, and aimed it straight at Lovitt. Rodriguez pulled the trigger instinctively, spewing 9mm rounds about the cabin. Glass crackled and collapsed. Lovitt ducked, clutching his forearm where he'd been hit. With a growl, he threw himself at Gabe, who'd shoved Rodriguez hard enough to send him flying to the opposite wall.

As Lovitt barreled into Gabe, they fell crashing onto the digital readouts. Lovitt managed to get an arm around Gabe's neck. He hauled Gabe off the instruments, grappling for his own weapon. In the brief reprieve, Gabe struck out a foot and hit the ship's throttle, kicking it forward. The PC accelerated suddenly, knocking the CO off balance. He staggered backward, dragging Gabe with him. With a crunch, they hit the rear wall together.

The stranglehold on Gabe's neck loosened abruptly. He twisted free in time to see Lovitt crumple from a standing position. The man had hit the key box projecting from the wall, hard enough to knock himself senseless. Gabe snatched the 9mm pistol from Lovitt's limp fingers.

Rodriguez had recovered and was taking aim at him. At the flash of fire in the muzzle, Gabe dropped and rolled, returning fire. With a satisfying thud, a 9mm bullet pierced Rodriguez's chest. The man's weapon clattered to the floor, and a stunned expression stole over his face.

Gabe leaned over and seized the submachine gun. "You're a piece of shit," he informed the man. Tucking the smaller weapon into his waistband, he stepped over Lovitt, who was still unconscious, and locked the pilothouse doors, keeping the other men out, at least for the moment. He picked up the radio handset, making note of his coordinates. "This is the USS *Nor'easter*, PC 5. I have a Mayday. Do you read?"

"We read you, *Nor'easter*. What's your Mayday?"

Keeping his eyes peeled for any sign of the three remaining renegades, Gabe relayed his situation as best he could. "There are two men down," he added, "and three hostiles aboard the ship. Friendly is in the pilothouse and cornered. Copy."

"What are your coordinates, *Nor'easter*?"

Gabe quickly provided the necessary information. A shadow flickered by the doorway, and he ducked under the display dash, taking the handset with him. It was only a matter of time before the renegades shot the door down and came after him. Given their training, they would overpower him instantly. Damn it, he ought to have broken cover and jumped overboard. The ocean was the best place for a SEAL to hide.

"Repeat," he whispered. "The three hostiles aboard the ship are highly trained. Send in Special Operations Forces to overtake them."

Thud! Gabe tensed for action, but it was only Rodriguez who'd fainted from his gun wound and slipped into a prone position.

Gabe snaked out of his hiding place to drag the man toward him. Leaving a streak of blood on the floor, he pulled the traitor on top of him, using the man's body as a shield. With a fine tremor in his fingers and his eyes trained on either door, he waited for the inevitable.

Helen, he thought as the silhouette of a tango sidled up to the rectangle of glass at the door. *Forgive me for being so ignorant that I didn't see this coming. If I die here today, don't grieve me, baby. Not everyone is given a second chance. I'm thankful for the opportunity to have loved you the way you deserve to be loved.*

Chapter Twenty-one

Master Chief and a squad of four men found the XO at the Special Operations Building and no one else. Jason Miller sat at his desk staring blindly at its contents. When Westy and Sebastian leaned into his open door, he scarcely glanced up at them.

"Where's the lieutenant, XO?" Sebastian demanded, not bothering to pitch his question in deferential tones.

Miller remained glassy-eyed. "The CO took him out on the PC," he said, subdued. Without another word, he began emptying his desk's contents into the trash can.

Westy and Sebastian shared a knowing look. There would definitely be some changes in personnel soon.

"We've got to get to the PC before it heads out to sea," Sebastian said, heading for the door.

"Roger that." Westy ran past him, setting a faster pace. Throwing open the exit, they came face-to-face with Helen, Leila, and Mallory looking white-faced and very determined.

Sebastian was startled to greet Leila while in his master chief mode. "The CO has taken Jaguar to the PC," he told

Helen, injecting as much reassurance in his tone as he could. "Rodriguez is watching his back," he added, seeing panic flare in her eyes. "I want you to stay here," he added firmly, "out of the way!" God, just the thought of Leila going anywhere near an armed situation made him panic. "Do you understand me?"

"Yes," said Helen, answering for them.

He suffered the terrible suspicion that she'd heard, but she wasn't listening. In that case, they'd just have to outrun her. "Let's go." The SEALs leapt into their vehicles and sped away. Ten minutes later, they arrived at the waterfront. It wasn't merely raining now, it was pouring. They jumped from their vehicles, gazes fixed with dismay on the empty berth where the USS *Nor'easter* normally sat at anchor.

"What now, Master Chief?" Vinny asked.

Sebastian's gaze raked the array of sea vessels, mostly amphibious craft rocking in their moorings. His heart beat fast and thready.

"There's a helo on the LCU," Westy noted, pointing toward the Landing Craft Unit, a 135-foot amphibious craft. Its normal cargo was tanks, cranes, and food supplies, but today, as if put there by providence, sat an MV-22 Osprey, multiengine helicopter.

"Takes two men to fly it." Sebastian eyed Luther, who'd been trained to aviate. "What do you say, sir?"

Luther hesitated, casting an uneasy glance at the operations building. They didn't have time to solicit an official request. Seizing military transport without authorization could have serious ramifications. On the other hand, the SEALs would never forgive themselves if they let their platoon leader die.

"I don't see what choice we have," Luther agreed.

"Let's go." They ran along the pier toward the LCU. The

petty officer standing guard fell back, too intimidated to try to stop them.

Once on the LCU, the SEALs scrambled into the helicopter, leaving the copilot's seat for Sebastian, who unlatched the bird from its moorings. He leapt nimbly aboard.

"Hang on!" Luther shouted as he started up the engine. "We're in for a rough ride."

The Osprey rose with a *whop whop whop* of the main rotors. The gusting wind caught its tail and swung it about, narrowly missing the radio antennae on the landing craft. As they rose into the air, rain spewed into the open cargo hold, wetting the floor where Westy, Vinny, and Teddy crouched. None of the men even noticed.

Each one of them grappled with the bizarre reality that their commander was not the man they'd thought, that he'd lured one of their own out to sea to finish what he'd failed to do in Pyongyang.

The last time they had huddled together thinking of Jaguar, it had been pitch-black. They'd been called in to sift through the remains of the warehouse, looking for some piece of him to take home. It was a SEAL tradition never to leave a body or a man behind. That had been the night they'd found Jaguar's tooth.

"I think we'll need these," Westy shouted, from the rear of the helicopter. He tossed a pair of wool-lined gloves at each of the SEALs.

The men donned the gloves with relief. Fast-roping onto the PC was their best option for attack. The deck wasn't big enough for the helo to land.

Westy tested the sixty-foot French-braided fast rope that would speed each man toward the deck.

"There's the PC!" Luther shouted, maneuvering the helo so that it veered east.

The men prepared themselves, hearts pounding, minds completely focused.

Master Chief abandoned the copilot's seat to join them. "Listen up," he said. "Here's the plan." He lived by the tenet of the six-Ps: positive prior planning prevented piss-poor performance.

As he laid it out for them, the men gave him their full attention. "We have no idea how many men are on board, but you can expect them to be trained, probably former SEALs. Debilitating shots, but not fatal," he added. "These men are going to answer for their crimes, especially the CO. We'll drop onto the stern and move our way forward. Any questions?"

The men kept silent. No, the plan was pretty clear. It wasn't the most optimal takeover, but it wasn't like they had a lot of options right now.

Luther brought the Osprey around, pulling it into position over the PC. Wind buffeted the helicopter, making it difficult to flare the chopper—lower the back end.

"We've been spotted!" he shouted.

Seconds later, bullets strafed the side of the Osprey. Westy snatched up an MP5 and aimed it at the solitary figure on the deck, driving him out of sight with a short burst of fire.

"Go, go, go!" Master Chief shouted.

One by one the men dropped out of sight, zinging down the rope that trailed onto the *Nor'easter*'s narrow stern. Westy provided cover as the gunman reappeared, taking shots at Vinny, who was the second man to descend.

"Now you!" Sebastian called, signaling that he would cover Westy.

As the chief made his descent, Sebastian spared a word with their pilot. "Pull away the minute I'm down," he shouted.

Luther nodded. He knew as well as the master chief that the PC's MK 38 225-millimeter chain gun would make short work of the helicopter.

With a final shot off at the gunman, Sebastian gripped the rope and dropped off the Osprey backward. He flew down the medium, feeling the heat generated by friction right through his lined gloves. His descent was faster than that of his men—mostly because he'd had more practice but also because he didn't want to think that they might be too late.

Gabe heard the whopping of the helo's blades and grinned. No way could the military police have responded that quickly. He had enough confidence in his men to assume it was them, coming after him. With the psychic force that they'd always shared, they'd known he was in trouble. Hot damn!

All he really needed was the distraction they offered. The shadows at the doorway melted away as his would-be murderers turned their attention to the interlopers.

Gabe squirmed out from underneath Rodriguez's body. With a weapon in either hand, he unlocked one pilothouse door and peered outside. The bridge wing was clear. At the same time he could hear gunfire over the chopping of the helo's blades. With his back pressed against the bridge, he inched toward the rear of the ship.

He grinned as he caught sight of Westy diving and rolling and returning fire all at the same time. The CT SEAL took cover behind a rope keel, his broad shoulders barely protected by the narrow projection. Gabe's grin faded as he realized his men lacked the protection that the bridge afforded to Lovitt's men. They were at a dangerous disadvantage.

He could hear someone above him now, shooting toward

the aft portion of the boat, threatening his squad's safety. Gabe tucked his second weapon in his belt to free a hand. Ascending a ladder, he peeked onto the second deck. The cop that had tried to run him over, the one that had disappeared off the front stoop of the information office, was emptying his ammunition clip at an alarming rate, while taking cover behind a radar box.

With a grim smile, Gabe aimed his Glock at the man's right buttock and fired. *Take that, bastard.* The renegade leapt in astonishment, spun around, and returned fire. *Ping.* The bullet ricocheted off the deck, narrowly missing Gabe's ear.

Gabe fired a second time, this time knocking the pistol from his opponent's hand. It flew out of sight to splash into the ocean on the far side of the vessel. With a growl of frustration, the man tried to retreat, but Gabe shot him again, in the left butt cheek this time. The man collapsed, arching in a heap of misery.

That one's for my daughter, you son of a bitch.

Feeling better, Gabe pulled himself onto the second deck. With a bird's-eye view of the ship beneath him, he spotted another renegade hobbling toward the deck rail, leaving a trail of blood behind him. To Gabe's amazement, the man never slowed down. He flipped abruptly over the rail of the boat and into the water. It was obvious he'd been given orders not to be taken. Vinny, who'd shot him, gaped in astonishment.

Gabe pivoted, wondering about the man he'd just debilitated. The deck behind him stood deserted. That man, too, had disappeared, using his last ounce of strength to slip into the ocean where he preferred to drown than to account for his transgressions.

A rapid burst of gunfire jerked Gabe's attention to the

front of the boat. Someone had positioned himself at the PC's most powerful weapon, the MK 38 225-millimeter chain gun, and was taking aim at the chopper as it scuttled off to a safe distance.

With a renewed sense of urgency, Gabe slipped down a ladder and rounded the bridge to the forecastle. The figure hefting the mounted gun was nothing but a gray blur, but as Gabe ran at him, his gun raised to shoot, he realized it was Lovitt. The CO must have regained consciousness, and even with an injured forearm, he handled the unwieldy gun with lethal accuracy.

"Hey!" Gabe shouted, distracting him from firing.

Startled, Lovitt peered over his shoulder. His gray eyes flashed with determination, and he turned back, swiveling the machine gun toward the Osprey and firing.

Rat-tat-tat-tat-tat! Fire leapt out of the muzzle as it spewed rounds at the helicopter. The Osprey was already buffeted by the winds. To Gabe's horror, the rounds made contact with the rear rotor of the helo, making the bird impossible to control. Through the gray drizzle and across the distance between them, Gabe couldn't tell who the pilot was, but he suspected it was Luther, their only trained aviator. The tail of the helo swung left and right.

Jump! Gabe thought, tearing his gaze from the chopper in distress to the madman who had paused to watch it flounder. Gabe was too close to shoot Lovitt without killing him, and killing him was not his intent.

"You're the murderer, not me," he growled, stowing his weapon. Then he tackled the CO, coiling an arm around Lovitt's neck and squeezing. Unfortunately, Lovitt's fingertips were still on the trigger and, to Gabe's dismay, he got off a few more rounds.

The helo tilted at an unnatural angle, then fell like a stone, streaming smoke behind it: It hit the roiling waves with a noisy crash.

Gabe gaped in disbelief. That was *his* man that had just gone down. Luther Lindstrom—a man without a mean bone in his body, who'd turned down gobs of money playing football because he was a patriot first.

Gabe's grip closed off Lovitt's windpipe. He could feel the CO struggling feebly, yet his hold didn't loosen. Visions of the warehouse exploding, of his yearlong incarceration kept him rigid. He was barely cognizant of the fact that his men had set cover for each other and were picking their way forward.

"Jaguar!" Master Chief was the first to reach him, shaking Gabe by the shoulders to break him out of his trance. "Let go, sir." He tried to pry Lovitt free of Gabe's death grip. Regaining his senses with a start, Gabe released the CO abruptly. Lovitt hit the deck with a thud. With a cough and a wheeze, the man revived. Gabe stared at him dispassionately. Rainwater splattered the commander's face.

"He'll live," said Master Chief, sounding a little disappointed. He gave Gabe a probing look. "You okay, sir?"

Gabe's gaze strayed out into the choppy gray waters. "Luther," he said, in a strained voice.

"I saw him jump," Sebastian assured him. "He'll be all right. Rodriguez, on the other hand, is dead."

"He betrayed me," Gabe added, handing Sebastian Rodriguez's weapon. "Apparently he was part of Lovitt's little scheme."

He and the master chief shared a dark look. Gabe severed their gazes as Westy and Vinny appeared, looking harried. "Both of them fucking jumped ship," Westy exclaimed.

Gabe's scalp prickled. "Where's the third one?" he asked. Master Chief swung around. "There were three?"

"Three in addition to Rodriguez and Lovitt," Gabe confirmed. He leapt to his feet. "I'm all over it," he added, determined to avenge all that had been done to him. He spared Lovitt a glance. "You mind dragging that asshole into the bridge for me?"

"Not at all," Sebastian drawled.

Helen, Leila, and Mallory waited for the SEALs to pull out of sight before they followed them. By the time they arrived at Little Creek, it was swarming with military police, gunning their small patrol boats in preparation for a trip out to sea.

"Oh, my God," Helen breathed, seeing it as a bad sign. Something had happened to Gabe. Life was just too perfect right now; she knew it couldn't stay that way.

Catching sight of a familiar face among the MPs, she pulled her two companions toward a patrol boat. "Artie!" she called. It was Artie Coonz, a faithful attendee of her lunchtime fitness class. "Can you tell us what's happening?" she asked.

Artie squinted up at her. "Got a Mayday from a PC," he shouted over the engine.

Helen's knees trembled. "You have to take us with you," she insisted.

"No, ma'am. I'm not carrying civilians into a situation."

"Pretend you don't see us," Helen retorted, urging Mallory and Leila to jump on board.

Artie grumbled something about losing his stripes. "Get into the cabin and stay out of sight," he relented.

With the feeling that none of this could be real, Helen leaned against the shelter's wall, clinging to her companions, as Artie guided them out into the water. The little boat slammed through the waves. A siren screamed over their heads; the deck jerked beneath their feet. Mallory looked green about the gills. Leila squeezed Helen's hand.

Helen closed her eyes, praying all this haste would be for nothing. How could a man who'd made it to the rank of commander betray his own men?

She opened her eyes to see the PC directly ahead, a larger craft than the one she was on. It bobbed in the choppy waters, going nowhere. Cold fear gripped her as she saw smoke rising from the water some distance away. Even standing in the enclosed cabin of the police craft, she could smell gunfire. She glanced at Mallory, who was searching the few figures aboard the PC for signs of Gabe.

Someone aboard the bigger craft waved at them, summoning them closer.

"It's Sebastian," Leila cried with a telling hitch in her voice.

As the patrol boats approached the hull of the PC, the MPs tossed up grapple lines, securing the smaller boats to the larger boat's side. Helen recognized Westy who was helping on his end. But where was Gabe?

Too impatient to wait, she ordered Leila and Mallory to stay put and stepped out of the cabin. The rain had subsided to a drizzle, but the sirens were still wailing, and men were shouting over the throbbing of engines. Military police shinnied up the sides of the PC on Jacob's ladders.

Helen grasped the rail of the patrol boat. "Vinny!" she called, catching a glimpse of a familiar dark head.

He peered over the edge of the *Nor'easter*.

"Where's Gabe?"

He looked disconcerted to see her. "He's okay," he shouted back. "We're looking for a missing tango. Stay out of sight!"

A missing tango. That meant one of the bad guys was not

accounted for. Helen turned to beat a retreat into the cabin, when she caught sight of a figure rising up out of a cargo hold near the rear of the PC. He sprang into sight like a nightmare jack-in-the-box, an antitank gun on one shoulder.

"Oh, my God," she whispered as fear gripped her. She'd seen enough war movies to know what a weapon that size could do.

To her horror, the cold-eyed renegade pointed his weapon down the length of the PC, at the pilothouse where most of the activity was going on.

Dear Lord. He's going to blow up the ship and take everyone with it, including himself! She took an astonished step backward, trodding on Mallory's toes as her daughter came up behind her. "Mom?" Mallory queried.

Helen didn't wait for someone aboard the PC to notice the threat and eliminate it. Pulling Gabe's Glock from beneath her shirt, she aimed at the would-be assassin. Never in her life had she pointed a weapon at a person. But this was different. Her hands were remarkably steady as she squeezed the trigger, thinking, *Over my dead body!*

On board the *Nor'easter*, Gabe was closing in on his prey. Technically, now that the MPs had arrived, he could leave it to them to hunt down the last tango. The man might have bailed ship like the others, but he'd learned from experience never to assume anything. He might well be plotting an offensive belowdecks.

Just to make sure, Gabe skulked along the narrow passageway, past the sleeping quarters, the showers, and the mess. At the end of the corridor, he came to the artillery storage area. A tug on the airlock revealed that it'd been jammed from the inside. Coincidence, or not? There was only one other means of entering or escaping that area of the ship, and that was through a hatch that opened onto the deck above.

With a jolt of horror, Gabe realized that the renegade could have come this way to arm himself. There were a number of lethal weapons in the room beyond. If the man escaped through the hatch on deck, he could wreak unspeakable havoc.

Jesus! Gabe changed direction, sprinting toward the exit, shouting raw warnings to anyone who might hear him. As he burst onto the deck, his gaze flew toward the rear of the ship. He was horrified to see that he was right. The renegade had popped out of the hold with an AT-4 antitank weapon on his shoulder. He was aiming it straight at the heart of the ship. Any second now, Gabe would see a ball of fire streaking toward him, and then . . . nothing.

The crack of a pistol rent the air, and Gabe flinched, expecting scalding pain. To his astonishment, the enemy faltered, clutching a hand to his abdomen. He fell to one knee. *Christ, someone had shot the man,* Gabe realized.

But he wasn't dead yet. His finger tensed convulsively about the trigger, and the antitank gun discharged with a roar. Gabe dived for cover as the shaped charge rocketed over his head. He expected the deck to buckle beneath him, expected to be swallowed in an upwelling of shrapnel and heat, but instead the PC merely bucked and rolled. Water showered the deck, telling him that the antitank round had exploded underwater.

Weak with relief, Gabe dragged himself up again. The renegade was injured but still a threat. The man struggled to his feet, fighting to center the AT-4 on his shoulder. Gabe didn't wait for him to fire again. With a roar of denial, he charged the man, firing as he ran. Three bullets punctured the man's chest before he finally collapsed, his weapon clanging loudly as it hit the steel deck.

Approaching the dead outlaw, Gabe slanted a look to his left, curious to know who had shot him in the first place. What he saw made him stop dead in his tracks.

There stood Helen aboard an MP patrol boat bobbing at the PC's side. She stood as stiff as a statue, pistol still gripped between both hands.

His wife had shot the freaking renegade. She'd kept the *Nor'easter* from going up in a fireball and ultimately saved every single soul aboard the PC.

The strength leaked out of Gabe's legs. He staggered toward the rail and gaped down at the trio below. "What the hell are you all doing here!" he roared, envisioning with horror what had nearly happened.

Helen tucked the weapon back into her shorts and offered up a shaky smile. "Hi, honey," she called. "We thought you might need help."

Jesus, God. Terror gave way to relief. Gabe's legs went out completely, making it necessary to turn around and sit down fast, his back to the rail.

"Honey?" Helen shouted up at him. "Are you okay?"

She sounded so distressed that he forced himself to rise again, though his legs wobbled precariously. "Stay there," he said, pointing a finger so she would know exactly where *there* was. "Sebastian!" he roared, summoning the master chief from the forecastle.

Sebastian raced to Gabe's side and looked quizzically overboard. "Yes, sir?" Seeing Leila with the other women, his jaw fell open and the blood drained from his tan face.

"I think she loves you," Gabe said as he clambered over the rail. He descended the Jacob's ladder, still weak with relief, and jumped the last few rungs. In two long strides, he

closed the distance between himself and his family, engulf-
ing Helen and Mallory in a rib-crushing embrace. The urge
to berate his wife battled with the realization that he and
everyone aboard the PC owed their life to her.

Torn by conflicting urges, he did the only other thing he
could think of. He crushed his mouth to hers, kissing her with
every ounce of frustration and love that roiled in him.

By some form of mutual consent the sirens aboard the
three patrol boats fell suddenly mute. Someone aboard the
PC whistled in approval. Gabe lifted his head to regard Helen
with amazement. "You just saved my life, woman," he exclaimed. "Mine and every other goddamn person aboard the
ship. Don't you *ever* follow me into danger again!" he yelled.

She shook her head apologetically. "We didn't want to
lose you, Gabe."

He looked at Mallory, whose level look implied that they
would have shot a hundred bad guys just to save his sorry
hide.

"You'll never lose me," he growled, squeezing them both.
"Chief," he said, turning to Artie, who hovered behind them,
"let's take this craft and search the area for my junior lieutenant. He jumped from the helo several minutes ago."

"Aye, aye, sir." Artie responded to the authority in Gabe's
tone, calling several men off the bigger ship to join them. Sebastian climbed stiffly down the Jacob's ladder and helped
unhook the grapple lines. He kept his back turned to Leila.

Artie shooed the women back into the pilothouse, and
they chugged away to begin the heart-thudding search for
Luther Lindstrom.

"He's furious with me," Leila commented with a stricken
expression.

Helen put an arm around her. "Well, if you missed it,
Gabe was mad at me too. It's a good sign, really it is."

"What if he never speaks to me again?" Leila added, sounding truly alarmed at the prospect.

"He will," Helen swore. "He's just rattled, that's all, and he doesn't appreciate being rattled in front of his men."

Shouts outside the cabin wrenched their attention to the front of the boat. Artie hefted a life buoy in one hand and was preparing to hurl it overboard. Helen strained on tiptoe to see over the fore portion of the boat. At the same time an ocean swell lifted Luther into view. Other than the fact that he was soaked and shaken, he looked no worse off for having jumped from a flailing helicopter.

With a whispered prayer of gratitude, Helen slumped back against her companions. This day's events could have ended in a number of horrific tragedies, but they hadn't. Righteousness had prevailed, just the way it was supposed to.

Epilogue

L abor Day gave Echo Platoon an excuse to celebrate
their victory over corruption. The weather could not
have been more amenable to a party on Gabe and
Helen's newly stained deck. The breeze rolling off the ocean
kept the sun from broiling them. In the event that one of the
revelers still became overheated, there was plenty of iced
tea, beer, and wine coolers to refresh them. There was also
the promise of the waves, spilling gently onto shore a mere
hundred yards away.

Gabe was king of the grill. He'd cooked up burgers that
disappeared in record time and was now turning the barbecued ribs. As Helen oversaw the distribution of chips and
napkins, her gaze strayed repeatedly to Gabe's handsome
profile. She relived again the nightmare that had occurred
two weeks ago, marveling at how closely they'd come to losing all that they'd rediscovered in each other's arms.

In the two weeks since, she'd been so blissfully happy that
it was hard to remember when she and Gabe had ever been
emotionally distant. While she was sorry for the suffering

he'd endured in North Korea, she was grateful for the changes it had wrought in him. Gabe was the most considerate, most compassionate, and the sexiest husband in the whole wide world. And she was the luckiest of all women.

Passing a bowl of chips to Westy, she gave a start at the directness of his gaze. The slightest of smiles hovered at the corners of his mouth, though it was hard to tell for sure with that goatee.

Still, she got the impression that Westy was happy for her. Helen smiled shyly back, rousing from her satisfaction long enough to reflect on the circumstances of others.

Why was Chief McCaffrey alone? Beneath his fearsome facade she sensed a heart as big as the wild, wild west for which he was named. He was intensely attractive in a dangerous sort of way. Yet, according to Gabe, Westy struck up affairs with married women to avoid the marriage trap. Being a counterterrorist SEAL, she supposed it was better in his line of work not to have a family of his own. Still, it seemed a shame. She sensed he would love a woman the way Gabe now loved her—completely, no holds barred.

Carrying the bowl of chips across the deck to Luther Lindstrom, her thoughts continued along the same vein. Luther sat directly beside his fiancée, Veronica, but the strained silence between them hinted at underlying issues. Gabe and the others were placing secret bets as to how much longer the couple would last.

Luther helped himself to a fistful of chips. "Thanks," he said, flashing a boyish smile. Veronica, with her eyes concealed by dark sunglasses, declined the offering.

Helen crossed the deck toward Leila, who stood off to one side. She'd come only at Helen's insistence, keeping as much distance between herself and the master chief as possible. Ever since the episode aboard the *Nor'easter*, Sebastian had seemed emotionally aloof. Confused by his apparent change in attitude, Leila was also withdrawn. It was apparent to Helen that both stubborn souls were waiting for the other to break the ice.

"I think I need to go, Helen," Leila said, taking a couple of chips from Helen's bowl. The ache in her voice told Helen that Sebastian's continued silence was taking its toll.

"Oh, come on. One of you needs to back down first. Just go up to him and get this stalemate over with!"

"What if he doesn't want me anymore?" Leila agonized.

Helen snorted in disbelief. "I guess you haven't noticed those fierce looks he's been shooting at you for an hour now?"

"What looks?"

"Oh, Lord. Just walk over there and ask him what his problem is."

Leila darted a look at Sebastian's taut form. "I'm afraid he's still angry with me," she admitted.

"He isn't. He's upset with himself now for pushing you away," Helen reasoned.

"You think so?" Leila blew out a steadying breath. "Okay, just give me a minute."

Satisfied that her friend would find the courage to bridge the gap, Helen returned to Gabe's side just as he raised his plastic cup. "I propose a toast," he called.

The men responded enthusiastically, reaching for their drinks.

"Here's to Master Chief, who kept me from choking Lovitt to death," Gabe began. "Without your intervention, my sorry ass would be in jail."

"Hear, hear!" the men confirmed.

Sebastian spared them a distracted smile and raised his cup.

"To Lieutenant Lindstrom," Gabe continued, acknowledging the oversized SEAL, "who can dodge any kind of tackle, even a tackle by an Osprey."

"Hoo-yah," said Vinny.

Veronica swiveled her head in his direction.

"To our XO, Jason Miller," Gabe continued, on a sarcastic note, "who did this country a great service in retiring."

The men groaned and shrugged off their memories of Jason Miller. The man had resigned his commission without explanation. He'd refused to say a word against Lovitt, even though the Naval Criminal Investigation Service pressured him continuously for a statement. He'd also kept mum about the incident last year, failing to acknowledge any role in Gabe's disappearance.

"And also," Gabe added, his tone turning serious, "a toast to Hannah Geary, wherever she is. God keep her safe until she's found."

The men murmured their agreement and took a sip of their drinks. Silence fell over the bunch as they contemplated the disappearance of the DIA analyst. The notebook she'd carried in her possession was needed to corroborate Commander Lovitt's crimes. While the CO had been interrogated concerning the incident aboard the *Nor'easter*, there was no hard evidence that could tie him to weapons seizure and sales, not without the notebook Geary had disappeared with. The thugs who'd backed him up on the PC were either dead or missing. True to his threat, Lovitt was insisting that Gabe was the one responsible for the fiasco aboard the boat, having succumbed to a paranoid attack. Until the NCIS completed their investigation, it wasn't clear who was going to face charges: Lovitt, Gabe, or even Luther and the master chief for appropriating and destroying military property.

Nonetheless, the men had faith in the system. The NCIS

was bound to bring the hammer of justice down hard over Lovitt's head. It was simply a matter of time.

But what about Hannah Geary, who'd been seen entering the gates of the US Marine base, Quantico? Her car was discovered outside the Military Police Headquarters, where two officers had been on duty that day. Neither one had reported any face-to-face contact with a flaming redhead.

It was a sobering scenario. That a woman could be whisked away on a military base without a soul noticing raised some serious questions. Who had pulled what strings to enable such a neat abduction?

The loose ends suggested the corruption didn't begin and end with Edward Lovitt. There were bad guys that hadn't been identified yet, but since Gabe didn't know who they were, he figured he was safe from any vendettas. Just in case, his men remained vigilant, rotating duty as they guarded Gabe and his family.

It maddened Gabe that his memory of that night in Pyongyang eluded him, still. He could not remember Miller turning on him. He could not even recall what he'd done to make Lovitt so wary of him that he'd ordered Miller to finish him off.

Perhaps it was better this way, Noel Terrien had suggested. The blow to Gabe's cheek had left a void that served to protect him. With that part of his memory permanently lost, Gabe was less likely to be targeted again.

"A toast to the members of Echo Platoon," Gabe continued, breaking the heavy spell that had fallen over the group. "Specifically, my favorite squad." He raised his cup toward them. "There isn't a finer group of men in the service. Hopefully I'll be working with you soon."

The men roused from their contemplative moods to smack their cups and bottles together, drinking heartily to

Gabe's toasts. With Dr. Terrien's clearance, Gabe had been recommended for active duty. It was up to Admiral Johansen, the base commander, whether he'd be struck from the disabled list and placed on active duty, and whether he'd be put on the same team or not.

"To the new XO of SEAL Team Twelve," Vinny countered, giving voice to the men's hope that Gabe would be slated to replace Miller.

"Hear, hear!" the men said in unison.

"One more toast," Gabe added. "This one's for my wife and my daughter." He reached for Helen, pulling her snug against him. Mallory, who was supposedly listening to CDs on a headset, looked up, proving she'd been attentive all the while.

"I have this to say to you two: I once was lost but now I'm found." His yellow-green eyes glinted in the sun as he smiled self-consciously. "I wouldn't be here today if it weren't for you ladies. You gave me a reason to resist the enemy and to survive. That's why I'm not ashamed to say it in front of God and everyone: I love you both, I really do."

Helen's breath caught. Gabe had pledged his love privately and repeatedly in the past few weeks. But proclaiming it before his men was a deliberate gesture. He was making it clear to Helen that his commitment to the SEALs would never surpass his commitment to his family. His dual identity as SEAL and a family man were intricately bound up in each other. Loving his family had given him superhuman strength and courage. With their help, he was nearly whole. He would soon be a SEAL again, but the team wouldn't take him away this time. His heart would remain at home with the ones he loved.

Gabe sealed his proclamation with a kiss. As was their

custom, he and Helen kept their eyes open, ensuring their connection was complete.

In her peripheral vision, Helen saw Leila make her way cautiously toward Sebastian. Their gazes locked, and they came together like two magnets. Wordlessly, and to everyone's astonishment, Sebastian snatched up Leila's hand and pulled her swiftly toward the stairs.

Half a dozen pairs of eyes watched them leave. No one dared say anything, but the expressions of amazement on their faces made Helen's ribs ache. *Oh, Leila! May you find the joy that you deserve with the one you love!*

With a satisfied smile, she went back to kissing Gabe, sharing private laughter that danced in their eyes. Their future was secure; their bond as true and fast as the surest link ever made. Nothing would ever come between them.

Mallory, who in a few weeks' time would be Mallory Renault, gave it her best shot. "Um, excuse me," she said, peering through chestnut bangs. "I'm supposed to be in on this."

"Well, come on in." Gabe threw an arm around her shoulders, bringing her into their circle.

With a lump in her throat, Helen recalled the first time Mal and Gabe had hugged since their reunion—in the hospital, the day they'd gone to pick him up. It had been that hug that convinced Helen to give Gabe another chance.

Thank heaven she did!

About the Author

Daughter of a U.S. foreign service officer, Marliss Melton enjoyed a unique childhood growing up overseas. As one of five children, she was encouraged to think creatively and wrote her first book at age thirteen. In addition to writing, Marliss taught high school for a decade. She now teaches Linguistics at the college of William and Mary. A Golden Heart and RITA finalist, Marliss writes both medieval romance (as Marliss Moon) and romantic suspense. Her husband, a warfare technology specialist, is her real-life hero. Together, they have six children and a Bassett hound.

More

Marliss Melton!

Please turn this page

for a preview of

IN THE DARK

available in

bookstores everywhere.

With the surf playing drum line to the melody of cicadas, Hannah fell into uneasy slumber. Deep into the night, her lids sprang open, and cold prickles of foreboding danced across her skin. She peered into the shadows of her prison cell, ears straining to discover what had awakened her.

A thumbnail moon shone through the grille at her window, casting a meager glow. The buzzing of insects nearly masked the shuffle of feet outside her door. The fine hairs on Hannah's body rose slowly to attention.

Someone was out there, standing on just the other side of her door. Was it the armed guard who'd eyed her so lasciviously or Pinzón himself?

She groped under her pillow for the simple weapon she'd engineered—a strip of sturdy linen torn off the edge of her mosquito netting. She swiftly coiled the ends of the strip about her fists, stilling as the lock released and the door swung open.

The naked light bulb in the hall cast the man's silhouette into relief. It was the guard. She recognized him at once by the mop of curly hair on his head. Even at this time of night, he was still in his uniform, but he'd parted with his hat . . . *and his gun!* she realized with a leaping of her heart.

It came to her in that instant, that if he was weaponless, she could overcome him and escape—no need to barter for her freedom with the naive hope that Pinzón would release her.

She held absolutely still, even as her visitor slipped through the door and shut it behind him, extinguishing the light. Her eyes, better adjusted to the dark than his, made out his shadow creeping toward her. She heard him fumbling with his zipper, making his intentions clear. Her heart pounded in her chest, rocking her entire body. She fought the urge to leap out of bed and evade him. Instead, she waited, every nerve fraying as his shadow came closer . . . and encountered the barrier of her mosquito netting.

With her arms over her head, Hannah waited, holding her breath as he fumbled with the gauzy net. He lifted it at last to crawl beneath. The moment his head appeared over hers, she whipped her arms down, coiling the length of linen around his neck. He reared back in alarm, and she used his momentum to throw them both off the bed, dragging the netting down over them.

They hit the stone floor with a thud. Hannah levered herself up and over him, pulling the line as taut as her strength allowed. He twisted to his knees. Hannah clung to him, locking her legs about his hips as he bucked and thrashed. She held the line tight for what seemed an eternity. Suddenly, he collapsed, and she pitched forward, letting go to catch her fall.

Leaping up, she pulled the line tight again, pressing a knee against his spine. He lay as limp as a throw rug, having apparently passed out. Wary of a ruse, she released the line, little by little.

He didn't inhale.

She nudged him, waiting for him to suck air into his lungs. Nothing. He'd stopped breathing.

She'd killed him! The realization stunned her. Dear God in heaven! She jumped off him, scuttling backward like a crab. She stared at his unmoving form, turning hot then cold as she grappled with the fact that she'd taken a life. She'd killed a man.

But then, the instinct for self-preservation roused her

from shock. This was her chance to escape. She scrambled to her feet and backed toward the door. Groping for the latch, she peeked into the deserted hallway. She locked the body inside and pocketed the key.

Then she ran, down the hall with its flaking paint, toward the stairs that led to the outdoor kitchen. It was via this route that Maria brought the food.

There were voices at the base of the stairs. Hannah peeked over the banister, spying two uniformed soldiers by the door. Pulling the key from her pocket, she threw it down the stairwell, prompting an immediate stir. As the guards stormed the second level, Hannah tucked herself into an alcove and slipped past them, her bare feet silent on the steps.

She'd had two weeks to study the layout of Pinzón's estate, determining the exact location of the movement-sensitive halogen lights and how far away one had to stay to avoid detection.

The buzz of insects masked her furtive dash toward the outdoor kitchens. Over the thudding of her heart came the clanging of pots and the sound of running water. She scraped her elbow on the cinderblock wall as she headed toward the rear of the compound.

There were still more guards, three of them, lighting cigarettes by the fountain and conferring. The shadows would be dark enough to hide her, but if she set off even a single light, it would all be over.

She paused at the corner of the building. This was the tricky part, making her way across the open courtyard to the small banana tree closest to the outer perimeter, a ten-foot wall.

At that moment, a cry of alarm came from a second-story window—*her* window, she determined, glancing up. The guard's body had been found. "*Ay, está muerto!*" a voice cried out—he's dead!

And, look, the woman is missing.

Great, now the whole place would light up like the D.C. Mall at Christmas, and the search would be on. She would have to do this fast and hope to God she'd done her calculations right.

The soldiers tossed down their cigarettes and reached for their rifles, looking around haphazardly. As one of them ran toward the house, Hannah darted out into the open.

One, two, three, four steps forward. Turn right and count to ten. Smaller steps, smaller steps! She reined herself in. Had she gone too far? In the dark, she gauged her distance from the spotlight jutting out of the dirt ahead of her.

The sound she dreaded reached her ears. "*Allí está!*" The two remaining guards had spotted her. Her shirt, apparently, wasn't dirty enough. "*Párate,*" the other one shouted. "*Alto! Manos arriba!*"

Dear God, they were taking aim at her! Forget the spotlights. Head for a tree! Hannah bolted, but her stride felt sluggish, her muscles weak from her incarceration. The banana tree seemd miles away.

Rat-a-tat-tat! The guards opened fire. Bullets whizzed by, missing her by several feet. Still, they had the power to motivate. She hit the tree at full throttle, looped her arms and legs around it, and tried to shimmy upward.

She'd had no idea banana bark was so damn slippery.

The guards were running toward her, chipping the cement wall as they emptied the clips on their semi-automatics. Hannah clung to the tree, doing her best to inch upward. The wall looked as high as the Great Wall of China. She knew with a sinking of her heart that she wasn't going to make it. Damn, damn, damn! To be foiled by tree bark. It was utterly unfair.

With a sob of defeat, she squeezed her eyes shut, waiting to be shot to death, grabbed, or both.

Thoop. Thoop.

Thud. Thud.

Those unexpected sounds brought her eyes open. Hannah peeked around the tree and found her pursuers flat on their backs, dead.

She whipped her head in the direction that the bullets had come from. Someone had shot the soldiers with a silenced weapon. She couldn't see anything but the outline of palm fronds, draped over the wall. Suddenly a hand came out of the leaves, then an entire arm and a powerful shoulder. She made out her rescuer by the whites of his eyes and realized he was lying on the wall's ledge just feet away, camouflaged.

"Take my hand," he commanded brusquely.

She groped for it, thrilled that he had spoken English.

The grip that closed over hers made her wince. Her invisible companion shook off the leaves and hauled her up beside him. Even sitting next to him she could scarcely make him out. He was dressed in black from head to toe, with his face painted. Still, she got the impression he was huge, muscular, and just a little pissed off.

"Hannah Geary?" he clipped, saying her name just as her father used to when she'd done something bad.

"Yes, who are—"

But he didn't let her finish. He swung her down on the opposite side, where a pair of waiting arms helped her to the ground. Then he leapt nimbly down beside her. "Let's go," he said, scooping her up into a fireman hold, eliciting a screech of surprise. "Quiet!"

"I can walk on my own!" she hissed, utterly disoriented in her pitch-black surroundings and hanging upside down.

"Can you see in the dark?" He was moving fast, and she had to appreciate that fact because the estate was seething with commotion now: shouting, a woman's scream, another burst of gunfire.

See in the dark? No, but apparently he could. He had to be wearing night-vision goggles—NVGs—to be moving through the undergrowth so quickly. His companion was somewhere up ahead of them, but damned if she could hear him at all.

They broke free of the tree line, and the pace changed as her rescuer lumbered down a sandy cliff while skirting enormous boulders. The noise behind them swelled as the shouting continued. A thick beam of light shot out over the ebony waves. Perhaps once a beacon for ships, it was now being used to hunt her down.

Amazingly, she wasn't afraid anymore. The man beneath her moved with the sinuous confidence of a super athlete. She already knew he carried a weapon, and when he jogged with her along the surf's edge, he covered ground *fast*, and she could scarcely hear him running—pretty impressive considering his size.

The land beneath them curved like a sickle. At last he stopped and tipped her to her feet into ankle-deep water. Hannah peered about, making out an inflatable raft, which the other man pushed across the sand into the surf. He held it in place and motioned for them to clamber aboard.

Hannah sprawled into the bottom of the boat, finding it wet and slippery. The men took up positions on either end and rowed them into deeper water, away from the light that strafed the shore.

They hit the surf. Up and over the waves they went,

higher and higher. She'd thought the water was relatively calm within the Bay of Santiago. Wrong. Every time the raft was tossed, Hannah feared she was going to fly off. She clung to the straps on the boat's bottom, her mouth clamped firmly shut. She would not scream like a sissy and embarrass herself in front of these men.

Who were they? And how had they found her?

The noises on the shoreline faded. Eventually the only sound was that of the paddles sliding in and out of the water. As the surface grew placid, Hannah pried her stiff fingers from the straps and heaved a sigh of relief. "Thank you," she said, thinking it was safe to speak.

The big man put his paddle down and leaned in, his painted face scary in the darkness. "You want to tell me what that was all about?" he demanded, sounding—again— just like her father.

"Which part?" she asked warily.

He gestured with disbelief. "What were you doing running across the compound with guards shooting at you?"

"Er, trying to escape?" She pointed out the obvious.

"You could have been killed!" he said incredulously.

Duh! "Yes, well, I realize that. But the alternative really sucked and I decided to take my chances."

"Three hours," he cut in irately, "and we would have had you out without a single witness."

She took exception to his patronizing tone. "Well, I didn't want to wait another three hours—how's that? You should have rescued me days ago. Who are you, anyway?"

At the other end of the raft, the second man chuckled. "Navy SEALs, ma'am, from Team Twelve. The lieutenant's just upset because you messed with his plans. He doesn't like surprises."

"I'm upset because no one was supposed to know we

were there. I laid out two men so they wouldn't shoot her. Tell me *that's* not going to get the Cubans up in arms and prompt an inquiry." He directed his flashing eyes at Hannah. "I heard someone shout that another man was dead. What do you know about that?"

Hannah winced. "I didn't mean to," she breathed. "It was the guard. He came into my cell and tried to ... to you know."

He sat back, clearly just realizing what a harrowing experience she'd just had. "Christ," he said, regarding her for a stunned moment. "Wow, okay, so you killed him. Good, good. He deserved it. You're okay now, right?"

Of course I'm okay, she wanted to say, only her teeth had started to chatter, and she was afraid she would bite her tongue.

Flipping a switch on a transmitter, the lieutenant spouted naval code-speak to request a pickup.

"Roger that. It'll take us twenty minutes to get there. Sit tight."

Hannah's whole body began to shake. The chills were uncontrollable—an aftereffect of too much adrenaline. Reviewing the last two weeks, she realized how narrowly she'd escaped violation and death. Emotions crested inside her, as high and frightening as the swells they'd traversed.

The SEAL put the handset down. "My name's Luther," he said, regarding her steadily. "My partner there is Westy."

Hannah glanced from Westy, who boasted a goatee of all things, to the long-fingered hand extended her way. Still shuddering, she accepted it.

His grip was warm, firm, and utterly sincere. "Are you cold? Westy, hand me a blanket." He tossed a blanket over her shoulders, adjusting it to cover her completely. Self-pity assailed Hannah. She'd been drugged and thrown into a boat, dropped off in a third world country, and been accosted. She'd had to kill to defend herself; she'd run and been shot at. To her horror, a sob escaped her pressured chest.

"Hey," said the big SEAL. He shifted closer, pulling her snugly against him. "All right, I've got you. It's behind you now."

The blessed security of that thick arm banding around her robbed Hannah of her composure. She pushed her face into his rubber wet suit and—to her undying shame—sobbed again.

"I've got you," he repeated, holding her tight.

Struggling to get a handle on herself, Hannah was aware of his body heat even through the rubber of the wet suit. Nor could the slick layer conceal the awesome proportions of his physique. He was powerfully built without a hint of softness anywhere. It felt delicious to be held by him. Unfortunately, the fact that he saw himself performing some noble service made it impossible for her to enjoy herself. Hannah didn't need comfort; she just needed a moment.

With a sniff, she withdrew from his embrace and scooted away. "I'm okay," she informed him. She raised her eyes to the sky, aware that the SEAL was watching her curiously. Offshore, the clouds had thinned to reveal a sky glittering with stars. "I'm good," she added, marveling at their brilliance. Strange how everything seemed sharper in the aftermath of high adventure.

Only, it wasn't over yet, was it? Gooseflesh rippled over her wet skin. She wasn't going to rot away in a Cuban prison, but now she was more of a threat than ever to Lovitt. If he ever caught wind of her escape he would surely want her dead this time. Hannah turned wary eyes on her two companions. They were, after all, under Lovitt's command. "How'd you know where to find me?"

"The FBI caught on to Lovitt's Cuban connection. They sent us in to get you out."

"I see," she said. "So, you're not loyal to Lovitt."

"No ma'am," said Luther with an edge to his voice.

Leaning against the raft's inflatable edge, with his dark eyes glittering, Luther the SEAL struck her as formidable, despite his gentleness moments ago.

"We sure could use your partner's notebook to corroborate his crimes, but I suppose it's gone."

"It's gone," she sighed, "along with my purse and my . . . my watch," she added sadly. "The creep who abducted me took everything."

The lieutenant seemed attuned to the strain in her voice. "Did he hurt you?" he asked gently.

"No, thank God," she admitted, amazed by her good fortune. "I spent three days on a boat with him and he stayed away for the most part."

"Patrol's coming," the SEAL named Westy announced.

Straining her ears, Hannah heard only water lapping at the raft, but the lieutenant went instantly to work. Pulling a device from a Velcro-sealed pocket on the raft, he sent a series of flashes out over the waves. At last, she detected the hum of a motor approaching.

Very cool, Hannah thought, determined to stick as close to these men as possible. They were definitely on her side. She could trust them to protect her while she pondered Lovitt's purpose in sending her to Cuba. Whatever his reason for not killing her as he'd killed Ernie, he was going to regret it. Together with these SEALs, she would drive Lovitt to his knees and earn the right—at last—to do fieldwork.

THE EDITOR'S DIARY

Dear Reader,

Love at first sight is nice. But love the second time around is even sweeter—especially if it's with the same person. From a blissful return to young love to a second chance at life, come see how two is better than one is these new Warner Forever titles this December.

Ever daydream about what happened to your childhood sweetheart? Well, wipe the sleep from your eyes as we present **Mary McBride's** latest **SAY IT AGAIN, SAM**, a romp bound to jump-start your heart and spice up your fantasies. *Bookpage* called her last book "sparkling" and "irresistible" so prepare to be dazzled. Weird things have been happening at Heart Lake. Strange things are being stolen—a trophy in a high school collection and even tuna fish from a local market—and everybody is jumpy. So Sam Mendenhall, former Delta Force operator, is called in to keep the peace. Little does he know that the chaos is just beginning as Beth Simon, his childhood sweetheart, is back in town. They were the perfect couple years ago . . . until Sam proposed, Beth refused, and Sam married someone else. Now single and hot on the trail of the person behind the mysterious thefts, he can't resist when the spark between them ignites, leading them to the little cabin in the woods where they fell in love years ago.

What would you do if your Navy SEAL husband who is presumed dead suddenly reappears, but with absolutely no memory of you, your daughter, or the life you shared? Helen Renault from **Marliss Melton's FORGET ME**

NOT has no idea what to do. She was just standing on her own two feet at last—and proud of it—when Gabe returns. Though she cares for him, they married young and for all the wrong reasons. But as she nurses him back to health from both his physical and mental trauma, she can't help but see he is a very different man now. Gone is the distant, secretive husband he once was. This new Gabe is a man she could finally fall in love with. But as his memory returns, bit by bit, a governmental cover-up is exposed, putting all three lives in danger . . . and jeopardizing their second chance at love. I hope you don't have other plans for today because, as *New York Times* bestselling author Lisa Jackson says, "FORGET ME NOT will pull you in and never let you go."

To find out more about Warner Forever, these December titles, and the author, visit us at www.warnerforever.com.

With warmest wishes,

Karen Kosztolnyik

Karen Kosztolnyik, Senior Editor

P.S. The New Year is just around the corner and here are two little resolutions you can't help but keep. **Kathryn Caskie** pens the witty and charming story of a lady's maid whose tingle cream—and her romance with a Scottish marquis—sets the ton abuzz in **LADY IN WAITING**; and **Shari Anton** delivers the spellbinding and sensual tale of a widow who hires a mercenary to keep her daughter and her village safe, only to pay with her heart in **AT HER SERVICE**.

Want to know more about romances at Grand Central Publishing and Forever? Get the scoop online!

GRAND CENTRAL PUBLISHING'S ROMANCE HOMEPAGE

Visit us at www.hachettebookgroupusa.com/romance for all the latest news, reviews, and chapter excerpts!

NEW AND UPCOMING TITLES

Each month we feature our new titles and reader favorites.

CONTESTS AND GIVEAWAYS

We give away galleys, autographed copies, and all kinds of fun stuff.

AUTHOR INFO

You'll find bios, articles, and links to personal websites for all your favorite authors—and so much more!

THE BUZZ

Sign up for our monthly romance newsletter, and be the first to read all about it!